Dangerous in Diamonds

"This one is a sparkling gem! . . . With strong undercurrents that are both comic and dark, *Dangerous in Diamonds* will keep you dazzled with reading pleasure!"   —*Fresh Fiction*

"Hunter . . . masterfully weaves a sensual web . . . Fans will be delighted."   —*Publishers Weekly*

"A terrific historical . . . a delightful series."   —*Midwest Book Review*

Sinful in Satin

"Hunter deftly sifts intrigue and exquisite sensuality into the plot of the third book in her exceptionally entertaining quartet."   —*Booklist*

Provocative in Pearls

"Hunter gifts readers with a fantastic story that reaches into the heart of relationships and allows her to deliver a deep-sigh read."   —*RT Book Reviews* (Top Pick)

Ravishing in Red

"Richly spiced with wicked wit and masterfully threaded with danger and desire, the superbly sexy first book in Hunter's new Regency historical quartet is irresistible and wonderfully entertaining."   —*Booklist* (starred review)

The Conquest
of Lady Cassandra

MADELINE HUNTER

JOVE BOOKS, NEW YORK

THE BERKLEY PUBLISHING GROUP
Published by the Penguin Group
Penguin Group (USA) Inc.
375 Hudson Street, New York, New York 10014, USA

Penguin Group (Canada), 90 Eglinton Avenue East, Suite 700, Toronto, Ontario M4P 2Y3, Canada (a division of Pearson Penguin Canada Inc.) • Penguin Books Ltd, 80 Strand, London WC2R 0RL, England • Penguin Ireland, 25 St Stephen's Green, Dublin 2, Ireland (a division of Penguin Books Ltd) • Penguin Group (Australia), 707 Collins Street, Melbourne, Victoria 3008, Australia (a division of Pearson Australia Group Pty Ltd) • Penguin Books India Pvt Ltd, 11 Community Centre, Panchsheel Park, New Delhi–110 017, India • Penguin Group (NZ), 67 Apollo Drive, Rosedale, Auckland 0632, New Zealand (a division of Pearson New Zealand Ltd) • Penguin Books (South Africa), Rosebank Office Park, 181 Jan Smuts Avenue, Parktown North 2193, South Africa • Penguin China, B7 Jiaming Center, 27 East Third Ring Road North, Chaoyang District, Beijing 100020, China

Penguin Books Ltd., Registered Offices: 80 Strand, London WC2R 0RL, England

This is a work of fiction. Names, characters, places, and incidents either are the product of the author's imagination or are used fictitiously, and any resemblance to actual persons, living or dead, business establishments, events, or locales is entirely coincidental. The publisher does not have control over and does not have any responsibility for author or third-party websites or their content.

THE CONQUEST OF LADY CASSANDRA

A Jove Book / published by arrangement with the author

PUBLISHING HISTORY
Jove mass-market edition / March 2013

Copyright © 2013 by Madeline Hunter.
Excerpt from *The Surrender of Miss Fairbourne* copyright © 2012 by Madeline Hunter.
Cover photography by Claudio Marinesco.
Text design by Laura K. Corless.

ISBN: 978-0-515-15111-4

JOVE®
Jove Books are published by The Berkley Publishing Group,
a division of Penguin Group (USA) Inc.,
375 Hudson Street, New York, New York 10014.
JOVE® is a registered trademark of Penguin Group (USA) Inc.
The "J" design is a trademark of Penguin Group (USA) Inc.

PRINTED IN THE UNITED STATES OF AMERICA

10 9 8 7 6 5 4 3 2 1

ALWAYS LEARNING   **PEARSON**

The Conquest
of Lady Cassandra

Chapter 1

•

"With each passing minute, I am more relieved that it will be a small wedding," Emma admitted. She gazed into her looking glass while her maid fitted a headpiece onto her golden-brown crown.

"I am wishing with each passing minute that it were larger," Cassandra said. She gestured for the maid to move aside and took over with the headdress. Covered in white silk and decorated with tiny pearls and a discreet white feather, the confection looked stylish but subdued, and appropriate for a bride who was a mature woman and not some girl fresh from her first Season.

Emma's age was one reason for the small wedding. The others were the location in the country, the dispersal of good society throughout the realm in August, and perhaps a desire on Emma's part not to be the center of an assembly.

"At a large wedding, one can avoid people whom one wants to avoid without being obvious," Cassandra continued while she worked two hairpins into place. "You, as the bride, can't, of course. But a guest can."

Emma looked at her in the reflection. "Do you anticipate being cut by some of them? Is that why you did not come down from town until yesterday?"

"Actually, I was thinking there may be some guests that *I* might want to avoid," Cassandra said, with a laugh. "I delayed because my brother insisted on visiting. You are a good friend to concern yourself with my reception by society, but you worry for naught. Southwaite's relatives and friends would never insult him and you that way."

She wished she could share with Emma the real reason she had delayed leaving London. Emma possessed great sense, and could advise her on how to handle the threats her brother Gerald, the Earl of Barrowmore, had made about Aunt Sophie. A year ago, Emma might have found a way to loan her the money, which had suddenly become so critical if she were to thwart Gerald's nefarious plans.

But it would be selfish to darken a friend's wedding day with tales of woe. Emma was about to become the new Countess of Southwaite, and her freedom to help a friend was circumscribed by larger duties. Also by a husband who did not much like that friend.

Emma turned in the chair. Her expression suggested she guessed at Cassandra's inner turmoil. She pulled Cassandra into an embrace and rested her head against Cassandra's body.

"Thank you for coming, even if it was later than planned. Had you not, I would have prepared all alone today, with only a maid, and had no one to laugh with me to keep my nerves calm."

Cassandra stroked her hand down Emma's head and along the curls that fell over her shoulder. At twenty-five, Emma was older by two years, but when it came to worldly things, Cassandra had often thought of Emma as a younger sister. She savored their embrace, especially because if she could find the means to take Aunt Sophie out of Gerald's reach, there would not be many more.

"You are my best friend, Emma, and a most exceptional friend you are too." Among Emma's remarkable qualities had been the ability to disapprove without scolding, and to accept a friend's choices without demanding explanations. "Nothing could have kept me away." She reached for her reticule where it rested on a chair. "Now, a bit of paint on your cheeks and lips."

"You know I do not paint."

"Just a touch, Emma. Only this once, so you do not look like a terrified ghost."

Emma made a face at herself in the looking glass. "I am a bit pale, aren't I? Do I really appear a little terrified too?"

"More than a little. There is no accounting for it either. It is not as if a great mystery waits for you when you go to your chamber afterward. Has he been a gentleman this last week, and stayed away so that he did not leave your bed the morning of the ceremony?"

Emma blushed. "How did you guess? He behaved most properly."

"How annoying that must have been."

Emma's face turned bright red. They caught each other's eyes and laughed.

"He probably wants to make you eager for the *official* first time," Cassandra teased.

"I think the presence of his aunts and sister restrained him. He became a paragon of virtue the day they arrived."

"That is because his aunts are ruthless gossips. They probably assume that only your being with child would explain this wedding at all. I would not be shocked to learn they took turns keeping watch at night to see if they could catch him sneaking in your door."

"Hortense probably brought a spyglass just for that purpose." Emma giggled. "In truth, though, more likely Darius did not want to scandalize Lydia."

Cassandra dabbed some paint and rubbed Emma's cheeks until it faded to a light blush. The Earl of Southwaite, whom Emma would marry within the hour, treated his sister Lydia like a schoolgirl, even though she was twenty-two. In order to preserve her innocence, he had forbidden her to be friends with Cassandra, which was one of several reasons why Cassandra did not overly favor him.

Considering Southwaite's prejudice against her, she had not expected an invitation to this wedding. Emma had obviously prevailed. Despite his faults, he did love Emma to the point of intoxication.

It remained to be seen if, a few months hence, the husband still indulged his wife should Cassandra remain in England. She did not expect either of those things to come to pass. As a result, these preparations with Emma possessed a poignant quality.

"All done." She moved so Emma could see the looking glass again.

Although not a great beauty, Emma's eyes held beguiling sparks, and her attention compelled one with its directness. She now focused deeply on her own reflection.

"It is time, and I am as ready as I will ever be. Will you walk down with me, Cassandra? If I falter when I see the guests, you must pinch me and push me forward."

"The man you love is waiting for you there, dear friend. He is all you will care about when the doors open." She fell into step with Emma anyway, so that they would face the waiting world together at least one more time.

A man had only to look at Lady Cassandra Vernham to begin imagining scandalous things. That rumors claimed she at least dabbled in the art of pleasure did nothing to discourage such thoughts when they invaded.

She stood near tall windows upon which rain formed arabesque rivulets. She had just disengaged from one conversation, and now examined the guests, planning her next social sortie.

Her dark curls in their fashionable, reckless abandon appeared almost black in the overcast light. Her large blue eyes implied an innocence that the full redness of her lips contradicted. The creamy, frothy dress flattered her body too well, emphasizing its feminine lushness.

Not for the first time in his life, Yates Elliston, Viscount Ambury and heir to the Earl of Highburton, thought that Cassandra Vernham looked good enough to eat. The room's colors and sounds blurred as his imagination feasted. His mouth kissed and tasted shapely, snowy legs, and moved up her body while his hands raised the creamy dress to reveal—

"Damn bold of her to come."

The pleasant fantasy, which had reached the curve of an extremely sensual thigh, vanished. Yates turned to see his friend Viscount Kendale glaring in Cassandra's direction.

"The bride invited her. They are very close friends," Yates said. The noise in the drawing room reasserted itself, rising around him like an orchestra tuning its instruments.

"She has to know that Southwaite dislikes her."

"He permitted her invitation in order to indulge Emma," Yates said. "If he does not mind her presence, why should you?"

"I am not blinded by love the way he is, that is why. I saw the way you were looking at her just now, for example. With all the women available to you, and damned eager to accommodate you from what I can tell, there is no need to set your sights on *that* one."

Kendale alluded to the fact that six years ago Cassandra had refused to marry Baron Lakewood, one of their friends, after he had compromised her. Both of their reputations had paid a high price for her capriciousness. Worse, the prior spring, Lakewood had died fighting a duel over a woman. Presumably that woman had been Cassandra, since he had never stopped loving her.

"I was merely considering some business that I need to conclude with her, and planning how to do so." The delay in settling that business had been inexcusable, even if family duties made it explainable.

"The hell you were. I know that look. Unless—you are not contemplating seduction as an act of revenge, are you?"

Not at the moment, but the unworthy idea had entered his mind more than once over the years. It had been the ignoble attempt of a randy mind to find excuses to do what should not be done. Cassandra Vernham had never married. A gentleman should not seduce her innocence, even if the latest *on dit* said she no longer had any.

From the looks of him, Kendale could not decide whether to disapprove of the idea, which meant he appreciated the conundrum. Normally Kendale adhered to rigid notions of honor, but Cassandra's suspicious independence put her outside any strict way of viewing those ideals.

"It is a different sort of business that I must conclude with her. Much less pleasurable."

Across the drawing room, Cassandra strolled away from the windows. With the grace and self-possession befitting the daughter of an earl, she attached herself to a small knot of guests. Within two minutes, she was at its center. After her addition to the group, both the conversation and guests' expressions changed from careful and wary to free and lively.

"Hell of a way for Southwaite to start his marriage. Now it will be almost impossible to force the break between his wife and that woman," Kendale said.

Yates almost explained the obvious—that Southwaite was too much in love to refuse his new wife anything. He had married Miss Fairbourne, hadn't he? Despite her common birth? Most of the guests did not approve of that any more than they did Cassandra Vernham.

"I suppose we must do our duty as charged." Kendale raked his dark hair back with his fingers. "Hell of a thing."

"She is holding her own without our help."

"We promised the bride."

"So be it. Fortunately, you will be at your post only until breakfast. I must take over then. We should line up in a quarter hour, I think."

"What am I supposed to talk about? Should I ask her about the most recent gossip attached to her name?"

"Are you even aware of it? I had no idea you followed the scandal sheets, Kendale."

"I read nothing and heard nothing. Yet I still know what the gossip would say. As do you."

Indeed, Yates did. "The rumors remain vague. The men remain nameless," he said, thinking aloud, once more calculating his obligations as a gentleman.

He would not mind knowing how true those rumors had been. While not complete, her fall had been far enough to make her fair game for his imagination, and thus unacceptable as a friend for the new Lady Southwaite. Presumably Southwaite would deal with that problem in the following weeks.

Cassandra smiled and sparkled as she extricated herself from her current group and walked away, greeting all whom she passed.

Kendale forced his scowl to fade. "Here I go. Fifteen minutes, you said. You must take over if it is one second more."

Cassandra prayed that the servants would call the party to breakfast. *Now.*

Until ten minutes ago, she had managed the forty guests in the drawing room very well. Then her situation had turned hellish. For reasons she could not fathom, Viscount Kendale, one of Southwaite's best friends, had not only addressed her but had decided to stick to her side.

She walked this way and that, and he followed like a shadow. She tried to engage other guests in conversation, and his face hovered above her shoulder. Anyone generous enough to throw a question his way received a minimal response. To say that polite conversation was not one of Lord Kendale's skills would be a kind way to describe his lack of social grace.

He had served in the army, so one expected better of him. Most officers were very amiable. Presumably, those who were not avoided society. Kendale's unexpected inheritance of the title meant he could hide no longer. Someone must have advised that at parties he attach himself to a woman who could cover his artlessness.

It appeared that today he had chosen her.

She stopped trying to converse with others, in order to spare everyone. She and Kendale stood near the windows while a long silence stretched.

"Regrettable weather." It was the third time he had commented on the rain. His handsome face remained a stoic blank, and his green eyes looked over the gathering.

"Fortunately, this is an expansive and comfortable house, so inclement weather will not dull the festivities." If he insisted on that topic, she would make the best of it. "Also, the storm should keep any boats carrying spies from trying to slip to the coast, and thus ensure that Southwaite and you do not have to leave, and ride out to save the realm in the middle of his wedding day."

Kendale's expression firmed. His eyes turned steely. "Our efforts to secure the coast from uninvited guests are small and uncelebrated, but I trust not worthy of your mockery."

"I do not mock you, Lord Kendale. Indeed, I am one of the few who knows enough about your activities to give what celebration there may be. Your bravery in this summer's earlier adventure has been described to me. Also, I would never insult a man whom I know my dear friend Emma holds in such high esteem."

His gaze shifted to the bride and groom. "I would have preferred if Miss Fairbourne had been discreet about that.

It should not be fodder for gossip by—" He caught himself. He drank more punch.

By such as you. That was what he had started saying before better sense stopped him. That, or something worse perhaps.

Really, the man was not to be borne. Here she was, doing a good deed by tolerating him, and he had the effrontery to almost insult her outright.

"Do you fear that I am going to whisper about you to my lovers, Lord Kendale? Sell your name to a French spy?"

"Nowadays, there is no telling who is a French friend or a French spy, when you get down to it."

"Then let me reassure you, sir. Emma's confidences are never fodder for my gossip, to *anyone*. Even notorious women have their loyalties. Your own experiences with members of the fairer sex have taught you that by now, haven't they?"

"I have been spared experiences with women who are determined to be notorious. Considering the consequences that I have seen for other men, I do not regret whatever else I may have forgone as a result."

"How fortunate for you. I should conclude that you are very particular about your feminine acquaintances and be flattered by your attention today. Although, instead I am tempted to wonder if you have had experiences with *any* women, besides your relatives and governess, that is."

Kendale's eyes narrowed. He opened his mouth to respond. A hand came to rest on his shoulder in a gesture of bonhomie, stopping him.

"Forgive me for interrupting, but it appeared you two were about to have a spectacular row." Viscount Ambury smiled at his friend, then at Cassandra. "If there will be fisticuffs, we should all repair to the privacy of the terrace. I will referee, and the rain be damned."

Kendale's face flushed. His embarrassment only made him angrier. Cassandra looked toward Emma to see if the little argument had been noted by the dear friend whose wedding day should never be so blemished.

She tried to cover the awkward tension with humor. "I dare not damn the rain, Lord Ambury. This dress would not survive a drizzle, let alone the downpour out there now."

Ambury's remarkable blue eyes inspected her from head to toe. His gaze lingered on how the diaphanous, filmy cream silk flowed from the high waistline of her dress.

"Too true. I daresay that when wet that dress would stick to you like the garments do on Greek statues. Alluring to be sure, but perhaps not appropriate for a wedding party." He turned to his friend, who had retreated into surly silence. "Kendale, perhaps you would take Lady Lydia something to drink. She appears parched over there."

Lord Kendale left. Cassandra rather wished he hadn't. Ambury was one of the people she had been trying to avoid. Now here he was, right in front of her, wearing a sardonic smile that had her wondering just how bad this was going to be.

She did not know Kendale well, but she did know Ambury. For a good many years, until this summer, their conversations had been restricted to brief greetings. During the last few months a private subject had arisen, however, that required more words.

When she had sold her jewels last spring at Fairbourne's auction house, Ambury had won the best pieces, a pair of sapphire-and-diamond earrings. Ever since, he had put off paying for them.

Their communications on the matter had been in writing, and stiffly polite. However, in a fit of panic after her brother's visit two days ago, after deciding to help Aunt Sophie run away, she had jotted off an intemperate missive full of demands and accusations.

With any luck, he had not read it yet. Not that his reaction would change the essential truth of the history they shared, and the real reason for the silence as they faced off right now. Ambury detested her because of the role she had played in the life of one of his friends.

His gaze and stance communicated the expected disdain, but also an undeniable masculine interest that surprised her. His presence exuded challenge, and his eyes dared her to— what? Play with the fire that smoldered in spite of their both knowing it should not? A touch warmer, a bit more dangerous, and his attention would imply that she could be had for a smile, and was amenable to whatever he contemplated.

"Thank you for arranging for my escape," she said. "I so want to speak with Lady Hollenfield, but I dared not bring Lord Kendale along." She angled her body away so he would know his further attendance was not required.

"Forgive Kendale. We are hard at work improving his manners. I am confident that in a year or two he should not provoke more than three rows at any wedding he attends."

She laughed lightly at his wit. To her dismay, he took that as an invitation to walk with her. She glanced askance at his profile. "Did you come down from town yesterday, Ambury?"

"I arrived yesterday, but I rode in from Essex."

"Then you have not been in town for a while?"

"I am still involved in family matters that keep me from town most weeks, as I explained in my letters."

If he had not been in town, he probably had not seen *her* letter, in which she accused him of using his family as an excuse in order to avoid paying her for the jewels.

"Are you riding back to town after the breakfast?"

"I still have business at the family seat. I expect to be in town by Monday, however."

At which point he would read a letter that had been in his house for more than a week. Forthright would be a diplomatic word with which to describe its tone.

The musicians ended one piece. The absence of music left a sudden void.

"Will you be playing today?" she asked, seeking a safer subject. Ambury was known to be a superb violinist. It was an unexpected talent for a man-about-town reputed to have no productive avocation.

"I rarely do in public."

"Not even for your good friend and his bride?"

"I have already played for them. Privately."

"That must have been very romantic."

"Perhaps. I would not know."

"Come now, do you expect me to believe that you have never used your music to make a lady pliable? You are not known as a man to resist pressing his advantage in the games of love."

"Is that how we will pass the time? Comparing each other's reputations? Or will I be constrained as a gentleman from participating in that topic?"

What a prickly response! Deeming polite discourse impossible, she began easing away in the direction of Lady Hollenfield.

Ambury remained with her step for step.

"I do not know why Kendale addressed me at all," she said when it became clear he would not leave. "He does not care for me any more than the rest of your circle do. You are now being suspiciously solicitous in his stead. Surely, with all the women here, you can entertain yourself for the remaining time with more appealing company than me."

"I doubt that. The very appealing image of that dress soaked in rain has lodged in my head now, giving you the advantage over the others."

"If you focus on the history of the woman who wears it, that should remove the image quickly enough."

He frowned, as if trying to follow her instructions. Those blue eyes scrutinized her slowly. The examination proved so thorough that she felt naked when he finally gazed in her eyes. He flashed a devastating, devilish smile. "Alas, your advice made it worse. Now the dress has a lovely body inside it, and I'm damned if anything else matters."

"I am not a schoolgirl mesmerized by your charm, Ambury. All the bold flirting that you can muster will not make your attention any less peculiar."

He laughed lightly, but his eyes told another story. Ambury could smile ever so amiably while the daggers within his wit sliced one to shreds. She worried that he honed the edges of those blades now.

"You are too clever for us. The truth is that Lady Southwaite asked Kendale and me to make sure you were not left stranded, what with her new husband's relatives making up most of the party. Do not let her know I told you. She meant well."

How like Emma to arrange this. Unfortunately, Emma did not know that Kendale and Ambury were the last people in this chamber to choose for the mission.

She gave her full attention to the man dragooned into what had undoubtedly been an unwelcomed duty. Too handsome for his own good, and far too charming for most women's safety, Ambury turned heads when he walked into a chamber. As was often the unfair case with such men, maturity only made him more appealing.

He must be over thirty now, but his dark hair had not thinned at all. The faint lines that had begun to etch paths on either side of his mouth only brought attention to how masculine and well formed that mouth appeared. His lean strength flattered the current fashions, which he wore with a flair that managed to convey both fastidious care and self-confident indifference.

His dark blue, deep-set eyes regarded her just as directly as she did him. Everyone always said that his eyes reflected his good humor, but his amusement right now contained much that did not flatter her.

"Emma does not know why you two would never welcome such an obligation," she said. "You could have explained it and been free of the chore."

"Far be it from me to describe your fall from grace to her if you chose not to do so. I did think it an odd omission in a friendship so close."

"Emma does not care about ancient history or stale gossip. She is a rare person, who accepts people as she finds them and who forms her own judgments without the influence of others. It was generous of you to agree to her request. I do not require your aid, however."

"We gave our word. You are stuck with one of us."

If she had to suffer Lord Kendale again, there really might be a row. Since it appeared Ambury had not read her letter yet . . . "How long must we tolerate each other's company?"

"She requested our attendance on you through breakfast."

"That long?"

"Afraid so."

He would be at her elbow for hours, it seemed. What a discomforting nuisance.

Chapter 2

"I hope you do not mind leaving through this door," Lydia said as she led the way through a passage angling toward the northern side of the manor house. "I would prefer to avoid the eyes and questions of my aunts."

Cassandra assumed those questions would be about the advisability of riding with Cassandra as a companion. Although Lydia was old enough to be on the shelf, she lived under the supervision of a host of adults. Cassandra knew that her own family itched to treat her the same way. She only possessed the freedom that she enjoyed because Aunt Sophie had given her a home.

"I am just happy that the rain stopped," she said. "A good ride followed by bathing in the sea will be wonderful."

Cassandra held her skirt up so she would not trip on the rose-hued riding dress that she had borrowed from her friend. Lydia's greater height explained some of the excess material, but the skirt was overlong by design to ensure modesty on the saddle. She noted with misgivings that it did not fit properly in other ways either. The fabric strained over her breasts.

"I told the servants to have a sure-footed mare brought for you, so the mud should not be a problem," Lydia said as she turned the latch on a heavy door.

Lydia would not require such care herself. Lydia was an expert horsewoman, due in part to being the sister of a man who owned one of the finest horse farms in England.

Two grooms waited outside, holding their mounts. As they were helped onto the saddles, Cassandra noted another reason why Lydia did not want her aunts viewing this departure. Lydia wore pantaloons under her skirt, and settled on a saddle that required her to ride astride. Cassandra's own sidesaddle permitted a more decorous seat but promised a pace that she doubted Lydia would enjoy much.

They avoided the main lane that connected the house with the road, riding cross-country. The sun shone brightly, and the damp formed a fine mist.

"I was delighted when you suggested this, Lydia, but I hope you will think it worth it if your brother discovers our outing."

Lydia smiled. Unlike her public smiles that appeared as false as they were, this one animated her entire face. Her dark eyes and hair, and her face's delicate but clear bone structure, gave her a lovely, somewhat poetic countenance.

"I believe my brother will be very occupied this afternoon, and not thinking about me. He did not wait to take his pleasure, but I do not think he will mind doing so again."

Cassandra laughed. "I did not know you were aware of that."

"I am not supposed to know, but I am not stupid."

Lydia guided their horses north on the coastal road, once they reached it. The mud seemed even worse, filling the wheel ruts that had baked into the dirt. Cassandra hoped conditions improved by morning, or it could take her days to get back to London.

"I read about you in a scandal sheet last week," Lydia said.

"That is hardly new." For years now the scandal columns alluded to all kinds of bad behavior by her. It was all innuendo, and mostly made out of whole cloth, but there were people who believed all of it—in particular, her own family.

"It was reported that you have not been seen gambling for months now. That is new for you—being notorious for giving up a vice. I hope that you are not reforming. I shall cry if that ever happens."

"On this one thing, I fear that I must. The losses I suffered in the spring have taught me to trust neither my luck at the tables nor the honor of those I play against."

That garnered Lydia's attention enough that she slowed the pace of her horse. "I heard you had to sell your jewels to recover. Are you saying you think your opponents cheated?"

"I am almost sure of it. I dare not say so publicly, and it can never be proven, however."

"Are you sure it cannot be proven?"

"Only if they are caught while doing it again."

"Yes, I suppose nothing less will do."

"Alas, even that will not return my money to me." All kinds of trouble had resulted from that big loss. She had been forced to sell the jewels to pay off tradesmen who were dunning her. Now she wished she had ignored their threats a few months more and held on to the auction proceeds.

"You must tell me what happened. I will put my mind to finding a way to exact revenge. It will give me something to do when I am imprisoned by my brother. Now that he has come down to Crownhill, the rest of the summer will be a terrible bore."

"You complain too much, Lydia. Compared to my brother, yours is a saint. At least he has your best interests at heart. I increasingly fear that Gerald does not, but I do not know why."

"Has he been cruel? What more can he do? He does not give you a penny, and he has all but disowned you."

"He has been looking for ways to coerce me to obey

him." He had found a good one, too. She longed to confide, but to do so carelessly could spawn gossip that would help Gerald's plan. This outing was a reunion of sorts with Lydia, but the truth was they had not been good friends for a long time now.

"The scoundrel. Surely he cannot hope to succeed in forcing you to marry after all this time."

"I fear he believes he can."

"Then he is a fool, and has never realized what he has in you. If you would not let Lakewood do the right thing, and have survived the consequences for six years, you are hardly going to be impressed with whatever threats Gerald makes now."

Lydia's assessment flattered her more than she deserved. It also missed the danger of the current development. Gerald had realized that while threats against Cassandra herself had borne no fruit, those against Aunt Sophie might reap a good harvest.

Nausea fluttered as she remembered the smirk with which Gerald had offered his judgment that Aunt Sophie's mental faculties were failing and that she required care and watching. He had preened at his own brilliance in discovering a new front on which to fight their war. She hoped that he had believed the lack of concern she had pretended when she dismissed his threats as not only dishonorable but impossible.

In truth, she had been dying inside, and trembling from the realization of Aunt Sophie's vulnerability. Relatives were put away all the time. Officially, her brother had no authority over her aunt, but as the closest male relative, and an earl at that, he would probably succeed if he tried.

He counted on her accepting his authority to spare her aunt. He wanted her married and silenced and out of London and society forever, so he would be spared the embarrassment of her.

She imagined her life if she agreed to his demands. She

would be tied forever to some kind, dull fellow who liked to hunt quail and hated the Season. She would be buried on some country estate. Even Lakewood would have been preferable, and she had never liked or trusted Lakewood.

"Aunt Hortense considered joining us," Lydia said. "Thank goodness she decided the afternoon was too warm to come out. She would have only ruined our fun."

"Did you tell her that we are going to bathe in the sea as well as ride?"

"That was my mistake. It appealed to her. If she had come, she would have insisted on a pavilion being set up on the shore and an army of servants to attend on her. Hours would have been lost in preparation."

Cassandra took the answer to mean that no servants would attend on them, and there would be no pavilion. "It is a private spot, you said."

"Are you worried for your modesty? Have no fear. No one even knows the way down to the water except me, and the cove is such that even fishing boats cannot see the shore. Follow me. I will show you."

Lydia turned her horse toward the coast and an unpromising stretch of rough, high ground. Cassandra followed, impatient to bathe in the sea. The storm had not refreshed the air the way summer storms could. Now the sun created a steam off the ground that only increased the discomfort.

"We need to go up this rise, then down the other side," Lydia said. "Do not worry about the horse's footing. She will not fall."

"Is it as steep on the other side as this one?"

"More so. Once we are in the sea, you will agree it was worth it, I promise."

Lydia guided her horse up a path that only she could see. Cassandra followed with misgivings. She was not a bad horsewoman if her mount traversed London's parks. She imagined falling into the rocks and brush that she passed.

Her horse and her prayers absorbed her attention until

the path leveled and she came up beside Lydia. To her dismay, the little plateau on which they stood appeared to fall away in a cliff in front of her.

She groped for courage while she stared at the steep decline. "Let us stop here a minute, if you do not mind."

"I think there is no choice," Lydia said.

Cassandra looked at her. Lydia gazed down, with her lids lowered and her expression one of engrossed curiosity. Cassandra followed the direction of that gaze.

Others had also decided to bathe in the sea. Ambury and Kendale stood down by the water, stripping off their clothes. Their horses had been tied to a marooned ruin of a ship's mast close by the rock face.

"I thought you said only you knew about this spot, Lydia."

"I suppose my brother does too. He must have brought them at some time in the past."

Ambury had just thrown aside his waistcoat and was unfastening his shirtsleeves. At the moment, with the breeze tossing his hair and dressed in only shirt, pantaloons, and boots, he appeared like a buccaneer. In a few moments, he would appear like a naked sea god.

Cassandra vaguely noted that Kendale was further along. His shirt had already been removed, revealing a strong, muscular back that displayed some odd scars. Soon Ambury's own back came into view too, as he pulled off his shirt.

The muscles in his shoulders knotted and moved with a most appealing tension when he sat down and stretched to remove his boots. He said something to Kendale, and both men laughed. It sounded different from any laugh that Cassandra had ever heard. It was a masculine laugh, shared only with their own kind.

Spying on this private camaraderie captivated her. So did Ambury's body when he stood again. He had loosened his pantaloons. He slid them down his hips, along with his small clothes. He bent to pull the garments off his body.

A sharp intake of breath sounded in her ear. She turned to see Lydia wide-eyed.

"Close your eyes, Lydia! You should not be—"

"Oh, stop," Lydia said. "You sound like my aunts or, worse, my brother. You are looking and you are unmarried. Why can't I?"

"I should not either."

"Yet you are staring so hard you might be doing sketches of them."

"My reputation is already tainted. Yours is not. Furthermore, if it becomes known you were here, *I* will end up blamed." Imagining Southwaite's withering accusation, Cassandra leaned over and stretched out her arm so she could cover Lydia's eyes with her hand. Lydia laughed and paced her horse away so Cassandra could not reach.

"Lydia! Really."

"Oh, tosh. I believe that I am too old to be as ignorant as I am, and rumor says you have not been so ignorant in years. If we are caught, we will be damned together."

"If either of them turns around, you must look away. Do you hear me? I will not be responsible for that bit of ignorance being lost by you."

"Such delicacy. I think I like the Cassandra of the scandal sheets more than the real one."

"*Lydia.*"

"I promise. By the by, I had no idea, none at all, that a man's bum could look like that. Sort of molded from stone. The shape suggests softness like ours, but there is much that implies enough hardness to cause an arrow to bounce off."

Cassandra assessed the bums in question. Ambury's, in particular, arrested her attention. It was indeed a very hard one, well formed and charmingly swelled. "I have heard that not all men possess posteriors of such aesthetic superiority, Lydia. Soft men will be softer there too, I expect."

"You have heard that, have you?"

"Yes. That is the rumor."

"I think I should not enjoy a soft man so much, then. I think those indentations on either side adorable."

One man who was not soft at all stood in naked splendor now, gazing out to sea. Sun glistened off the water behind his form, and even off his hair and body. White ripples nibbled at his feet from the surf's eddies. Legs separated and limbs tense, Ambury raised both his arms and grasped his hands over his head. He stretched as if waking from the night, and all those taut muscles responded. Even the admired ones of his hard bum tightened more.

"Mercy, but the sun has become hot today," Cassandra muttered.

"I was just thinking the same thing," Lydia said.

Kendale was already in the water, with only his shoulders and arms visible as he swam against the waves. Ambury waded in. Inch by inch, water covered him. First his feet and lower legs. Then his thighs. Finally, he was submerged to his waist. He kept walking deeper, with his hands trailing through the water at his sides.

He stopped. Kendale called something and swam farther out. Ambury just stood there with the sun carving his back into planes and ridges and his hands pushing against the sea so that his shoulders tightened.

Lydia turned her horse. "We must go. Now! He knows we are here, I think."

"He has been looking east the whole time, Lydia." Cassandra began to turn her horse too. It took a bit of doing on the little plateau.

While she struggled with the reins, she saw out of the corner of her eye that Ambury had turned around. That distracted her enough that she gave the horse its head to find the way down on its own. She twisted to admire the front of the torso rising out of the sea, and a very well-formed torso she considered it to be.

She did not know if he saw her, or if he even looked where she and Lydia had been watching. In the next instant, he was on his back in the water, floating toward Kendale. Churning water obscured that which she had insisted Lydia not see, but not totally. Cassandra looked away, in part because her horse had decided to take the hill faster than she dared allow it.

Lydia waited at the bottom. She burst out laughing as Cassandra bounced toward her. "I hope my brother is enjoying his wedding day as much as we are."

"You must tell no one."

"I know that, but I shall burst. When we arrive home and Hortense asks how our afternoon went despite the loss of her company, I may choke. Do you think either one of them saw us up there?"

"I do not think so."

"What if one did? What if something is said?"

"Nothing will be said." At least, not to Lydia. "Some oblique teasing might come from Ambury, but I expect only stoic silence from Kendale. However, should either of them, or anyone else, so much as allude to it, you must pretend total ignorance of what they mean. No giggles, Lydia. No blushes. Look through them as if they are made of glass, and do not react at all."

"That is easy. I can do that."

Of course she could. Lydia spent most of her days doing that.

"Since we did not get to go into the sea, baths in our chambers are in order after this ride," Cassandra said. "Let us return to the house so I can call for one."

A nice cold one.

"I'm telling you someone was up there," Kendale said as he and Yates directed their mounts up the steep hill.

"I saw no one."

"I sensed it. We were not alone."

Yates had sensed it too. Right before Kendale had called

out a warning, he had felt the presence of others, and of being watched.

"I think it was *that* woman."

"She has a name, Kendale. If she was there, and I do not think she was, she would have been there in the hopes of coming down to bathe too."

"Perhaps, but having seen us there, she should have left. Instead, she watched."

"You do not know that."

"I think that I saw bits of color through the brush and trees, and not huge flowers. Someone else was there too."

Yates preferred to avoid where this was going. If *that woman* saw them stripping, it would be bad enough. If Southwaite's sister had . . .

"Since you are not certain about any of it, let us assume no one was there. It is the conclusion any gentleman would make."

Kendale rode on. His expression displayed his consternation. "When we see them next, it will be difficult to act as if nothing happened."

"Yet we must, since nothing did happen for certain."

"That woman will probably let us know she saw us, without saying so directly. She will be clever and arch about it, but she will let us know."

"If she does, you must not react in any way. Appear confused if necessary, but better to look through her as if she were made of glass and her allusion has no meaning to you at all."

Kendale nodded, but hardly appeared appeased.

They crested the hill and started down to the road snaking below. Two colorful dots, pink and blue, moved along it, heading south. The close proximity of the ladies in question did not bode well for Ambury's insistence that no one had watched from the ridge.

Kendale's posture turned military and rigid. His jaw squared. His face took on more color.

"It would help if you did not look guilty, Kendale. I said you must not react at all. Instead, you are blushing like a schoolboy, and we are still a good seven hundred yards away from them."

"I don't like it, is all."

"No one likes such discomforting situations, but—"

"Not the awkwardness. I do not like that a woman saw me naked but I did not see her naked. There is disadvantage in that, you must admit."

"Are you concerned that they were judging us the way we might judge them, regarding the aesthetics of that particular view?"

"Hell, no."

"Then I do not understand why—"

"Women don't do that. Look at men that way, I mean." Kendale laughed. "The idea is unnatural."

"Do they not? And you know this for a fact because of your vast familiarity with women, I assume. Having been naked with scores of them, you noticed that not a single one ever reacted warmly to the sight of your body? By Zeus, I stand corrected then."

Kendale's jaw firmed again.

Yates noticed that their pace had slowed to where, if Kendale had his way, they would never catch up with the ladies in question.

"If you say women might look at men that way, I must concede it could happen, since you probably *have* been with scores of them. It is a definite possibility with one of the women in question, I will grant you that." Kendale picked up the thread of the conversation as if several minutes had not passed. He had been chewing over the revelation all the while, it seemed. "If so, I am definitely not concerned. Unlike you, I do not spend my time in hedonistic pursuits, but lead an active life. If any judgments on bodies took place, I am confident that I, at least, passed muster."

"Then I guess all eyes were on you today. I am relieved

to know it. Now I can converse with either lady without the slightest embarrassment."

While Kendale absorbed the implications of *that*, Yates kicked his horse into a gallop.

"We have company," Lydia said, her gaze aiming to the northeast.

A horse had just descended the hill and now galloped in their direction, its hooves throwing up clods of mud. Another rider came slower and aimed south toward the house and not at them.

"I think it is Ambury," Cassandra said.

"Oh, dear, it is. He has seen us and is coming to join our outing." Lydia turned her horse. "Forgive me, Cassandra, but I cannot face him so soon after—I dare not stay. If I do, I am sure to giggle."

With that, Lydia galloped away.

Vexed at being abandoned, Cassandra turned her attention to Ambury. If he found it odd that Lydia had chosen that moment to exercise her horse, his expression did not reveal it. He pulled up his horse just as Lydia disappeared into a copse to the north.

His gaze contained no indications that he knew she and Lydia had been on that ridge. None at all. And yet, in that instant, she knew that he knew she had been there. She could not identify what about him told her that, but it was in him as plain as could be.

She looked back as blandly as he looked at her. She was sure that she revealed no more than he did. All the same, it passed between them in that gaze—the mutual acknowledgment that she had watched him undress and that he knew she had.

An image flashed in her head of this man walking into the sea naked. Then another one, of him naked right now on that horse. She pushed both pictures away, lest she betray herself with a flush.

"Lady Cassandra, I see that you can call up the weather's obedience at your command. I am sure everyone in the party is grateful that you ordered the sun to appear."

"My command had little influence. It was a gesture of mercy on the sun's part, so Lydia and I could steal away to avoid having to entertain Southwaite's aunts. Both ladies would have been discomforted by my presence."

"I see Lydia has now decided everyone would be discomforted by *her* presence."

"She loves to ride hard. I was holding her back."

"Then allow me to accompany your return to the house. We will hope the sun remains generous."

Cassandra looked for Lydia again, but she was well gone. She moved her horse forward. Ambury fell in beside her.

"Finding you out here, away from the wedding party, was fortuitous," he said. "I want to thank you for your forbearance and discretion about the auction. It was gracious of you not to mention it at the party or at breakfast. You have been extraordinarily patient."

She thought about the letter she had sent. It had been a blazing example of patience abandoned. "Will more time be required? Please do not be insulted by my question. I truly need to know. I sold those earrings out of necessity, and my situation has not changed. I have not sold them elsewhere, because you promised to settle within a few weeks, but rather more time has passed than that."

"The delay in paying up was not caused by lack of funds, if that is what you think."

It was exactly what she thought. Everyone knew that Ambury's father, the Earl of Highburton, kept his heir short of the kind of allowance a man in his position might expect. It was the financial expression of an estrangement between them.

"I have not mentioned this in our correspondence, but

perhaps I should have, so you did not doubt my word regarding family matters preoccupying me. My father is very ill," Ambury said. "Gravely so. I have spent all of the time I could spare this summer with him and the solicitor, helping them to get his affairs in order."

"I am sorry to hear that. It is wise to involve yourself, I suppose, and take care of it while he can help."

"He thought to do most of it himself. However, he lacks the strength, so more has fallen to me these last months than I expected."

"Is that where you were this week?"

"Yes."

"You are taking great care in this duty to him, it appears."

"It matters to him that everything is in perfect order."

"Is it your peace offering? Your attempt to mend the differences that grew over the years?"

He looked at her as if she had just said something surprising. He appeared almost vulnerable for a moment. "A small attempt, perhaps."

"The reasons for those differences probably seem very insignificant now that time is running out."

"Yes. Damned insignificant."

So this was the reason for the repeated delays over the last months, as he put her off again and again. The harsh accusations in that letter now mortified her. Under the circumstances, they would read as unfair and cruel.

"The earrings are exquisite, and I, of course, will be glad to pay what I bid for them and finally take possession," he said. "How did you come by them?"

"Almost all the jewels that I sold at Fairbourne's were given to me by my aunt."

"Were those earrings among the jewels that you received from her?"

The question sounded rather pointed. Now that she thought about it, he had asked this in one of those earlier communications too.

"Why do you want to know?"

He shrugged. "Fairbourne's is very careful about the provenance and history of the paintings it sells. Less so about the jewelry."

"The provenance is very clear. They came from *me.*"

"And before you?"

"A ruby is a ruby. A diamond is a diamond. The provenance, or history of ownership, is not needed to support the claim of what it is, like collectors expect with a Raphael drawing."

"I suppose not. Still, I would like to know more of their history. Part of the pleasure of owning something rare and beautiful is knowing its history," he said. "At least it is for me."

She could tell him. There was no real point in not doing so. So why did she find herself hesitating, and feeling very suspicious? Perhaps because right now, for all his pleasantness, he did not really appear friendly. His best features, his eyes and that mouth, betrayed him in nuanced ways.

They rode along another hundred feet before he spoke again. "Then you did receive them from your aunt?"

His persistence made her ill ease increase. Her grip tightened on her reins. "You are too boring with your questions."

He laughed. "Forgive me. I will try to entertain you with different ones. For example, how long were you up on that rise, watching me disrobe?"

He caught her off her guard completely. She flushed and stammered and acted just as she had scolded Lydia not to. "I am sure I do not know what you are talking about," she finally choked out.

His blue eyes twinkled. He enjoyed her disadvantage too obviously. "It was very naughty of you, but I do not mind. It relieves me of a difficult decision I was facing."

She was afraid to ask, but of course she had to. "What decision?"

"Whether to add you to my conquests. The plain evidence that you are indeed a woman of the world absolves me of some irritating points of honor on the question that have made me hesitate."

She felt herself flush again. Thoroughly, down to her toes. "Do you always announce your intentions so boldly?"

"Not usually. I thought it would save considerable time on this occasion."

She pulled herself together. The man was having too much fun at her expense. "Do you expect me to faint from anticipation, Ambury? Wait for your sly moves for weeks on end? You are not even serious. You are playing a game and trying to make a fool of me, as a way of expressing your disapproval and disdain." She turned her horse. "Now I will take my leave of you. Perhaps you would be useful and see if you can find Lydia before it rains again. I will ride alone the rest of the way back."

He leaned and caught her horse's bridle in his hand, keeping her in place. "I will call on you when I return to town."

"I prefer you not do that. Fighting off such a cynical seduction would be tedious."

"I will not call to seduce you. I do not announce my intentions *that* boldly. I need to settle about the earrings. Remember?"

The earrings. Of course.

"Perhaps your aunt will receive me too, for a short visit."

They were back to that now, were they? "She never receives now."

"I am sure that you can cajole her to make an exception for me."

"I can't imagine why I would." Indeed, she could think of several reasons why she would not. She jerked her horse free. "I have changed my mind. I will continue riding, and find Lydia myself. As for our business, I will expect to see you early next week in town."

Chapter 3

Cassandra examined the garden, looking for the plain straw bonnet that her aunt wore when she tended the plants. She spied its deep brim bobbing up and down behind some high rosebushes.

Both she and Aunt Sophie had modest incomes, but they could have a gardener if they chose. A man was hired in the spring and autumn to do the heavier work, but Aunt Sophie preferred to save his fees and devote herself to the daily maintenance. Since she no longer made morning calls or attended parties, she had plenty of time to do so.

Cassandra made her way on the paths to that straw bonnet. As she drew closer, her aunt's face showed with rhythmic regularity, framed by green leaves and red blooms. It was a handsome face still, despite its thinning skin and deepening lines. A little fuller now, just as Aunt Sophie's body had thickened these last two years. The current styles did not hide that the way the corsets and stomachers of the past had done. Not that Cassandra expected to find her aunt in a stylish column of muslin and a high waist. Sophie had not updated her wardrobe in ten years, but she no longer bothered with bone and lacing.

Did she only imagine that Sophie's eyes appeared distracted by thoughts far away from these plantings? She wondered if her aunt's mind dwelled in the past more vividly than normal memories would explain. That was what Gerald had said at that ugly meeting last week. That Aunt Sophie's mind was not entirely with them anymore.

Cassandra's chest grew heavy again with the worry his words had planted. She hated that her brother had turned his cruelty on Sophie. Not only worry saddened her, however. Guilt did too, and not only for being the cause of trouble for her aunt.

Ever since Gerald had raised the question, she found herself wondering if he were correct. Little things not noticed before—distant, vacant expressions such as Sophie wore now, loomed larger. Moments of forgetfulness carried more weight. Even Sophie's choice to retire from society— Cassandra had never questioned the reasons in the past, but Gerald had her wondering about them now.

She paced forward with determination. She would not allow Gerald to do this to her. To both of them. There was nothing wrong with Aunt Sophie's mind or judgments. Gerald would be grateful to be so sharp when he was past sixty years in age.

Turning around the roses, she found her aunt bending to pull out a vine that had assaulted the bed. Cassandra doubted a male gardener could have displayed more energy. Sophie's work gloves grasped and entwined that long, green invader while one booted foot braced her weight into the effort. The roots gave way just as Cassandra arrived. Sophie nearly fell from the sudden surrender that burst through the soil.

Sophie threw the vine into a basket, picked up her shears, and began eyeing the rosebushes.

"Late summer is the best time for flowers," she said, as

if Cassandra had been by her side all morning. "I think I will ravish these bushes and fill the house with roses today. Autumn's sad fading will be here all too soon."

"I will help. You cut, and I will put them in the basket."

Sophie began her snipping. A fussy woman when it came to objects of beauty, she did not take just any bloom. She considered and debated for a few moments before each cut.

Cassandra laid each fragrant rose in the basket. The pile began growing.

"I need your advice, Aunt Sophie," she said. "I have done something on impulse that I regret."

Sophie eyed the bush, choosing her next trophy. "I hope you found pleasure in it at least. I have always thought impulsive pleasure was the best kind."

Cassandra glanced askance at her aunt. It was advice of this nature from Sophie that made her mother and brother want her to come home.

"The impulse had nothing to do with—this is not about pleasure. Not in any way. I wrote a letter to someone that was indiscreet."

"Did I not tell you that letters can cause trouble? Words, once written, cannot be retracted. It is hard for them to even be forgotten. I warned you many times to never, ever, write when your emotions are stirred."

"You warned me, but you were speaking about affairs of the heart."

"If you want to call them that, I will not shock you by calling them something else. Please tell me that you did not either in this letter. I believe that a woman should be forward when necessary if she wants a man, but not on paper."

"I did not write to a man and declare my lust, let alone my love. Nor did I write to a lover already conquered and allude to our pleasure. I hope that I learned something from you all these years."

That made Sophie happier. She began to snip the next rose, but stopped. She suddenly appeared more substantial and alert. More *there*. "What was this letter you wrote, if not indiscretions to a lover?"

"I had some business with a man, and he was slow to conclude it. In a fit of pique, I wrote to him and demanded just that."

Sophie dropped her shears into the basket. She pulled the gloves off her snowy white hands. "I suppose having a solicitor write would have been more delicate, but I do not think you need to feel you behaved badly."

"I made accusations that in hindsight were rash. I suggested the delay was no accident. I used words that he might consider insulting. It would be better if he did not read it. I have reason to think he has not yet. I am wondering if I should offer his servant a bribe to find the letter and return it to me."

"Do you have a particular sympathy with this servant?"

"I do not know him at all."

Sophie strolled toward the house. "You should save your money, and not become distraught over this. Tradesmen are often called names, by each other and by customers. A degree of insult goes with the profit. This one will not react as badly as you think, and will probably even still welcome your patronage."

"That would be good news, if this were a tradesman. I regret to admit it is a gentleman."

"I see. May I ask which gentleman?"

"Does it matter to the advice you will give?"

"Oh, yes. It matters a great deal. One can't anticipate his reaction unless one knows his name. Hopefully it is a stupid fellow who will manage to read flattery into your insults out of a desperate desire to be pursued by a beautiful woman."

"I regret to say the gentleman is neither stupid nor desperate. It is Viscount Ambury."

Sophie's eyebrows rose. "Highburton's heir? That handsome young man with the blue eyes? Your dealings with him are financial in some way, and not those of lovers?"

"Definitely not those of lovers."

"What a shame. He is delicious. Don't look at me like that. The day I stop noticing is the day I hope someone shoots me."

"That letter will anger him. Bribing the servant is probably my only choice. How much will it take, do you think?"

"His manservant will never accept a small bribe. Ambury's good opinion and recommendation are too valuable to risk for less than twenty pounds, is my guess."

If she had an extra twenty pounds, she would not have written that letter to start. "Then I must do something else. *Soon.*"

She held the door so her aunt could enter the house with her bounty of blooms. Sophie set the basket down on a worktable in the cool cellar kitchen, took several containers off a shelf, then sat down to arrange her flowers.

Sophie eyed the composition she created in a French porcelain pitcher. With the precision of an artist, she broke the stem of one final rose and added it to the front, just so. She set the pitcher aside and pulled a fat round blue transfer vase toward her. Cassandra watched, and wondered if the topic of their conversation had drifted out of Aunt Sophie's mind entirely.

Finally her aunt had finished with the blue vase too. She sighed heavily as she reached for a pewter bowl.

"Good heavens, Cassandra, what were you thinking in sending a missive full of insults to Highburton's heir? If you are going to throw down a gauntlet before such a man, at least be sure there is an army positioned over the next hill to ride to the rescue."

Cassandra laughed. The evidence Sophie had been considering the dilemma heartened her. She hoped her aunt had concocted a solution while playing with all those roses. "Perhaps you know where I can find an army."

"In my youth, I could have summoned one with a smile," Sophie said wistfully. "Now—there is no army, dear. There is only me."

*   *   *

"This is the first time you have left the house in almost a year, and you are going dressed like that?" Cassandra said when Sophie emerged from her chamber late that afternoon.

Her aunt had been known for her style when she circulated in society, both at home and abroad. Today, however, she looked like an aging governess. Her old-fashioned gray dress lacked any adornments. She wore no jewelry. A large white cap with limited lace hid most of her hair.

"I am not leaving the house. Not officially. I am going as your companion. Let him think I am a servant. You are not to introduce me. I will be a lady's maid who is beneath his notice."

"I think it would be better if you were who you are. You could dazzle him so his brain is too numb to realize just how poor my bribe actually is."

"If I come at all, I come like this."

Wishing Aunt Sophie had primped more, Cassandra led the way down the stairs. A hired coach waited on the street. She helped Sophie in and settled across from her. She handed the coachman a piece of paper through the window.

"You are sure this is where Ambury has his chambers?" she asked Sophie. Her aunt had ruminated for four hours before revealing her advice and her plan. Cassandra was not convinced it was a good one.

They were to call on Ambury while he was still out of town, but pretend they believed him to be in residence. While insisting on an audience, Cassandra would broach the matter of the letter with a servant or whoever served as caretaker of the building. The hope was that a small bribe would be accepted and the letter produced merely to be rid of their presence.

"I do not make calls or accept invitations, but I am not

without friends," Sophie said. "I obtained the address with one short letter."

The coach started to bump and roll on the lanes.

"Do you remember that time in Saint Petersburg when we called on the Countess Petrovnik and you so impressed her?" Sophie asked.

"Her brother was in attendance, as I remember."

"You captivated them both with your beauty and vivacity. They completely forgot I was in the chamber."

"You exaggerate."

"Not at all. I am not speaking with any resentment. I am reminding you that my days of dazzling anyone are over, and it will be up to you to impress whomever we confront today. I am only accompanying you because it might be seen as odd if I do not. We cannot have you entering Ambury's chambers all alone, in broad daylight."

Cassandra wanted to say that a simple explanation would solve that problem, except it almost never did. There had been a perfectly logical explanation when she had been compromised by Lakewood. Everyone could see that her absence with Lakewood had been unavoidable, and not some assignation. All the same, they were both expected to snuff any flames of scandal by marrying.

What a stupid world it was. Yet it was the world in which they lived, and Aunt Sophie was correct. Ambury was not in town, but if someone saw her visit his chambers alone today, there would be hell to pay.

"Why are you smiling?" Aunt Sophie asked. "Something has put you in a merry mood."

"Just imagining what you alluded to makes me laugh. It would be a fine thing to end up compromised when the man isn't even in the same town as I am."

"Odd for you, but odder for him. Picture him returning to learn he stands accused of something he never even had the pleasure of consummating." Sophie's expression mimicked

Ambury's confusion, then shocked surprise. They both laughed.

"Maybe Gerald would call him out if he did not do the right thing," Cassandra said. "I say, Ambury! I demand satisfaction!"

"Damnation, sir, I was not even in the same county!" Sophie responded gruffly. "I know there may be celebratory rumors regarding my seductive powers, but even I can't bed a woman in London when I am in Essex."

"Your excuses will not restore my family's honor. Name your second, or be known as a coward!"

"I'll be damned if I will fight over her without having had her!"

"Then have her, sir, and we will meet the following morning!"

Cassandra wiped her eyes of tears brought on by her laughter. She found the exchange all the more hilarious because it was not entirely far-fetched.

Aunt Sophie's clever repartee also raised her spirits. This was the Aunt Sophie she knew and loved, the one who had given her a home after she had refused to marry Lakewood, the celebrated beauty who had taken her on a lengthy tour of the Continent's capitals. There was nothing distracted or vague to her right now. She was still the vivacious and somewhat bawdy sophisticate who had entertained princes and their courts for decades.

The coach stopped, and so did their fun. Sophie looked out at the house. "His chambers are said to be on the second level, carved out of the house's public rooms when it was made into gentlemen's apartments."

It appeared a nice enough building on a nice enough street, but one could tell that Ambury's living situation was modest. "Not what one would expect for an earl's heir."

"That is just Highburton's pride punishing a son who will not fit the family mold, I expect," Sophie said. "He will get it all in the end, so he probably has lengthy tallies all over town awaiting that day."

No doubt Ambury's expectations would allow a great deal of credit to accumulate. Perhaps he had assumed she would await that day, too, like all those tradesmen.

The coachmen handed them out, and they approached the door. Aunt Sophie stayed two steps behind, assuming the role of a shadow.

"My business with Lord Ambury cannot be delayed." Cassandra spoke haughtily, hoping to awe the balding, tall, thin man peering at her through spectacles.

He was having none of it. "As I explained, he is not at home."

"I have had reports of him being seen about town, so I know he is in residence here."

"I am his valet, and I think I know better where he is than whoever has given false reports."

"More likely he told you he wants to avoid me, and instructed you to help him do so. Go to him and explain that I will not be put off. It is time for him to give me satisfaction regarding his debt to me."

The word *debt* made him flush. "I cannot go to a man who is not in the building."

"Then I will wait for him to return." She looked past him, to the doors that would lead to the apartment's chambers. She felt Sophie at her back. A direct poke hit her spine. Taking the cue, she walked forward.

"My dear lady, I fear that you will wait in vain," the valet said as he scurried alongside her. "If you would leave your card—"

"He will never return the call if he is avoiding me now. I will wait. He is in town even if it has not been noted in the papers, and I expect he must return here at some time today."

Aunt Sophie moved into sight on her other side. *Dazzle*, she mouthed while the servant looked to heaven for patience.

Cassandra stopped before she reached the doors. She gazed in the valet's eyes and tried to appear in need of sympathy. The valet flushed a deep red.

"Might I know whom I am addressing, sir, since you have been kind enough to allow me to wait for Lord Ambury?"

"Robert Higgins, at your service." A half smile formed before the entirety of her statement penetrated. "As for your waiting, I did not—"

"The drawing room, I think you said. That would be these large doors here, I assume."

"Did I say that?" He truly did not seem to know. "Hardly fit to be called a drawing room in the normal way. More of a sitting room, if you will, but comfortable for my lord, I believe."

"I am sure it will be comfortable for me as well." Cassandra opened the doors. "Oh, most comfortable. Is this appealing arrangement of the chairs your doing, Mr. Higgins? Or does Lord Ambury have other servants?"

Higgins bowed his head modestly. "I do for my lord alone. Even a bit of cooking, if I may say so."

Cassandra sat on a nice bench near the fireplace. Aunt Sophie sat on a chair even closer to it, and her gray self seemed to blend into the gray stones of the hearth.

"I do not intend to be a burden. I will wait here and be quiet as a mouse," Cassandra said.

"I hate to think that you will waste a whole afternoon waiting for an arrival that will never occur."

"I doubt it will be wasted. I have much to think about, and this chamber is pleasant enough to encourage serious contemplation. In fact, you are so helpful and kind, perhaps you would consider giving me some advice on a matter that concerns me deeply."

He coughed and composed himself. "If I can be of service to you, then of course I must be."

"I had a little argument with a friend on a question of etiquette. Or maybe it was a question of morals. My friend faced a peculiar dilemma—" A tap on her arm distracted her. Sophie leaned toward her and whispered in her ear.

"Mr. Higgins, my servant sees the library through those doors. She is something of a bluestocking. Indeed, that is how she came to be a paid companion—all that reading made her unfit for marriage. Would you mind if she perused the volumes on the shelves? She promises not to touch any."

"Of course she may. Nor do I think my lord would mind if she removed one or two to look more closely. The best bindery is used, as she will soon see."

Without a word, the gray ghost rose and drifted across the chamber to the library door. Mr. Higgins watched. A puzzled frown formed on his face.

Cassandra claimed his attention again. "As I was saying, my friend had a dilemma. She wrote a letter to her mother, and posted it, but soon regretted its contents. She told me that she planned to intercept the letter prior to her mother reading it. Well, I said that was stealing. She insisted it was not. She claimed that until her mother opened it, the letter was still in transit. Which of us was correct, do you think?"

"I suppose, once posted, it belongs to the postal service, until it is delivered and paid for by the recipient, at which time it belongs to the recipient."

"So you agree that if intercepted, it is not stealing?"

"Not from her mother, if it is done before delivery. Of course, that would not be possible. The postal service does not hand over the mail."

"No. I suppose not." Behind Mr. Higgins, a gray form floated this way and that in the library. "Here was the situation that my friend faced. If she intercepted that letter, she would be doing a kindness. If her mother read it, the contents would only bring grief. You can see the moral quandary, I am sure."

Mr. Higgins nodded and looked sympathetic. "I do not envy her the choice. How did she resolve it?"

"She had her mother's maid remove it from the delivered mail and return it before her mother saw it."

Higgins frowned on hearing that a servant had stolen the letter.

"Now she wants to give the maid a gift. A token of her appreciation in sparing her mother all that sorrow. What so you think, Mr. Higgins? Can she do this without it tainting the maid's good intentions?"

"I suppose, since the maid risked her mistress's displeasure, a small gift might be in order."

"How small? If it were you, for example, what would you think was in order, but not so much as to smell of payment for services rendered?"

"*Me?* I would never do such a thing, so no amount would be in order."

"Not even to spare your master great anguish?"

"I can't imagine a letter would ever cause Lord Ambury *anguish.*"

"Perhaps a letter would lead him to challenge a man, and end up dead. Would it not be worth a slight deception to avoid that?"

"Dead! Goodness, what was in that letter your friend wrote to her mother? Something very shocking, I am beginning to suspect, if you equate it with an insult so severe as to require a duel."

Cassandra looked from one side to the other, as if checking to be sure no one would hear. The only other person in the chambers had disappeared in the library. Mr. Higgins leaned forward, more interested in the answer than he would probably want to admit.

"She had confessed to a liaison with a man," Cassandra whispered.

"No!"

"A most illustrious man. I dare not say his name, but I

assure you that this man is very well-known to *everyone* in the realm."

"You mean . . . Surely not . . . Goodness, she put this in writing? How indiscreet, even if it was to a mother."

"Exactly. So you can see the dilemma. For her, it was a matter of life and death in a way, and the prospect of a huge scandal loomed that would affect her whole family and even the reputation of—but I must not say! Surely it was as significant as an insult that would cause a duel, I think you will agree."

"Oh, my, *yes*."

"That servant did a good turn not only to my friend, but to England itself, I think."

"By, Zeus, it was a most noble deception."

"How well you put it. So, how much of a gift would be appropriate? If it were you who performed such a noble deception, for example?"

Higgins debated the matter. "Hard to say. One risks being sacked, doesn't one? There would be no recommendation either. Indeed, one's livelihood might be over for good. Noble or not, such a deception has huge risks, and the gift might reflect that."

Cassandra worried that Higgins increased the size of the "gift" with each mutter. "But it should not be so large as to appear to be a bribe, I think."

"Of course. Of course. Still—"

"I think we must go now, my lady." The frail declaration interrupted. The old woman who uttered it stood right behind Mr. Higgins.

He turned, startled by the reminder that he and Cassandra were not alone.

"In a few minutes, we shall," Cassandra said. She had Higgins close to naming a figure.

"I do not feel well, my lady. I am quite faint."

Higgins was at her side at once. "You should sit. I have salts here somewhere. I will—"

"Fresh air is all I require, thank you." Aunt Sophie sent a glare Cassandra's way.

"Of course," Cassandra said. "How unkind of me not to understand that if you spoke up at all, it was most necessary." She walked over to Sophie and slid an arm around her back. "Thank you, Mr. Higgins. For all your kind advice. I am rather glad that Lord Ambury was not at home. You have helped me enormously, and my business with him can be concluded another day."

With much fussing and worry on Higgins's part, they helped Aunt Sophie down to the waiting coach. As soon as Mr. Higgins returned to the chambers, Cassandra expressed her displeasure.

"I had him three-quarters there. He was about to name a sum, and I would then broach my situation and—"

"As it happened, that was not necessary." Aunt Sophie opened her reticule. She removed a letter and set it on Cassandra's lap.

It was her letter to Ambury.

"You stole it!"

"By your own explanation, and that of Mr. Higgins, it was not Ambury's until he read it."

"Until it was *delivered*."

"Oh, I missed that part. Goodness, how careless of me. Tell the man to turn this coach around, and we will return it at once."

Cassandra was hardly going to do that. Nor should she upbraid her aunt, no matter how disgraceful this theft had been. She now held the letter in her hand, instead of it lying in those chambers waiting for Ambury to see it.

She turned it over to break the seal and see if its language was as insulting as her memory insisted. The seal, however, was already broken.

"Aunt Sophie, I wish you had not read it. I understand your curiosity, but now I am embarrassed that you know just how immoderate I was."

Sophie's sharp interest snapped to Cassandra's face, then to the letter in her hand. "I did not open it. I slipped it out of a large stack of mail on a desk in the library and stuck it in my reticule without looking at it much at all."

That was not good news. The seal was broken. It was unthinkable that Higgins had pried into his master's mail.

Probably the seal had accidentally broken in transit. Yes, that was what happened.

The alternative did not bear thinking about.

Chapter 4

The house on Adams Street was a small abode on a lane toward the northern edge of Mayfair. Yates judged from its exterior that it provided comfort for Lady Cassandra and her aunt, but not luxury. It rose only three stories and looked all the more modest due to the two larger, wider houses that flanked it.

There would be servants, but not many. Possibly some sort of carriage was available, but only one, and not a grand coach.

He knew all about the economies such an existence required. His own father's lack of generosity left him living the masculine equivalent of this house. A man, however, had the option of supplementing his income, although, as the heir to a peer, strict discretion was in order when he sought employment. Fortunately, he had discovered in investigative missions an occupation that not only stimulated his intellect and provided some adventure, but one where the client desired discretion as much as he did.

No butler or footman opened the door, but rather a woman who appeared to be a housekeeper. She took him to a small drawing room upstairs and walked away with his card.

The chamber proved less feminine than he expected. Fabrics the colors of jewels covered the furniture. Dark wood abounded. One wall sported three framed prints by Piranesi. Not views of Rome, such as his father owned. Rather these were the bizarre prison engravings with their skeins of oppressive stairways leading nowhere.

Did they belong to Cassandra or the aunt? The images reflected a deep streak of independent taste and thinking.

In Cassandra's case, she was not merely independent, he now knew, but irreverent. Irresponsible. Irritating. She was probably guilty of all the bad behavior all the *ir-* words in the language alluded to.

He had cause to believe Cassandra Vernham had crossed the line from bold to brazen, and held no respect for even the basic proprieties and rules. It changed everything, and he no longer felt an obligation to couch his dealings with her in the sort of pleasantries that would save her pride.

"Lord Ambury. How good of you to call." Lady Cassandra addressed him immediately on entering the chamber. With her tumbling dark curls and ivory skin, and her body draped in a diaphanous, Grecian inspired pale yellow dress that floated with each step, she appeared both lush and luscious. "I trust all is well with your father."

"He is better. He is insisting on returning to town, so he will be close to any developments in the war."

"Even so, it is a sad time for you. I am sorry for that."

She appeared sincere. For a few moments, he allowed the balm of her sympathy to soothe the ragged emotions that the situation with his father had carved. Then he set that aside. His righteous irritation with her rose again.

"Have you reconsidered allowing me to see your aunt?"

"It is not my decision. She is not some old lady under my

care." She gestured for the woman who had met him at the door and who now stood near the wall, waiting to serve if called. She handed over his card. "Merriweather, bring this to my aunt. Tell her that Viscount Ambury has called on her."

It did not take Merriweather more than a minute to return and say that Lady Sophie could not receive today.

Cassandra dismissed the maid. "My aunt is jealous of her privacy now. Please do not take it personally, Lord Ambury."

She spoke sweetly. Innocently. The sparkle in her eyes could entrance a man who was not careful.

"I do take it personally. According to my man Higgins, she is hardly the recluse you say."

She batted those thick lashes at him. She widened her blue eyes. "Whatever do you mean?"

Damnation, the woman was treating him like a fool. "He said an old retainer accompanied you to my chambers yesterday. Your aunt, I assume."

"You assume a great deal, but then you have the reputation for doing so with women."

"Are you saying your chaperone yesterday was not your aunt?"

"Higgins's description of her as a servant should settle it for you. Surely your man can spot the difference between a servant and a lady."

"Not if the lady is working hard to appear as a servant."

"You give Mr. Higgins too little credit."

"On the contrary, I give you and your aunt a great deal of it. If the two of you set out to deceive Higgins, he would not have stood a chance." He moved closer to her. "Did you flirt with him? Were you that bold? That shameless? Did you captivate him with your attention and flatter him by insisting on conversation? Did you press your advantage as his better to throw him off his guard?"

"What peculiar accusations you make, Lord Ambury.

I called to press for a conclusion of our business, not to press my advantage."

"I doubt that. Having written that letter, you would not want to witness my reaction to it."

She stilled. She blinked twice. She donned a mask of innocence. "Letter? What letter?"

"You know what letter. The angry, demanding, insulting one in which you accused me of being a scoundrel, a blackguard, a fraud, a—what was it? Oh, yes, a *liar*. The letter you stole from my library yesterday."

He could see her flush from the edge of her bodice to her hairline. "Oh," she said. "That letter."

A mbury dominated the sitting room's space and air. His vitality imposed itself on every damned inch of it. A tall dark column of lithe strength, his presence and energy barely left Cassandra room to stand.

Yet stand she did. She had no choice. She had a lot of practice in facing down people like Ambury, and it helped her now.

His eyes smoldered so hotly that their blue color could not be seen. His jaws appeared carved out of rock. The line of his mouth looked almost as hard.

"Higgins said you were not in residence," she said. "It was my hope to retrieve the letter before you read it."

"I stopped here for a day only before going to Essex. I have not taken up residence of a public nature. Nor does it matter. Whether you took it before I read it, or after, it was not *retrieved*. It was *stolen*."

"I was most distraught when I wrote that, and I regretted it almost at once. It was very wrong to write those things. However—"

"However?"

"My apology about taking the letter stands, but I will not

apologize at all for insisting that you pay me what is owed. I have waited months for you to settle up on those earrings. I consigned them and the other jewels to that auction because I needed the funds. I am not some tradesman who can extend credit indefinitely, and due to circumstances that I cannot explain, my frustration got the better of me. So I apologize for the letter's worst insults, but I do not regret making sure that you attend to this matter now instead of months from now."

He glared at her. She steeled her spine so she would not flinch.

"So have you come to settle today, or only to berate me about my behavior?" she finally asked. "If I must still wait until next week, so be it, but that is the extent of my patience."

He shook his head in exasperation. "You are too bold by half."

"Bold enough to sell the earrings elsewhere if I must, along with the ring you left with me after the auction as surety."

"Even if you sell all of it, you will never get what I bid."

"That is why I have waited. But I can wait no longer and must do what is necessary."

A scowl still marred his brow, but it furrowed more in thought than anger now. "I simply want to know how your aunt came to own the earrings. Once I document the jewels' history, I will settle everything immediately."

"I never said those earrings came from my aunt."

"You never said they did not, so I assumed—"

"Too much, once again. However, I will admit to that part of their history now."

"Then establishing their provenance should not take long at all. Since she will not see me, I ask that you raise the matter with her."

"And if I refuse?"

"In bidding on those earrings, I was buying information as well as jewels. Without the information, I have received only half a loaf."

"My consignment at the auction was *jewelry*, not information. You are too much trouble. I will sell them elsewhere and—"

"I have been told that the earrings may have been stolen, you see. I am sure that you do not want to trade in stolen goods. The law frowns on that." He tossed out that accusation ever so calmly.

It took her a few moments to realize she had heard correctly. "*Stolen?* Who told you something so outrageous?"

"I cannot say. I am sure you see my problem, however. I would not want to give them to someone, only to have a claim made by someone else."

"I think I see a man putting me off again and finding a new game to do so."

He was right in front of her with four long strides. To her shock, he took her chin in his hand and tilted her head so he could look right into her eyes. "Do not insult me again. You may not be a man, and I cannot call you out, but there are other duels besides those of arms, and you are within a hairsbreadth of requiring one."

"Do your worst, Ambury. See what short work I make of whatever weapons you think you have. I have battled better than you."

It was a big risk to double back his own dare at him. Sophie would probably scold, and say bedazzlement would have been the better choice. Only she did not want to dazzle Ambury. She just wanted her damned money.

They stood locked in a mutual challenge. Slowly, she turned her head, demanding that he release his hold on her chin. Belatedly, he did so. It felt as if she had to yank herself out of his fingers. Free, she stepped away, then turned to face him squarely.

Ambury hardly appeared friendly, but he retreated enough to speak with firm calm. "You need only have your aunt tell you what she knows of the earrings' history to end any game."

She tried to see into his mind. Would it really be that simple?

More to the point, did he think *her aunt* had stolen the earrings? Aunt Sophie had purloined the letter right out of his library, after all. He had to be wondering if she had experience in such things.

First Gerald and now Ambury. Poor Aunt Sophie. The only person protecting her was Cassandra herself, and every plan for doing so required more money than she had, until Ambury paid for those jewels.

Rather suddenly the air of danger left him. He became the amiable Ambury that the world knew. He gave her a charming smile.

"I know you have waited too long, and are suspicious about ever seeing a conclusion to this. To reassure you, I suggest giving the price of the earrings to a solicitor to hold, along with the earrings, until this is resolved. It should not take long. You have only to put a few questions to your aunt, and all will be settled. That is fair, don't you agree?"

It was fair. Suspiciously so. There was more to this. She sensed that, mostly due to the intensity with which Ambury looked at her.

"Why do I feel as though you have backed me into the corner of a chamber?"

"I only do that with women in very private chambers, and for very different purposes."

"Yet I am feeling importuned all the same, Ambury."

"It is in both of our interests for this to be settled well, don't you think?"

She debated it. "I will do what I can, but I will not press the question if she chooses not to answer."

"I only ask that you try. I will arrange for us to meet with a solicitor when I return to town Monday, and write to you with the time. You bring the earrings, and I will bring the payment, and he will hold both until you learn what I need to know, or until I learn it another way if you cannot."

"That could take forever. I cannot wait too long."

"Shall we say a month from today? If I know no more than I do now, you will receive the earrings back."

It seemed a big delay, but it would probably take at least that long to make travel arrangements to get Sophie away from Gerald.

She reluctantly agreed to his proposal.

"I cannot promise that my aunt can satisfy your curiosity, Ambury," she said as he began to take his leave of her. "You may have to give up on the earrings if you require so many details before you make a gift of them to your future bride. The person who filled your ear with gossip about their being stolen is probably waiting to buy them from me on the cheap."

He cocked his head. "Why do you say that I bought them for a future bride?"

"It is past time for you to marry. Considering their price, I assume that you have found your future countess. But do not worry. I promise to start no gossip."

Yates perused the documents on the desk in front of him. Another stack waited on a nearby table. He judged that he would be lucky to finish with all of them before Christmas.

Scents of the late country summer blew in through the window on a breeze that tickled the edges of several pages. He moved a weight to ensure the careful arrangement would not be disturbed. He felt a bit like those documents himself, weighted in place by responsibility.

He did not mind the duty he had committed to, but it was not one with any joy. Even the fact that he would inherit the estate being so meticulously examined did not raise his spirits when he came down from town and made his way to this study in Elmswood Manor. The whole business made him feel too much like an executor before the fact of his father's passing, and the ill health of the earl cast a pall over the entire household.

They had spent more than eight months on this now, and would spend more, perhaps whatever months were left. As his physical side wasted away, the earl seemed to cling all the more to the part of him that had no end. What energy he possessed, he spent on the title and estate, on the parts of his life that made him one Highburton in an ongoing line of them.

Is it your peace offering? Your attempt to mend the differences that grew over the years? Cassandra Vernham might be irreverent and irritating, but she possessed a quick insight. It was an attempt at doing just that. A poor one, but it was all he had.

Thinking of her led him to pull the papers forward that dealt with those earrings. If he coerced Cassandra to learn what she could from her aunt, it was past time to learn what he could from this household. Normally, unraveling a mystery fascinated him, and in his discreet investigations he did not shirk from asking the questions necessary. But then normally the questions did not have to be asked of his own family.

He reviewed the papers, set them down, and stood. As he left the chamber, he passed the violin case that had lived here with him for too long now. The temptation to stop and play tugged. Deciding he could put off the next chore for a short while, he picked up the instrument and tuned it.

A tutor had introduced him to playing the violin when he was ten. For years he had only dabbled, but at university, the exercise suddenly had greater appeal. He went through a period of several years back then when he practiced hours every day, taking as much satisfaction in mastering a new piece of music as he did in hitting the marks when he shot his pistol.

He picked up the bow, and within ten notes, he hit his stride. He barely felt the strings as his fingers moved over them. The bow served as an extension of himself. The music formed a cloud that hovered above the world and in which he floated. On good days like today, it proved so dense that nothing seemed to exist outside of it.

Sometimes even his own thoughts did not survive the sound. The notes would intrude and merge with his consciousness. They would dissolve him. That was a rare occurrence, and not something he especially enjoyed. He could not predict it either, which made performing too capricious.

Today that did not happen. Instead, the progressions and skill disciplined his thoughts. The separateness of the cloud provided a rare isolation that permitted clear thinking. There was no chaos in music.

His mind took the opportunity to categorize things done and things that needed doing. He exerted no effort and did not direct his thoughts. It just happened. Playing aided his obligations to the estate just as they had aided his studies. In his investigative work, he came to rely on the way an hour with the bow helped him see patterns he had not noticed on his own, and explanations obscured by too many facts. Something similar happened now, regarding those earrings.

When he finished the piece, he set the violin aside and left the study to do his duty.

The door to his father's chambers stood ajar. He looked in and saw his father sleeping in a chair set near a window of his sitting room.

His mother sat in another chair nearby. Tall, thin, and white-haired, with sharp features and sharper eyes, she was a formidable woman. Right now her eyes were closed, but her posture remained rigid. The control symbolized her life and her nature. The daughter of a marquess, she had always been even more upright than his father, if that were possible. It had been a good match, if mutual severity could ever make one.

Her eyes opened on his entry. "Surely it can wait, Yates," she said softly. "He has just fallen asleep."

"I did not come to see him. I would like to speak with you, if you don't mind."

With a sigh she stood. "I expected you to temper his zeal regarding the estate, not encourage it."

"It is important to him. He only rests because he knows I do it in his stead."

She walked over and joined him at the door. "I hope that when I see the end coming, I do not waste the time left counting hairpins. That is all this is when you get down to it. Counting and organizing hairpins."

He could not disagree. The vast majority of the estate had been handed down with precise documentation. Good lands and high rents waited for Yates, just as they had for his father. The stacks up on that desk were indeed the hairpins of Highburton's legacy, not the jewels. For the most part.

His mother followed him toward the library. They passed through the gallery on the way. Yates stopped midway.

He pointed up at a portrait hung high, near the ceiling, the uppermost in one of the rows of paintings that covered the wall. "I was always told that I look like her."

His mother tipped her head back and squinted. "It needs to be cleaned. She is barely visible. But your great-grandmother was a handsome woman and, yes, you do look like her."

"That is probably why I always noticed the painting when we came down here to Elmswood Manor, despite its location and dark varnish. Because people always said that. She is wearing earrings. Blue-and-gold ones. Sapphires, I would guess."

"Your eyes are much better than mine."

"Don't you recognize them? You received the earrings when you married. Just as Grandmother had when she married Grandfather."

"Perhaps. I received boxes of jewels, most of them too old-fashioned to wear, just as those are."

"They were in Grandfather's inventory. Sapphire-and-diamond-and-gold earrings."

His mother started toward the library again. "If you say so. Now, what is it you need to talk about?"

He waited until they were sitting in the library before he answered. "I want to talk about those earrings. As I said, they were in the inventory taken by Grandfather five years before his death. However, they are no longer in any of those boxes you received."

"You have gone into my jewels?" Her tone was indignant. Expressing annoyance was unusual for her. She had never been a woman to show her emotions. Not to his father, and not to him. His parents' union had been an arranged marriage, and his had been an arranged birth. Other than the arguments he had caused with his father, there had been little in the way of temper or love expressed within the family, which only made those rows more dramatic.

"Highburton's jewels," he corrected. "Father instructed the solicitor to do another inventory last winter."

"He wants to count every single hairpin, it appears. Is poor Prebles making lists of the silver service and linens?"

"Yes."

"Goodness, did Prebles count my stays and corsets too?"

"I expect not, since your personal property is not the concern of this endless endeavor."

"I did not lose the earrings, if that is what you want to know."

"Father thinks they were stolen. He charged me with finding out what happened to them."

That surprised her.

"What a lot of bother over some ugly earrings. I have never even worn them."

"They are worth hundreds, mother. He has tracts of land not as valuable. The diamonds are of good size."

Yates remembered the dismay in his father's tired eyes when he learned of the missing earrings.

Yates had thought that buying the jewels at the auction would take care of it. They would return to the estate, after all. His father had expressed anger at the solution, and surprise that they had found their way into Cassandra Vernham's possession. *Damnation, someone has betrayed this family. Find out from the chit how she got them.*

"Did you by any chance pawn them?" he asked.

His mother leveled a gaze at him such as he had not been subjected to in years. Not since gossip about his first mistress had circulated ten years ago, and she had learned that the woman was the married daughter of one of her friends.

Her demeanor turned imperious. "I have no reason to pawn jewels, or anything else. A Countess of Highburton does not gamble. She does not spend more than her pin money, and she certainly does not sell family jewels that are not hers to sell. She honors the family traditions of abstemious and moral behavior that her position has inherited, even if her son does not do the same regarding his more exalted expectations."

There was much he could say in response, unpleasant things mostly, but he would not. She had been a good countess, and even now she sat with the earl for hours on end. There may have never been a great passion between them, but few could surpass her when it came to performing her duties.

"Do not dare accuse my maid of theft, if that is your next intention, Yates. She has been with me for decades, and I will not have you browbeat her. I have heard about your secret avocation of turning over rocks, looking for dirt, and I will not tolerate your playing that sordid role with this family."

"I will not accuse her of anything, merely talk to her. Father has asked me to find out what happened. I don't give a damn myself, but I will give him this if he wants it."

It was not really true that he did not give a damn. The matter seemed most peculiar. Then again, perhaps he had become too much the investigator, and could not resist untangling the knot to see how the earrings in that portrait ended up at Fairbourne's auction.

The weariness of the last six months could be heard in her next words. "Do what you must, of course." She stood, and he rose as well. "Before he slept, he again spoke of returning to town. I could not dissuade him from the notion. Perhaps this evening you will try instead."

He would try, but it would do no good. Word had just come this morning that French forces had landed in Ireland. In the morning, he and his father would pack up all those documents and remove to London. Now that his father felt a little better, he would not be kept from the discussions taking place in the government about this disastrous development. He was Highburton.

Chapter 5

London emptied of society in August. Even the theater people and other members of artistic circles who might hold parties were scarce. Last August, Cassandra had been able to visit with Emma at least, but now Emma was in the country too.

All of this left her with too much time to ponder Ambury's unspoken insinuations. She was all too tempted to sell the earrings to someone else and to hell with Ambury. Unfortunately, it was unlikely she would get the same price from someone else, and she badly needed every penny those earrings would bring.

That Sunday Cassandra pondered her dilemma while she drank lemonade on the terrace where she sat with Aunt Sophie.

"The weather is too hot even for August," Aunt Sophie said. She looked up from her book and gazed out at the riot of color in the flower beds. Those plantings knew no restraint and possessed a lush, vivid beauty, much like Sophie herself.

"Of course, not nearly as hot as that August that I spent in Naples. Goodness, I was naked the better part of most days, and all of the nights, back then, but still the heat was not to be borne. Although, perhaps it felt especially warm that month because of Leonardo." She puzzled over it for a moment, then smiled to herself at the memory and returned to her book.

Cassandra had never heard of Leonardo before. There had been other men who had made other months unseasonably warm for her aunt over the years, and Cassandra was enough aware of them to take mention of Leonardo in stride.

She watched the pages of Sophie's book turn with regularity beneath a few dangling curls of her aunt's fashionably dressed, graying dark hair. Obviously her mind handled the content of that book perfectly. Nothing supported Gerald's claim that Sophie's faculties had become impaired. True, her aunt lived a peculiar, reclusive life now, but after all of the Leonardos, perhaps that was to be expected. A woman with such a colorful, energetic past might be tired by the time she reached sixty-four years in age.

"Aunt Sophie, how much money do you have?"

"Not enough to lend you any, dear." Sophie did not even look up from her book. "That is what is meant when it is said one has a respectable income, as I do. There is enough for a decent, if modest, life, and even the occasional luxury, but never enough to make ill-advised loans."

"I do not want to borrow. I was thinking that if, between the two of us, we had enough, we might sail to the Continent before autumn sets in."

"There is a war on the Continent. Paris is out of the question, and I have no desire to visit Vienna now that Franz has married. It would be bad form for me to do so."

Franz was another Leonardo, a man from Sophie's past. "Perhaps Naples then, or—"

"I never thought I would say it, but I have had my fill of travel. Besides, I gave you most of my jewels, and there is little else to pawn."

"I believe it would be healthier if we went to the country, at least. Perhaps we can visit the lake district."

"I am touched by your concern for me, but you worry too much." Aunt Sophie no longer read her book. Rather she peered over and read Cassandra. Her handsome face firmed while her eyes turned remarkably shrewd. "Your brother does not frighten *me,* Cassandra. He will never be so bold as to make a move. Should he find the courage to try, your mother will stop him."

Cassandra did not think they could depend on either of those assumptions. Gerald had developed an arrogance during the last few years that exceeded anything she ever expected to see. As for their mother—Aunt Sophie did not need to know how often Mama wrote letters scolding Cassandra for living under Sophie's roof and influence.

Cassandra patted her aunt's hand, as if agreeing with her. The skin of that hand felt very thin and cool, and the hand itself frail. Sophie had aged rather suddenly, the way that women did sometimes when time caught up with them. The face under Sophie's lace-edged cap still reflected the great beauty she had been, however, and her eyes, while paler now, often contained the sparks of wit and life that had made men by the score fall in love with her.

Two years ago, Cassandra would have never doubted that Aunt Sophie could keep Gerald at bay with one withering joke. Today, however, that hand felt very small and her aunt seemed vulnerable, and indeed in need of care and protection.

If the Continent was too risky, they would go to America. Cassandra thought she would not mind escaping England. The world was changing around her, and she felt herself being nudged more and more to the edges of society. She tried not to mind that—she had all but asked for it, after all—but digging in her heels had become tiresome.

Her aunt's attention became distracted by the garden again. This time it seemed those blue eyes grew paler yet. A girlish smile only made Sophie appear more distant.

"Yes, if Gerald does not behave, I will have to talk to the earl about him," she mused.

"Gerald is the earl now. Papa is gone."

Sophie blinked. "Of course he is. My mind was still on Leonardo, and I misspoke."

She lifted her book again. Cassandra tried not to watch for a page to turn, but she knew too much relief when one finally did.

Yes, it was time to clear up the history of those earrings so Ambury did not put off paying for them any longer, and she could move ahead with her plans

"Aunt Sophie, I am curious about something. Last spring, when I said I had to sell some jewels, you were most particular about which ones they could be."

"I was?"

"You insisted on looking at them all. Don't you remember? It was back in March, and we spread all the jewels out on the carpet in the library. You strolled among them, pointing to the ones I should not consign to the auction."

"Now I remember. I thought they enhanced the carpet so much. I thought jeweled carpets might become a new fashion, except that they would be difficult to walk on." She frowned, as if the notion puzzled her. "Were they all on the carpet? Every one?"

"That is what you told me to do. Even the ones with the little notes were there." Aunt Sophie had provided instructions with some of the jewels regarding when and where they should not be worn. One, for example, said, "Not to be worn in Vienna." Cassandra assumed it had been a gift from Franz.

"Of course I did. I remember."

Cassandra studied her aunt's face, trying to decide whether Sophie really did remember. She hated how she checked things like that all the time now. Even if Gerald did not win this game, he had scored heavily just in playing it.

"Do you remember the sapphire-and-diamond earrings? They were old-fashioned but in the best way. The center diamond on each was quite large."

"You would have appeared stunning in those. They would have flattered your eyes." Sophie blinked. "You sold them with the others?"

"They went for a very high price." Cassandra tried to speak lightly. *Ambury bought them. He says they were stolen, and I think he suspects you were the thief.* It would be a kindness to leave all of that unsaid. "Who gave you those earrings? Was it Leonardo perhaps?"

"Goodness, Leonardo was too poor to give me gifts like that. However, he was such a considerate lover that a woman could hardly mind. He had this wonderful trick he did with his—but I should not scandalize you. We don't want to give your brother more reasons to disapprove of your living here, do we? Now, where did I get those earrings?" She frowned as she pondered the matter. "Perhaps I bought them. Yes, I am almost sure it was those earrings that I purchased that winter."

"They must have cost a fortune."

"I found those earrings at a pawnshop, and not nearly as dear as you would expect. Perhaps the pawnbroker thought the diamonds were merely paste."

Sophie picked up her book again.

Cassandra sipped her lemonade. She had asked, and she had her answer. She could in good conscience tell Ambury at least part of the jewels' history. The only point from the conversation left unexplained was what Leonardo's trick had involved.

Yes, this should settle things nicely, provided she ignored the feeling that Aunt Sophie had just lied to her.

* * *

Two days later a letter from Ambury came in the morning post, asking Cassandra to call at his family's house at two in the afternoon. The solicitor would be in attendance, and their business could be conducted with total discretion.

Another letter came at the same time. Emma wrote, telling Cassandra that she had returned to town. She asked Cassandra to call at her family's auction house at noon.

Curious as to what brought Emma back to London so soon after her wedding, Cassandra presented herself at the auction house at eleven o'clock. She had feared she might never see Emma after the wedding and yet here they were, meeting as they had so often in the past.

The tall, cavernous exhibition chamber proved empty, its gray walls devoid of even a single painting. The wooden floor still displayed evidence of the scrubbing with sand that had heralded the end of the Season a few months earlier. None of the employees were about.

She followed sounds to the office at the far end of the gallery. Emma sat at a big desk there. The wooden surface in front of her had been turned into a field of jewels.

"I could not imagine what would draw you back to the city, Emma. I should have guessed it was rarities such as those." Cassandra lifted a particularly eye-catching ruby suspended on a chain. The setting was simple, but such a jewel required little adornment.

She put it down. "You are supposed to be enjoying married life. I am surprised that Southwaite agreed to return to London."

Emma poked at earrings consisting of little more than two perfect pearls. "He did not want to come, but felt obligated after learning the most recent war developments. Of course I did not want to be parted from him."

Cassandra gestured to the desk. "Does he know about these?"

"I may have neglected to mention them. Once I learned I would return, I arranged for their delivery. Temporary, of course, while I evaluate them."

"And your brother? It is his auction house now. Should he not be—"

"He is ill. A summer fever. Nor does he know much about jewels. Even less than I, and I am no expert. Which is why I needed you."

Cassandra turned her attention to the jewelry. She had learned about precious stones and settings from Aunt Sophie. During those first few years together, when she traveled with her aunt, Sophie had pointed out the very best gems adorning society on the Continent and given lessons on how to assess quality and value.

"Most of it is fairly recent, set perhaps twenty years ago." She picked up a few pieces and held them to the light of the window. "The settings are very restrained. The value is in the stones. Most have excellent clarity. Where did you get them?"

"Marielle found them."

"Let us pray that she found them in the legitimate possession of their owners." Marielle was a young Frenchwoman, an émigré who had escaped the revolution when only a girl. She had become an agent for Fairbourne's, serving as a go-between for other émigrés who wished to sell valuables brought out of France.

"The owners have agreed to be named, so we are probably safe there. What do you think? Are they as good as they appear?"

"They are worthy of Fairbourne's. If you wait until autumn, I think they will fetch at least seven hundred in toto. If you try to sell them now, it will be half as much, if you are lucky."

"Marielle says her friends can wait if I promise to include them when we start up again. Our next auction will be in mid-September, I think."

Cassandra continued examining the jewels, returning each to the table in one of several rows that she formed. "Why has Southwaite returned to town?"

"You will hear about it soon enough. The situation in Ireland had taken a bad turn. French troops have landed in County Mayo. It is not known how many, but rebels are joining them, and on last report, they had not yet been routed."

It was indeed shocking news, yet a development for which the whole country had been bracing. "All this fear about the southeastern coast, and they go to Ireland instead."

Cassandra continued examining the jewels. The news that Fairbourne's would hold an auction next month relieved her. If Ambury should prove yet more of a problem, she could put those earrings up for sale again.

"Will Southwaite be angry if he knows you met with me today?" she asked.

Emma came around the desk and embraced her. "I have explained to him how dear you are to me, and how we have a true friendship and not merely the sort of tolerance that I am likely to receive from the women in his circles." Emma pressed her lips lightly to Cassandra's temple. "He has not forbidden it. I had hoped that your invitation to the wedding would make that clear."

Emma's loyalty touched Cassandra deeply. Her throat burned. She pointed to the jewels. "Left rows to right are low values to high."

Emma returned to her chair, removed a sheet of paper from a drawer, and began jotting notes. "Lydia has come back to town too."

"I would expect her to remain at Crownhill if her brother did not. She prefers it there if she is alone. Why did she come to town?"

"I am not sure, but—I believe she did so to see you."

Six months ago, Cassandra would have expressed naughty joy, and perhaps even included Emma on any plans to circumvent Southwaite's interference with the friendship. Now, however, Emma's loyalties had become complicated.

"More likely she wants to see her other friends, or place orders for a new wardrobe." She picked up her reticule. "Now, I must leave you. I have promised to rendezvous with someone in half an hour."

The mansion owned by the Earl of Highburton could not fail to impress, situated as it was on Pall Mall, near Marlborough House. A property with impeccable pedigree, it was of a size and luxury befitting peers who had prospered by living with moral restraint and by managing to align themselves with the winning side of most political controversies over the last few centuries.

The morning paper had reported that Highburton had returned to London and was in residence. Normally Cassandra would feel uncomfortable intruding into the home of a dying man, but the earl surely had an expansive apartment and inviolable privacy inside this huge pile of stone. She doubted that he would even be aware of her appearance at the door.

When the footman escorted her into the drawing room, Ambury was already there.

He greeted her with a smile and bow. She noted again, as she curtsied, how maturity suited him. His father was still famous for his handsome face, and the son took after him in that at least, even if everyone knew their minds had little in common. His disagreement with his father on almost everything of importance had created a rift even before he left university.

That Ambury lived outside the strict and conservative notions of behavior that his family had long espoused had not helped matters, she supposed. Even generations ago, when most everyone of their class enjoyed a degree of licentiousness, the Earls of Highburton and their families had been famous for their uprightness. Ambury, however, had the reputation for being a libertine. The notes about him in the scandal sheets were not at all ambiguous. Unlike his friend Southwaite, he was not even especially discreet about his affairs.

"Won't you sit? The solicitor will be here very soon." Ambury gestured to one of a pair of chairs set quite close to each other.

Cassandra did not want to perch there if this man intended to put his hard bum on the cushion next to it. He looked too handsome today for comfort. The kind of handsome that turned a woman all tingly and silly. She needed to keep her wits about her.

"The solicitor will not be necessary. I have asked my aunt about the earrings. She remembers purchasing them from a pawnbroker some years back. How they came to be in his possession is anyone's guess."

"Some years back? Two years? Thirty?"

"She did not say."

"Which pawnbroker was it?"

"She did not say that either."

"It is all very ambiguous. Is your aunt getting vague in her memories in a general way, Lady Cassandra? Sometimes—"

"Not at all. Why would you suggest such a thing? She is as sound of mind as you are. I did not quiz her closely on the earrings. It would be rude to do so." She withdrew a little velvet sack from her reticule and set it down on a table. "Now at the risk of being extremely indelicate, I will give you the earrings, and you will give me the money."

He turned one of his smiles on her. She tried not to allow it to affect her, because she guessed it heralded trouble.

"First I must ask that you attempt to learn more from your aunt about when and where she found the earrings."

"She has told me all she knows."

"I doubt that. They are not the kind of jewels that one forgets obtaining."

"Are you daring to say my aunt lied?"

"I am suggesting that she answered your discreet question and offered nothing more. By your own admission you did not ask for details. I am sure that she would be more forthcoming if I broached the subject. Since she will not see me, I ask that you raise the matter again, with less circumspection."

She could tell he would not budge. He was going to hold off on payment until she either discovered the entire history or the month had passed. In a gesture of pique, she snatched up the velvet sack and stuffed it back into her reticule.

She paced slowly around the chamber. "There has been some recent redecorating here. The obvious Pompeii influence is gone."

He glanced about as if he had not noticed before. "I forget that you visited several times during your first Season. I suppose there have been changes since then."

She paused to admire a chair that displayed restrained Gothic elements in the carving on its arms. The countess must be trying out this style to see if it suited her and the drawing room. "I was here not only during my first Season. I attended a few salons with my aunt after I went to live with her. I do not think that your mother really wanted my presence, but Aunt Sophie managed to extract invitations for me."

"My parents always had a fondness for her, despite her unusual life. My father was a friend of your father, and had reason to be tolerant of his friend's sister."

"How generous of him. Perhaps your parents hoped to redeem her."

"You sound bitter. Your aunt did not seem to mind how society viewed her, so there is no reason for you to do so."

No, no reason. Yet she did.

"Perhaps it is not your aunt's reception that makes you frown, but your own," he said.

She stopped admiring the furnishings and stared at him.

He had not said that with sarcasm or cruelty. He had merely made an observation that shot like an arrow into her heart.

"I think you are correct." She feigned a lightness of humor. "However, I confess that it is more envy causing the frown. My aunt never married, and lived freely, and somehow it was accepted. Perhaps the world dared not forbid her to do as she wished."

He strolled to where she stood near a window. He appeared to be giving the matter some honest thought. "It was a different time. Also, everyone knew she did not marry because her fiancé died."

"Ah, of course. That is the difference. She almost did it right, while I refused to from the start. Yes, that explains everything, I expect."

He gazed at her too seriously. That made her uncomfortable. And tingly and silly too.

A servant entered then, and held the door wide. A gray-haired man walked in. Everything about him, from his formal bearing to his serious expression, from his conservative coats to his spectacles, bespoke his profession. The solicitor had arrived.

Chapter 6

Yates introduced Mr. Prebles, who had descended from his labors above punctually, much as he performed every service. Mr. Prebles bowed deeply to Cassandra, then stood there just like the footman did, near the wall, awaiting directions.

"You are the earl's solicitor, Mr. Prebles?" Cassandra asked.

"I am so honored, yes."

She turned to Yates with a skeptical expression. "Would it not make more sense to find a third party who puts neither of us at a disadvantage?"

"Mr. Prebles, Lady Cassandra is worried that should this agreement not work out to my liking, you will prove less than objective in its resolution. It is a fair concern, I think."

"It is indeed, sir. Let me reassure you, Lady Cassandra, that whatever is agreed to today will be how the matter is handled by me. I have been the earl's solicitor as long as I have due to my strict honesty, which, as the world knows, the earl practices himself."

Yates thought Prebles might have been good enough to add "as does his son" to the end of the little speech. The truth was that Prebles did not know the son well. Even their months sequestered with accounts and deeds had not forged anything resembling ease with each other. Of course, Prebles had been the one sent to the son to deliver a father's scolds in years past, about gambling, about women, about politics, about—many things.

Cassandra dug into her reticule and extracted the little velvet sack again. She spilled its contents on a table set beside a window. Gold glinted. Lights flew from the two diamonds that would rest on a woman's earlobes, and three sapphires dangled on gold filigree below each one.

"The understanding, Mr. Prebles, is that you will hold these, and the amount that Ambury bid on them, for thirty days at the most, until we are satisfied that the earrings should go to Ambury and the money to me. If you do not so hear, on the thirty-first day, the earrings are to be returned to me."

Prebles looked at Yates for confirmation, then picked up the earrings and returned them to their little sack.

Yates walked over and handed him the wrapped banknotes.

After Prebles made his retreat, Cassandra began to make hers. "You did not ask why I did not bring the ring," she said.

"To have asked would have invited an answer that Prebles did not need to hear." Yates had not even thought about the ring. He had left it after the auction as surety, to be sold if he did not pay up.

She gazed around the chamber once more, not giving the answer, perhaps because he still had not asked the question. "I always admired this drawing room," she said. "Also the gallery next to the ballroom. I remember during my first

Season how there were palms placed near the north corners of it when your family hosted a ball. More than one girl had her first kiss behind them."

"Are you feeling nostalgic?"

"I did not say I had my first kiss behind them."

Unless Lakewood had lied, she had, however. For an instant, Yates saw her again at one of those balls, in a gown very different in style from what she wore today. It was as blue as her eyes, and shaped like an hourglass instead of the current narrow columns of fabric. Her hair had been dressed in tight ringlets, not today's natural curls. Matrons gossiped that she painted those lips even back then.

"Come with me," he said. "We will revisit the scene of your first worldly triumphs."

"My first Season was hardly triumphant," she objected. However, she joined him as he left the chamber. "You were the one scoring victories that spring. I daresay poor Amanda Stockton has never recovered from her minute in that corner."

"You know about that, do you?"

"Everyone knew, Ambury. She swooned, for goodness' sake."

"It was only one kiss."

"It ruined her for life. Her suitors seemed sadly ordinary after that." She glanced over at him and laughed. "Stop that preening."

"I am not preening. I have been told I kiss better than most, but I am astonished to find myself accused of ruining Miss Stockton's chance for happiness with another man."

"Better than most? Odd that I never heard that rumor, you conceited man."

The gallery ran the length of the house, flanking the southern ballroom on its northern side. Like the one at Elms-wood Manor, it held some portraits of ancestors and family members, but these were the more recent ones.

Nothing had changed here since that Season six years

ago. Cassandra paced down the polished wooden floor, glancing this way and that, taking it all in. She paused at one of the portraits that caught her eye.

"My grandfather, on my father's side," he offered, standing next to her.

"He is handsome, but he appears a bit stern."

"That is a family trait."

"With all but you," she teased, walking on. She looked over her shoulder and gave the portrait one last glance. "And yet—one wonders, Ambury, if you will not turn stern too in time. Staid as well, as is also the family trait. I think I see it in you already. I doubt you would kiss Miss Stockton behind the palms now."

Her observation nettled him. Perhaps she was right and he was turning a bit stern. She poked at an awareness, emphasized of late by duty and obligations, that the best years of youth had passed, along with its freedoms.

They were near the spot where those palms had stood. It was not a moment to look at her, but he did, just as the light filtering into the gallery from open windows beyond the door found her. So did a breeze that flicked at her hair's tendrils and at the ribbon ends that dangled down her dress.

"You are correct on one count. I would not kiss a Miss Stockton now, but only because I am six years older, and have no interest in girls in their first Seasons."

"Then you had better hold on to the woman for whom you bought the earrings, Ambury, and be glad she lets you think she is dazzled. The more we women gain in years, the less likely we are to swoon, no matter how well you kiss."

The goad threw dry straw on a fire. "You really should not cast down gauntlets like that when you are all alone with a man."

That elicited peals of laughter. "Oh, no. Mercy, are you going to try and conquer me now, as you threatened? You despise me, Ambury. We both know that I am safe enough."

Her words should have stopped him, alluding to what

they did. Instead, they had the effect of obliterating what little resolve he had mustered.

"Not safe enough. Not really safe at all." He swung her around and pulled her into his arms.

She gazed up, startled. Then her thick lashes lowered and her red lips parted and, no doubt, a scold began forming.

He silenced her with a kiss.

The kiss could not be called staid. Cassandra vaguely noted that with the part of her mind that did not succumb to astonishment. A bit stern, perhaps, but not in a bad way. She had been kissed often enough to appreciate the nuances, and how his handling of her communicated both sweet seduction and command.

She tried to grope her way out of the fog of sensation he created, but common sense kept slipping away as soon as she found it. The most delightful pleasures trickled through her body, urging her to let them do their worst. Warmth flushed her skin, then permeated to her core.

His embrace truly undid her. Strong arms wrapped her, holding her close . . . a caress too bold, but scandalously welcomed, trailed down her back, firm enough that the heat of his hand made her dress fabric disappear . . . he lifted her enough that his mouth could reach her neck, then her décolletage . . .

She should not. She knew it. This could never be right. Yet it had been too long since she had been enlivened with feminine excitement and she forgot for a while that the man inciting it could be up to no good. The pleasure refreshed her, awed her. She might indeed be behind the palms during her first Season, being kissed for the first time.

She did not resist soon enough. She knew that even as she delayed. He took it for compliance, of course. Nips on her lips heralded further intimacy. Even the preliminaries to deeper passion caused a thrill to resonate through the center of her body, luring her to recklessness.

She turned her head to stop the kisses. Her cheek felt the superfine wool of his coat, and her ear heard the low throb of his heart. They stood like that, his embrace still holding her, for ten seconds at most, during which she ignored the truth of the moment and allowed herself to savor the illusion of being cared for.

She stepped back. His arms fell at the same time. She should turn and walk away. She should pretend it had not happened, or that he had importuned her, which he had in a way, at first at least. She should—

"Why?" His gaze focused on her so intently that she dared not move. The family sternness could be seen in him clearly now.

She sought the Cassandra the world knew, and tried to dredge up a clever response. *Because I am wild, of course. Because I have been kissed so often that one more is a small thing.*

"Why did you refuse?" he pressed. "He had compromised you. It was unintentional, and quite innocent, but it still happened. Why did you refuse him when he sought to do the right thing?"

The real meaning of his *Why?* startled her. No one had ever asked before. Not outright. Assumptions and conclusions were drawn instead, about both her and Lakewood. Even as the world expressed horror that she would not agree to marriage, it had also whispered and wondered about what happened to cause her to refuse. A man must have shown his true colors in ways most appalling for a young woman to risk ruin rather than accept social salvation as his wife.

A little cloud of dishonor had darkened Lakewood's path after that. His friends, Southwaite and Kendale, and even Ambury, blamed her. To them, her behavior must have seemed childish, spoiled, and cruel. It probably still did.

"I did not want him." It was the truth but not the whole truth. "It was indeed innocent enough, and did not warrant such an extreme measure as marriage."

"He was in love with you. His intentions were always to—"

"I. Did. Not. Want. Him," she enunciated slowly, angry now. No one seemed to care about this part of it. No one ever had. "As for his love and his intentions, there is much you do not know. Now that he is gone, no one knows except me."

He cocked his head, suddenly curious. Too curious. She cursed herself for allowing him to draw her into this.

"I must take my leave." She tried to sound brisk, but the effects of the kiss still lingered, and her voice came out with a tremor.

She walked away from him and his questions and his damnable ability to turn her into a silly girl. "I will press my aunt to the extent that I can, to learn more about the earrings. I need your solicitor to release the money to me as soon as possible."

Chapter 7

Yates's thoughts would not remain on the documents spread in front of him, no matter how hard he tried to force the proper concentration. He found his mind dwelling instead on a stolen kiss in a shadowed gallery. Inevitably that led to consideration of the conversation that followed.

That kiss had been an impulse, but one a long time coming. The question about Lakewood had been too.

There is much you do not know. Undoubtedly. He had always assumed that what he did not know was due to Lakewood's discretion. Now it seemed there may have been more to it than that.

In the years that followed, he had stared down men who slurred speculations, when in their cups, about what had really happened when the Baron Lakewood had found himself alone with Lady Cassandra Vernham. He closed ranks with Southwaite and Kendale and, yes, even Penthurst, and had done what friends do when one of their own is the object of damning suppositions.

The rumors had blown like an ill wind at first, and even now the breeze could be felt. He had forced her, it was said. He had succumbed to a rage when she refused his hand and lost control. It had been her own fault for being a flirt, but still . . .

Had it happened that way?

He stood up, disgusted even to be considering the possibility that Lakewood might have been dishonorable, when he was not there to defend himself. It was a hell of a thing if a few kisses could lure him to be disloyal so easily.

All the same, his thoughts wandered again, back to the shadowed gallery, as if pulled there by a capricious spirit. He felt Cassandra pressed against him, as warm and soft and sensual as she appeared.

The door opened and Prebles entered. He paused and peered at Yates from behind his spectacles. Then he walked over and looked at the documents spread on the desk.

"Ah," Prebles said with a nod. "I understand now why you appear annoyed, sir. The situation with that property is vexing, I agree."

This was news to Yates. What situation with which property? What had he missed?

Prebles helped him out by lifting one of the deeds, then pointing to a map. "Did you visit it? Is it the dearth of evidence of rents that upsets you?"

Yates recognized the deed as one for a swath of property amid the swamps of the southern coast. "I went north, not south. Are there a dearth of rents because the land is not worked?"

"In part. It is not the best land, what with the sea so close and parts of it too wet for farming."

"But there is more?"

"It seems that there is the chance, even the likelihood, that there may be another claim on it. See, look here at this earlier map. The land is clearly marked as Highburton's. But on this newer one there is the notation that it may be contested."

Yates noted the maps, then inspected the deed. The date on the vellum, written in a flourish even more dramatic than Prebles's own hand, marked its transfer to the Earl of Highburton in the year 1693.

"If there is another deed, it would be peculiar if it predated this," he said.

"That is what I thought. I have never found evidence it was sold, so the note on the newer map is unexplained. Yet there it is."

Yates folded the deed and set it aside. "When next I speak with my father, I will mention it. Any rents collected would be minor, of course, and probably not worth spending the cost of time and money to go to court."

"No doubt, sir. No doubt."

"Do you want all of them? Every one?" Merriweather asked. Her chin held a stack of boxes steady as she carried them from the dressing room.

"All of them." Cassandra eased the stack out of her arms and placed them on her bed.

After Merriweather made another trip, Cassandra sent her away, then sat down on the bed to examine the part of the legacy that Aunt Sophie had given her in advance of actually dying.

First she opened the two largest wooden boxes. Inside lay little velvet sacks and a variety of trinket boxes. These were the boxes that had held the jewels that she sold at Fairbourne's last spring. The sacks and boxes were empty now.

That was not true with the other two containers. A rainbow of stones and a small fortune in settings greeted her inspections there. Not only jewelry rested in the trinket boxes, however. Little pieces of paper did as well.

She plucked one of the tiny notes and unfolded it. "Not to be worn when the Count of Emilia is in England," it said, in Aunt Sophie's hand. She placed it back with the garnet

ring it accompanied, then lifted an organza sack and tipped
it into her palm.

A fine golden filigree necklace, more valuable in its work-
manship than its metal, poured down. So did another little
note. "Best to wear this only when Sir Charles and Lady
Lightbown are abroad." Several others also named specific
individuals. A number simply instructed, "Not to be sold
unless the jewels are reset."

The notes implied the jewels had been gifts from lovers
whose wives and family might object. They had tempered
her excitement about receiving Sophie's gifts. She had not
cared for the notion of checking who was and was not in
London, or likely to attend a party, before donning a piece
of jewelry.

What if she made a mistake? Would some man be horrified to see her walk in wearing his love gift? Would the
man's wife guess the jewels had been bestowed on a lover
by her husband?

It was good of Aunt Sophie to take such care with others'
happiness, but Cassandra's reaction had been to never wear
any of these baubles herself.

She reached for the first box again. One by one, she
opened all the empty boxes. A few of them had notes too.
She read each one. No names were mentioned, and all of
them appeared to warn against wearing in various Continen-
tal capitals rather than in England. Three, however, merely
said "Can be pawned or sold if necessary, but not to be
worn." At the time she first read them, Cassandra had
assumed that was Aunt Sophie's way of giving a lesson in
taste and fashion.

She tried to remember which box or sack had held the
diamond-and-sapphire earrings. Had it been one with a note?
Perhaps one of the three that could be sold but not worn?

Her memory failed her. Nor could she recall the details
of that day when she had spread all the jewels on the carpet
and Sophie had pointed to this one and that and allowed

their sale. Cassandra had requested the exercise because of the history of this jewelry, or much of it. She had not wanted to make a mistake.

Now she wondered if she had, and if Aunt Sophie had as well. Maybe the jewels had lured Aunt Sophie into her memories, and her attention had been distracted from the task at hand.

She put all the jewels away and closed all the boxes. She wished she could just burn those notes and not wonder what they meant. Worse, she worried that perhaps they did not refer to lovers and gifts after all.

She suspected that if Ambury knew about them, he would think they did not too.

Looking at those boxes made her miserable, because her thoughts were turning in directions that were disloyal to the only family member who had remained a friend.

Merriweather returned to the chamber, carrying a card. "You've a visitor."

She took the card. Lydia had called.

She went below and greeted her. "Emma said you had come up to town. It is good to see you. Are you here to shop?"

"That and other things. I have decided to become accomplished at more than riding and sketching, Cassandra. And you get to help!"

Yates opened the door to his father's apartment slowly. He stepped inside silently. That was how he always approached his father now, in careful movements and soft footfalls. There was no reason for it, yet everyone acted the same way.

The earl sat in a chair by a closed window in the sitting room. The physicians feared summer fevers claiming his ailing body, and wanted him in the country. The earl had always preferred town, however, and now, with the news out of Ireland, he had found the perfect excuse to return.

The prime minister had visited yesterday to discuss the matter. It had been a symbolic act to acknowledge the role of the Earls of Highburton down through the years. The current earl could no more effect politics now than he could rise from that chair alone, but Pitt had pretended matters could not be resolved without his sage advice.

His father's eyes opened. "What have you there?" He nodded to the papers in Yates's hand.

Yates sat in the chair. "More of the same. Questions that Prebles could not answer."

Yates waited for him to ask for the questions, or to sleep.

"What do you think of this Irish mess?" the earl queried instead.

They had not spoken of politics since winter. It had been an unspoken pact. They would take care of the estate together but avoid the topics that had caused so much rancor between them.

"I have not thought about it much at all."

Something like a laugh choked out. "The hell you haven't. You have an opinion on most everything, so this would be no different."

He should tell the earl what the earl wanted to hear and claim to agree with his father's own opinion. It would be a kindness, perhaps. A gift.

"Don't be feeding me mush like the physicians do. My stomach is bad, but my head is still fine."

"I think the mess is the result of one very foolish man thinking he will be a hero. It would be an error to punish an entire people for his crime."

The earl shook his head. "What I expected you to say."

"I am who I am."

"That's the truth, although soon you will be Highburton, and then you are not only who you are. So you counsel restraint, do you? Pitt told me there are others saying that. Even Penthurst, who can be a hard man when it is warranted. You must be influencing him, and not to the good."

Yates did not influence the Duke of Penthurst at all these days, not that he thought he ever had. His father did not know about the rift that had formed between him and that friend. Other than a few formal conversations on strictly official matters, he had not spoken to Penthurst since last March.

"No doubt you know his trial is next month," his father added. "I told Pitt that it was nonsense, that he had been challenged by Lakewood and the duel was a point of honor and everyone knew it. Important that there be no special treatment, he said, so the lords will take it up." He made a face of disapproval, but it dissolved, and he shrugged. "There is no danger, so you are not to worry for him. Gentlemen understand these things, but the people must have their shows."

The effort at reassurance touched him, even as he reacted badly to the assumptions his father made about another friend. But then the earl had never liked the man who had died in that duel for which Penthurst would answer to his fellow peers.

This was how their arguments started in years past. He swallowed his reaction so one would not start now.

His father seemed to drift off. Yates was beginning to ease out of the chair when the earl's eyes opened again. His pale hand gestured to the papers. "What questions?"

How minor these details seemed now. Hairpins, his mother had called them.

"There is this property on the coast. I have not been there yet. However, it is apparent from the records that no rents have come from it in years, if ever. Prebles cannot account for it. I thought perhaps you can."

The earl held out an unsteady hand. He took the deed. Angling the vellum so the window light washed it, he squinted.

"Ah, this one." He nodded, as if remembering an old puzzle. "There is said to be another deed that challenges this one."

"Have you seen the other deed?"

He shook his head. "The tenants send rents to him who holds it, however. Not much income from there. Half of the land is swamp."

"I should tell Prebles to address it. So you know what is what."

An exhausted sigh issued from his father. Yet his eyes appeared less filmed and distant for a moment, even as that sound hung in the air. The mind was being engaged, and the sight of it raised Yates's spirits.

While he watched his father consider the question and had a glimpse of the man he had once battled and defied, a profound emotion filled his heart. He wished there were a pact with the Creator that the current Earl of Highburton would not die until every tiny question were answered, and that there would be years of questions to settle.

"It would cost thousands to claim this property," his father said, handing the vellum back. "Not worth it. I left it be. When you inherit, you can reconsider, but I think you will decide as I did."

It was an odd response from a man who did not favor ambiguity on any matter, least of all the honor of Highburton. A measured one, and probably financially sound, but it disheartened Yates anyway. He had rather hoped settling the challenge to this property would become a crusade. They would spend hours plotting strategy, and he would see alertness and life in those eyes again and again.

"Open the window a little, Yates. Damned physicians worry that a fever will kill me. That is a joke. They have no idea how feeling the sun and the breeze—it is a comfort and a treasure. Perhaps it is also a preparation. A way of calling one home."

Yates opened the window so the breeze could enter. His father turned his face to it and smiled with private pleasure.

"Have you learned anything about those jewels?" he asked in a voice half asleep.

"A little. Not how they left their box here."

"Stolen," his father muttered. "Sure of it. No other possible explanation that makes sense. Hell of a thing. Who would have guessed it?" Slowly, his body sank as sleep robbed him of alertness to his posture.

Yates did not leave at once. He stayed and shared the breeze for a while.

Chapter 8

There is not much for a man-about-town to do in London in August. Especially a man looking for distraction from a heaviness of the spirit. Yates therefore went for a walk after spending more hours with the deeds and accounts. Even a long respite making music had not relieved the mood that had overtaken him that afternoon while visiting his father.

While he strolled, he allowed himself to dwell on the memory of kissing Cassandra Vernham. He wondered how she would react if he called on her now. At this hour, there could be no mistake why he had done so. Nothing about their business together required a meeting at eleven o'clock at night.

He wanted to believe she would debate sending him away for at least a few minutes before doing so, but he was sure she would not receive him. She had responded to the kisses. She was not immune, but as a woman of the world she knew better than to yield quickly, should she yield at all.

He spent some time plotting a strategy to that end. It

distracted him as even the cool night and exercise could not. Feeling more himself, but still in need of some society, he turned his direction toward a house where he knew some friends would undoubtedly be in attendance.

He mounted the steps of the building with something like a light heart. That was what contemplating the seduction of a lovely woman could do for a man.

She was still much on his mind when he entered the drawing room that served as Mrs. Burton's discreet and elite gaming salon. Enough that when he spied her standing near a table, it did not surprise him. Then he remembered that Cassandra Vernham had not been gambling of late. He hoped his delay in paying for the earrings had not driven her to it again.

He walked toward her. While he did, he admired the dress she wore. Its barely pink fabric and its narrow skirt skimmed around her curves. Her dark lashes appeared very thick in the candlelight, and her eyes were sapphire pools gazing down at the table.

The other patrons moved enough for him to see the Duke of Penthurst standing on the other side of her, also watching the card play. With occasional smiles, she acknowledged His Grace's presence.

Seeing them together ruined his mood. Cassandra's name had never been connected to Penthurst's in any romantic sense, but the trial Penthurst would soon endure might change that. Hell, for all he knew, she had been Penthurst's mistress for years now.

She frowned deeply and squeezed the shoulder of the woman sitting in front of her. That shoulder shrugged off her touch as if it were an insect. Cassandra's hand went back, rather decidedly. The other woman turned her head to complain.

It was Southwaite's sister Lydia. She did not appear her normal distant, soulful self tonight. Rather she looked half mad.

He knew that look. It meant only one thing in such a place.

Cassandra turned her head away from her friend's giddy excitement. She saw him. Rather than pretend he was not there, she made a desperate face and gestured for him to come over.

She stepped back just as he arrived, so they were not right on Lydia's back. Bodies filled in the hole, obscuring Penthurst.

"It is always a happy day when I see you, Lady Cassandra. Even a happier one when you don't mind seeing me."

"As it happens, I am relieved to see you. You must help me with Lydia."

His smug satisfaction that she turned to him for help instead of Penthurst did not entirely conquer the dark resentments resurrected on seeing them together. "Lady Lydia appears to be enjoying herself. I hope so, since her brother will lock her away for a year if he learns of this. As for you, and your leading her down the path to ruin, I have no idea what he will do."

"She was determined. Either I brought her here, or she would ask some hackney driver to bring her anywhere with gaming and end up in the worst hell. I decided it could not hurt for a few hours. We would come, she would lose, that would discourage her, and it would all be over."

"Only it is not over?"

She bit her bottom lip and looked adorably distraught. "None of it has gone according to my plan. For one thing, she is winning."

"A lot?"

"A ridiculous amount. At least seven hundred thus far, even with the small amounts I insist she restrict herself to. She can't lose, Ambury. She makes the stupidest choices, she plays badly, and wins. I have even whispered deliberately wrong advice, and when she takes it, she *still wins*."

A squeal came from the table. Lydia's arms rose into the

air. She looked over her shoulder at Cassandra. "I risked rather more this time." Her big smile said it had gone well too.

"Do you see what I mean? I need to remove her from here before her luck turns, or she will go down deeper than she was up, I fear. Only I have given her the signal several times, and she ignores me."

"Is that how you played? Unable to quit when you were losing?"

She did not appreciate the query. "She is drunk on it. I never was that bad."

"Yet you lost big, did you not? Perhaps she will prove more disciplined."

"I did not lose for lack of discipline. Are you going to help me with her or not? Her brother is your good friend. I think he would expect you to stop her."

"I was not the person who introduced her to Mrs. Burton's drawing room, so do not pretend she is my responsibility. As for helping you, what do you propose?"

"Go over there, look at her severely and tell her it is time to stop."

He laughed out loud. "Would that stop *you* if you were winning hundreds?"

"Of course not. But Lydia is accustomed to obeying orders from her brother, and she may obey you as his surrogate."

Right now Lydia did not look like a woman inclined to obey anyone who interfered with her triumph. Yates rather wished Southwaite could see her. Darius worried that his sister had turned remote and emotionless. It was questionable whether he would appreciate just how alive she seemed right now, of course.

Yates made his way around the table so that he watched Lydia from the side and could catch her eye. She beamed with pride and gestured to her winnings. "It appears I am brilliant at this, Ambury. Who would have ever guessed?"

"It is called luck, and it turns easily. It is wise to quit while you are ahead."

"I think it is wiser to ride with luck while it favors you," she replied with a laugh.

"Allow me to call for a carriage and take you home."

"Oh, tosh. The night is young, and I am having a wonderful time. Mrs. Burton's is much more fun than the parties my aunts insist I attend."

He looked at Cassandra, who rolled her eyes. She took her place behind Lydia and firmly squeezed her friend's shoulder. "It is time to go. I am very tired."

Lydia shook off that hand yet again. "Then go if you must. I am sure I will be safe." She gestured for the dealer to give her another card.

The player beside Lydia left then. Yates waited to see if Cassandra would take the chair. Instead a man moved from the edge of the circle of watchers and sat himself down. Lydia took no note of him, but Yates did. So did Cassandra. So did the other three people sitting in the other chairs.

Penthurst stood out from the others by his dress and manner. The dark queue that had not been cropped marked him, as did the brocade waistcoat that was far richer and more old-fashioned than the other garments worn tonight by the men. The distinctions sat on him well. He managed to make others feel out of place. His demeanor said it could never be the other way around.

Yates had to admire the aplomb with which he carried it off. The antiquated appearance was an affectation, of course. A way of saying some men were slaves to fashion and the opinions of others but the very best do not concern themselves with such trivialities.

The dealer bowed to the newcomer. "Your Grace."

Lydia turned her head and stared at the noble, handsome man whose shoulder brushed her own. Her color rose.

The Duke of Penthurst favored the dealer with acknowledgment by barely nodding his head. Another nod went to Lydia and the other players. Then the gaze of his golden-brown eyes stayed on the table.

Another round was played. Lydia won again. She happily took her winnings and added them to her stack.

"Luck seems to favor you tonight," Penthurst said, his deep, quiet voice carrying surprisingly well in the noise of the drawing room.

"So it seems."

"You should not waste such good fortune on small stakes like this." He gestured to the dealer. "A deck, if you do not mind."

The dealer handed over a deck of cards, then stood back. No more vingt-et-un would be dealt now, it appeared. As if dismissed by a king, the other players left their chairs.

Penthurst set the stack on the table in front of him. "Do you enjoy risk, Lady Lydia? Do you find gambling exciting?"

"About as much as most people, I suppose."

"You have just shy of eight hundred there. What if I wagered you ten thousand against it, decided by the chance draw of cards? Would you take the wager?"

"My eight hundred against your ten thousand? You stand to lose much more than you stand to gain. That is a very odd wager."

"I think that your eight hundred means more to you than my ten thousand means to me, so the greater risk, and the greater excitement, is still yours."

"I would be a fool not to take the wager, since I stand to win so much."

"That is what gamblers always think. However, I require that you risk something in addition to the eight hundred in order to win my ten thousand, so we each play for a worthwhile prize." He leaned over an inch and spoke again, too quietly for anyone but Lydia to hear.

Lydia frowned at what he said, as if puzzling out a foreign language. Then her eyes widened. She glanced at him, aghast. Her old detachment fell like a curtain over her face. She stood abruptly and walked away from the table.

Cassandra watched her go, then stared at the table. All Lydia's winnings still sat there. She began scooping them up.

Penthurst helped her push it all into her reticule. "Her presence here was your doing, wasn't it?" he asked.

"Believe what you like, Your Grace, but she is not a child and is capable of making her own decisions." With that, Cassandra hurried off to look for her friend.

Penthurst looked over at Yates. "She will let you take her home soon, Ambury. You might tell Southwaite to keep an eye on her. That is a restless woman looking for ruinous adventure, and I have at best delayed her finding it by a fortnight."

"What did he say to you?" Cassandra demanded. "I do not want to speak of it. Oh, dear, I left all the money."

"I have it here." Cassandra patted her reticule. She resented the way Penthurst had so quickly blamed her for Lydia's behavior. Ambury did too. So would Southwaite. It was not fair, since Lydia had all but blackmailed her into it.

"He has ruined my night, and it appears he is going to remain," Lydia said. "I never liked him when he was friends with my brother. He always lorded it over everyone, and spoke to me like I was a child."

"Is that what he did tonight? Speak to you that way, and scold?"

Lydia's face reddened. "No."

Ambury was pushing his way toward them. His expression said that he expected Cassandra to stay put until he got to her.

"I walked here," he said when he reached them. "However, I have told the footman at the door to get a hackney. I will see you both home."

"I do not want to leave immediately," Lydia said. "If I do, Penthurst will think he chased me away, and I refuse to allow that. I am going to watch the hazard play for a while. Then I will leave."

"Oh, Lydia, please—"

"I will not play, Cassandra. I promise. I am only going to watch."

Before she or Ambury could object further, Lydia marched away, aiming for the hazard tables. Over at the vingt-et-un, Penthurst noted her progress.

"We will give her a quarter hour so she can save her pride, Ambury. I will meet you at those tables then. I will drag her out by her hair if I must after that," Cassandra said.

She excused herself and retreated from the chamber, in order to seek less noise and some fresh air. The crowd at Mrs. Burton's had made the drawing room uncomfortably warm.

She tried the library, but a clutch of ladies gossiped there. She found a small sitting room that was deserted. She threw open the window and lifted the curls on her neck so she might cool off.

A hand took the curls from her. Another removed the fan from her other hand. A wonderful breeze bathed her neck as the fan flicked behind her.

"We could go down to the terrace," Ambury said. "It is very pleasant outside."

"I am not such a fool as to go to a dark terrace with you." Being alone with him in this chamber was no smarter. She could hear the murmur of the women gossiping in the nearby library.

"Are you afraid that I will kiss you again?"

She turned to face him. She took the fan. "You do not frighten me."

"Not at all? How insulting."

He made it a joke, but she could see in the moonlight that he did not believe her. Nor was she telling the truth. His kisses had lured her too well, and she was in danger of doing something stupid if she permitted that again. Worse, however, he frightened her for reasons that had nothing to do with pleasure and embraces.

He was up to something with those earrings. She was almost sure of it now. She had begun to suspect the information was all that really mattered, and that he did not care about the jewels at all.

"My aunt and I will be going abroad soon," she said, turning back to the window. "She thinks the Continent is too unsettled. I have proposed America. What do you think?"

"I think that you will not be happy either place." His voice was right behind her. His head all but touched her own. She felt him there, very close to her, looking out as she did at the city square bathed in moonlight.

"I have been to the Continent before, and was happy enough. I traveled there with my aunt after my first Season." She had gone after she had refused to marry Lakewood. That sorry episode had caused enough scandal that there would be no second Season. There had been no reason to remain in England, so she had journeyed with Sophie to Vienna and Saint Petersburg and other capitals. She had returned as a woman, not a girl. A woman of the world, as Ambury called her.

"That was temporary," he said. "It was not forever."

"We were gone three years. I am practiced in meeting new people, and putting down roots quickly, so this much longer journey does not frighten me. I do worry that my aunt would find America too different, however. Too rustic."

"It is said the cities there are not so different. Still, you would know no one in America. You would be forever removed from your friends and family."

"Perhaps that would be a good thing." She would miss Emma, and Lydia, and a few others, of course. Mama too, but even that tie had loosened so much in the last six years, and after tonight, for all she knew, Southwaite might decree that Emma and Lydia were lost to her.

"Why are you telling me that you are leaving? Is it supposed to be the reason why you won't let me kiss you?"

Once more he teased, but she heard a serious note in the question.

I am telling you so that you will leave my aunt alone, if you think she has done something wrong. I am hoping that if you know she is going away, you will not care about whatever she did. She wished she could just say that. Only he had not really indicated that he thought Aunt Sophie had done something wrong. She was the one who worried about that.

A hand raised her curls again, startling her. Another breeze drifted over her neck. A warm one, from a human breath. Pressure on her nape, firm but also soft, made her tense. His kiss caused thrills to travel arabesque paths down her body. Enticing little pleasures prodded awake her sensuality.

She closed her eyes and noted every stimulation and what it did to her. How the warm kiss on her neck stole her breath, and how her breasts grew heavy when his mouth moved to her shoulder. The sweetness tempted her badly, but there could never be a simple pleasure with this man.

"You surprise me, Ambury. You are not the sort of man to pursue a woman he does not care for. Do you sacrifice yourself to make me pliable for some reason?"

His hands rested on her shoulders, then caressed down her arms. "If you think I do not want you, you are wrong." His voice spoke right near her ear, and his breath made her own catch.

"I said you do not care for me, not that you do not want me. All men want all women, when you get down to it."

"Not like this. I have wanted you for years."

That touched her, although she should not allow it to. Deep inside, a corner of her essence trembled. It would be very nice if it were true. It moved her that perhaps someone had thought about her at all these last years, for any purpose other than silly gossip.

She turned around, lest she melt completely. Only that brought her face-to-face with him in the moonlight, very close. He appeared unbearably handsome. She wanted desperately to believe he did not just toy with her, or manipulate her, or merely seek to make her one more conquest, but she dared not.

"Years? It has taken you a long time to let me know. You are not known for timidity in your pursuits either, so that is odd." She tipped up her head and looked him right in the eyes. "Do you feel free to act now because he is dead? Or because you have decided that I am indeed a woman of the world, and inclined to permit it?"

She expected her taunt to put him off. To anger him. To remind him why she had the reputation she did, and why he had avoided her for six years. A deeper intensity entered his eyes, and she braced for his wit to slice.

Instead, to her shock, he took her face in his hands. His lips brushed hers. "You incited me to act with your talk of leaving England. If I do not do this now, I might never have the chance." He kissed her again. "I would go to my grave regretting that."

What nonsense. Still, she let him kiss her one more time, and savored the titillation more than she ought. Then she covered his hands with her own and removed them from her face.

"I must go to Lydia and take her home," she said.

He did not appear inclined to let her move away. She half hoped he would not. After a hesitation, he stepped aside. She left the sitting room alone, unseen, and unremarked. He was a discreet fifteen steps behind her when she entered the drawing room.

"Open your reticule," Cassandra said to Lydia. "I need to move the money from mine to yours."

"You keep it. I don't want it."

Cassandra stared at Lydia's profile, dark beside her despite the moonlight coming in the windows of the coach. After everything else tonight, Lydia's indifference to the money tested her temper badly. "I cannot take it. Now, *open your reticule.*"

Lydia gazed sightlessly out the window. The remoteness that had descended on her at the vingt-et-un table had not lifted.

Cassandra was in no mood to indulge her. She took the reticule and handed it to Ambury, sitting on the facing bench. "Hold this open, please."

The two of them managed to transfer the night's winnings from Cassandra's reticule to its owner's own just as the coach stopped in front of Southwaite's house.

Ambury hopped down and handed Lydia out. "I will take you to the door. If Southwaite finds out about this, we will tell him that we both found ourselves at the same party."

"He will not discover us. The servants do not tell on me, and my brother has been in bed for hours now. That is all he does of an evening. Go to bed with Emma." She turned to Cassandra. "I think he is insatiable. Is that common?"

"Initially, I think perhaps so," Cassandra said through the window.

"I do not think I would like a husband who was insatiable." Lydia shook her head. "Poor Emma."

It was not so much the conversation itself that made Yates uncomfortable but the husband under discussion, and the ladies who were doing the discussing

Once Lydia had been dispensed with, he returned to the carriage, where Cassandra looked at him through the window. When he reached for the door's latch, she rapped her fan against his knuckles, stopping him.

"I will allow you back in if you promise to behave yourself."

He crossed his forearms on the window's lower edge. "How is it you want me to behave?"

"You know what I mean. You have been too bold."

"Have I? I thought you were too sophisticated to require long wooing and empty words. I assumed you live like your aunt did, free of concern about the opinions of others and open to experiences that make me far from bold thus far. If I erred, then you are indeed merely wild, and only in need of taming."

He expected her to react with playful wit or vexed indignation. Instead she just looked at him, her eyes black in the night.

"Taming?" She said the word curiously, as if she had never heard its sound before. "Did my brother put you up to this, Ambury?"

The question stunned him. During the moment when he was at a disadvantage, she reached out and rapped her fan on the outside of the coach.

The hackney driver snapped the ribbons. They drove off, leaving Yates to find his way home alone.

Chapter 9

Yates entered Brooks's and surveyed the parties that had already formed. Pitt was holding forth to a thick collection of ministers and peers over to the left, his voice low and their expressions rapt. Presumably the war with France was being dissected, or perhaps the Irish situation.

One of those figures moved his attention from the prime minister. Penthurst noted Yates's arrival, then angled his head ever so slightly. Yates instinctively followed the direction, and his gaze lit upon Kendale and Southwaite sitting thirty feet away.

"I am surprised to see you," Yates said to Southwaite as he took a chair with them. "I had heard you returned to town, but duty does not require your presence at your clubs."

"I am reclaiming the patterns of my life at my wife's insistence."

"He means he was overstaying his welcome in her bed, I think," Kendale said. "However, he has not said much since he came in, so I think his mind remained there even if his body did not."

"I did not overstay any welcome," Southwaite said with clear measure. "However, the rest of your suspicions are accurate. How did you know?"

"The damned self-satisfied smile gave you away," Kendale said.

"We all look forward to the day when you smile thus, Kendale," Yates said.

Actually, they looked forward to when Kendale smiled more than once a week. Prior to his older brother's untimely demise, Kendale had served in the army, as was common for second sons of peers. Only instead of a jovial regiment of Horse Guards, he had insisted on a commission with a regiment that saw action. He left that service far more serious than when he entered.

"Do not hold your breath. I haven't a romantic drop of blood in me, and will never be as drunk on a woman as our friend is now with his bride."

Southwaite raised his glass of brandy in salute. "May you never fall, for if you do, I fear the earth will shake due to the heights from which you tumble."

"Oh, he will fall," Yates said. "He is too proud to heed our lessons and practice the feints and dodges required of a man determined to remain free."

"Fine lessons they are, for all the good they did him." Kendale jabbed a thumb in Southwaite's direction.

"He was not caught unawares, as you will be. Next Season, some sweet girl with a shrewd mama is going to run you to ground before you even know the hounds have been let free. You won't know what happened until you see your own tail nailed to her boudoir wall."

"What shit," Kendale muttered. "Feel free to continue, however. Unlike him, you are somewhat entertaining."

"Has he been boring you? Southwaite, why not follow your mind's directions and go home? You have forever to reclaim the patterns of your life, and probably only another fortnight or so more of enthusiastic interest from your new wife."

Southwaite frowned. "If anyone knows why I am here, it is you, Ambury."

"I do?"

"Have you forgotten the messenger you sent? He said you wanted to speak with me on a matter of personal importance. It sounded urgent. I knew I might find you here tonight." He folded his hands and waited. "It had better be good, especially after that warning about only another fortnight."

Yates had sent no messenger. He thought he knew who had, however. He turned his head until his eye caught the view of Penthurst saying something to Pitt and his group.

How like the man to issue an order, then arrange to ensure the order would be obeyed.

"You may consider what I have to say a matter of interfering where I am not wanted. I have thought twice about doing so. Three times, in fact."

Southwaite's sobriety turned to concern. "If it even crossed your mind once, you need to tell me. You are not one to consider such a thing lightly to begin with."

Kendale watched with keen interest. Southwaite's expression made it clear there was no turning back.

"It has to do with your sister. She was at Mrs. Burton's the other night. Gambling."

Kendale whistled between his teeth.

Southwaite closed his eyes. "How much did she lose?"

"Nothing. She won."

His eyes opened. "She won?"

"Seven hundred, I think. At least."

"How is that bad news?" Kendale asked. "Please bring me such sorry tidings tomorrow, Ambury."

"She may not win next time," Yates said. "She was drunk from the excitement too." He cleared his throat. "At least one onlooker commented to me that she was looking for adventure. I found the description apt, and thought I should inform you."

"Well that you did. It must stop, of course. Be nipped at once. Although, I confess I would have liked to see her excited about something. Anything." Southwaite shook his head. "Did you bring her, so that she would have someone watching out for her? If so, I owe you my gratitude."

"I found her there. I did see her home, however."

"Please tell me she was not so rash as to go alone."

"No, I do not believe so."

"A man brought her? Who is he? Give me the scoundrel's name. I swear I will—"

"She came with another woman, I think."

It took a three count, no longer, for both Southwaite and Kendale to guess who that woman had been.

Kendale glanced his way with an I-told-you-so look. Southwaite closed his eyes in forbearance again.

"Thank you, Ambury. I will deal with all of this immediately."

"How?" Kendale asked. "You let your wife be friends with that woman. How do you explain to your sister that she can't be?"

The undeniable logic of the question hung in the air. Southwaite frowned while they ground through the conundrum. They all drank more brandy to douse the turning wheels.

"There is only one solution that I can see," Kendale offered. "If you are not going to forbid Cassandra Vernham's friendship to both of them—"

"If he does, it may be the shortest fortnight of pleasure known to a man," Yates said.

"And you are not going to permit your sister to be friends with a woman of her reputation—"

"There is rather more to it than that," Southwaite said.

"We do not know that for certain. We suspect she was at the heart of that duel, but we do not know," Yates said. "And even if she was, the equity issue is the same, regarding your wife."

"I suppose that is correct, in one manner of speaking."

"*As I was saying,* if those two choices are out of the question, there is only one other. I dislike the woman so much that I hesitate to point it out, but you need to find a way to rehabilitate Lady Cassandra's reputation so her friendship does not reflect badly on your sister or your wife."

"Kendale, you have a delightfully simple, if misguided, view of the world," Yates said.

"I think he makes good sense," Southwaite said. "She is not truly ruined. She has not been totally ostracized by good society. There are those who receive her and invite her to parties. Who is to say if any of the rumors have been true? They have mostly been vague references to vague liaisons with unnamed men. She need only marry and—"

"I am sure her family has traveled that path often enough, to no avail."

Southwaite's wheels turned some more. "That would be the easiest way, but not the only possible one. An idea is forming. I need to speak with Emma." He stood. "I think I will go home and discuss the entire situation with her now."

Penthurst noticed Southwaite passing on the way out. He glanced down at Yates. A vague tip of his head acknowledged that duty had been served.

"He doesn't have another idea to discuss with his wife," Kendale said. "He just wants to get back into bed."

"You are both right and wrong. He needs to raise a delicate matter with his bride. Debates with women always go better if they are pleasured first, Kendale. Consider that another bit of wisdom that you should tuck away regarding women, should the day ever come when you deign to court one."

Cassandra received the letter in the midmorning post the next day. *"Meet me in Hyde Park. One o'clock. Emma."* It appeared to have been jotted in a hurry, and the handwriting communicated urgency. Worried, Cassandra dressed and prepared to comply.

She found Emma pacing back and forth, right inside the corner entrance.

"What has you so distraught?" Cassandra asked. "Have you discovered that Marielle's jewels will not be offered to Fairbourne's?"

"Jewels? Oh, goodness, I do not want to talk about that. I need to discuss something else entirely."

Cassandra twined her arm through Emma's and began strolling. "You will still be holding an auction in September, however?"

"I expect so."

"Good. I may have another lot for it."

"Wonderful," Emma muttered.

"Your mind is elsewhere, I can see. Is your brother worse?"

"He is hale and fit enough to leave town to go shooting up in Yorkshire. He acts as if Fairbourne's can manage itself." She made a shooing gesture, pushing the topic away. "Better he be gone than in the way. Nor do I care when he returns. I have enough on my mind without debating his course or worth."

"What has you in such a state?"

"You will laugh when you hear it. You will not think it dire at all. Darius has suggested that we host a dinner party." She looked Cassandra in the eyes. "I have never hosted a party for good society. Nor will this be a friendly one. He wants to entertain some of the peers who have come to town, and their wives, and his aunts, and—" She threw up her hands helplessly.

"It is rather soon after your wedding."

"That is what I thought!"

"Although there is little for society to do now, so I am sure it will be welcomed."

"That is what he said."

"However, it is more worry than you need."

"I thought so too."

"On the other hand, if you put it off, you will probably get with child, and your condition will only make it more burdensome."

"His words exactly."

Cassandra laughed. "You did a lot of thinking, and he did all the talking. It is not like you to withhold your opinions."

"I mostly thought after he talked. An hour or so later, my mind marshaled my arguments very neatly, only it was too late."

"Did he become all lordly and masterful with you? Is that what put you off clear thinking?" Southwaite had a tendency to issue decrees and assume he knew best about things. Cassandra had rather hoped he would control that for at least a year or so with Emma, so that Emma was prepared to give as good as she received.

"In a manner of speaking, only it is not what you think." Emma went very red, and she was not a woman to blush easily. "He was very solicitous about his idea. Charming. The moment he chose to broach it, however . . . I was at a disadvantage."

"And not thinking clearly, I believe you said."

"Yes."

"Your mind was preoccupied."

"Exactly."

"May I assume that you were inclined to believe the world a blissful, happy place when this subject came up?"

Emma nodded

"Just how much of a disadvantage did he create first?"

"A rather large one."

The scoundrel.

"I will be happy to help you with this, if that is why you wanted to meet. With the aid of your servants, this is not nearly as complicated as it may appear now. You must start them cleaning immediately, however. The open windows in summer will have let in a lot of dust."

"Thank you. I will be grateful to have your help and advice. However . . . that is not the reason I asked to meet today."

Emma stopped walking. Cassandra braced herself to hear the true reason for the rendezvous. Southwaite had probably learned about Lydia being at Mrs. Burton's, and had instructed Emma to warn Cassandra off the friendship.

"You are to be invited," Emma said. "I wanted you to know that. Not only has he agreed to permit our friendship, he has decided to receive you in the proper fashion henceforth."

It was a most unexpected announcement. "I am touched. And very relieved for us both, but mostly for me."

"You will attend, then? I am overjoyed. Your aunt must come too. Darius was very specific about that."

"I think it unlikely that my aunt will come."

"Can you cajole her? Darius wants her company for his aunts. Please try to convince her, just this once."

"I will try, but I doubt that I will be successful. When is the grand event to take place?"

"Five days hence. Darius's secretary is penning the invitations right now."

"That does not give me long to convince her."

"It would probably be best if she came. There is a bit more that I did not tell you yet."

Cassandra heard a dubious note in Emma's voice. "I am not going to like this bit more, am I? Speak plainly, Emma, as you are normally proud to do."

"I saw the guest list after Darius added to my small one. There is one name that I do not think you will care to have present."

The memory of kisses on her neck and shoulder turned

vividly real, and of a warm voice near her ear. "You must refer to Ambury. Do not let it concern you. I am not nearly as pliable as he may think."

"Ambury? What has he to do with anything? I am speaking of someone whom you dislike far more than him. Darius will be inviting your brother to the party."

"Gerald?" That was bad news. "He will be even less pleased to see me there than I to see him. He rather counts on society pushing me to its margins."

"That is why you must come. I think that Darius aims to allow you to step out of the margins, Cassandra. I believe he hopes to allow you to claim a place other than that influenced by the scandal sheets."

Was that Southwaite's goal? If so, it was Emma he hoped to serve with it. If Cassandra became less notorious, Emma's friendship would be less embarrassing. And Lydia's too.

Cassandra found it hard to believe that Southwaite was concocting a scheme to salvage her reputation, but that might be the result of whatever else he was concocting all the same.

The notion appealed more than she ever thought it would. She had known the price of standing her ground when she refused Lakewood six years ago. She had not complained as she paid it. She had grown used to being fodder for the rumor mills, and even developed pride in being her own woman, confident in knowing herself no matter what others believed. Now, however, as the possibility of salvation glowed on the horizon, she admitted she experienced fatigue from the weight of carrying that exaggerated reputation.

"I can manage Gerald, Emma. I have for years. You are not to worry about our being there together."

"It is a relief to hear you say that, Cassandra. I have been troubled since I saw the list after breakfast." She slid her arm through Cassandra's and set them strolling again. "Now, before I leave, you must explain what you meant when you said that Ambury thought you were—what was the word you used?" She glanced over slyly. "Now I remember— *pliable*."

"I do not remember which pawnbroker it was, dear. It was years ago." Aunt Sophie dismissed Cassandra's query out of hand, then eyed the cook's doings from her seat at the worktable in the kitchen. "A bit more salt than that, senora."

Eagle-eyed and skinny, Senora Paolini, the cook Sophie had brought back from Naples on returning from one of her tours, kept her back to her mistress. She pinched a bit more salt and threw it in the soup with a gesture that spoke her opinion of the command.

"I would appreciate it if you tried to remember anyway," Cassandra said.

"You are very curious about those earrings now that you have sold them, despite showing no interest at all when you owned them."

Cassandra debated explaining why she had all this interest now. Would Sophie be sympathetic or insulted? It was unlikely Sophie would miss the implications of Ambury's suspicions.

She decided to admit to part of it. "The person who bought them at auction is curious about their history. They are clearly old. I think it is hoped they are from the crown jewels of some country you visited." The last was not a lie as such. Not really. Well, yes really, but a fib told for the best of reasons.

"You will have to disabuse her of such speculations." Sophie stretched to see what senora was doing at the hearth. "I would never give away the crown jewels bestowed on me by royalty."

"Did you keep any crown jewels, or are they among what you gave to me?"

"Do not cover that rabbit yet, senora. It will steam instead of browning properly." Sophie turned back to Cassandra. "The best ones went back recently. You remember last spring, when I returned Alexis's necklace to the agent he sent. There may be a piece or two more from the collections of small countries."

Alexis had sent his man to England to auction a collection of art. Fairbourne's had performed the service, to Emma's triumph. The agent, Herr Werner, had been the only visitor Sophie had received all year, and Cassandra indeed had to remove an item from her own auction lots in order for Sophie to return it to him.

"About that pawnbroker . . ."

"Really, dear, at my age the mind starts throwing away insignificant details. Even so, I will try and remember." She closed her eyes. "Let me see—I can summon up sensations more than names or buildings. I believe, I am almost sure, that the pawnbroker's establishment was off the Strand a few doors. Back then, the door to the shop was blue. I see blue very clearly in my mind." She opened her eyes and shrugged off the effort. "That is all I remember. Tell the buyer to have the jewels reset if she has some silly concern about their history."

Sophie stood and walked over to the hearth. She peered into the soup pot, then bent to the sizzling pan of rabbit. Senora Paolini waited for the daily inspection to be done. She grasped a wooden spoon like she would not mind using it for a purpose other than stirring.

"Come, Cassandra, let us leave senora to her art. It would not do to interfere."

Cassandra looked back as she followed her aunt up the stairs. Senora was shaking that spoon at them.

"You interfere each day, Aunt Sophie. You really should leave her alone. You are no cook yourself," she said when they settled into the library.

"That would be unkind. She depends on my going down there. I am the only friend senora has. Now, I want to tell

you that the oddest thing happened. I received an invitation
to a party from Lord and Lady Southwaite. I did not even
know there was a Lady Southwaite. I wonder who brought
that proud man low."

Thank goodness Gerald was not here. "That is my friend
Emma. You remember—I went to the wedding two weeks
ago, and was gone for several days."

"The one in Kent? Fairbourne's daughter? Why did you
not tell me she was marrying Southwaite? So he married a
tradesman's daughter? Well, well . . . I expect he got her
with child and did the noble thing."

"She is not yet with child."

"It is a love match? How strange the world has become,
when such a man marries such a woman because of love. In
my day, it was handled quite differently."

"I was invited to the party too. We can go together."

"I think not."

"Gerald will be there, I believe. If you came and it was
obvious to all that you are fine, if you showed yourself in
public and there were all those witnesses to your health, he
would have a more difficult time trying to do what he
threatened."

Sophie gave that considerable thought. At least Cassandra
hoped that was what suddenly preoccupied her as she sat on
the divan, gazing at nothing much at all.

"What you say is true, Cassandra. This party would be an
opportunity to put Gerald in his place. I could attend and
be witty and sharp, and he would have to retreat entirely from
his threats and stop insinuating that my mind is failing."

"Then you will come? It will be something of a resur-
rection for me too, and I confess that I will feel better if you
are there."

Sophie patted the place beside her. Cassandra went over
to sit by her side.

"I think you will do better alone. It is possible I would
more than acquit myself well. I want to think that I would.

However, let us be honest and admit that it might turn out very differently." She took Cassandra's hand and held it. "Do not pretend you have not noticed. If I go, we both know that I will flirt with danger. Instead of proving your brother wrong, I may say something that gives him, and the whole world, evidence that he is correct."

Cassandra gripped her aunt's hand. "I have noticed a little bit. Not much."

"It is only a little bit. Not much. But enough for his purposes." Sophie reached over and moved a tendril of hair off Cassandra's cheek in a motherly gesture. "A memory does it to me, or a scent, or even an object. Suddenly the past is real in ways it should not be. The memories lure me to let them have their way. I never have forgotten where I am. I have been aware of it all. It is as if the barriers break down, however, and time flows in both directions too freely."

"Surely that is normal. If you are aware it is happening, and do not lose hold of an anchor in the present, who cares how much you float to the past?"

"For most aging people, I expect no one much cares."

Only Aunt Sophie was not most people.

"It is my fault he is doing this." Cassandra held on to her shaky composure by allowing her anger to spike. Her swallowed tears burned her throat. "I will not allow him to succeed." She embraced her aunt. "You will see. I will take care of you just as you have taken care of me. You will be safe and you will be free. Whatever it takes, I will make sure of that."

Her aunt did not resist the embrace, or make any attempt to respond. Instead, her head tipped just enough to rest on Cassandra's shoulder, and her hand never left Cassandra's own.

Chapter 10

Cassandra picked through the jewelry Aunt Sophie had given her, seeking a discreet but attractive necklace that did not have any little notes warning that it not be flaunted in London. She decided that a simple gold chain sporting a cluster of small dangling pearls would do, especially since it was only off limits in Saint Petersburg.

Her maid fastened it so the pearls dotted the flesh exposed by the neckline of her blue dress. A blue, gold, and red patterned turban, tied in the broad, artistic style favored on the Continent, gave her ensemble a dramatic flair. She eyed herself in the looking glass and hoped her appearance reflected her determination to cooperate tonight, but only up to a point.

Merriweather showed in the mirror suddenly, her cap a garish white blotch above the turban's exotic depths. "A caller, m'lady."

Cassandra took the card and the accompanying note. "Allow me to escort you and your aunt, so the two of you do not enter the lion's den alone and unprotected. Ambury."

Had he turned his carriage here on a whim, while on the way to the party? It was irregular to arrive and offer such service at the last minute.

Of course, she was irregular too, so perhaps he thought he did not need to stand on ceremony. Or maybe those kisses had led him to assume their brief intimacies had breached any need for formality.

She had worked hard to avoid thinking about his mouth on her skin and his hands on her body. The memory did silly things to her. The way it could renew the chills and flutters she had experienced at that window was the least of it. When Ambury kissed a woman, it became very easy for her to forget how unwise it would be to allow him such liberties in the future.

He made it ridiculously tempting to pretend he pursued a serious flirtation, and that no old histories darkened his motivations or colored his views of her. He was well practiced in using pleasure and flattery to conquer feminine caution.

She considered having Merriweather tell him his escort would not be needed. Only she really did not want to go alone. This night's assembly would be harder to enter than the wedding, and that had taken a good deal of courage. Tonight there would be no way for cuts to be subtle. The truth was she dreaded the possible humiliation she might endure. She would not go at all if anyone but Emma had invited her.

Instead of sending Merriweather down with a message, she grabbed her reticule and her wrap and descended herself.

She found Ambury in the small chamber near the door that served as a reception hall. He appeared devilishly handsome in the light of the small candelabra that Merriweather had left with him. The golden glow flattered the angles of his face and the deep blue of his eyes. Surprise showed in his expression for an instant when she entered. Then his gaze took her in from head to toe, with alarming thoroughness.

"Is something amiss?" she asked, too aware of the flush

rising on her face. "Did my maid leave a hairpin dangling over my nose?"

"I am admiring how you deck yourself in garments that fit you so well."

"That is why I hire dressmakers. So my garments will fit me."

"I was not speaking of how they fit your body, but your style. Although—" Again his gaze traveled a leisurely path over her dress. "That other fit appears perfect too."

The small chamber grew smaller yet. Her sensuality stirred. She could call the sensation nothing else, the arousal proved that distinct and obvious. She began reconsidering her decision to ride with him.

"My aunt will not be attending."

"That is unfortunate. I hope she is not ill."

"Not at all. She merely chooses not to attend. Since she will not join us, I will hire a hackney."

"I am charmed by your attempts to hide behind propriety. One might think you had never been kissed before."

"One might think that only if one were very stupid. I am not hiding. I am trying to spare you unnecessary gossip."

"Gossip follows me just as it does you. We have that in common. After the first five or so scandalous rumors, one ceases to care. Don't you agree?"

Her clever retort died on her lips. He knew, she realized. He suspected that most of the gossip was not true.

"The party is only a few streets away," he said. "I will not be seducing you in the short time it takes to get there." He offered his arm. "Shall we go?"

"I think it is going well," Emma whispered. She appeared poised as she stopped near Cassandra's chair to share a few words, but her gaze darted around the drawing room, looking for pending disaster.

"I told you it would be less trouble than planning one of

Fairbourne's grand previews. Fewer people. More organized movement. Not to mention you had an army of servants to help."

"It was your help that I relied on, Cassandra. Your advice on the menu was perfect." She placed a hand on Cassandra's arm. "Please tell me that it has been bearable for you. I tried to convince Darius to strike your brother from the list, but he was most firm about keeping his name on it."

"I am having a lovely evening. Do not worry about Gerald. He and I can share a meal and a few hours under the same roof. Your husband no doubt had political reasons to invite him, as he did with most of the other men here."

Those men would arrive soon from the dining room, where they had sequestered themselves after the meal. Cassandra wondered how things would go with Gerald once the rituals of the evening relaxed.

Probably just as well as they were going with Southwaite's aunts.

The two of them, steely haired and formidable in their height, bore down on her now. Neither had addressed Cassandra most of the night, except in the most formal way, but it appeared a decision had been made to have a conversation.

Emma did not abandon her, but stayed by the side of her chair. Hortense and Amelia lowered themselves into other chairs nearby.

"That is a stunning hat," Cassandra said to Amelia. She was the shyer of the two, and she blushed at the compliment and fondly patted the green turban on her crown. "May I ask which milliner made it?"

They spoke of hats and fashions for a few minutes. The two aunts appeared grateful that a topic had been supplied. As conversation waned, however, Hortense began looking formidable again. Lips pursed, and with a gaze surprisingly warm, she leaned forward confidentially.

"I have missed your aunt, Cassandra. Sophie was always

so lively. Her presence refreshed any party, and I hoped to see her here tonight. How is she faring these days?"

"She is faring very well. I will be sure to tell her that you asked after her."

"She does not receive visitors at all, it is said."

"Very rarely."

"Nor even take walks in the park."

"She prefers her garden."

Amelia frowned. "She let you sell her jewels. That is most odd. She always loved her jewels."

"She gave them to me when she retired from society."

Hortense looked at Amelia. They both glanced to the door.

"Your brother confided his concerns about her before you arrived. He expressed doubts she would venture out, because she is not well. We could hardly gainsay him when we have not seen her in many months. We had hoped . . ."

Cassandra tensed as anger flooded her. Still standing by her side, Emma gently pressed her shoulder with a calming hand.

"I have seen her," Emma said. "When I visit Cassandra, her aunt is often there. You are quite correct. Her presence is always refreshing, and her distinctive outlook on life is clever and lively."

Cassandra welcomed Emma's lie from the depths of her heart. "And, of course, I see her daily," she said with a big smile. "My brother does not. Gerald has never been comfortable with my aunt's choices in life, so he is unlikely to understand her current ones." She angled closer and shared a knowing look with Hortense. "You know how vain a man can be. If a woman does not flatter his sense of his own importance, she must be ill. My brother's view is swayed by my aunt's refusal to receive him along with everyone else, that is all."

Hortense and Amelia smiled like conspirators. Cassandra could not tell if they were relieved or disappointed to learn that all was well with Sophie, however. Cursing Gerald in her mind, she began plotting how to handle the gossip that might spread after this party.

As she did, the door opened and the men arrived. Gerald appeared in deep conversation with Southwaite, who listened politely. Emma left her post beside Cassandra and advanced to welcome her guests.

People moved. Conversations began. Some guests took to playing whist. Cassandra watched Gerald and wondered if she would escape a conversation with him.

Ambury made his way over and sat in a chair he moved to her side. "You appear vexed. Has someone been rude?"

Gerald was still on her mind, and in her sight, as she answered. "No one has been rude. If I appear vexed, it is because I learned something tonight that I had been ignorant of before. I am vexed with myself for being naïve, although I want to believe my trust in human nature speaks well of me."

"What is this great discovery?"

"That the matrons of society will overlook much if I am received in a good house."

It was another lie. She had always known it would not take much to reclaim full respectability. If she had been damned, these women would have missed Emma's wedding rather than be seen in the same chamber with her. The cuts would not have been subtle, but direct, and Southwaite would never have permitted Emma's friendship to continue.

No, today's discovery was far more devastating, so much that her heart broke. She had always assumed that the gossip about her came from the idle speculation of bored minds. She had never suspected that instead it might be the result of someone's concerted effort to humiliate her.

She looked at Gerald. He had their father's eyes. Sophie's eyes. Only he always looked to be peering hard at the world. That killed their warmth. It affected his whole face. Not a bad face in its features, but there was nothing friendly about it. His countenance and body had a rigidity that made him unappealing.

Had he done it? Was his current game regarding Sophie a new tack after an old one had not worked as well as he hoped? Had he ensured that her reputation for being too wild and too independent took as big a toll as possible? He had wasted no time today to gossip about Aunt Sophie. Perhaps he had been planting gossip for years.

He appeared to be a man who could do that. Even his smiles looked like they could cut stone. And his manner— she remembered a full-faced boy who got into mischief too easily. Now she observed a severe lord who would most likely whip that boy if he ran into him.

Gerald noticed her watching him. To her horror, he began walking in her direction.

"You appear faint," Ambury said. "Perhaps you would like to go out to the terrace and get some air."

Escape held enormous appeal. Only it was too late. In the next moment, Gerald stood in front of her, gazing down as a father might on an errant child. "You appear lovely tonight, Cassandra."

"I was just thinking the same thing," Ambury said. That forced Gerald to acknowledge that Ambury sat close enough to be included.

"The turban is a little too dramatic, however," Gerald said. "I cannot decide if it is the style, the fabric, or the way it makes you look like an ancient sibyl from the Near East."

"The world is never hurt by a little drama, Barrowmore. It is rude to flatter a woman in one breath and insult her in the next, even if she is a sister."

Her heart swelled with gratitude that Ambury defended her. He appeared amiable and casual, but his attention possessed a sharpness that suggested his daggers were ready, should they be needed.

Perhaps Emma had requested his aid again, in looking out for her friend. If so, Emma could never have expected the worst of the night to come from Gerald.

Gerald should have let Ambury's rebuke pass, but, being

Gerald, he could not. "Because she is my sister, Ambury, and because all that she does, and is, reflects on me and my family, it is my duty to correct her if I see the need."

"That has worked so well in the past, Barrowmore, that of course you would want to continue. However, a hat? You feel the need to correct her regarding that? The world is at war, the French breeched our borders, the economy is going to hell, and you concern yourself with your sister's turban."

Gerald flushed to his ears. "It is symbolic of much more."

"It is? Who knew? You must tell Southwaite's aunt that. She too wears a turban, and I doubt she guesses its meaning. When you do speak to her of it, what will you explain it symbolizes?"

Gerald's gaze narrowed on Ambury, then shifted to her. "Is he the latest? Or has he only just joined the queue?"

She was horrified he would say such a thing in Emma's drawing room. Their conversation had drawn attention too. Out of the corner of her eye she could see others darting glances at them.

Ambury's smile did not waver, but only a fool would misread his temper now. "In insulting your sister further, you also impugn me now. You are being unforgivably rude to our host and hostess by abusing their hospitality with family squabbles."

"Squabbles? Your arguments with your father were family squabbles. Rather more is at stake between Cassandra and me."

Cassandra's breath caught at the mention of Ambury's father. Real danger entered his eyes on hearing it, but he acted as if Gerald only bored him. "If more is at stake, that is even better reason to avoid such conversations in public, Barrowmore."

"See here. I hardly need lectures from *you*, of all men, on comportment."

"Don't you? Perhaps you should move on before you cross what line is left."

"I gladly will take my leave of your company. However, I need to speak further with my sister. Privately."

Ambury looked around. "I would say that privacy is nigh impossible tonight."

"In here, yes. With you eavesdropping, yes. However—Cassandra, I will wait for you on the terrace." With that, Gerald turned on his heel and marched away.

"Don't go," Ambury said. "I angered him, and he looks to be the sort to take it out on you."

She stood. "It would be unwise to refuse to hear what he has to say, or to risk a row here that will embarrass Emma. As for enduring his anger, it will be a price worth paying for having seen you slice his pomposity to shreds."

Gerald waited in a corner of the terrace, arms clasped behind him and posture straight as an iron rod. Shadows obscured the details, but she knew his stance boded ill. Indignation poured off him. Cassandra wondered if the few other guests who had come outside noticed how his mood ruined a beautiful night.

"Here I am, Gerald."

"Yes, indeed. Here you are. For now, while the blush of passion is still fresh with our host. Soon Southwaite will come to his senses about his marriage and not allow his common bride to lead him by the nose into such indiscretions as allowing your friendship and permitting your attendance at dinners where ministers eat."

"I told Emma that you would be confounded by it all. That you would never understand. She was going to cross you off the list to avoid any spectacles, but I convinced her to let you come too." A third lie for the night, but oh, she enjoyed this one.

He found the notion that he, not she, might have been excluded so shocking that he startled. He hid his reaction by crossing his arms and peering through the night in what she assumed would be a very severe stare if she could see it.

"I am told Aunt Sophie was invited as well. I had hoped to see her."

"She decided not to attend."

"Did she fear her condition would become too apparent if she had to spend hours in the company of others?"

She hated him for putting it into words. "She has no fear of company. She merely does not care for the superficialities of society any longer. People like you have made parties too boring for a bright spirit such as she."

"See here—"

"I will leave at once if you get puffed up and tedious. You demanded to speak to me, so speak. You did not need privacy to inquire after our aunt's whereabouts tonight."

He did not speak. Not right away. He unfolded his arms and tapped his fingertips on the low terrace wall beside where he stood. He watched those fingers, as if making sure he played the correct tune on the stone.

"Mother wants you to come down to Anseln Abbey," he said.

"Tell her that I will see her when she comes to town next month. She always makes at least one visit in autumn, to attend the theater and see her dressmakers."

"I want you to come down too. I must insist on it. I will send my coach to bring you and Sophie. You need only stay a week if you prefer."

He sounded so reasonable that this might appear to be a casual conversation between a brother and sister who enjoyed each other's company. Alarm throbbed in Cassandra's head anyway.

"Sophie will never agree to it."

"I think you can convince her."

"I am sure I cannot."

His teeth flashed in the dark as he smiled. "Then you will come alone, if that is how it must be."

124   **Madeline Hunter**

"Why do you want me there?"

"Mother—"

"Mother knows that if she wants me there, I would be more likely to come if she made the request herself. Yet it comes from you. So why do *you* want me there?"

More finger tapping. A new tune. A faster one. "I need you to meet someone."

"Oh, Gerald. Please, *no.* Who is it this time? Some second son in need of a settlement who is willing to take your scandalous sister off your hands?"

"It is past time for you to wed. Mother agrees. If not for Aunt Sophie—"

"If not for Aunt Sophie, you and mother might have browbeat me into marrying Lakewood, and I would have never forgiven either of you. As for now, Aunt Sophie is not what stands between you and me. She has nothing to do with it."

"She has everything to do with it, only not the way I thought."

"What does that mean?"

"I assumed she influenced you badly. Spoke against marriage since she has never married. Advocated certain . . . freedoms of a shameful nature because she is reputed to have enjoyed them. Your behavior has suggested as much."

"You have realized your error in that? I am heartened, Gerald."

"Oh, she influenced you, but it was not her doing. It was your own. Nor is it why you have refused every gentleman's offer that has come along in the last few years."

"You are correct there. My refusals were entirely my own doing, influenced only by the fact those gentlemen were uninteresting and, in truth, uninterested."

"I don't think so."

"They wanted a settlement and connections, but not me, and were not even clever enough to pretend for politeness' sake."

"Well, a woman with your history cannot be too particular. But I think you really refuse to marry because she needs you. She needs your care. She protected you, and now you think to protect her. You dare not let her live on her own. You probably worry when you leave her for a few days, or even of an evening now."

He was terribly close to the truth. So close that it frightened her. "You speak nonsense. She will bury you and me both, and her mind is twice as clear as Mother's. She does not require that I devote my life to protecting her."

"I am sure that I am correct." He lowered his head so his face was very close to hers. "I'll not have it, Cassandra."

A chill shivered down her spine. "Leave her alone, Gerald. It is cruel and ignoble of you to involve her in your designs for me."

"I do not plan to involve her. I plan to remove her for her own good, as is my duty as her closest male relative. I have found a home for her. It is not too far from Anseln Abbey, and run by a doctor who is assisted by his two sisters. It is—"

"Don't you dare!"

"Lower your voice. You are creating a spectacle. Now, as I was explaining . . ."

His unctuous voice droned into her ear in its sotto voce confidences. She battled the urge to create a very big spectacle indeed. She wanted to hit Gerald, or scratch at his face. She wanted to tell him how insufferable he was. Her mind upbraided him in the strongest words she knew while she stood there mute and impotent.

She pictured Aunt Sophie reading at home, unaware of just how far Gerald's scheme had progressed. She had promised to protect her aunt, but her brother was leaving little time for that.

"We will do it in a fortnight," he repeated. "Write and let me know if you will have her things packed and ready, or if I should send servants."

"You must not. It is unfair."

"It is necessary. It is for the best. You will see that soon enough, once your emotions calm." He pushed away from the terrace wall, to return to the party.

"I will not allow it." Tears swelled her throat, and she barely got the words out before he was out of hearing.

He paused. Light from a terrace lamp washed his face, revealing his smug smile. "I am Barrowmore. You are my rebellious, disobedient sister. No one cares what you think to allow."

Yates kept his eyes on the terrace doors while he chatted with Southwaite and Kendale. Cassandra and her brother had been out there a good while. Whatever Barrowmore was telling her, it had led to more discussion than one would expect from siblings who were estranged.

"I think it is going well," Southwaite said, surveying his guests.

"Your lady has more than acquitted herself well," Kendale agreed.

Southwaite gave him a friendly look that still contained a degree of exasperation. "She has managed larger affairs than this over the years. There was no question that she would acquit herself well as a hostess. I referred to other things."

"He is speaking of Lady Cassandra, Kendale," Yates said. "The company has been very accepting of her presence."

"They had no choice, unless they wanted to insult Southwaite and Barrowmore as well as the lady."

"They did not have to attend at all," Southwaite pointed out. "No doubt some hoped to enjoy the discomfort of both Cassandra and her brother, but instead it appears that a rapprochement is under way on the terrace. Word of that should spread as fast as the post can carry it."

Southwaite appeared very satisfied with his efforts to make Cassandra's reputation safer for Emma's friendship.

Yates looked to the other lady who would enjoy Cassandra's company once gossip did its work.

Lydia sat at the card table, across from her Aunt Hortense. Hortense had recently joined the play, but Lydia had been in her chair for more than an hour now.

"Your sister has taken to whist, it appears," he said.

"With Hortense as a partner, she should fare well enough for a novice."

"Actually, she has been winning all night," Kendale said.

The three of them watched the play from afar.

"Are they wagering?" Southwaite asked, squinting to see.

"No point in playing if you don't," Kendale said. "It is only pennies."

"That does not look like a stack of pennies in front of my sister."

"Shillings, then. No one will go to the poorhouse," Kendale said.

Southwaite set his glass down on a table. "It is not the amount that draws her, but the thrill. I think it would be better if that stack shrank a good deal. Ambury, come with me. We will insert ourselves in opposition to her and Hortense and ensure that my sister experiences the despair of defeat that inevitably comes in gaming."

Just then the terrace door opened. Barrowmore walked in. Everything about the man, from his bearing to his bright eyes to the smile on his face, said that he had just enjoyed defeating an opponent more than was decent.

"Take Kendale if you want to teach her such a lesson. I do not have the heart for it."

He was halfway to the terrace door before the last words had left his mouth.

Chapter 11

Cassandra stood in a far corner of the terrace, near the low ribbon of wall that marked its edge overlooking the garden. No light from the lamps reached her, but she was clearly visible as a very pale column.

She did not move while he watched her. She just stood there, facing the summer plantings. Her posture and immobility suggested she reflected on something and did not see the dots of white amid the flowers below that glowed as much as she did.

He waited for her to compose herself, if that was what she was doing. Instead, the opposite happened. The thin pale lines of her gloved arms rose, and she buried her face in her hands.

He walked over, making it a point to put his body between her and two women who chatted near the center of that wall.

"Are you unwell?" he asked, keeping his voice low.

She shook her head, but her hands did not leave her eyes. With a loud sniff that stopped the conversation behind him, she composed herself. Her hands dropped. Tiny stars glinted on her face as the moonlight reflected off her tears.

"I am going home," she whispered. "I cannot bear to go back in there. If I see him again, I shall do something that will finally give the gossips facts to savage me for, instead of fancy." She opened her reticule, removed a handkerchief, and dabbed her cheeks. "Please tell Emma that I will explain all tomorrow. I will write to her."

"I will call for the coach and—"

She was already moving, however. She descended the long stone stairs leading down from her corner of the terrace. The garden's shadows swallowed her.

Yates returned to the drawing room. He could not see Emma. Over at the whist table, Southwaite peered severely at his cards. His sister Lydia played one of hers and smiled broadly at the consternation that her move caused Kendale.

"Please tell your wife that Lady Cassandra has chosen to return home," Yates said quietly into Southwaite's ear.

Southwaite nodded, barely paying attention while he debated what card to play. As Yates walked away, he noticed that Lydia's stack of shillings had not shrunk at all. Rather the opposite.

The evening air soothed her body, but its calming caress could not reach inside her heart. She damned Gerald in mutters that only caused her agitation to grow. She stoked her anger with curses because beneath it a desolate emptiness threatened to swallow her.

She had been on her own for six years, but she had never felt as alone as she did right now, assessing her weakness and her brother's power.

They had been close as children, playmates and confidants. When had Gerald become so mean? Probably by the time he inherited. She had been so absorbed with her pending first Season that she had not noticed him much back then. Yet a formality descended between them after Papa died.

She had attributed the new demeanor to his new responsibilities. Surely, once he grew comfortable in the role of earl, he would be normal again. Only he had never reverted back to the brother she knew. Instead, he had become more full of himself by the day, and more unkind to her too.

Now he planned to execute the threat he had dangled. Her head wanted to burst from the outrage of knowing he would succeed. Who would stop him? Mama? Perhaps their mother did not even know.

She latched on to that idea. Mama and Sophie had been very close when they were younger. Hadn't Sophie even gone with Mama to wait out the birth of Gerald in the country? As soon as she arrived home, she would write to Mama and tell her everything, and urge her to shame Gerald into putting aside his plans.

Having her own plan gave her some relief. Her head cleared, and her heart's pounding slowed to a pace more normal. It was then that she heard the steps behind her, closing fast.

Panic pounded through her, urging flight. It had been very stupid to walk home, even if it would be faster than waiting for a servant to go for a hackney. Dear heavens, if she were attacked by a footpad, Gerald would probably put her away in that home along with dear Aunt Sophie.

"Wait. Do not run away."

The voice reached her just as she hitched up her skirt to run. She knew that voice. She dropped her skirt and turned. Ambury strode the hundred feet still separating them.

"I have called for my coach. You should not be walking," he said.

"I am not ill. I want to walk. If I have to sit still, I will end up screaming." She turned on her heel and forged on.

His boots fell into step beside her. "Then I will escort you, to make sure you come to no harm." He raised his hand to his mouth and a shrill whistle shattered the silence. She turned her head and saw the lamp of a carriage slowly grow larger. The clipped sounds of horse hooves sounded down the lane.

She did not have the will to object, nor any good reason other than she wanted to be alone. The carriage caught up, then slowed and followed at a discreet distance.

"What did he say to make you weep?" Ambury asked.

"Nothing rude, if that is what you think. He did not upbraid me for my behavior, or throw the recent gossip in my face and treat it as fact." She took a deep breath. "He did not scold me that I have dishonored the family and broken my mother's heart. He did not call up my father's memory and speak of how distraught he would be if he were alive and I were unmarried and so suspiciously independent." The litany of Gerald's normal scolds poured out, bitterly.

"Yet he left you in tears."

The worst of her frustrated fury deserted her, leaving only sorrow and a sense of impending doom in her heart. And beneath it all, an exhaustion from fighting the world all alone.

"He wants me to go down to see my mother. Also to meet some man he has decided I should marry."

"It cannot be the first time he has tried matchmaking."

"It is as predictable as the rising sun. It is the worst during the Season. Then the fellows come here to town, and he is not constrained by whether he can lure me to the country. Last Season, every time I turned around, there one would be, presented by a friend or my mother or some relative. But I knew Gerald had arranged it all." She tipped her head and gazed up at the sky. "A man should have a bigger quest in life than marrying off his spinster sister, I think."

"He may just want what he believes is best for you."

"Do you believe that? Do you think that Gerald is a good brother doing his duty as he sees it?"

Ambury gave it a few moments' thought. "I think that he has decided it is what is best for *him*."

"I fear even that reason gives him too much credit for thoughtfulness. There are men for whom being the winner in any contest is of paramount importance. I think he is such a man, and he will do anything to achieve that victory, even if it is over a woman and a sister. It is sad, and does not speak well of him, but that is what I am concluding."

"Whatever his motivations, his goal is not unlike Southwaite's tonight—to pull you back from the edge of society, so that you are not the subject of rumors merely because you refuse to obey the rules."

She wanted to explain that it was more than that, only she did not know what it was instead.

Gerald's behavior would appear very normal to most people. Ambury's assumptions about the goal made perfect sense. Yet it did not explain the intensity of her brother's dogged insistence that she submit to his plans, in all their details. It did not explain his willingness to sacrifice Aunt Sophie to get his way.

"It is not marriage alone he wants for me. It is marriage to the man *he chooses*," she said, speaking aloud an insight that suddenly came to her. "He never forgave me for refusing Lakewood, for example. He came close to beating me into it when I refused the first proposal."

"But he did not, I trust."

"No. He managed it another way. He plotted to make the choice not mine at all."

They had reached Aunt Sophie's house. The carriage stopped down the street.

"Thank you, Ambury. Although we did not see another soul on foot all the way here, it is probably just as well I did not make the walk alone."

She mounted the few steps and opened the door. Merriweather had left a lamp burning in the little reception chamber to the left, and it allowed her to see her way. To her surprise, a hand grasped the door's edge so she could not close it.

Ambury stepped into the house. The lamp's light found him and revealed an expression sharp with curiosity. "What do you mean, he plotted to make the choice not yours at all?"

His demand startled her. Her mind scrambled for the best way to step back from a place that she had carelessly wandered.

"Lakewood was your friend," she said. This could not end well no matter what she said.

"He was a good friend for years."

"Then it would be wise for us both not to talk of this. I am sorry that my emotions over my brother led me to be too familiar, and to confide about him. It would be best if we—"

"What did you mean?" He took two long strides until he stood right in front of her.

He was so close that she had to look up to see his face. The lamp's dull light carved his face into hard planes. It gathered in his eyes, showing them as sapphire jewels. Bright and faceted, they concentrated on her and those careless words.

She had never told anyone about that horrendous day with Lakewood. She had let people think what they chose. Ambury now insisted on knowing, but he really wanted to think what he chose to.

She could explain it all, but he would not believe her. When it came down to either accepting the truth of her words or defending the honor of a dead friend, he would choose the latter to preserve the memories.

He waited, hard, strict, and uncompromising. She tried feeding him only a bit of the loaf because he would never swallow all of it.

"He had proposed and I had refused him. I have reason to believe that Gerald encouraged Lakewood to compromise me in order to ensure I would accept his proposal when he made it again, this time to do the right thing and spare me the scandal."

She saw his outrage. Felt it.

"That is a damnable accusation."

She had known he would not believe her, but she had hoped . . . perhaps she had hoped that he already had guessed.

"You will believe what you will, Ambury, along with everyone else. However, you demanded to know what I meant. Now you do."

"What everyone believes is that a willful, rebellious girl tainted her name and that of a good man who tried to spare them both, damn it."

Heavens, the man was no better than all those gray matrons who shook their heads over her behavior. Well, if he saw the world through the pages of the scandal sheets, so be it.

She donned the face that she wore in public. The one with which she faced down the world. Tonight she faced down only one man, which should have been easier. It was not.

"Being married to him would have spared me much, that is true, but I decided the cost was too high. I much prefer the life I had instead anyway. Being somewhat notorious has its benefits."

His eyes narrowed. "Does it now?"

"Most definitely."

"It also has its danger."

She did not ask what danger he meant, because suddenly it filled the chamber as his anger took on a sensual texture.

His expression altered subtly. Still hard. Still intense, but his gaze lost its cold fury and warmed. He looked at her differently, but no less directly and no more safely.

"I do not know if I believe it happened as you say it did," he said. "That is because one thought conquers every other in my head when you look at me like that." His head dipped and his lips brushed hers, surprising her. He inhaled deeply. "One taste and suddenly I am glad that you did not marry him, whatever the reason, which makes me a very poor friend."

"There are those who disdain me for it, and think I should have retreated into shame."

"Not me. What a waste that would be."

His lips brushed hers again. Warm. Teasing. Too sweet to bear. "When I see your mouth, I have to kiss it," he muttered. "Because it is soft and red, and because it utters challenges to which a man must respond." The next soft kiss was more seductive than the most erotic touch. It soothed the sadness she had borne out of the party. It distracted her from tomorrow's problems and dangers.

One thought conquers every other. She knew what some of the others were, and they were such that she should stop this love play. But he cupped her face in strong hands that held her with such care and overwhelmed her battered emotions with refreshing sensations that brought unexpected joy.

"But it is your eyes that truly undo me, Cassandra, and make me forget myself. They incite the best in me, and the worst. I keep imagining your eyes looking up at me, wide and bright and reflecting your pleasure, while I have you in bed."

He kissed her more fully. *Not by me.* No, he did not disdain her, at least not for these kisses. The liberties he took and intended did not insult the woman he knew her to be now. He was a man of the world who was glad she was a woman of the world, that was all.

Little whispers clustered in her mind, almost too quiet to notice while he distracted her with thrilling little bites and lures on her lips. They overlapped in a litany of soft warnings and reminders. They wanted to interfere with the melody lifting her spirits. *Another time*, she thought. *Later I will list all the evidence that he is not only moved by honest passion.* Right now she could ignore the loneliness and dread for a little while if she did not think at all.

His embrace enfolded her. Strong arms held her close and upright so he could kiss her neck, her chest, then her lips again.

She let herself sink into his support. She luxuriated in her reactions, and the changes in her body and skin. It had been longer since a man had held her than Ambury would ever guess, and forever since one had done so with such seductive skill.

It could not remain a soft, sweet game. He was a man, kissing and caressing a woman who offered no resistance. She could not claim surprise when he sat and pulled her onto his lap.

Less luring then. His caresses spoke assumptions that only a fool would ignore. His kiss turned invasive, insinuating the intimacies he envisioned. The pleasure had already conquered her, however, and a yearning for closeness, for the embrace to last until it destroyed her isolation, silenced the last of those whispers. She lost herself more than she suspected he ever did. Scandalous images and desires filled her mind too, of what he might do and what she might feel, of anticipation of pleasure so incredible it was worth being damned for.

He caressed her breast, as she had been silently urging. She moaned from the intensity of the sensation. It was many times more exquisite and powerful than she remembered. He touched in ways that left her breathless and praying it would not stop. She did not try to keep her body from flexing in the rhythm of need that moved her. Her bottom pressed against his thighs, and her hip against his arousal.

In response, his kisses warmed the tops of her breasts while his hand worked against her back. Her dress loosened, giving her body a welcomed freedom. He stopped kissing her and eased the bodice down. She wore only a petticoat beneath, and he slowly lowered that too.

His fingertips slid slowly over her exposed breasts. She looked down and watched that hand glide and bit the tip of her tongue to keep from crying from how good it felt. Pleasure's torture between her thighs became insistent, pulsing, and wanting. His fingers glanced across her taut nipples, and she could barely contain what it did to her. Her breasts swelled even more as that light touch made her mad with desire. She almost begged for him to use his mouth.

She did not have to. His tongue flicked and laved one tip while his palm skimmed the other. The fog of sensual delirium settled on her. She tried to bury her cries in his shoulder, but they escaped anyway in impatient, awed sounds.

His mouth closed on her breast more forcefully. Sharper pleasures speared down her body. His caresses moved up her hose, under her dress, until his warm palm smoothed over her thigh.

That intimate touch absorbed all of her, mind and body. She waited for him to seek the hollow itch that was the center of her breathtaking torment. Skirt high and bodice low, half naked now in the soft candle glow, she shifted how she sat and dropped one leg to make it easier.

He kissed her cheek, and she felt him smile against it. His embracing arm lowered her back to make it easier yet. The caress on her inner thigh firmed, then rose and cupped her. The pressure unhinged her, and she pressed against it for relief. Instead, a long stroke within that cleft shattered what was left of her self-possession.

"Cassandra? Is that you, dear?"

The call from the stairs bounced off the remnants of her mind. It sounded far away at first, then blasted like a horn through the night's silence.

She froze. Ambury did too. She felt a new tension enter him as he reacted to the interruption.

"Cassandra?" Her aunt sounded worried now.

She sat upright. "It is I, Aunt Sophie. I am just returning from the party. All is well." She prayed the response did not sound as strangled as it felt.

"Thank goodness. Be sure to bolt the door, dear."

She listened for sounds that indicated her aunt returned up the stairs. Soon the dull thud of light footsteps could be heard on the boards.

She tried to adjust to the world all around her, much like she took stock when awakening from a dream. Her skirt fell and covered most of her legs. Ambury raised her petticoat to cover her breasts.

They sat there, two thwarted sybarites, resisting the evidence that neither would be satisfied tonight.

"I fear we were too loud, if we woke her," she said finally.

He kissed her cheek.

She stood and turned her back to him. "You had better fix my dress, in case she is awake when I go above."

He worked the fasteners, then turned her around. "If I were a groom and you a kitchen maid, I would suggest I go out and climb in your chamber window."

" 'Tis a pity then that you are an earl's son, and I an earl's daughter." She tried to make light of it, but the physical intimacies still affected them, and had bred a mood that required acknowledgment of some kind.

Just what kind confounded her, and perhaps him as well. He kissed her soundly, deeply, as if giving a promise that they would share this again. Then he walked to the door. She bolted it after he left.

Still in a sensual fog, she mounted the steps and walked to the main bedchambers at the back of the house. Aunt Sophie's door was open but no lamp shone there. She found her aunt sitting up in bed, wide awake, her white cap catching the moon rays entering through a crack in her drapes.

"Who was that?" her aunt asked.

"How did you know it was anyone?"

"I saw him. You were too enthralled to notice, but I came all the way down and looked in."

"It was discreet of you to pretend you had not. I appreciate your consideration." She sat on the bed's edge. "It was Ambury."

"Well, that absolves you. He is handsome as his father was, and could always be charming as the devil. One could see it in him even when he was a boy. Any woman would be susceptible." She cocked her head. "Is he as skilled as his face and manner imply?"

"Aunt Sophie!"

"There is little more disappointing than a man who looks like he will know what he is about, then one discovers he does not understand the subtleties. It would be such a waste if after all of Ambury's practice, he were such a man."

Cassandra did not miss her aunt's own subtleties, and the reminder that Ambury had a rakish reputation. "I do not believe he wasted his practice."

"That is good news indeed. And he has called on you at least once, so it is not as if he tried to seduce you tonight because he could not think of anything else to do with his time."

Less subtle this time. "Are you scolding me? Or perhaps warning me?"

"I am not such a hypocrite as to scold. If you hear a warning, it is not because I question your taste in men. However, passion played out on the carpet of a reception hall, which was where that was going, is never going to end well. I apologize if you think I should not have interfered."

"At the moment, I rather wish you had not."

"If in the morning you wish the same thing, then enjoy him, dear. Only bring him to your chamber and have some comfort in it. I promise to sleep very soundly."

Cassandra wondered if she would still wish it in the morning, when she had slept off the pleasure and thought about Ambury and all the parts of their recent meetings.

"How was the party?" Aunt Sophie asked.

"You were missed. I wish you had come."

"And Gerald? Did he behave himself?"

Cassandra gritted her teeth against the resurgence of anger and worry that her brother's name evoked. "He and I spoke for a while. The others probably thought we had a pleasant chat and that all is forgiven between us."

"But all is not, from your tone."

"Gerald is Gerald, isn't he?" Only she would ever know just how much Gerald had been Gerald tonight.

"If word spreads that all is forgiven, you will know," Sophie said. "You will receive invitations from the hostesses who have not sent them these last years. You must let me know if you do."

Cassandra stood. She bent and kissed her aunt on her crown. "You should sleep, and I should as well."

"Try not to dream of him all night," Sophie said with a little laugh.

Cassandra decided she would not let Ambury invade her dreams at all. Aunt Sophie had reminded her of exactly what that passion in the reception hall had been—not even the beginnings of a romantic liaison, but merely impulsive pleasure between two people who did not obey the rules.

Chapter 12

Two mornings later, the damp that had settled on Hyde Park during the night refused to lift. London's famous fog still hung low, even at eleven o'clock, when Yates rode his horse beside Southwaite and Kendale to meet two other gentlemen who had come up from the coast for a few days.

A citizens' militia drilled beside the Serpentine, its red uniforms blazing through the gray light. It had become impossible to visit the park these last weeks without some group or other preparing for the huge invasion that never came. The trouble in Ireland had only doubled the efforts.

Yates did not think such an invasion likely. It carried too much risk, and the French had extended this war in so many directions that such an effort would involve resources he did not think they could muster. That he considered it unlikely to happen did not mean he thought the preparations should not take place, however. Logic said they would not be needed, but one never knew if the enemy would be logical.

His companions rode in silence, perhaps thinking as he

did of the larger issues affecting their world. They were meeting men who brought a report from the network of watchers they had organized on the coast. That probably explained Kendale's seriousness. He scrutinized the citizens' troupe as they passed, his military eye assessing their formation.

Southwaite's sobriety was less expected.

Suddenly Kendale stopped his horse. "I cannot do it, Southwaite. I know you asked me to pretend nothing had changed, but it is a lie, and I'll be damned if I am such an actor as to pull it off."

Yates turned his horse at the outburst.

Southwaite stopped too. "No good will come from this. A friend knows when to keep silent."

"It seems to me that a friend speaks plainly, so that unspoken resentments do not fester," Yates offered.

Southwaite closed his eyes in strained forbearance. "How philosophical of you, Ambury. No doubt my wife would agree, since she also prefers plain speaking. Unfortunately, Kendale's plainness is more plain than even hers, and the sort of plainness to create more trouble than clarity."

Yates did not disagree, but thought saying that in front of Kendale was more plain than warranted.

Kendale's face hardened. "So I am just to let it all pass, because it is convenient to your purposes and his pleasure?"

Yates tried to lighten what had suddenly become a sharp conversation. "Whoever this friend is, you should let it pass if it is a small thing. If it might harm the friendship, speaking up may be the better course."

Southwaite lowered his lids. "Far be it from me to attempt to argue against such sage advice from a man who is adept at maintaining his amiability even when perhaps he ought not."

"What is that supposed to mean?"

"It means that there are times to be friendly and amiable, and times to be restrained and discreet."

Confused, Yates looked from one to the other. They both looked back. For a while, they all just exchanged gazes. The knowing ones that passed between Kendale and Southwaite gave Yates his first suspicion of what was amiss.

Kendale looked away and raked his hair with his fingers. "Damnation, it is bad enough that she is being invited to dine in Southwaite's home."

"I explained *that*. Damn me if you want, but when I weigh old loyalties and insults against Emma's happiness, there will be only one possible decision."

"He is not married and has no new loyalties to make him forget the old ones," Kendale snarled.

Yates realized that he was the unknown friend at the heart of this dispute, mostly because Kendale poked his finger in his direction.

"What are you talking about? I have not been disloyal to you."

"Not *me*."

Southwaite held up a hand, telling Kendale to say nothing more. He then turned to Yates. "You were seen."

They were talking about Cassandra, of course, but now the reason for all the silence and knowing glances made sense.

"Seen?" He feigned an innocence he did not feel.

"On the terrace, by some. That you left in her wake was noted by others. That you arrived together has now taken on new meaning," Southwaite said.

"You were also seen leaving her damned house in the middle of the damned night," Kendale added.

Hell. The first bits could be explained away. But if he had been seen leaving . . .

He searched his memory. The vague sounds of a carriage rolling down the street while he strode from Cassandra's house seemed to emerge. He could not be sure. The only thing he truly remembered about that forced retreat was savage, blinding sexual frustration.

"Seen by whom?"

"Does it matter whom?" Kendale asked.

"Hell, yes, it matters."

Kendale turned to Southwaite. "You and your *gossip does not make something a fact.* I told you it was true. He is fucking that woman."

Yates allowed his irritation to show in the stare he gave Kendale. "First, you are not to speak of her in that manner. Ever. Second, as it happens, that is not true. I swear it as a gentleman. I have not had Lady Cassandra Vernham."

That took the wind out of Kendale's sails, fast. His expression fell. "I apologize. I should have known you would not—that is, you were a better friend of Lakewood than I was, so it goes without saying that you would never take up with her."

Southwaite's expression turned carefully bland. A side-long glance at Yates said one friend was not nearly as convinced about intentions, even if he accepted the baldly stated claim of lack of success.

"My loyalty to Lakewood does not extend to condemning a woman for something I do not know for certain she did," Yates said. "I raise that as a matter apart from your accusations about two nights ago."

Kendale appeared suspicious again. "Now you are making excuses for her."

"I am saying I do not know for certain over whom that duel was fought, and it has been wrong to blame her without knowing. Since Southwaite here has received her, and is allowing his wife and sister to be her friends, it is time to admit that any suspicions about that duel are only that, and not firmly grounded in anything except our dim knowledge of the women in Lakewood's life."

"You *are* making excuses for her."

"What he is saying is true. I have come to the same place in my head," Southwaite said. "I was Kenwood's second.

He never gave me the name of the woman he challenged Penthurst over.''

Kendale's expression indicated he did not like having this other front open unexpectedly in his little war. "There was only one woman for him. Unlike Ambury here, who has liaisons by the dozen, Lakewood loved once and he loved forever."

It was an astonishingly romantic view of Lakewood—or any man, when you got down to it. It sounded startling coming from Kendale who, Yates would have sworn, did not have the slightest experience with love, and who had always displayed evidence of a very cynical view of romance.

He felt guilty questioning the illusion. "None of us really know that, is all I am saying. Six years is a very long time to pine for any woman, let alone wait to die for her."

Nothing more was said for several minutes. Then they fell in next to each other and continued on their way. Up ahead, two figures emerged out of the mist, riding their own horses. One man hailed them, and the two groups began converging.

"None of us really knows that duel *wasn't* over her either," Kendale said, getting in the last word just before they reached the others.

Yates could not disagree, much as he wanted to.

Cassandra did not wake the next morning sorry that Aunt Sophie had interrupted her and Ambury. Instead, she faced the dawn breathless with astonishment at her own rashness, and spent the day itemizing just how foolish she had been.

This was the man questioning the earrings, after all. The man who had no doubt bought those earrings to gift them to a woman far more important to him than she was.

This was the person responsible for withholding the

money that would allow her to run away with Aunt Sophie. She had assumed the month's delay in settling the sale of the earrings would not matter. She had been wrong.

Nor had he absolved her about Lakewood. Even as he kissed her, that question had remained open. He might have wondered over the years about the oddities of that story of compromise, but when he lured her into pleasure, he had not yet accepted the truth of it.

I want you, he had said at Mrs. Burton's. It was not special that he wanted her. Men were quick to lust over women, and she was accustomed to being wanted in that way. So was he, she guessed.

All of these discouraging thoughts turned over in her mind a hundred times. They left her with no excuse and no way to pretty up what had happened. She had behaved just as wildly as all those rumors said she did. Except for Aunt Sophie's timely interference, she would have finally deserved the worst of the gossip.

Two days after the party, still ruminating over that passion and trying hard to convince herself she had not even enjoyed it much, she made her way to the Strand. It was past time to see if she could find the pawnbroker from whom Sophie said she had bought the earrings.

The broker would surely recognize such fine jewelry from the drawing she had brought. He would certainly remember from whom he obtained such distinctive items, even though it had been years ago. No doubt it had been a member of a good family whose integrity was unquestioned. She would hand Ambury all of that information, and he would finally hand her the money. She and Aunt Sophie would be gone by week's end.

That was her plan, at least.

Three hours later, she had been directed to four different pawnbrokers whose establishments might be described as a few doors off the Strand. None had a blue door, but doors can get painted different colors over time. The first three proprietors could not help her at all. The fourth one looked at her drawing a long time, raising her hopes.

"Did you have them?" she asked. "It would have been years ago."

He shook his head. He still wore his dark hair in a queue, but the better part of his head was bald. His dark eyes reminded her of a hawk.

She pointed to her drawing. "That is a diamond. You may have thought it was paste."

"I know the difference. I'd not been surviving all this time if I didn'."

"You appear to recognize them."

"Not recognize as such. I've never seen them." He handed her the drawing. "You are not the first to ask after them, is all. I've had earbobs much like this described to me recently, so your drawing took me by some surprise."

He returned to weighing the silver spoon that had been on his scale when she entered. She tucked the drawing back into her reticule. "Who else asked about them?"

He stacked some weights to balance the spoon. "Would be indiscreet for me to say. My profession requires secrecy. If I gossiped about who walks through my door, soon no one with real valuables would again."

"I thought this person only asked you questions."

"True. Just as you did. Should I tell the world you came here with that drawing and asked questions?" He must have seen her dislike of that notion, because he smiled and dropped another tiny weight on the tray. "Anyway, I don't know who he was. A gentleman, though."

"An old gentleman?"

He thought over the question, then shrugged. "Not old. No gray yet. And no—" he patted his bald pate.

"Was he—"

He held up a hand. "It is all I know and more than I should have said. You will have to pardon me now, unless you have something you want to pawn."

She swallowed her curiosity, but it was hard not to press him for more. *Was he handsome as sin? Did he come in a fine coach with a matched pair of white horses? Were his eyes more blue than the best sapphires? Could his smile charm the skin off a snake?*

The pawnbroker was not going to tell her anything else. She left to meet Emma as they had arranged, sure she knew the answers to her questions anyway. Ambury was not waiting for her to learn the earrings' history. He was seeking it on his own.

Emma opened the storage chamber at Fairbourne's auction house to reveal two dozen paintings stacked against the wall.

"My brother has acquitted himself very well in one duty to this business," she said. "He is proving very adept at spending considerable time at places where people with rarities are apt to gather. My father's name and reputation are having him received in ways most men in trade would never be, and he is enjoying it to the fullest."

"Is he proving skilled at the rest of that part of the trade?" Cassandra asked. "Are these paintings consigned to Fairbourne's now, through his efforts?"

Emma tipped one painting back to examine the one under it. "They are. Three are copies of old masters. Two are middling, but one is quite good. The rest are by the hands of respectable artists, mostly Dutch and English. He wants to establish regular weekly auctions by October. I have told him that he will have to do more than wait for consignors to come to him at parties in order to do so. He will have to aggressively pursue patrons and clients." She looked over her shoulder. "That is not as much fun as making morning calls and going to assemblies."

"Do you still expect to open your season in mid-September?"

"I think so. Marielle has promised those jewels, and also the cameos she brought to me last spring. We have been offered a large library too, and Aunt Hortense has said she wants to sell some of her objets d'art. My brother is turning up his nose at most of it, since he wants to auction only art, but even my father had not yet achieved that consistency, and it is unlikely we will do so for a long while, especially if we establish weekly sales."

"You need agents who mingle with better than your brother does."

"Like you? I have not forgotten that the best paintings in our last auction came to us through you."

"Through my aunt, if we are particular about the details. Had Herr Werner not come to ask for the necklace back, I would never have had the chance to point him to you for consigning Count Alexis's collection."

Emma set the painting back in its stack. "How is your aunt? I have not seen her in so long now."

"She is very well. Why do you ask?" Cassandra regretted her sharp tone as soon as the words left her mouth.

Emma was not easily hurt. From her expression, she also was not quickly put off. "At the party, your brother spoke of her not being well. You heard Hortense as well as I did. I only sought to be polite in asking after her, Cassandra."

"No doubt Gerald expressed concerns in a most solicitous manner. No doubt everyone thinks he is a most generous and dutiful nephew."

Emma opened the door, and they strolled into the cavernous exhibition hall. "From your words and your eyes, I think that the rumors of reconciliation at my party are much exaggerated."

"For now, let the rumors stand, Emma. Allow your husband to think he succeeded where so many have failed. However, not only was there no reconciliation, there was almost a spectacular row out on the terrace. He has found another man he wants me to marry, and he seeks to separate me from my aunt in order to encourage my agreement."

Emma took her hands and squeezed them. "I am sorry to hear that. Not for myself, but for you. I had hoped he had softened his views."

"Let us not talk of it. I much prefer helping you plot Fairbourne's future. If I have any chance to send consignors your way, I will do so. I am not alone in finding the agent's percentage helpful either."

Emma nodded, while she eyed the gray walls of the hall. "You are probably correct. Now help me decide something. I think we should paint in here. What do you think?"

"You are not enthused enough about my idea. I think it is brilliant. With some discreet recruiting, you could have a dozen pairs of eyes assessing the paintings in country homes that they visit. In the least, you should recruit Ambury, who would be discreet. His expectations may be high, but he is still kept short of funds by his father."

Emma squinted at the walls. "He has already found a way to supplement that miserly allowance, so he is not a good choice."

"Being your agent is more secure than taking his chances at the tables."

"Not the tables," Emma said, still distracted by her walls. "Blue, I think. Not too dark or bright a hue though. It would have to be just the right one."

"Blue it is. How is he enhancing his allowance, if not by gaming?"

The question confused Emma a moment, until she found the thread of thought in her mind. "You mean Ambury? Darius says he does investigative missions for people, very discreetly. He first did it as a favor for a friend, and proved to have the talent and found it interesting. Now he is sought out, and the most discreet compensation is offered for his services. You must not tell anyone, Cassandra. Promise you will not."

Cassandra turned her own gaze to the walls, but the only color she saw on them was red. She did not fight her surging anger, because it kept in check another emotion that weighed inside her, thick and sour.

The scoundrel. He was not merely curious about the history of the earrings. He did not only want to ensure there would be no embarrassment if he gave them to someone. He was *investigating* their history, which was another matter entirely. He was digging into their past for someone who had told him they were probably stolen. He probably had been hired to find the thief.

That was why he had gone to the pawnbrokers too. No wonder he was being so relentless about the whole matter. She had been a fool not to pay more attention to how odd his determination first seemed.

Even his kisses were part of the scheme. He had distracted her from the start with his flirting.

He had been pointed about confirming they had come from Aunt Sophie too. Which meant that now he was investigating her.

The thought horrified her. She thought she would be sick. If Ambury did this for pay, anyone might hire him.

Even Gerald.

"I wonder if a hue close to primrose would be better than blue," Emma said, tapping her chin thoughtfully. "Do you think so?"

"Primrose would be lovely. It is the perfect choice. Now, might we go sit in the garden? I have a favor I must ask of you. It is a big one, I am afraid."

The summons came that evening. Yates had not been formally commanded to attend on his father in months, so the footman's message surprised him.

He set aside the map on which he was charting a visit to that disputed land on the southern coast. The plan had not progressed far. Left alone with his thoughts, they turned to Cassandra too often. An hour would then be lost in memories of her firm, snowy breasts in his hand and his mouth, and of the adorable, arousing way she tried in vain to hold in her sounds of pleasure.

In the day since Kendale and Southwaite had alerted him that he had been seen leaving her house, nothing more had developed. That did not mean the story had not spread. Scandal could quietly pass around this circle or that for a long time before it emerged as a public spectacle.

It had been madness to try and take her. Ill-timed and ill-advised. Careless and ignoble on several counts.

She had just accused Lakewood of dishonorable behavior.

Had desire led him to grab at the chance to think the worst? Had he used those doubts as an excuse to have a way of possessing her? He only remembered his anger in a blink, turning into a different fury and succumbing to an urge to conquer the voice and person who had just threatened memories from half a lifetime. That he had wanted Cassandra Vernham almost as long hardly absolved him.

He was not above seducing a woman, but normally he planned it with more ceremony. There had been no planning at all this time, just the impulse to have what he wanted and the instinct to know he probably could.

He owed Cassandra an apology, unless he wanted what had happened to be an insult he neither intended nor wanted to stand. Before he went down to his father, he penned a quick note and gave it to a footman to deliver.

Chapter 13

Cassandra found her aunt in the little library of their house with her face buried in a voluptuous collection of blooms that overloaded their vase.

"Heavenly," Sophie sighed. "Roses and hydrangeas. What a lovely and unexpected combination."

"Where did you get them?"

"A footman delivered them. Merriweather was putting them in this vase when I came in after supper. This came with them."

Cassandra picked up and read the folded paper to which Aunt Sophie pointed. "I will call on you tomorrow. Please receive me. Ambury."

Aunt Sophie shot her a sly glance. "Thank goodness he is not going to pretend it never happened. Men who do that are so annoying. One should not sin if one is not willing to own the sin."

"It would be better if he did pretend. I do not expect any

weight on his conscience, but mere common sense says he should not call."

"What nonsense. Flowers change everything. They absolve all presumptions. Had he pretended it had not happened, that would be insulting enough to call him out. If you had a male relative brave and honorable enough to do so, that is."

Which she did not have. Perhaps Sophie was correct, and the flowers absolved any presumption or insult implied by that night. They did not truly alleviate either, however.

She had not conquered one whit of her suspicions about Ambury, and she really wished he had not sent these flowers.

"You must receive him. Will it be easier if I do as well?" Aunt Sophie asked. "I can sit with you when he arrives, and stay a few minutes."

The offer astonished Cassandra. She embraced the dear woman who would leave the safety of her retirement in order to make the visit from Ambury less awkward.

She held Sophie a moment, smelling the lavender in her hair. She kissed her aunt's cheek. "I can manage Ambury alone. I thank you for loving me enough to offer. I will receive him as you advise, this one time."

Her aunt patted her face in approval, then buried her face in the huge bouquet again. Then Aunt Sophie picked up a basket and headed to the garden to tend her own blooms.

When a man has seen a woman naked, it changes the way he views her forever.

Ambury noted the truth of that old lesson when he entered Cassandra's drawing room.

She appeared proper, respectable, and even demure as she greeted him. He might have been Pitt coming to call, she proceeded so formally. Yet in her eyes he saw the same familiarity he felt, and he knew the ongoing sense of intimacy was mutual.

They continued to pretend it was not. He smiled and spoke as he might if this were a call on Southwaite's wife. All the while, Cassandra's clothes were peeling off in his mind until she sat on her straight-backed chair totally naked, with the hard tips of her breasts beckoning him to lick until she screamed from pleasure.

"I appreciate your receiving me today," he said. "I need to leave town, and wanted to see you before I did."

"More duties to your father's estate?"

"Yes. A border dispute between tenants up north. He told me that he wants me to tend to it personally. He thinks it will accustom the tenants to accepting my authority."

"How does he fare?"

"There has been a small revival that is heartening. It is subtle but visible."

"That is good news." She idly twisted her forefinger in a curl dangling down her shoulder. "If you came to learn if I have discovered more about the earrings, I fear I have nothing to give you. I am making inquiries, but to no avail. I think the month will end without more information for you."

"That is not why I am here." She knew it wasn't. She had just let him know that she wondered if the two things—his interest in the earrings and his seduction of her—were in some way related, however.

She looked at him with those blue eyes, waiting. She appeared to be daring him to speak of it, and warning him not to at the same time.

"I need to apologize for importuning you the other night. It was reckless impulse, but that hardly excuses me." There. It was done.

She thought over his words as if weighing each one. "So you had never planned on more than a stolen kiss or two? You had never thought about seducing me, despite your bald announcement the afternoon of Emma's wedding?"

"I can see that you have decided not to make this easy for

me. As a gentleman, I must accept responsibility, of course, however you choose to interpret my actions and intentions."

"Even though you do not feel totally responsible. Do you?" Her voice challenged him like someone looking for a good row.

"I do not engage in games of blame about such actions," he said. "If you do, allow me to accept all of it."

She studied him, as if trying to decide something important. Perhaps she only wondered if he were the least sincere.

"I accept your apology," she only said. "Let us not speak of it again."

"That may not be possible. There has been some talk about us. Did no one tell you that yet?"

Her face fell. A tiny panic entered her eyes, but it only lasted a moment before disappearing. "No. However, I have only seen Emma, and she is not yet a part of circles where talk would begin."

"It is mild. Unformed. I expect it will all come to naught."

"I am not too concerned. I will brave this out as I have before."

She was taking it very well. Surprisingly so. "I will not permit lies to attach to you regarding what happened." He stood to take his leave. "I will call on you when I return. We will see how things stand then."

"You need only write. You do not have to call."

"I will call on you anyway."

To his surprise, she accompanied him to the door. They stood before it, mere feet from where passion had overruled good sense so recently.

She looked up at him after he made his bow. Neither her eyes nor her expression held the mocking humor that so often served as her shield. "Kiss me good-bye, Ambury, so we part as friends."

It was her first acknowledgment of the intimacy that bound them now. Her first words that were not arch and indifferent and spoken like a woman who gladly accepted being slightly notorious.

He lifted her chin and touched her lips with his. He lingered, because it had not entirely been a momentary impulse that night, and they parted now as more than mere friends.

"Go now," she said, stepping back. "Duty waits and cannot be denied."

He opened the door, then looked back at her. She stood in the shadow beyond the sunlight pouring through the opening. She gave him a vague, sad smile, then closed the door after him.

"Here is the letter for Ambury," Cassandra said. "Here is the one for the lawyer, Mr. Prebles, who now holds the jewels. And this one is for you, in which I give you permission to auction the earrings again should I remain down at Anseln Abbey longer than initially planned."

Emma took all three sealed letters and set them on the corner of the desk at Fairbourne's.

"Please allow me to simply give you the money."

"It is better this way."

"I do not understand why. But then I do not understand why Ambury did not pay for them. I told you after the auction that Darius offered to cover the bid if you needed the funds right away. Of course, he did not expect Ambury to wait months to make good, just as you did not."

"Do not think ill of him for the delay. He has been much distracted by family matters." She did not know why she defended Ambury. He had put it off a long time by any accounting. Since he bid on the earrings and investigated their history for someone else, as an agent, he did not even have the excuse of his father's illness.

You defend him because his last kiss was sweet, and because he promised to defend you. He might well prove to

be a scoundrel in the end, but right now, as she put in place
the means to escape London, nostalgic feelings about him
dulled her mood.

That emotion was one more reflection of a sadness that
would not leave her. She had to go, of course. She had to take
Aunt Sophie far away. The tickets on the ship had already
been bought with the money given to her by Emma, who
had not even asked the purpose of the loan before agreeing
to provide it.

The settlement regarding the jewels had now been arranged. When the month was up, and Ambury had no information, Emma would give him the letter reminding him of
the pact. She would send the lawyer, Prebles, the letter
demanding the jewels be released. Then Emma would add
the earrings to her first auction and repay herself with the
proceeds.

Emma's fingertips rested on that last letter. "This was
unnecessary. I do not need a signed promise from you about
that loan, if you insist it be a loan at all."

"I prefer to do it this way. I am sure your husband would
prefer it too, if he knew. Does he?"

Emma blushed. As Cassandra had assumed, Southwaite
did not know.

"When are you going down to your family's estate?"

"Tomorrow." She had decided to visit her mother one last
time. It would be a surprise, and for only a few days. Gerald
was in town, so Mama and she could spend the time privately. Upon her return, she and Sophie would use a hired
coach to travel to Liverpool, and they would be gone.

She looked at Emma and her heart ached. She remembered the first time they met, in front of a painting at a Royal
Academy exhibition. They had argued whether the artist
deserved the prize he had won. There had been no deference
in Emma's frank manner, even when she later learned she
was talking to an earl's daughter. The argument had turned

into a long walk, and eventually into a deep friendship. The only close one that Cassandra had.

There was a fourth letter, in addition to the three now on the desk. It would be mailed from Liverpool the day she and Aunt Sophie sailed. She hoped Emma, who had never blamed or judged, who had accepted a friend's rebellious views even when she did not hold them herself, would understand why there had been no good-bye other than the one that, unbeknownst to Emma, they would have today.

Emma lifted a delicate watch from the surface of the desk. "I hope that you will stay awhile longer. I am expecting a very important consignment to arrive any minute now, and I want you to see it."

"Is your brother bringing it?"

"He knows nothing about it yet, but he will be delighted if it is as good as I hope." She set the watch down, then stood and went to the door to peer out into the exhibition hall impatiently.

Cassandra joined her there. Men were busy painting the walls in preparation for the autumn auctions. Mr. Nightingale, Fairbourne's exquisitely handsome exhibition hall manager, directed them. Even in shirtsleeves and waistcoat he appeared too perfectly beautiful to be real. He rebuked one painter for using strokes that were sure to show streaks when the light hit the wall from an angle.

The door to Albemarle Street opened. Emma's gaze shot there expectantly. Her face fell when the person who entered was her own auctioneer, the short, slight, and graying Obediah Riggles. He greeted Cassandra with a bow on his way to the storage chamber next to the office.

Emma fretted. "Perhaps it will not be today after all."

"It must be a fine collection if you are so excited."

"It is reputed to be. I will need to see the paintings myself before I know for certain."

"From whom are you receiving them?"

"Did I not say? Marielle is bringing them."

"It is odd for her to find paintings for you. Jewels and cameos, and even drawings and books, are easily brought over by the émigrés, but paintings do not easily fit on the boats by which they cross the channel."

"These are very small ones. They are very rare, she says. Do not look so skeptical. She has promised the provenance is all in order and that the owner—ah, here she is now!"

A lovely young woman wearing a dress two decades out of style walked in. The sunlight blazed off her light brown hair before the door closed. Cassandra had always thought it very unfair that Marielle Lyon could appear elegant and delicate dressed in old mended silk decorated with torn lace.

She hailed Emma with a wave. In her other hand she carried a framed panel not much larger than a dressing-room looking glass.

"The others are in the carriage outside," she said to Emma as she handed it over. "Perhaps that pretty man can bring them in. The hackney also wants to be paid."

Emma fished a coin from her reticule and gave it to Mr. Nightingale. He flashed a gleaming smile at Marielle and went to get the paintings.

Marielle flipped her long curls over her shoulders while Emma assessed the painting. It had brilliant colors and showed a primitive Deposition from the Cross. The figures appeared angular and emaciated, and very different from the rounded and real-looking ones seen in the Renaissance art favored by collectors.

"It is odd, no?" Marielle said. "I did not think such a thing of value, but the man who owns it said it is very old and rare. Perhaps some English lord will buy it for a few pounds."

"A sophisticated collector will find it of great interest," Emma said. It was obvious that she did too.

"Here come the others. I like this one better." Marielle took a painting from Mr. Nightingale and held it in front of her, displaying it for Emma. It showed the interior of an old house, and a garden in the background. A man and a woman sat at a table, and all of it appeared so real that one was sure one could get splinters from the wood depicted.

"That is much more recent," Emma said. "Seventeenth century. It is Dutch. It will bring a very good price."

"The same terms, yes?" Marielle asked.

"Of course." Emma told Mr. Nightingale to put the other paintings in the office and followed him to see them in the light that flowed in through the window there.

Marielle admired the new wall color. Mr. Nightingale returned and admired Marielle. Cassandra sidled beside them both.

"That is a lot of paintings to be smuggled out of France."

Marielle shrugged. "People are clever when they need to be."

Cassandra had always found this daughter of France a little too mysterious. An émigré herself, and the niece of a comte, there were those among her own people who believed her to be a charlatan. Cassandra had not decided yet, but at least one émigré had confided to her that he did not believe Marielle was even French.

Emma could be too trusting sometimes. If she liked someone as she liked Marielle, her normal shrewdness could abandon her.

"You know that Emma is married to the Earl of Southwaite now, don't you?" Cassandra said. "It happened a few weeks ago. You appear surprised. It was in all the London newspapers."

"That is happy news. I knew they were affianced, but I thought it would be some time."

"I am sure that Emma will tell him everything about Fairbourne's now. We must make sure that every item we bring her is impeccably legal."

Marielle nodded. "*D'accord*." She looked Cassandra right in the eyes. "Both of us must be most careful in the future. Especially when it comes to jewels, I think. *N'est-ce pas?*"

Cassandra tried not to let that direct gaze make her uncomfortable. Marielle was warning her just as she had warned Marielle.

"I go now," Marielle said. "Tell Emma that I will bring the man who owns the paintings to her soon."

Cassandra returned to the office. Emma sat at the desk, with the small painting propped upright in front of her, angled so the window's light washed it. Cassandra watched for a minute, branding her memory with Emma practicing the skills taught to her by her father, using her expert eye to see more than most people ever would in a work of art.

"Marielle is gone," she said.

Emma looked up. "So soon?"

"I must leave as well. You can examine every inch of these paintings at your leisure then."

"I admit that I want to. I have never seen anything like this small one. I judge it to be at least four hundred years old."

Bracing herself to control the emotions that threatened to inundate her, she stepped around the desk. She bent and embraced Emma. She held her a moment longer than she might have otherwise, then straightened and kissed her cheek.

Emma looked up with a little frown. "Is something amiss, Cassandra?"

"Not at all. If I appear less than happy, it is because I am already anticipating listening to my mother's criticisms."

"I will see you when you return, dear friend. Be safe on this little journey that you take."

Chapter 14

Cassandra faced her mother across the table that the servants had set on the terrace. Silver and crystal glittered in the sun on the linen that separated them. Refreshments arrived, coffee for her and cocoa for Mama.

They drank in silence while bees made free with flowers growing in a nearby bed. Since she spent most of her time in town, Cassandra always found the silence in the country strangely vacant. That she could hear bees only reminded her how little happened out here.

"I expect London is full of talk of nothing except the invasion." Her mother said it like the French had landed in Ireland merely to provide an excuse for politics to bore everyone for weeks on end.

"I would not say that. Nelson's victory on the Nile is still discussed, and there is always a spot of gossip here and there to enliven things, even in summer."

"Anyone I know?"

Someone you know very well. "I do not think so."

More silence. More buzzing bees. If she listened very, very hard, she was sure she would hear mice crawling and ants climbing.

"I plan to go to town in a fortnight for a few days, for my wardrobe. You could return with me."

"I am only here for three days, as I told you. I must leave tomorrow."

"Three days. Why even bother?"

"I bothered in order to see you, Mama. Why else?"

Mama flushed. She looked away. Plumpness had settled on Mama the last few years. That often softened an older woman's face and made her appear amiable, but it had done the opposite with Mama.

When had they become such strangers to each other? When had silence become welcome and conversations awkward? It could probably be traced to the same event that had changed so much in her life. Mama had been even harsher than Gerald when she refused Lakewood.

"I also want to talk to you about Aunt Sophie," she said.

"Sophie has become a trial, Cassandra. It is very unfair of her."

"She bothers no one. She does not call on others, nor receive. She tends her garden and reads her books and exasperates the cook. How can she possibly be a trial to you?"

"Her hold on you has not loosened, I see. It was bad enough she was so reckless with her own life and reputation. It is unforgivable that she has led you to do the same."

It was an old argument, and Cassandra did not want a row today. "It is not her life and her past that I want to talk about, but her future. You may not know of Gerald's designs, but I believe I must share them now. He has become very direct, and I fear that only you will be able to dissuade him."

Mama did not appear confused or curious about this little speech. She did not even look over to show attention. Instead, she concentrated on folding her napkin, pressing each step with her palms. "I am aware of his concerns regarding her. And his plans."

"You must stop him. It is wrong for him to do this, and very unfair."

"Unfair? *Unfair?* Sophie has lured you away from me, and you think your brother is unfair?"

"She did not lure. She gave me a home when this one became inhospitable."

"She dragged you all over the Continent and exposed you to the most disreputable behavior. She encouraged your disobedience and rebellion. Do not expect me to risk Barrowmore's displeasure by defending her. I have no idea what I could even say."

"She was your friend, Mama. Does that count for nothing? You met Papa because of her, and she encouraged her brother to make the match." She reached across the table and grasped her mother's hand. "She was at your side when Gerald came. Have you forgotten that summer together with her? She has not. Do years of friendship and love count for nothing?"

Mama's composure cracked. She turned her head and closed her eyes. Her expression turned slack and, finally, soft.

Cassandra waited, hoping this emotion meant she would have an ally. Finally Mama's head shook ever so slightly.

"Barrowmore will not listen to me, Cassandra. He has resolved to force a break between you and Sophie. He is very determined. He wants what is best, even if his means might be harsh."

"So you will not help me? And her?"

"I cannot help. Nor is it really about you, or her." Mama looked over, sadly. "You have never understood, but this is bigger than that. It is about the honor of Barrowmore."

"If I am such a stain on that honor, he can disown me, and I will no longer matter. He does not have to threaten Aunt Sophie."

Her mother gazed away with misting eyes. "You do not understand."

"If you will not or cannot stop him, I will take her away. Both she and I will be out of his life."

Her mother's attention sharpened on her. "He said that was your plan. I did not believe him. Do we mean so little to you now that you would abandon us? Is that why you are here? To say good-bye? Or did you not even intend to do so as you left?"

"I am here, aren't I? You cannot mean so little if I came to see you." A sick sensation had lodged in Cassandra's stomach at her mother's first words. "When did he tell you that he guessed it was my plan?"

"Before he went up to town this time." Her mother looked guilty, as if she had spoken out of turn. "I am not sure, but I do not think he intends to permit you to take her away."

Panic pounded in Cassandra's head. Gerald had spoken of a fortnight before he came for Sophie, but he already had his own plans for her in place. If he had guessed she might flee . . . if the rumors about Ambury had angered him . . .

She had been a fool. A stupid fool. She had left Sophie alone with Merriweather. Neither one could stand against Gerald. Maybe she could not either, but at least she could try.

She stood. "I must go back to town. At once. He might be up to no good there. Please loan me one of the carriages and a coachman. If you were ever Sophie's friend, help me to return quickly."

"It is too late. He wrote yesterday that he would return here today. He knows you are visiting, and commanded that I keep you here."

"How does he know? Did you write and tell him?"

"He knows because he did not find you at Sophie's house." Guilt colored her mother's voice, but so did resignation. "It has already happened, Cassandra."

* * *

Yates moved his horse to a gallop on the ground that flanked the road out of London. He sped past the long line of carts, wagons, and carriages that had poured through the gates and into the country. He kept up the pace until he left the town far behind and had passed the knots of conveyances that slowly picked their way along the dusty road.

On the other side of the road, Kendale kept pace. They would keep each other company until Kendale turned away toward his property in Buckinghamshire.

The horses tired just as the road cleared. They met in its center and continued on at a leisurely pace.

"So, are you going to Ireland?" Yates asked. Kendale's army experience and title meant he could obtain a commission if he chose.

"No."

"That surprises me. You have just cost me a hundred pounds."

"You wagered on it?"

"I thought it was a sure way to grow a hundred pounds richer. I did not think you could resist, especially since the enemy had the audacity to land on British soil."

"If I would only be fighting Frenchmen, I would not hesitate."

"The others are rebels. Traitors."

"I am not needed in this campaign. It has become apparent I am not needed in any of them."

Yates never expected Kendale to reconcile to leaving the army when his brother died. This new acceptance surprised him.

"It is a fair day. I can smell autumn already," Kendale said. "Let us not speak of wars and invasions. I am escaping London because I tire of the talk of it."

"I think you merely tire of talk itself. You do not want to

speak of politics, investments, or society. You have never joined conversations about natural science, philosophy, or literature. Now that I think about it, I was a fool to suggest we ride together, since you are unlikely to help the time pass."

"That is not true. There are many topics I am willing to discuss."

"Name one."

Kendale thought it over. Expecting nothing more to be said for many miles, Yates let his own mind wander.

As was common these days, its path meandered back to Cassandra very quickly.

She had been very cool when he called on her. Perhaps he had been a fool to worry that she had been insulted. If she had been, she overcame it quickly enough.

The whole time they sat and spoke, invisible and inaudible language had passed between them, however. The memories of the pleasure created tethers, and even the desire itself. They might both deny its power. They might agree they had been rash. They might resolve to set their dealings with each other back in time, even to before the wedding. None of that changed the truth that intimacy had destroyed most barriers between them in ways even distance and time would not rebuild totally.

"Lady Cassandra Vernham."

Yates startled at hearing the woman in his thoughts named aloud. He looked over to where Kendale rode, back straight and profile firm.

"What about her?" Yates asked.

"That is a topic I will discuss. You said to name one."

"That was ten minutes ago."

"It was a long list that I considered. She was not at its top, but I discarded the others before her as too tedious."

"Have you taken a liking to gossip? Is that why she was not too tedious a topic too?"

"I am not interested in the gossip, but in the facts of the

situation. What you are doing is common in the army. Not our army so much, although there are episodes that are known but not spoken of. It is very common on the Continent. The French favor it, among others. It is as old as war itself, I suppose."

"What in hell are you talking about?"

"Treating women as the spoils of war. Proving victory by claiming a woman. She defeated Lakewood, and now you conquer her in order to avenge him and raise the flag."

"You are not making any sense. I have not set out to conquer her." Except he had. Only that war was a different one, and even older than military conflicts.

"Forgive my choice of words. You pursue her. You seduce her. You beguile her. You—"

"Lakewood has nothing to do with it either."

"Doesn't he? How can he not? In the heat of passion, he may be far from your mind, but vengeance is the only explanation for your interest in her to begin with. There is little about her that is attractive, and much that is not."

"Are you mad? Made of stone? Blind? She is beautiful. Zeus, those eyes—that mouth. How can you speak such nonsense?"

Kendale looked at him as if *he* were mad. "If both of you found her so bedazzling, I will have to accept that some men do. I do not see it myself. As for revenge, it is the assumed explanation, and I see no way to disabuse the world of that."

Riding suddenly became inconvenient to this conversation. "*Stop.* Now. Right here."

Kendale commanded his horse to stand.

"What do you mean the *assumed explanation*?" Yates asked. "Why would you think that?"

"I have heard them speak of it. Two days ago, in Brooks's, several members were assessing it. Last night I had dinner with friends in the Horse Guards, and it was mentioned. Hell, while I was tying my horse on Oxford Street, I overheard two women gossiping about it as they passed."

"I thought you were unaware of the gossip?"

"I said I was uninterested in the gossip. It would be impossible to be unaware at this point. Did you not know?"

"No." He had been sequestered in the damned study examining damned leases in preparation for this damned journey.

"I did not see the clouds blow in, but the rain started around the fashionable hour two days ago," Kendale said.

If even Kendale was hearing the rainfall, a deluge must be under way.

He turned his horse.

"Where are you going?"

"Back to town."

He could not leave Cassandra to drown all alone.

Chapter 15

Anseln Abbey showed all the signs of being the seat of a family with more prestige than money to its name. Barrowmore was an ancient title, and Yates assumed this land had come to them under King Henry, when so many monasteries were absorbed by peers.

A year ago, he might not have noticed the evidence of poor maintenance, but examining Highburton's estate had honed his perspective. As he rode toward the jumble of eaves and walls, he itemized the obvious lack of improvements and the toll that was taking.

An ancient gutter promised a damp attic, and the mortar around the stones needed tending. At least one chimney stack needed to be rebuilt, and another would only be good for a few years longer.

Cassandra's brother should not have wanted her to marry Lakewood, who had little fortune of his own. Although that might have been the appeal, if by chance Barrowmore welcomed the match. Lakewood's demands might be far less than another man's when it came to the settlement, since he had little to offer on his own side.

He truly wished that old friend did not invade his thoughts today. He wanted to believe he had reconciled himself to all the ambiguities surrounding Lakewood's death, and the open question of whether it had involved Cassandra's name or person. He liked to think he had achieved a philosophical view and buried any resentments. He would continue wondering for a while, he expected. He trusted the day would come when he no longer did.

He presented his card and asked to speak with Lady Cassandra, half expecting to be told she was not in residence. Her intention was to go abroad, and her unexpected absence from London could indicate that was where she had gone now, despite what she had told Emma.

The servant bore the card away. Another footman came five minutes later and escorted him to the drawing room. One could tell the chamber was original to the abbey, perhaps its refectory, from its size. Redecorating over the years had given it a proper ceiling and floor, but it still retained its medieval character in its small casement windows and uneven walls.

He waited with some anticipation to see her. He wanted evidence that she was still here, and not on a ship to America. He also wanted her vitality to make the day more interesting than days had been for some time now, except when she was in them.

He smiled at himself. It was not love, but at least he was fascinated in ways that happened with less frequency these last few years. Thank God for that.

As soon as she entered the chamber, he knew something was wrong. She smiled brightly and her eyes sparkled, but she wore her manner like a wax mask that would melt if the sun shone too brightly. It was not Cassandra who greeted him, but an actress who played a role she had studied for years.

"Have you come to congratulate me, Ambury?"

"If congratulations are in order, I will gladly give them. It would be nice to know the reason."

"The whole world will know in a few days. Such news travels fast, even in late summer. I thought it had already." She held out her arms in a gesture of astonishment. "I am to be married! Can you believe it? He is an upstanding man from Northumberland. Or is it Cumbria? One of those counties at the end of the earth. I am assured that he is handsome enough and good enough, and once we are wed, I suppose he will be wealthy enough, since my reputation necessitated rather a large settlement. He and I will grow old together, raising sheep."

"It sounds idyllic. You must be delighted."

"It is exactly the life I envisioned for myself when I dreamt at night. If only Mr. Treedle—or is it Tweedly?—had shown up years ago so I did not waste so much time in town, telling myself I was having fun."

"It appears all it took was a man with an estate full of sheep to win you. Had the world but known, such a man might have even been found in Sussex or Kent, and not so far away. There are surely a few Mr. Treedle-Tweedlys in the south."

"No more than four thousand or so, I am told."

"Then a simple inquiry could have done the trick, and avoided so much grief."

The mask fell to reveal the true Cassandra on this most unusual day. Her eyes blazed with anger. "You are not going to make this easy, are you? You are going to gloat. I knew you would. Even as I agreed to the match, I thought, *Oh, Ambury and Kendale and Southwaite are going to love this.*"

"I find gloating of little appeal. I am more interested in learning the story behind this peculiar news."

"I am being a dutiful sister, which is not peculiar but expected. I do know how to be one, despite what people think."

"It is odd that you are accepting the will of a man you

do not trust, no matter what your blood ties." He advanced until he could look into her eyes and see behind the sparks, whether they be of wit or anger or false joy. "What has he done to make you agree to this, Cassandra? I cannot imagine. I would have wagered that even if he beat you, it would never happen."

She bore his scrutiny for a few moments, then turned away abruptly. She kneaded her hands together. She looked back at him defiantly, as if he were to blame for whatever distressed her, but then her expression broke and tears entered her eyes.

"He has her. My aunt. He has taken her and put her in some doctor's home with lunatics. She will end her days there unless I do as he commands. Of course I agreed to."

There was no *of course* to it. Many young women would have written a few letters of cheery condolences to the aunt and gone about their lives.

Barrowmore was a scoundrel.

"Are you sure she will be free if you make this marriage?"

"He has promised . . . he says he will allow her to live in her house in London with a proper companion who knows how to care for those who . . . those whose minds start sliding back. I do not trust him totally, but I must try to give her back her home and some kind of dignity." She sounded desperate, and very sad.

He again saw some blame in her gaze. If he had paid up on those earrings, this would not have happened. She and her aunt would probably have escaped London before Barrowmore executed his plan.

She composed herself, and put back on her mask to play the role of the Cassandra the world expected. "So what brings you here, if not to offer felicitations on my good fortune?"

"I came to see your brother."

"Government business, I expect. It is odd for Pitt to ask you to be the messenger if they need Gerald for some minor consultation."

"Other business." He gestured for the footman standing by the door and handed over a card. "Tell the earl that I have called."

"Please say nothing about what I told you," Cassandra pleaded when the servant returned for him. "It will only make him angry if you turn your wit on him, and then he may make all of this harder."

"I do not intend to say one word about your forthcoming engagement to Mr. Treedle, unless he mentions it himself."

Barrowmore received him in the library. Even as Yates entered, the earl wore the smug expression of a man who had proven himself right, once again, on a matter of importance to himself.

"Were you riding by, Ambury? I would not expect you to call otherwise. If you are looking for a night's lodging and a meal, we, of course, are happy to accommodate you."

"I am here specifically to see you, on a matter of considerable importance to both of us."

Barrowmore's expression altered in the oddest way. Caution flickered in his eyes. Yates wondered what matter might cause that reaction, since the two of them had little connection or contact. Except for Cassandra. And Lakewood, of course.

They sat and pretended to be comfortable with each other.

"I have come to ask for your sister's hand in marriage," Yates said. "She is of age to decide for herself, but I thought it best to observe the formalities."

Barrowmore's expression fell into one of shock. Yates might indeed have brought news of a French invasion.

"Surely you jest, Ambury."

"Not at all."

More astonishment. "Zeus. *Zeus.* Why?"

"She suits me." It was unseemly for Barrowmore to express such amazement, as if his sister really deserved nothing more than a Mr. Treedle.

Barrowmore tried to recover, but failed. He stood and paced away. Finally, his back straightened and his head rose. He turned around.

"I regret that you are too late. She is already engaged."

"Damnation, that is inconvenient. Who is the lucky man? I expect he is here if all this happened so quickly. I should like to meet him and offer the congratulations of a vanquished opponent."

"He is not here, so that is not possible. Nor do I think he would like to meet one of her . . . prior gentlemen."

"Ah, you have heard the gossip."

"It was already being whispered before I left town. It is why you are here, isn't it? To do the right thing by her. But you are too late, as I said."

"Like so much gossip, it is not true in the details, but of course no one cares. So, yes, it is one reason why I am here. If her intended is not, and the decision was so recent, I have to wonder if she is in fact engaged yet, or merely promised to him. If it is the latter, you would be a fool to disregard my offer. I suspect it is the better one."

"I prefer his."

"Under the circumstances, we both know that I am in a poor position to expect a large settlement, while presumably this fellow held a gun to your head to extract as much as possible to take her on. And I am a fellow peer. Why would you prefer his offer to mine?"

"For one thing, I do not like you. For another, her marriage to you would probably bring more scandal to this family. In fact, I think I would rather see her dead than as your wife."

Yates swallowed his building temper. It was not insult that he tasted, even though Barrowmore had insulted him well enough. Instead, he experienced a bloody outrage at Barrowmore's attitude toward Cassandra. Her brother wanted to punish her with this marriage. He wanted her isolated and invisible. He did not care if that left her unhappy and bound to a man who quite likely scorned her.

He wanted to thrash Barrowmore. Instead, he stood. "I have done my duty and attempted to rectify the consequences of my behavior. Since you will have none of it, I will take my leave and consider my business with you completed."

He walked out. Ignoring the footman's attempt to escort him, he strode back to the drawing room.

Cassandra struggled to remain composed. Seeing Ambury had been both horrible and a relief. Horrible because his presence reminded her of the irony of her situation, and also how he had interfered with her hopes of saving her aunt. A relief because she had needed someone to speak to and tell how cruel her brother was being.

He had mercifully left quickly, before she ended up wailing at her fate. That would have been embarrassing, especially since he probably would not be sympathetic. He might even think there was justice in her marriage to Mr. Treedle, or whatever his name was. She had turned down a baron, had lived on the edge of scandal, and now she merely reaped what she had sown. That would be everyone's view, she expected.

She closed her eyes and tried to find a respite of serenity in the chaos swirling in her head and heart. She wondered how Aunt Sophie fared at that doctor's house. She hoped Sophie's caretakers would acknowledge she did not belong there, and treat her as a friend instead of an inmate. She hoped they let her work in the garden . . .

Rest settled on her, the first she had known in two days. It felt delicious to hold the unhappiness aside for a spell. If she could do that for a few hours, perhaps she could find some way to fight this battle with Gerald instead of simply surrendering.

"Come with me now," a voice commanded. A firm hand grasped her wrist and pulled her to her feet.

She startled alert. Ambury strode away, pulling her along. She tripped after him as he aimed for the terrace doors.

"We need privacy," he said. "Show me a place in the garden that cannot be seen from the house."

Surprised and befuddled, she pointed to a shrubbery halfway down the garden on the left. Ambury proceeded there with her in tow.

He released his hold when they were in the shade of the bushes. She sat on a stone bench and remembered that she and Gerald used to play in this little secluded spot when they were children.

Ambury reached into his coat and removed a parchment. He dropped it on her lap. "That is a special license. I asked your brother for your hand just now. He refused to agree. However, his blessing is not needed, and I think you and I should just walk out the garden portal and—"

She held up her hands. "*Stop*, please. Allow me to hear one shocking sentence at a time."

He appeared impatient and angry. The first was with her, she guessed. The second probably was due to her brother's insult.

She poked at the document on her lap. "You came here with a special license and the intention to propose?"

"I did."

"I suppose that means that the gossip has not died down about us."

"It has not."

"Poor Ambury. It is a cruel irony to find yourself trapped by honor where I am concerned, I am sure."

"I came here to do what honor requires, that is true. I did not take it less seriously, or resent the obligation, because it was you."

It was a gallant thing to say. He almost had indicated that the notion did not horrify him too much.

"There is no need now, of course," she said. "Mr. Treedle will solve everything. That should be a relief to you."

"Mr. Treedle is an ass."

"You have not even met him."

"Nor have you. You don't even know if his name is Mr. Treedle."

"Goodness, you do not sound relieved at all. Are you annoyed that my stupid brother prefers Mr. Whoever to you?"

"Not annoyed. Mystified. My offer should be preferable in every way."

"It would be foolish to let pride lead you to folly. You may be mystified, but you are also spared an unwelcomed marriage."

Ambury sat down beside her. "See here, I was not joking. I think we should elope and let your brother swallow it. I am hardly a paragon, but I am not known to seduce young women who have never married. Even Mr. Tweedle can't clear your name of this. Only I can."

He meant it. That was sweet, and it touched her. "You are forgetting why I agreed to his plans. My aunt. Gerald will never let her go if I elope with you. For all the good that will do, I might as well marry no one at all."

He paced back and forth, his scowl showing exasperation with her reluctance. "Let us say I find a way for us to rescue your aunt."

"Is the price of that rescue my agreement to this marriage? You would not do it otherwise?"

"It would be pointless to do it otherwise. Your brother would get her back, and I would have no standing to do anything about it. If you and I are married, I could offer protection, legally and socially. In the least, I can muddy the waters. I would be acting on your behalf, but my actions and words will carry far more weight than yours."

"Indeed, they would carry at least as much as his," she

mused, seeing the idea in a clearer light and envisioning any challenges. "More, since your words will be better spoken and you are better liked."

So there it was. A choice of sorts. Not really a choice, if she did not want to be buried alive. Not a choice at all, if she wanted to protect Aunt Sophie. And yet . . .

Ambury appeared so serious as he made his case for a marriage he had never sought, with a woman he did not love. There was so much unspoken between them, about Aunt Sophie and his pursuit of information about those earrings. About Lakewood.

Perhaps Mr. Treedle would be the better choice when it came to living out the years ahead.

"Do you give your word that she can live with me, that you will never try to do what Gerald has done, even if she should become a little dotty?"

"If she ever needs special care, it will be in your home, not another."

"I want your word that you will protect her, no matter what."

He smiled ruefully. "I never swear to something so ambiguous as *no matter what*, Cassandra. I will, however, promise to protect her, no matter what, so long as it does not compromise my honor."

She could hardly say that was not good enough, even though it might not be.

She wished she could demand time to think about this. Her mind felt full of cotton, and too many emotions jumped around inside her. It wasn't fair that she had to do this now.

"Cassandra, it is good of you to think of your aunt. It is time to think of yourself too. I was seen leaving your house that night. The scandal is breaking hard in London, even as we sit here. There is a name attached to the gossip this time, and it is mine. You will not survive this as you have the vague rumors of the past. You will be ruined for sure, totally, and my honor will be impugned. I must demand that you allow me to do the right thing here."

"It means a lifetime, Ambury."

"The life you knew is over anyway."

That was harsh. True, but harsh. Nor did it address the life that would follow. "As dear Emma would say, let us speak frankly. You do not really like me, Ambury. You do not trust me. You blame me for your friend's tainted reputation. I have come to suspect you blame me for his death."

"I like you well enough. As for the rest, we will not speak of it. It was long ago."

From his tone, she guessed he meant the "not speak of it" started right now. Perhaps he was wise. Maybe they could just lock the topic away in a wardrobe. After a few years, Lakewood's ghost might stop rapping at the door, demanding attention.

"Will your parents not be appalled that you are marrying a woman reputed to have had a history of liaisons?"

"They expect me to act with honor and that is what I am doing. However—I do need to know, for their sake as well as my own, whether you have had a liaison recently."

"Ah. So you want to know the truth about my past."

He thought about that, then shook his head. "Only the recent past."

"The only recent thing that might be called a liaison ended last February. He was a French émigré. Do you need to know if I loved him?"

"No."

Of course not. This was not about romance, love, and jealousy. Ambury did not care if she had given herself to another, or even many others, so long as she did not present him with a son born too soon.

"The Highburton succession is in no danger," she said.

"Nor must it be in the future."

Rather suddenly they were down to significant negotiations. "I know that. I am an earl's daughter. However, after that succession is secured, I assume you will allow me my freedom, as is customary."

Another thoughtful pause. A rather long one. "I will consider it."

She hoped that meant he would be reasonable. She would not know until the day came.

"And you, Ambury? Is there someone who will be unhappy by this precipitous marriage of obligation? You do not like the question, I see. Perhaps all those rumors about you are something else we will not speak of."

"That might be best."

The life you knew is over anyway. Just how different it would be, and how powerless she would be, pressed on her. A panic pounded in her chest. She clung to the one good thing that she knew for certain she would see in this decision.

"How do you intend to find my aunt? We should move quickly if we are to move at all."

"I will query the coachman and grooms, and see where your brother went."

"They may not tell you."

"If he treats you badly, he treats them worse, you can be sure of it. I will bribe if necessary, but I expect to get the route he took out of them in the least."

"I will see if my mother knows anything."

He took her hand in his. "Then we are decided?"

Saying it was hard. After escaping such a marriage once, she never expected to find herself in another one. She might be agreeing to a terrible mistake.

It was not about her, however. Gerald had made promises that she could not trust him to keep. Ambury would rescue and protect Aunt Sophie if he promised to. She believed that, and it was all that mattered now.

"Yes, we are decided."

He surprised her then. After this most practical conversation, he kissed her. Not a sweet kiss sealing their engagement either. He kissed her fully, sensually, as if he had been waiting to do so. He held her head and embraced her body and pulled her close, so his hold encompassed her. He kissed her until sensations stirred that distracted her from her worries about Sophie.

The carnal implications of this marriage became explicit. It flittered through her mind how that could be horrible too, if one married the wrong man. She would just have to hope that it would not be.

When he stopped kissing her, he looked down, with his fingertips resting on her lips. His hand drifted down, skimming her chin and neck and breast. Finally, he released her.

"Go now. Meet me here in three hours."

Chapter 16

Doing the Right Thing was a lot like having a bad tooth pulled. Given the choice, one would not do it, but it had to be suffered as a necessity.

It struck Yates, as he made his way through the property to the carriage house and stables, that he should be in a darker mood than he was. Mostly that was because he anticipated having Cassandra soon. The notion of taking her to bed put a better light on just about everything.

The opportunity to put his investigative skills to use partly explained his high spirits too. He had not taken up the avocation with the intention of earning a few pounds. Rather, he found the hunt interesting, even exciting, and money had flowed to him almost by accident.

He approached the coach house in an investigative frame of mind, half of his brain sorting though the questions he would ask the servants. The other half just as naturally analyzed the potential pain of having this particular tooth extracted.

There would be undeniable risk in marrying Cassandra. She might be more licentious than even the worst rumors suggested. She might cuckold him within a fortnight. She could make his private life hell if she chose. He might learn that she still had rendezvous with her French lover. He might discover that she could not be trusted in any way.

He might uncover evidence that he was bringing a thief into the family.

I want your word that you will protect her, no matter what. Cassandra had guessed what he suspected. What his father claimed. Perhaps she had always known, but it was possible that his questions about the earrings had caused her to review the past with new eyes.

Until recently, her Aunt Sophie had led a colorful life of frequent travel and amorous adventure. Everyone assumed her famous jewels had been gifts from her many lovers. Once he considered the possibility, however, he had seen how easy it would be for a woman with Sophie's access to grand homes to help herself to a bauble or two, especially from the homes of those lovers. If Count Lover or Chevalier Lover discovered a jewel's absence, how would he prove he had not given it to his paramour freely?

Cassandra had been Sophie's companion for six years now. Wherever Sophie had gone, Cassandra had gone as well. She may have seen things that in hindsight took on new meaning.

For that matter, she may have helped, or followed in her aunt's footsteps. If Aunt Sophie had an opportunity to steal jewels, so did Cassandra.

His thinking went to that conclusion of its own accord. The idea emerged from the others much like his footfalls fell in logical rhythm. His stride stopped as soon as his mind landed on that particular bit of ground.

He gazed at the carriage house up ahead that needed a new thatched roof. He noted the lone youth outside working on some tack in the shade. While he made his plans, he tried to discard the thought of Cassandra's complicity as absurd.

The impulse to make excuses for her came not from any secure opinion of her character, or even from the new reality that she would soon be his wife. Rather, it had more to do with a wide red mouth and blue eyes that could appear both innocent and scandalously worldly at the same time. It also derived from his instincts. Lust and sensibilities were hardly sound reasons to form a judgment.

He walked on, trying not to contemplate the implications. In particular, he did not dwell on the one that suggested that in agreeing to marry him, Lady Cassandra Vernham had just found the best protection in the world from all of her possible past sins.

Yates found the coachman drinking beer at a table in a chamber at the rear of the carriage house. Open windows let in a breeze that had done little to dry the sweat that stained the man's shirt. His embellished coats hung on nearby pegs, ready to be grabbed. He still wore his boots and cravat and wig. The small keg from where he had filled his tumbler rested in a corner.

He startled when Yates entered, then frowned. His gaze quickly slid down his intruder's form, taking in the details. He stood. "Milord!" He reached for his coats. "No one told me you were visiting, sir. I'll go straightaway and take care of your coach and people."

"Do not dress," Yates said. "It is too warm, and I do not require your services. I did not come in a carriage."

That puzzled the coachman more. He waited to learn what was required, if not service.

Yates looked through the door to the carriages. "Lady Cassandra wants to take out the gig this afternoon. Since I was going to take a turn, I said I would inform you."

"I'll have it brought around."

"Actually, she will come here for it. Have it ready in two hours."

The coachman nodded. "Will she be wanting a footman?"

"No."

The coachman gave him a hooded, sidelong glance for that. "It will be ready."

Yates paced around the spare chamber. There were three beds against the walls, but no indication that two of them were in use. He eyed the coachman's periwig and pantaloons. "Are you expected to be in formal livery all day?"

"Milord prefers it. There is always the chance he will want a carriage. He does not like to wait."

It was not unusual, but normally an estate like this had more servants in the carriage house than Yates saw in evidence here. "It must be hard to keep livery clean while you in turn clean the carriages and repair them."

"That is done at night by me and a boy."

"And when the carriage is out very late, as it was three nights ago?"

"Then it is done before dawn by me alone."

"Better to take a faster road and know that you will get some sleep."

The fellow swallowed a derisive chuckle. "I take the road I'm told to take, even knowing it will add four hours to a day's journey and make it two nights I do not sleep coming from London, not one."

"I would think the quickest way from London is obvious to anyone, even Barrowmore."

The irreverence was not lost on the coachman, who permitted himself the barest smile. "He knows his roads as well as any gentleman. An errand required a change through Hertford. His aunt accompanied him, and we needed to bring her to her friends near St. Albans."

"She must have been grateful that her nephew inconvenienced himself for her."

The coachman flushed. "I wouldn't know. The footmen helped her with her things and such when we got there. I stayed with the coach. And with Milord."

So Barrowmore had not even had the decency to present Sophie to her gaoler. He had sat in the coach while footmen took her in. Yates was tempted to ask if Sophie had fought them. If she had, it would not have slowed them much. She was small enough that one footman could carry her without any strain.

The coachman's deep flush did not abate. Whether it was due to revealing his master's business, or to memories about that stop, Yates could not tell.

He felt in his pocket for some shillings. Too many and his informant would worry about his recent indiscretions. Too few and his future silence might not be bought. The latter mattered more, so he erred on the side of generosity. "Lady Cassandra asked me to give you this, for her calling for the gig so late in the day. It is her request that you be discreet about her riding out. She tires of her current company and wants to take some different air for a while. It would be best if you tied the gig outside and remained in here when she comes."

The man eyed the shillings. He hid whatever thoughts he might have about Cassandra riding alone with an unknown, unexpected gentleman. "I have never been instructed to report on the family's comings and goings. No reason to start now on my own inspiration."

"That was easy," Cassandra said as the gig jostled down the road with Ambury's horse in tow. "You have a talent for elopements, Ambury."

"We were fortunate that the coachman was cooperative. Otherwise we would be walking across fields until I found an equipage to hire."

Cassandra doubted that would have ever happened.

Ambury was a man who arranged things to his liking. His birth, charm, and manner ensured the whole world cooperated. "I expect praise for thinking to send your horse out of view so my brother did not wonder why you were still on the property."

He leaned over and kissed her cheek. "You were brilliant."

The afternoon was waning and the air cooling. The excitement of their dash to the carriage house and quick escape had left her in a lighthearted mood. She pictured her brother explaining to Mr. Treedle that things had turned out rather badly and there would be no marriage and hence no fat settlement.

She did not feel at all bad for Mr. Treedle. What kind of man agrees to such an arrangement without even meeting the woman? A very greedy one.

"My mother refused to tell me where my aunt is. I am sure she knows."

"I learned enough to find her. We will not be able to remove her until tomorrow, however. She is closer to London than she is to Anseln Abbey."

"You know where to go? You are the one who is brilliant."

"Not exactly where to go. I know enough, however. The rest is just a matter of asking questions. Any doctor who keeps patients in his home will be known in his area."

He sounded confident. Cassandra allowed herself to know relief and delight that at this time tomorrow she would have Sophie free.

"Will we ride all night? I do not mind," she said.

"There isn't enough moon. We will impose on Kendale tonight. His seat is not far into the next county."

Her spirits sank. Kendale would ruin their adventure. He would probably say all the wrong things about this elopement. He would try to convince Ambury to send her back to Gerald and let Aunt Sophie fend for herself.

"Can we not stay at an inn?"

"If you are worried that I plan to seduce you tonight and you do not want such intimacy under his roof, let me reassure you that I have decided to wait until after we marry."

"It isn't that. Of all of you, he hates me the most."

"I do not hate you at all, Cassandra. Nor does he."

Perhaps *hate* had been the wrong word, but she was sure he knew what she meant. Just as he knew why she had said it.

"His home will be more comfortable for you, and his vicar can perform the wedding in the morning. I promise that Kendale will not be rude, and he and his servants will ensure your brother does not try to interfere."

The logic of staying with Kendale barely sunk in. She was too startled by the discovery that Ambury planned to marry *in the morning*.

"You intend to say the vows so soon?"

"When you procure a special license and elope in a clandestine manner, it is customary to say the vows as soon as possible."

She turned her attention to the passing countryside while she tried to accommodate just how soon her life, as she knew it, would be over.

Ambury guided the horses on. "So the notion of intimacy under his roof does not worry you?"

That pulled her out of her thoughts. How like a man to remember that passing response out of this entire conversation. "Not at all. I expect you to do this well enough that I will not notice where I am."

"Damn. Now I am regretting my resolve to wait."

"If waiting means we rescue Aunt Sophie first, I do not think you will regret it." She moved her rump closer to his, and leaned over to nip and nibble his ear. Mention of intimacy had reminded her of one possible benefit of this marriage, and the implications swam in her head. Feeling devilish, she caressed his knee.

He suffered her taunts for a few minutes. "Hell." He reined in the horse. He took the ribbons in his left hand and embraced her with his right arm and pulled her into a savage kiss. His hand circled around and closed on her breast.

They sat there on the road while a little storm possessed them. Arousal teased her mercilessly, and she ensured with her caress of his thigh that he would be no more comfortable. It reached a point where they either had to stop or tie the horse up and go into the field.

He broke a kiss in midpassion. Forehead pressing hers, his gaze locked on her eyes. "Tomorrow night, no matter where we are, I want you naked. No dressing gowns, no ceremony, no pretense. When I come to you, I want to see your breasts and your legs and your desire for pleasure."

He released her and took the ribbons up again. She stayed near him and rested her head on his shoulder while she reminisced about a hard back and bum walking into the sea.

D ogs began barking a half mile before they reached the house. At least a dozen accompanied the gig the last hundred yards, and swarmed around it when it stopped in the dark drive.

Cassandra tucked herself closer to Yates, who held his whip at the ready, should Kendale's hounds display as little social grace as their master.

The door opened and a tall, dark form became a silhouette in the light pouring out of the building. After a long, silent gaze, the figure stepped out. "What in hell are you doing here, Ambury? And in such a clumsy carriage at that?"

"Seeking sanctuary." Yates hopped down and met Kendale halfway. The hounds followed, nipping at his boot heels and sniffing his legs. Kendale gave two curt orders that sent them scattering.

Kendale looked past him, to the carriage. "Is that Lady Cassandra?"

"It is."

"Should I bother to say that you are both courting

irredeemable scandal if you are traveling alone together at this hour in the middle of the country?"

"Do not waste your breath."

Kendale sighed. "Fine. Bring her in. There is no one here that will be corrupted by your boldness. Should I tell the servants you need one chamber or two?"

"Two, of course."

Kendale found that amusing. "Go and get her. Or should I extend a warm welcome to her too? Yes, I suppose I should." He strode forward and proved quite effusive in that welcome, apologizing for the rustic nature of the hospitality and the lack of feminine comforts. Yates was impressed. He had not heard Kendale combine so many words at one time before in the name of politeness. Cassandra's skeptical expression softened.

Yates helped Cassandra down. Once in the house, Kendale turned her over to an old housekeeper.

"She will be in the first chamber at the top of the stairs, on the second storey, if you go looking for her later tonight," Kendale said after she had left.

Yates would not mind seeking her chamber tonight. After what had happened on the road, he was sorely tempted. He would not, he decided, although he was not sure why. He followed Kendale into the library, where Kendale poured them both some brandy.

"What did you mean, you are seeking sanctuary?"

"There is the chance her brother will try to interfere. He may turn up here if he can follow us."

"Hell, let him come. Half my servants are ex-army. We could withstand a damned siege if we had to."

"I assumed as much. It is why we came here. Now sit and I will explain all. Oh, before I do—there is a vicar on this estate, isn't there?"

It took Kendale a few moments to understand the implication of the question. He shot Yates a good glare and reached for the brandy again.

* * *

On occasion, although not recently, Cassandra had imagined a wedding in which she was the bride. Although that fantasy had been distinctive in some particulars, it had not been unusual in its general unfolding. It had never included a wedding dress that was little more than a muslin bit of practicality, such as one might wear in the country on a hot summer day.

It definitely had not included a dour old housekeeper and a severe Lord Kendale as witnesses.

The vicar, a second cousin of Kendale who was new to his living, proved flustered and flushed and astonished to be called for such a duty. He required reassurance that the special license was authentic before taking his position in the drawing room.

Just as the ceremony began, a storm broke. Cassandra watched the downpour out of the corner of one eye. The opposite corner of the other eye noted that Ambury appeared the most tranquil person in the chamber.

He would be quite a catch under normal circumstances. A woman would have a hard time swallowing smug glee if he had proposed without a sword at his back, and if she did not have several unresolved matters with him that might bode ill for the future. They would not speak of them, he had decided, but that would not make them go away.

The moment came for the ring, and to her surprise, one emerged from Ambury's coat. She wondered where he had gotten it. The gesture and symbolism made the ceremony very real suddenly. Starkly so. All the bad nerves a bride might know over the entirety of her engagement assaulted Cassandra in one single moment when that ring came at her. Her hand shook so badly that Ambury had to clutch her wrist in order to catch her finger with the golden circle.

Then it was over. Done. No one moved for a long moment.

No one spoke. The vicar appeared frozen, his hopeful, cautious smile beaming her way.

Finally, Ambury placed his hands on her face and kissed her carefully, as if he guessed the terror in her heart. "I promise to take good care of you," he said quietly.

It was not the declaration of love from her girlhood fantasy, but it was more than some women ever could count on.

"And I promise to make sure you never turn staid and strict like your ancestors," she said.

He laughed, and the sound broke the awkwardness. People moved. The vicar offered his felicitations. Ambury took her arm, and they joined the tiny wedding party as it went to the dining room for breakfast.

"I do not think we can ever repay Kendale for his help," Cassandra said as the carriage rolled into St. Albans.

"We do not have to repay him. He is my friend." Ambury was more interested in the outskirts of the town than her comment.

Kendale had been a better friend than most might be. Not only had he hosted their wedding, he had loaned them this coach without Ambury asking. For a man who lived in masculine indifference to society's demands, Kendale had some unexpected insights, such as the one that said it would look very odd for Ambury to bring her to London in a stolen one-horse gig.

A gig with Aunt Sophie on the back step would be even odder. Cassandra decided she would let Kendale know how grateful she was that he had foreseen practicalities. The loan of two footmen and a coachman might be very welcomed too, before the day was out. She did not doubt that Ambury could intimidate any doctor into releasing Sophie when the time came, but it would not hurt if he had several strong men along.

"Wait here," Ambury said. He called for the coach to stop

and was out the door before it completely did. She peered out the window and watched him enter a tavern.

She waited a quarter hour before he returned and climbed back in. "I think the place we are looking for is on a side lane three miles south of town. The doctor who lives there keeps to himself, but there are reports that he has a variety of permanent guests."

Cassandra tightened with excitement and fear. "Have you decided how you are going to do this? Perhaps you should say my brother sent you to get her."

"I am not going to lie, of course. However, I may say that her family sent me to fetch her. Since you are her family . . ."

She hoped that would be good enough. She pictured the unfolding of this drama while the coach bore them forward.

The house on the side lane did not appear anything other than a good-sized cottage. There was nothing to indicate its purpose as they rolled up. The noise they caused changed that. Soon, pale faces appeared at the windows on the second level and in the attic. Eyes peered down on them. Cassandra looked from window to window, seeking Sophie. All she saw were ghostlike presences and eyes. Confused eyes. Mad eyes. Blank eyes.

"I must go in with you," she said.

"You will not."

"She will not believe you are here to help her. She may think you are doing Gerald's work for him and taking her to a more remote place. We will go in together, and if this doctor tries to stop her from leaving, then I will leave and you can return with these brawny footmen."

He thought it over. "We will try it your way. But . . ." He reached up and took down the pistol from its box in the carriage wall. "He may have brawny footmen too, and I'll not risk your safety."

The occupants of the house were waiting for their knock. The door opened immediately. A florid-faced gentleman wearing an old-fashioned periwig- and fawn-colored pantaloons and coats greeted them. A manservant, who appeared brawny enough, hovered behind him.

Ambury handed over his card. "We have come to call on Lady Sophie Vernham."

Filmy eyes peered at the card, then at Ambury, then at her. "I was not told she would have callers."

"And who are you, if I might ask?" Ambury said.

The fellow drew himself up tall. "Doctor Harold Wakely, physician. This is my home and my private hospital."

"Oh, dear, has she taken ill?" Cassandra asked. "Thank goodness I decided to make this detour to see her. How like Barrowmore to try and spare me."

Dr. Wakely did not know what to do, so he erred on the side of etiquette. Cassandra accepted his invitation to enter.

"If you will show me to her, I would greatly appreciate it," she said.

Dr. Wakely instead showed them into the sitting room. "I fear she has become worse since she came here. Her memory absorbs her in ill ways almost all day now. That is why your brother brought her to me. She is losing all control of her mental faculties."

"Oh, my." She looked at Ambury. "I must see her even so."

"She may not know you," Dr. Wakely said.

"We will risk that," Ambury said. "My wife was very close to her aunt and needs to offer her comfort if she can."

"Your wife? Her aunt?" Dr. Wakely looked at Cassandra with surprise. "My apologies, Viscountess. I did not know you were family. Yes, of course you must see her. If you will follow me."

He led the way through the house, to a door in the back that gave out to the garden. "She likes the flowers. She spends most of her time here if the weather is fair. Unlike some of our guests, she is no real trouble. Not insane, of course. Just entering her second childhood."

Cassandra spotted her aunt sitting on a bench under a

tree midway down the garden's main path. "Thank you. I would like some privacy with her."

Dr. Wakely stepped back. "I will be inside."

Cassandra and Ambury advanced on Aunt Sophie. Cassandra noted how her aunt did not move, and looked at nothing really. Her mind was elsewhere, the way it tended to be sometimes now.

Misgivings churned in her. Perhaps Sophie truly had gotten worse since she came here. Was that possible in only a few days? Maybe if one was in a house full of people who were very ill mentally, one found an escape in one's own mind.

They were very close before Sophie even heard them. She looked over, that filmy distance in her gaze that heralded old images occupied her too vividly.

"Ah, Anthony, it is you. I knew someone would come and rescue me, but never expected such a noble champion as Highburton."

Ambury took her hand and bowed to kiss it. "I am not Anthony, but his son. We look much alike, I am told."

Sophie blinked twice. Her eyes brightened and a shrewd smile formed. "You do indeed. You are much like him when he was younger." She accepted Cassandra's embrace. "How did you find me? I hope that Highburton's son beat it out of Gerald. The scoundrel abducted me from my own home. Can you believe it?"

Yates watched as Cassandra took stock of her aunt. Right now Sophie appeared normal enough, but a few minutes ago she had indeed been lost in her thoughts. She had truly mistaken him for his father, which indicated she dwelled in those memories quite thoroughly at times.

"You will tell me all once we have you away from here," Cassandra said. "Ambury and I are taking you home with us.

Gerald will not be allowed near you, and if he tries to do this again, we will go to court to stop him."

Sophie looked from Cassandra to Ambury, confused. Then her gaze fell on Cassandra's hand that rested on her shoulder. She saw the ring. "You are married?" She peered at Cassandra, then Ambury. "To you?"

"Yes. Just this morning," Ambury said. "Other than my friend Viscount Kendale, you are the first to learn of it."

"Well, well. Gerald is not going to like that at all. Indeed, it may distract him from bothering with me." She stood. "I have little personal property here, and we should not delay to retrieve it. I would suggest we merely walk out a garden gate, but I checked my first day here, and they are all locked. Dr. Wakely has two very big servants to help him deal with the poor souls who truly are in need of this retreat, so I hope you brought a pistol, sir."

"I did, but I am sure I will not need it."

"You have more faith in the common sense of others than I do, then." Regal, aging, but still beautiful, she appeared very alert to the world around her. "Shall we go? I daresay anyone who is sane would not remain such if left here too long."

Dr. Wakely was waiting for them right inside that back door. He appeared pleased to see Sophie so aware. "Your visit clearly has helped today, Viscountess. Are you feeling better, Lady Sophie?"

"I am in fine form, my good man. I have been all day, and yesterday, and the day before. Indeed, I told you I do not belong here many times."

"Of course, of course," Dr. Wakely cooed.

"I am taking Lady Sophie with us," Ambury said. "My wife will see to any care that she may need in the future."

That startled the doctor. "She was put in my care, sir. I am obligated to—"

"You have no obligations. The family has changed its mind regarding her care. I am sure that happens sometimes."

Wakely frowned. He moved so that he blocked the way

to the front. The big servant appeared at the end of the passageway. "I gave my word, sir."

"You will not be breaking it of your own will."

"The fees—"

"Are yours to keep, I think. Of course, the longer Barrowmore is not aware of this change, the more likely you are to in fact do so."

The servant took a few steps forward. Wakely's face turned red, and he more obviously blocked their path. "I cannot allow this. It is most irregular, and of suspect legality."

Yates moved his coat so the pistol showed. He fixed Wakely with a hard gaze. "Do not speak legalities to me. You have been party to an abduction. Barrowmore has no authority over Lady Sophie, and you had no business accepting her confinement here against her will, without proof he had been given her custody. She chooses to leave with us, and I will ensure that she does so. Now call off your man and move out of our way."

Wakely held his ground for a ten count. Then his arm went up in a gesture to the servant, and he himself stepped aside.

As Yates walked Sophie and Cassandra out of the house, Sophie tilted her head close to that of her niece. "See, dear? I told you he was delicious."

Chapter 17

Yates soon learned that Lady Sophie, in possession of all her mental faculties, was a woman to be reckoned with.

After putting ten miles between Wakely's home and their coach, they stopped at a staging inn for a meal. Yates decided they should forge on, even if it meant arriving in London after dark. The ladies accepted that. What they did not accept was his plan regarding what to do once they reached London.

He intended to bring both of them to his family home for at least a few days while he made arrangements to let a house. Sophie would be safe there, and Cassandra would have some privacy and comfort.

"I would prefer to return to my own home," Sophie said. "I refuse to be a burden on your parents, and would feel very awkward being their guest without their invitation."

"They will not mind, I assure you. This is an extraordinary situation, and we still do not know what Barrowmore may contemplate doing. If you are alone in your house, we could find you missing once again." He assumed she would see the logic of his plan.

"We can solve the Gerald problem easily enough. Leave these footmen with me, and give them orders to throw out anyone who tries to enter my home."

"They are Kendale's servants, not mine. They need to return to him, along with this coach."

"Lord Kendale will not mind your keeping them for a few days, I am sure."

"You do not even know him, so how are you sure?" His voice must have carried his growing exasperation, because Cassandra, whose hand rested under his, turned her palm and gave a little squeeze.

"I am sure because he is a gentleman, and Cassandra told me he was an officer. Having involved himself in your skirmish, he would never remove his troops if you still required them. Write to him and explain. You will see I am right."

So it was that Yates deposited Sophie and two footmen in her house on Adams Street. Cassandra took the opportunity to pack a portmanteau before joining him as the coach moved on to his family's home.

"Do you plan to explain about us tonight?" Cassandra said as she looked up at the dark façade. Enough lights glowed inside to indicate the household had not retired yet.

"That would be best."

"Do I have to come with you?"

"I think I will do it alone."

"I expect that is wise." She accepted his escort to the door. "Of all the things I have braved out over the years, I think this odd homecoming may turn out to be the hardest."

"You are the next Countess of Highburton, Cassandra. Every person under this roof will treat you as such."

"Your mother—"

"Especially my mother."

A footman did the duty at the door at this hour, but the butler soon relieved him. Yates explained that they would be staying a few days. "Put us in the third-storey apartment that overlooks the garden. Tell Mrs. Anderson to send someone up to help the lady. Send word to my chambers for Higgins to come here too."

The butler began giving out orders. Yates took Cassandra aside. "I must go to my father now, and hope he is awake. It would not do for the servants to know first."

"Of course. I will wait to thank you for today until I see you again."

Her mischievous smile did much to distract him from the audience he faced. His mind began calculating that his father probably was not awake and it could all wait for the morning, or even afternoon. He set that notion aside and began mounting the stairs, wondering how bad this audience might be.

His father had been moved to his bed. His mother sat in a chair nearby reading to him. Yates regretted interrupting the peaceful scene.

His mother set down her book as he approached. "It can wait for the morning, Yates. He is almost asleep."

"I'm awake enough," his father muttered. He struggled to sit up. Yates went over and helped him and set two pillows behind his back.

"So what is it that brings you here at this hour?" his father asked. "I thought you had left town."

"I just returned. There is something I must tell you, and it could not wait."

His mother began rising, to leave them to it.

"You should stay," Yates said. "It was fortunate to find you together."

Watching him cautiously, his mother sat again. "Did you lose big at the tables?"

"It is not that, although all the same, I will be needing some money. I was married this morning, by special license. To Cassandra Vernham."

His parents stared at him. No one spoke or moved. Of

the two, his father appeared more shocked. Yates hoped he was only stunned and this would not badly affect his health.

The silence hung awkwardly.

"I have brought her here. My chambers were not suitable."

"I should say not," his mother said. "Of course you had to bring her here."

"Of course," his father echoed.

His mother looked over and caught his father's eye. Some silent communication passed between them.

"Special license," his father said. "Was it an elopement? Did her family not approve?"

"Her brother was less than happy with my offer."

"I expect he was." His father found that amusing for some reason. "Well, it is done, so there is no purpose in discussing the wisdom of it." His head lulled back on the pillows. "Bring her to me tomorrow, so I can welcome her."

He seemed to doze off then.

"Come with me," his mother said. "He may be finished with you, but I have a bit more to say."

Yates followed her to the apartment's dressing room. As soon as he closed the door, she turned on him and let her shock show.

"Really, this is the kind of thing we worried you would do when you were twenty, not now. What were you thinking?"

"I am sure you have heard the talk, so that is an odd question."

"Of course I have heard it. There has been talk about each of you for years, so the current gossip is nothing new."

"What is new is that the talk is about the two of us together."

"So you had an affair. It was not your first, nor hers." She sank onto a chair and shook her head. "*Cassandra Vernham.* Of all the women in England, you had to get entangled with *her.*"

"Actually, we did not have an affair, but her name was compromised all the same. I know about the past rumors that have surrounded her, but this talk is not like that. It is specific as to evidence, and I am named. It would have ruined her. She has never married—"

"By her own choice. As to ruining her, she was well on the way already. I do not see why you have to be sacrificed for her sake."

"I cannot allow you to speak like that about her. Please do not do so again."

To his surprise, she began weeping. He did not think he had ever seen her cry before.

"Father understands even if you do not. I know that you are not happy. You probably had a whole list of matches for me that you would prefer."

"Dozens. Hundreds."

"I know her better than you do, and I think she will suit me very well. She is my wife now. I am sure that you will welcome her as Father will."

She wiped her eyes and collected herself. "Of course. There is nothing else to do. I expect you are taking over the large apartment on the third storey?"

"Until I find a house for us."

"I will tell him to give you the money for establishing a household. It is past time, and keeping the purse strings tight did not make any difference with you anyway."

He bent down and gave her a kiss on her cheek. She did not seem to mind, although it was not something he had done in years. Just as she had not patted his face the way she did while she peered intently at him with moist eyes.

"I will be kind to her, I promise."

He took his leave of her. He went to the library and found some port. He drank it while he looked out the window to the lamps dotting the dark.

It had gone better than he expected with the earl, and worse than he had anticipated with his mother.

Thoughts of Cassandra soon pushed aside any memories of those conversations. He resisted the inclination to stride up the stairs and have her at once. Instead, he finished the port while desire taunted him. He lingered fifteen minutes more after that, so she might have time to be settled in.

Then he could wait no longer.

The maid held a large linen as Cassandra stepped out of the cool bath. Eschewing heated water had left her time to linger before washing, and she felt refreshed as she wrapped herself in the towel.

She sat at the writing table, and the woman began unpinning her hair. While her locks fell, she jotted a note to Emma. "I married Ambury this morning. I will explain everything when I see you next."

After sealing the letter, she moved to the dressing room while her hair was brushed. Then she dismissed the woman and opened the wardrobe in which her few items of clothing had been placed. She tried to decide what to put on. The apartment had two bedchambers, and when Ambury walked the narrow connecting passage, she assumed he would be visiting for one purpose alone. Sexual pleasure would be his lone benefit in this marriage, aside from upholding his honor.

She did not expect him to stand on ceremony either. He had no need to seduce a virgin, did he? No requirement to pretend love, or even much affection. A man who does the right thing is a man coerced by society's rules. Had she been an innocent, he might have at least tried to be gentle, but a woman of the world did not need such care.

I want you naked. To take him literally would make for a vulgar beginning. Even his mistresses probably did not greet him totally nude. She flipped through her nightdresses and dressing gowns, and chose one that would perhaps do. Dropping the towel, she slid into it.

She had no idea how long he would be with his family.

There might be considerable discussions taking place regarding his unexpected marriage. It would be nice to find something to distract her, but she doubted he would take it well if he walked in and found her reading a book.

She returned to her bedchamber. The woman had turned down the bedclothes on one side. Apparently the servants still did not know that she and Ambury were married. She folded them down on the other side. The night was warm, and they would not be needed.

Finally, all was as prepared as it would ever be. Except her.

This was her wedding night, and its rituals spoke how her life had changed. This would be no impetuous passion raging out of control. Ambury would not be a man plying her with kisses and pleasure into agreement. There were no fantasies of love into which she could retreat.

Instead, tonight was about rights ceded and duties accepted. It could be nothing more than that. It might be cold and perfunctory.

Or not.

She sat waiting, her heart pounding hard, all of her senses shrilly alert, and wondered if she would have any say in which way it went. Perhaps so. Ambury assumed she was a woman of the world. It might be wise to act like one, instead of a frightened goose.

Returning to her dressing room, she removed the night-dress she wore, before slipping back on the sheer overdress. Back in the bedchamber, she laid in the center of the bed.

The waiting aroused her. The fabric veiling her body chafed gently against skin enlivened by anticipation. Memories of pleasure from their prior embraces and kisses teased her.

When she listened hard, she could hear faint sounds from other chambers that indicated someone moved about. It might only be his valet, but each muffled sound twisted her nervous excitement tighter.

Different sounds suddenly. Closer ones. She looked over,

and he was in her chamber, standing in the shadows. A prism of silver light leading through a nearby drape crossed his face and upper body. He wore a green robe de chambre of raw silk that hung loosely and freely. She doubted he wore anything beneath it. She remembered how he looked as he walked into the sea. The image made her stir with a deep, physical purr.

He came to the bed. He fingered the thin, transparent silk of the overdress's hem. That caused the two sides to part until one of her legs was uncovered up to her hip.

"It is elegant," he said.

"I thought it was bold."

His fingertips glided up the silk along her torso until they skimmed the dark circle of her nipple visible beneath the film. Her breath caught in her throat at the vague caress. Her breasts swelled even more. Her nipple tightened harder beneath his touch.

"It is bold too." With another pull, the fabric slid away, leaving half her body completely naked.

The way he looked at her created delicious prickles. She peeled back the other side of the overdress so his gaze would arouse her even more.

"You are beautiful, Cassandra. I have often thought you look good enough to eat." He cast off his robe.

She had been correct that he wore nothing beneath. Also, that there would be no standing on ceremony. He made no effort to cover himself or to slide into bed quickly so her delicate sensibilities would not be shocked. He stood there, aroused and naked, while the robe fell to the floor.

She could barely find her voice. "Good enough to eat? I will take that as a promise."

He knelt on the bed and leaned over her. "Definitely bold now. I will count on your giving as good as you get, once you are used to me." He lifted her shoulders and gathered her hair and piled it on the pillow above her head. "I am curious to discover just how worldly you already are."

Not worldly enough. Not so worldly as to feel sophisticated when his hips settled between her thighs and his shoulders loomed above her. Not nearly blasé when she felt the
evidence of his desire pressing against her and saw it in the
severity that passion gave his expression.

She had to force herself to remember what to do. Her
embrace of him was tentative. His warmth and physicality
startled her. The hard body she had admired walking into
the sea turned her into a small, vulnerable woman. The combination of nerves and arousal robbed her of the ability to
dispel her awe with conversation or humor. She could only
experience amazement as he began handling her in ways
that left her breathless. It was not her first time with a man,
but it was the first time that she was with a man who deliberately sought to drive her mad.

He knew how to do that. With kisses that claimed and
caresses that commanded, he vanquished every clever
thought that tried to form. Her body welcomed his mastery
too much. Her skin savored the rough warmth of his palm
and the hot press of his mouth. She opened her lips so he
could explore, and gasped when he turned his devastating
tongue and mouth to her breasts and created a building pleasure too delicious to bear.

He succeeded then in conquering what little hold she kept
on her self-control. Nothing mattered except the way her
body pulsed with ragged hunger. She arched her back so her
breasts rose to him. She fumbled a caress down his chest to
where their bodies met. He shifted so she could reach lower,
and she took his hardness in her hand. All of him tightened
more, and became tense like desire coiled inside him waiting to break free.

His teeth closed carefully but clearly on her nipple. A
sharp sensation shot low inside her, making her tremble over
and over as it echoed through her loins and hidden flesh. She
thought about nothing else after that, only that void that she
wanted him to fill and that carnal itch desperate for relief.

When he finally touched her down there, she almost wept from relief. She used her own hand more aggressively so he might not stop. She parted her legs shamelessly so he could stroke more deeply and freely. Again and again a torturous pleasure resonated around her vulva, until her whole consciousness cried.

Cassandra's cries filled Yates's head like a feminine melody contrasting with the hard staccato of his own mindless hunger. The barest thought drifted beneath both. That she was lush and beautiful and bold enough in the end. But not truly worldly, perhaps. Not vastly experienced.

He tried not to note the evidence of that, but it was there. He had bedded enough women to know the difference.

His body grew impatient. The heat in his head turned white hot. He moved over her again and embraced her so he could lave her breasts. His phallus swelled and hardened more in anticipation of the rest.

The smallest thought suggested he should not assume she intended an invitation with her arch response while he undressed, but he ignored it. He was too far gone to stop himself, and did not want to anyway.

He lowered his kisses down her body. Her breath shortened more with each inch of his path. She knew what he was about, he was sure. That alone silenced any gentlemanly whispers about restraint. He paused only long enough to use his fingers to stroke her until the new tension he felt in her flanking legs disappeared and she was ready for him.

He used his tongue gently at first, luring her while he anchored himself to some control. Then he lost himself in the scent and taste of her, and to the primitive pleasure consuming his consciousness.

She came with a series of deep groaning cries. His own release would not be denied much longer. He went up over her and pressed inside her slowly. When there was no resistance, he thrust deeply and gritted his teeth against the urge to ravish her.

He braced himself above her and moved. Her thick lashes rose. She watched him, her eyes full of passion's lights, her sighs keeping rhythm with their bodies' repeated joining.

E ven in her sated state, Cassandra remained astonished. She had known pleasure before, but not such free pleasure. There was something to be said for not having to worry that you were doing something wrong, or might find yourself with child out of wedlock.

That was one of several unformed thoughts that floated to her while she enjoyed a deliciously languid peace. She barely noticed Ambury's weight on her. His deep breaths seemed to encourage time to remain unnaturally slow.

He moved off her, and it broke the spell. Bit by bit, she accommodated her physical self again, and the existence of time and place.

He did not leave her the way she expected. Instead, he lay on his back, one arm crooked beneath his head. His eyes remained closed and his teeth slightly parted. He appeared contented enough, although, on second glance at his profile, she thought she saw the smallest frown.

Perhaps she had been too bold? It was possible that he believed she should have been less agreeable to what he had done. Men could think like that. They were not always fair in the way they judged such things. They could descend into idiocy even if it was not in their best interests.

Those unexpected nether kisses had been one astonishment, but another had been even more surprising. She tried to decide if she should speak of that one odd moment that now begged for clarification. She would let it pass if he did not appear contemplative, and if she did not suspect his thoughts were becoming very masculine in the least logical way.

"I think, as wedding nights go, this has been a better one than most women can hope to know," she said.

His expression softened. "Most men too, especially since it is not likely most brides bother with flattery afterward."

"That is because most brides are virgins, and know little pleasure on their wedding night. I was not, of course."

Silence.

Oh, yes, he was thinking like a man. Who would have expected this when it came to her, of all women?

"You were not sure about that, I think," she said. "You were surprisingly careful, just in case. That was thoughtful of you."

She received no response again. They would not speak of it, just as he had promised in the garden. He had not asked about her past then, and he would not now. He truly did not want to know. What a gem of a husband. Truly remarkable.

"Who was it?"

Not remarkable enough.

The question did not annoy her. She only wished that he had held this conversation when she invited it, before they wed.

"Not him."

She did not want to say more, but she was glad to be explicit regarding Lakewood. Perhaps Ambury would think better of her now that he knew for certain that nothing warranting marriage had occurred that day six years ago.

"If not him, then who?"

"You said you did not want to know my history."

"A day ago I did not, and a day hence I may not. Today I find myself very curious." He turned on his side and rose up on his arm. "You are not as experienced as the rumors imply. Bold is not the same thing as expert or jaded."

"I did not realize that you were taking stock of me so thoroughly, and forming judgments."

"Not judgments. Just questions."

He waited like a man entitled to answers. How irritating.

"Apparently you are not as worldly as you thought either," she said, "to care about such things."

"In these circumstances, that is true, and it is a surprising discovery. If you were a mistress and not a wife, no doubt I would not give a damn."

"It might be wise to think of me as the former, then."

"Tonight, at least, that is impossible."

She hoped he did not expect apologies and tears and a dramatic confession. She had never misled him.

"When I returned from the tour of Europe with my aunt, I met an army officer. He was very dashing. He impressed me by not caring about the scandal with Lakewood. I agreed to marry him. One day, he called and my aunt, who had not yet retired from society, was not home. He stole a kiss, and one thing led to another."

"Did the scoundrel abandon you after he had what he wanted?"

"You are very quick to think badly of him."

"That is because he proposed, you agreed, he seduced you, but he did not marry you."

"He tried to marry me. My brother refused his blessing, then threatened to ruin this officer's career if he married me anyway. That ended it."

"I thought your brother wanted you married. He should have welcomed the offer."

"He did not welcome yours, and it was far better than that of an army officer. My officer did not fit the plan, whatever it was."

"He sounds like a man who needs an avocation. Or a distraction." He reached out and laid his hand on her stomach. "He should marry. That will give him something to do with his time now that he can no longer scheme about you."

"That is a splendid idea. I think I will find him a bride. Some girl who shows the mark of developing into a shrew."

He laughed and rolled onto his back, then pushed up to sit against the headboard. "While you look for her, you can turn the table on him and introduce him to a dozen innocents and their mamas every week next Season. Make sure none of them has a superior fortune, if you want him miserable. He cannot afford to marry for love."

She tilted her head and looked up at him. "Why do you say that?"

"Anseln Abbey is badly in need of investment. He put it off too long. I assume he is short of funds."

Ambury had seen evidence she had missed, but she knew little about maintaining an estate. Gerald had given her nothing these last years, but Mama seemed to buy as much at the dressmakers as she ever did, and nothing had been said about strained finances.

A caress on her face pulled her out of her thoughts. Ambury carefully stroked her disheveled hair away from her face. She looked up at him and saw in his eyes the reason he had not left the bed.

He took her hand and coaxed her up. "Come here."

Yates had never been a jealous lover. A few women had told him that was one of his more endearing qualities. Many more had resented it. He took pride in that aspect of his character, however. Jealousy turned men into asses.

Yet here he was, still wondering about Cassandra. Only after he settled her so she faced him, kneeling with her bent legs flanking his hips, did the curiosity abate a little.

He caressed up those legs, and along the curved lines of her body, until he held her breasts in his hands. A day ago, when he said he did not need to know her history, he had meant it. But a day ago, he had not been married. She belonged to him now, and he did not like the idea that others had seen her like this, naked and beautiful, with stunning lights of desire in her eyes.

Not him. That was something at least. He had not liked the idea it had been Lakewood. He did not know why. He only knew that if Lakewood had possessed her first, it would complicate many things.

She resettled herself a bit closer. Her cleft pressed against his shaft now. He was not in her, but they were as close as possible short of that. He felt a sensual pulse in the unbearable softness nestled against him. She sat back and swept her warm, soft palms over his chest in slow delicate caresses that teased like feathers.

Bold enough, but not too bold. He could be excused for wondering if all of her experience had been nothing more than rumors. Even now she appeared fascinated with her own audacity in being this forward. When he had tasted her, he had felt and heard her surprise, even if he heard no objections. By the time he considered that she might talk a better game than she played, he was too far gone.

He touched her creamy white breasts. Round and high, their darks tips pointed erotically. Her lids lowered, but he could see her arousal in her expression, could see how the titillation made her vaguely smile, and how his caresses began causing a small frown of need.

He teased until the distress made her control crack. She moved in sensual sways that caused an incredible caress where they joined. Finally she embraced his neck and hung there, her breasts filling his hands. He made sure he pleasured them until she was undone completely.

She trembled when he entered her, then shifted her hips to absorb him deeply. His own mind dazed to everything except the tightening pleasure that coiled hotter and higher each time she rose up and lowered herself onto him.

She turned frantic, as if nothing was enough and relief would never come. She moved aggressively, roughly, seeking the connection that would satisfy him. He swelled all the more until he filled her and stretched her and his own relief flexed through him. "*Yes, yes,*" she whispered again and again while she rode his hard climax and let him pound into her.

Chapter 18

The footman jumped to his feet as soon as Cassandra entered the morning room at her aunt's house. With three long strides, he took a place near the wall.

Cassandra bent to kiss Aunt Sophie. As she did, she noticed an extra cup and plate on the table, then glanced at the footman. He was a hearty fellow, and handsome, with a tawny rough-hewn ruggedness. In his thirties, she guessed. He stared off into space.

She told him to leave. Sophie waved good-bye and smiled at him like a girl.

"Aunt Sophie, are you being too familiar with Lord Kendale's footmen?" Cassandra asked while she sat down.

"That depends on what you mean by too familiar."

Cassandra made a gesture at the extra cup and plate.

"I will admit to asking Sean to join me while I had my morning coffee, but nothing more."

"Sean?"

"That is the name of the Scottish masterpiece you just dismissed."

It was not clear if Sophie had asked nothing more of Sean than his company at breakfast, or whether she just would admit to nothing more.

It was a detail better ignored than clarified.

"I hope that you have not come to depend on him. He and Kendale's other servants will be leaving this afternoon with the carriage, and Highburton's footmen will be here instead after that."

"That is too bad. I rather like Sean and his brogue. I don't suppose Highburton has any Scottish footmen? I find myself with a taste for them suddenly, rather the way a hankering for marzipan can come over me when I least expect it. Normally I am not all that fond of marzipan."

"I do not know if any are Scottish. I can hardly ask. What would I say? Excuse me, Ambury, but it would be very nice if you would send any Scots in your household, so my aunt can indulge her taste for . . . marzipan?"

"I don't see why not. If you acquitted yourself even passing well last night, he should not refuse you anything today, least of all a Scottish footman."

Had she acquitted herself well? He had stayed in her bed most of the night, so she supposed perhaps she had. Only *she* had hardly bedazzled *him*, the way Sophie implied.

Sophie eyed her over the edge of her cup while she drank her coffee.

"How *did* your wedding night fare, dear?"

Cassandra felt her face getting red. Sophie laughed.

"Thank goodness, Cassandra. I prayed that he knew his way with a woman better than that supercilious Frenchman from last winter. What was his name? Jean?"

"Jacques. I have no desire to defend him, but you are very opinionated for someone who was not there."

"I saw the cut of him. He looked to be a man who thought only of himself. I prayed last night that Ambury had at least some consideration, what with your being married to him. A lifetime is too long to have a lover who is not generous."

"That was thoughtful of you."

"Were my prayers answered?"

They had been answered so well that Cassandra did not want to talk about it. Doing so might break the spell. "He will suit me in this one way at least, if you must know."

"That *is* good news." Sophie stood and reached for her bonnet. "I am going into the garden. Will you join me?"

"I must visit Emma, who is so shocked she may need salts. Her letter this morning was illegible. I came to tell you about the change in guard, and to assure you that your safety is being seen to, as promised. I am to tell you that you should not go out, if you have a sudden interest in doing so. Ambury says it will be much harder to keep Gerald from you if you are abroad in town."

"I never go out. You know that. I do, however, believe that having handsome footmen attend on me here is a brilliant idea. I wonder why I never considered it in the past."

Cassandra found not only Emma receiving her when she entered Southwaite's drawing room but also the earl himself. It was clear that Southwaite had no intention of waiting to hear the details from his wife, let alone from Ambury later in the day. Men could be such insatiable gossips, even though they would never admit such a thing.

"Your letter astonished us," Emma said. "I could barely hold a pen straight to respond. You must tell us what happened." She glanced meaningfully at her husband, then caught Cassandra's eye. *Leave out what you want while he is here, but later I expect to hear it all.*

Cassandra shared the story as simply as she could. She made it a point to express her gratitude that Ambury had been so noble and honorable.

Southwaite took it all in. "I am sure that I do not need to tell you what this means, and what is expected of you now."

She wanted to be good. Truly she did. But this man tended to bring out the worst in her when he used that arrogant tone.

"Rest assured that explaining my duties will not be necessary. My mother did the honors long ago. Not only was my education complete, but my new husband and I have reviewed the lessons very recently." She fished for her watch and looked at it. "Indeed, I was last schooled a mere four hours ago—quite memorably, in fact."

Southwaite flushed. He looked ready to explain that he referred to different duties than she did.

Emma giggled. Southwaite flushed all the more.

"I would not think of spelling it out," he said. "Should any drilling be necessary, I will leave it to Ambury."

As soon as he left, Emma burst out laughing. "He is rarely as bawdy as that parting comment, Cassandra. Now, I am bursting with questions, and I expect detailed answers."

"Not too detailed when it comes to my recent lesson, I think. Southwaite would have apoplexy. Or are we allowed to be bawdy ourselves now that I am married too?"

"I think it is more acceptable, at least. We will save that part, but otherwise you must tell me all. I finally heard the gossip about the two of you, and assumed you would brave it out as you always have. Whatever induced you to agree to marry him? He had no choice except to offer, of course, but—"

"It was either Ambury or living out my life counting sheep on the Scottish border. Worse, I failed my aunt in every way. My brother outflanked me, and this was the only way to save her from him."

She described the drama to Emma, including most of its scenes. She was just finishing when the door opened and Lydia strode in.

"I was on my way to call on you when the butler said you were here," Lydia said. "My maid said she heard the most astonishing rumor that you had married. You must tell me it isn't so."

"It is so, and in Ambury she has found a worthy match," Emma said.

Lydia threw herself into a chair and closed her eyes. "I cannot believe it. Not only a marriage after all these years, but a predictable one at that. How disappointed I am in you, Cassandra. Had it been an actor or a highwayman, even a writer, I would take consolation in your extraordinary choice, but Ambury—how dull for an earl's daughter to marry an earl's heir."

"Ambury is not dull, Lydia," Cassandra said.

"You are being very rude," Emma added. "At least take joy in knowing that now her friendship will not be denied you. Her dull, predictable marriage should have the predictable result with her reputation. No one will dare stand against Ambury on the matter. He has pulled her back from the brink, one might say."

Lydia opened her eyes. They brightened as she considered Emma's silver lining. "That is true, I suppose. We can still go out of an evening together. He will allow that, won't he? He is not going to treat a mature woman of your fame and experience like a child, I hope."

"I expect to have the same freedom of movement as in the past." She did not really know if she would. She had neglected to negotiate that part with Ambury before accepting his proposal. She had been at a disadvantage, and he had known it.

"I expect that I can accommodate myself to this, then. I am still disappointed, but I will muddle through."

"Oh, that is good news," Cassandra said.

Emma smirked, but Lydia missed the dry tone. "I hope that he proves to be a good lover," she said. "A marriage of obligation is probably much less horrible if the groom is skilled in that area." Lydia, calm now, played idly with the ends of her bonnet's ribbons. "And he has a very nice physique when he is naked, too, so that is a point in his favor.

Now you can admire his hard bum whenever you like, Cassandra."

Utter stillness descended in the chamber. Cassandra's breath caught, and she could not exhale. She felt Emma turn into an immobile statue beside her. Lydia toyed with her ribbons, oblivious to the grave error she had just made.

"Lydia, dear," Emma said, her voice thick as syrup. "How is it you know so much about naked physiques, hard bums, and skilled lovers?"

"Women of the world know all about those things. Don't we, Cassandra?"

Cassandra managed one deep breath. Mortified, she glanced askance at Emma. Emma appeared quite severe in the way she peered at Lydia.

"I think, Cassandra, that this marriage of yours has happened just in time to avert utter ruin," Emma whispered.

"I could have lived it down. If not for Aunt Sophie's situation with Gerald, I would have."

"I am not speaking of your ruin, but that of your partner in crime over there."

Pure sound penetrated the silence. Isolation, clarity, and precision built invisible walls and ladders. Yates indulged in the music's peace, and the structures formed on which thoughts organized themselves without effort.

The bow moved. The notes swam. Something like joy lightened him. That was rare, and almost odd. This had never been about pleasure.

Even so, mental patterns formed and arranged. Unexpected relationships presented themselves like bits of dreams. As always, a few perplexed him, but he knew better than to disregard the unexpected.

He let his mind float down a direction never seen before, curious where it would go. Much like the melody itself, variations unfolded regarding facts known too well.

The possibilities fascinated him. He tried to push them further, but suddenly the cloud in which he existed split down its center as if made of china. He stopped playing and looked around. The door of his dressing room that gave on to the apartment's passage stood ajar.

He set aside the instrument. Grabbing his coat from where he had thrown it, he walked down the passage to Cassandra's chambers.

The maid fussed with Cassandra's hair in the dressing room.

"I will be finished here soon," Cassandra said. "My bonnet took a bigger toll than normal this morning."

"I did not know you were going out."

"I called on Emma. An early letter came that begged for explanation, and she insisted I not stand on ceremony and wait for afternoon."

He wondered how that explanation to Emma had gone. *I was trapped by circumstances and have to make the best of it now.*

"Did you need me for something? If so, I apologize," she added while she waved the maid away.

"Only your company at breakfast."

She checked her reflection one more time, then stood. "Is that all? Then I am sure you did not mind my absence."

He had minded more than he would have expected. When he had told her last night that they would visit his father this afternoon, he had not expected her to disappear all morning. She had set aside their intimacy faster than he had, it seemed, and gone about her day with a most practical indifference to the events of the night.

"Will I do?" she asked, looking down on her muslin dress. It fell in a white column from the blue ribbon binding the high waist. Some filmy fabric filled the area above the neckline, hiding the upper swells of her breasts. He saw them in his mind anyway, and the rest of them rising as she arched her back and—

"He will think you are lovely, because you are."

"What am I to say to him? He disapproves of me and this marriage."

"I did not say he disapproves."

"You did not say all went well when you told him last night either." Her posture firmed. "Let us go now before I lose my courage."

He took her hand, and they walked to the stairs and descended to the earl's apartment.

"Did you come through the passage while I was playing?"

"I was waiting for the maid, and I thought to tell you about my visit to Emma. I did not mean to intrude. I will stay on my side of the apartment in the future."

"That is not necessary."

"You are kind to say so, but it may be best. Especially when you play, I think. I saw how it is a private experience, Ambury. I had not understood that before." They reached the doors to the earl's apartment. Her attention focused on the wooden panels. She bit her lower lip. "Will you stay with me during this ordeal, or am I to be left alone with him?"

He squeezed her hand. "I will stay with you."

Cassandra had not seen the Earl of Highburton up close in years. His poor health had restricted his public life for some time, and she had never moved in his circles anyway. Now she approached him with Ambury at her side. Her nerves ran riot with her composure. Only the training of a lifetime kept her collected and presentable.

The earl sat in a large upholstered chair near a window. The countess was nowhere to be seen. A valet blended into the far shadows. A voluminous robe de chambre enveloped the earl in garnet silk. A cravat swathed his neck, and the crisp linen of a shirt could be seen beneath it. His hair, fashionably cropped for a man his age, had not turned white yet.

Rather it had the mottled black and steely gray that made him appear younger than his years.

He turned his head when they neared. Even illness and the years could not make him anything but handsome, with his blue eyes and regular features. The resemblance of father and son struck her at once. Twenty or so years hence, her husband would appear much like the man waiting for them.

Ambury went over and opened the window. Then he introduced her as his wife. The earl gave her a good look, from head to toe.

"You can leave her with me, Yates. I would speak with my new daughter-in-law in privacy and come to know her."

"I think I will stay this time. The two of you can chat privately on other days."

The earl's dark scowl expressed his view of a disobedient son. He did not argue, but turned his attention on Cassandra.

"You probably think I am shocked that my son married you."

"It entered my mind that you might be, sir."

"Not so shocked. My wife told me about the gossip. I knew he would do what was right, for all his unconventional thinking. It probably helped that you are a very pretty woman."

She could think of no response.

"I knew your father. We were friends when we were young. We had drifted apart by the time he died, but I still mourned him. He was a fine man with a generous character."

A fit of coughing interrupted. The valet appeared at the earl's side, handkerchief at the ready. After a few minutes, the earl calmed, and the valet melted away.

"And his sister. Your aunt. How does she fare?" He spoke in a distracted tone, as if the coughing had robbed him of alertness.

"She flourishes, sir."

"Flourishes, does she? A good word for her, as I remember. It is good to know that she still flourishes." A critical gleam entered his filmy gaze. "As the next Countess of Highburton, it would be best if you did not flourish quite as dramatically as she did, of course."

So there it was—the scold that everyone felt obliged to give her, as if they thought she would be too stupid to know what was expected. *You had best not be careless with your reputation in the future, young woman.*

"At the same time, no one wants Cassandra's high spirits to desert her, I am sure," Ambury said. "It is her most attractive quality, and one I would never want her to lose."

She wanted to kiss him for defending her and speaking well of her at that moment. The firm smile that he gave his father perhaps did even more to curtail any further lessons.

"Your mother says you must have your own household now," the earl said to Ambury. "This will be yours so soon it seems more an inconvenience for you to establish another one for a mere few months."

"I do not think it will be a mere few months. Nor should you assume that."

"Perhaps. Perhaps. What do you say, Cassandra? Do you expect your own house? It will not be as large and fashionable as this one, that is certain. If you have a taste for luxury, you would do better to stay here."

"I will have my husband decide this question. Whatever he prefers will suit me."

The earl chortled. "She is clever enough, Yates. I will give you that. Clever and lovely and the daughter of a good man. You could do worse, I suppose. God knows that I expected you to." He raised his hand and gestured to her. "Come and give me a kiss, girl, and I will bless this marriage, such as it is."

She went over and bent down and kissed his cheek.

"You need to take her down to Elmswood Manor soon," the earl said. "Let the county neighbors meet her."

The earl's eyes closed, and Yates beckoned her away. As they were leaving, the valet appeared and reached for the casement window's knob.

"Leave it open," Yates said.

"The physician, sir—"

"The day is fair, the breeze is mild, and the physician is an ass. Leave it open."

Outside the apartment, Cassandra sank against the wall with relief. "I would rather face down all the patronesses of Almack's at the same time than ever do that again."

Ambury drew her into his embrace. "Come now, it was not that bad."

"Only because he was kind. He did not have to be, and I could not count on it. As it is, I know his acceptance is only resignation when facing a *fait accompli*."

"I do not care why he accepts, as long as he does." He gave her a kiss. "Clever, lovely, and high spirits. What he said was true. I could have done much worse."

It was a sweet thing to say. His embrace and kiss evoked echoes of the previous night's mood. The warmth woke the delicate emotional tethers that had formed, as if they were living things that had slept with dawn's rise but waited for a nudge to be active again.

She found her back pressed against the wall and her face cradled in his hands. He kissed again, differently. Deeply.

"Thank you for staying with me, so I did not face it alone," she said.

"We are in this together. This evening we will ride in the park and let the world see us that way. The announcement will be in the papers tomorrow, but word is spreading already."

"What will we do until we ride out?"

The way his body pressed hers said he had an answer to that. The next kiss was not very passionate, however. More apologetic.

"I know how I would like to pass the time. Unfortunately, you have one other visit to make today, and my company will not be tolerated on this one."

"Another visit? To whom?"

"My mother."

Chapter 19

"I can see that I am going to have to do all of this myself for the next half year or so," Kendale muttered as he snapped his riding crop lazily against his outstretched legs.

"Not that long," Southwaite said. He poured Yates more brandy, but did not even offer it to Kendale. Kendale would be on his horse for hours soon, and never drank when on a mission anyway.

"No more than five months, I would guess," Yates said.

"He is deliberately provoking you, Kendale. Forgive his high spirits. We both are grateful that you will make the ride to the coast that this letter demands."

"I would not want to have you abandon your wives so soon. Hell, who knows what dire things might happen if you were denied the pleasures of marriage for three or four days." Kendale rarely used a sarcastic tone when he mocked. The result was it often sounded like he was serious. Yates enjoyed pretending he was more often than not.

"Among the dangers is insanity," Yates said. "I read a

scientific paper on it. A groom parted too soon from his bride might go mad from the lack of release."

Kendale scowled at him. "That makes no sense. If a man could go insane from lack of release, catholic priests, university dons, armies at war, the entire naval service, and half the husbands married over three years would all be lunatics."

"One would think so, but it appears we grooms are special. The paper explained how the lack of release following the free assumption of enjoying said release was what could lead to insanity. The evidence of this truth is all around us. How often have we seen a man who, when thrown over by his mistress, turns mad? He threatens, he weeps, he stays drunk for days while he writes bad poetry and considers doing himself in." Yates sipped his brandy. "I hope you did not believe it was a broken heart causing that, Kendale, instead of something as vulgar as the anticipation of sexual frustration."

Kendale's gaze narrowed on him. Yates maintained his serious and innocent pose.

"He is taking advantage of your common sense, Kendale. Again," Southwaite said. "Neither Ambury nor I have any excuse for sending you to the coast instead of going ourselves, except our desire to—well, indulge our desire."

"It seems to me that you have both been doing that long enough to want a few days away. Don't correct me, Ambury. If you were any other man and she any other woman, perhaps your claims of innocence would have been believed. Both of you knew they would not be, so do not blame me for my assumptions."

"Then accept as my excuse my obligation to pursue a greater duty, so you do not leave thinking that I shirk that which takes you away."

"Ah, it is not pleasure that binds you here, but the need for an heir. How convenient for you that greater duty still requires you to bed your new wife."

"I referred to my need to go down to Elmswood. I have some work to do there that has been delayed by recent

events. I also need to introduce my wife to the people there."
It would be all the honeymoon Cassandra would have too.
Between his father's health and the dangers of war, they
would not be taking any lengthy journeys abroad, even
within England.

"I will end this conversation as I started it, by noting that
it will all fall to me for many months from the sounds of it."
He stood and buttoned his coat. "While I am in Kent, I will
make it clear that none of us is to be called unless the watchers have good cause. The letter you received sounded pan-
icked, Southwaite. Considering the high alarm of the country,
it is to be expected, but I grow weary of riding all that way
for nothing. My ass should not suffer for our watchers' poor
judgment."

"Do as you think best, of course," Southwaite said.

It was unnecessary to say, since Kendale always did what
he thought was best, even if the rest of them thought another
course of action would be better.

"I hope he can calm them down," Southwaite said after
Kendale left. He pawed over some letters stacked on the
table. "Some of the watchers are seeing ghost ships due to
looking too hard into the night. I spend hours each day writing back, pointing out that their breathless reports, in fact,
include nothing of note."

"Considering recent events, the network we put into place
is inadequate. It is time for the government to do something
official, and permanent."

"I believe that will happen soon. Do you remember that
series of towers that we proposed last year? Coastal defenses,
staffed by the war office, so that the watching is systematic
and the southeast coast is more secure?"

"I thought that plan had died."

"It was resurrected in early summer. The war office has
been working on a list of locations. It appears they will move
soon."

"That is good to know."

"I would have told you sooner, but you have been busy conquering Lady Cassandra and getting caught at it."

"I did not enjoy any conquest, as I told you."

"Allow me to believe you did. The idea that you found yourself obligated to marry a woman whom you did not even seduce is too dispiriting."

"The realization that she has now been redeemed and can be your wife's friend should raise your spirits enough. As for the rest that might dampen your delight, Kendale saw the situation clearly enough to host the wedding and stand witness. If he can accommodate this match, you should be able to."

Southwaite settled into the chair that Kendale had vacated and stretched out his booted legs much as Kendale had. "You entered this house this afternoon looking like a man drunk on new pleasure, so right now it appears this marriage suits you well enough, and that is what matters."

"By right now, you imply it may not when the experience ceases to be new and inebriating."

"I expect that is true of most marriages."

Not his, of course. Southwaite's confidence that his love match would never fail to suit him did not require expression. He gazed at his brandy for a spell but eventually turned his eyes toward Yates.

"Have you talked to her about Lakewood?"

"There isn't anything to say."

"Isn't there? Penthurst's upcoming trial has caused me to think about that duel quite frequently of late. I wonder if I assumed too much. I wonder if Lakewood intended for me to."

Yates did not like to think of that ugly, snowy day when Southwaite informed him and Kendale that Lakewood had just died. "As his second, surely your understanding was as sound as anyone's."

"He said Penthurst had insulted a lady. The love of his life, he said. Like you, I assumed that meant Cassandra

Vernham, but now . . ." He shrugged. "He had to be a fool to challenge Penthurst. Had he succeeded in killing a duke . . ."

"He probably did not intend to kill. Most duels do not end that way these days."

"Oh, he intended to kill. That was clear when we all met. Lakewood demanded the ultimate satisfaction. Even so, Penthurst, I am sure now, as I relive it often in my head, aimed high, for his shoulder, but Lakewood stepped into his own shot at just the wrong time." He shook his head sadly. "Hell of a thing. I suppose we will have more answers soon enough, when Penthurst goes before the lords. I will probably be called to give testimony. Hence my renewed efforts to sort out just what I saw and just what Lakewood said."

"Perhaps you think about it too much. It was what it was."

"You are more sure than I am about what it was. I would expect you to grab the ambiguity, now that you are married to her."

"I have decided she cannot be blamed for men killing each other."

"You are better than I am, if you can leave it at that."

Yates was not sure he was better at all. He had broached the topic in his head a few times, most recently last night, when, sated with her scent and softness, he had debated if clearing the air about Lakewood might be best. That old friend had become a ghost of late, a spirit that entered his mind carrying all those ambiguities like a long chain. He had told Cassandra they would not speak of it, but he wondered if the ghost would ever rest if they did not.

Now that he is dead, no one knows what really happened except me. That was what she had said. Wondering what she referred to had become yet one more link in that chain. A big one.

"I will be leaving town for two weeks," he said as he stood to take his leave. "I was not lying about having some business to address in the south."

"Your bride should be glad to escape town for a while."

"The news of our marriage has made drawing rooms more interesting of late, and a long line of ladies has called on her to satisfy their curiosity, so she is indeed looking forward to this little journey."

"I was thinking more in terms of escaping your mother."

"That is going better than hoped, but it is possible she may be glad for a holiday from that as well."

As he rode home, he considered that fortune had smiled on him regarding that last relationship. For once, his mother had decided to ignore any failings she saw. There had been no rows or awkwardness at Cassandra's first meeting with his mother, nor any since. Nor great warmth either, of course.

Their first week of marriage had progressed well. It was still new, but the comfortable familiarity forming spoke well for the years ahead. He should be more contented than he was.

He blamed himself for the irritations he experienced sometimes. They almost always afflicted him when he bumped into the hedgerows planted with his own words, when he had told her they would not speak of her past in general, and Lakewood in particular.

He had assumed that leaving all of that in the past would be best for the future. He might have been wrong.

Cassandra could tell that something was on Ambury's mind. His lovemaking was more aloof than normal. That he spoke little in the aftermath did not surprise her. That she could sense an internal distraction in him did.

She expected him to leave and devote himself to whatever occupied his head. He did not. Instead, he laid there beside her while the candles gutted and the room darkened. His right arm remained across her body, and his hand held her hip in an awkwardly possessive gesture, while his brain went wherever it might. She tried to sleep so she might not be too tired for the carriage ride down to Highburton's county seat in the morning.

"What was his name?"

Her eyes opened in surprise. She had not guessed he had been doing all that thinking about *her*.

"I am not going to tell you. You said we would not speak of it and already you have done so twice now."

"I have changed my mind."

"Change it again."

"I do not like the idea that I might meet him, and that he knows he had your love and I do not know he was the one who did."

"You will not meet him. He was not born to your circles. He is not with the kind of regiment that finds itself at your parties."

"I still want to know his name."

She sat up and pulled the sheet around her. He was little more than a collection of dark forms in the night, but she saw him clearly in her head. Saw the handsome face and the hard mouth unsoftened by one of his frequent smiles. Saw the taut muscles of the naked body that marriage gave her a right to admire now.

"I do not believe you will be any happier knowing his name, or anything about such things. I *do* know the names of some of your former lovers, and the knowing brings me no comfort. I would rather be ignorant."

"That is different. You are mine now."

Heavens, but men had such strange minds. Worse, they could be so annoying when they said things and did not hear what else their words meant. *You are mine.* He saw it going only one way, as most men did. He possessed her, but she did not possess him. *That is different.* In his mind, it *was* different, and the whole male world agreed.

"Yes, I am yours. Can you not be content with that? It is not as if you really care who he was or what I felt for him. I doubt you even resent that you were not the first. The truth is, you like having a wife that you can treat like a mistress instead of a virginal girl. You like that I am bold enough and worldly enough for more sophisticated pleasure. It is why you wanted me."

He looked at her through the dark, then sat up and reached for his robe. "Perhaps you know my mind better than I do, Cassandra. You certainly see the benefits of the marriage to me more clearly than I had. I will do as you suggest and enjoy my good fortune in the ways you recommend."

Chapter 20

Cassandra loved her bedchamber at Elmswood Manor. An abundance of windows let in beautiful northern light that filtered through trees until it assumed a cool, silvery cast. As a result, it was always dawn in the chamber, and restful and quiet.

Her apartment was larger than in London. It was all hers too. She could find no door or passage that connected to Ambury's chambers. Presumably, only the earl enjoyed such convenience with his wife here.

He found her anyway. He walked in while the maid assigned to her unpacked her portmanteau. He did not announce himself or say any word at all. He merely stood at the doorway to the dressing room until the maid noticed him and excused herself.

Thinking a husband's sense of privilege could be inconvenient sometimes, Cassandra began a bit of unpacking herself. Ambury watched with his shoulder resting against the wall and his arms crossed.

"We will dine at Trotwood Park with the Witherspoons. They are a prominent gentry family and important in the county," he said. "Tomorrow morning, we will ride out so the servants and tenants can see you."

"Then I should hang this out at once." She pulled out her riding dress and shook it out with a flourish. He did not get the hint that she was more likely to appear presentable if he allowed the maid back to do her duty.

"The next day, I will have to leave for a few days. I need to ride south to visit some property."

"Is this part of your obligations to your father and the estate?"

"One of the more inconvenient ones."

"I will use the time to get to know the people here. I may do better on my own anyway, since they are too much in awe of you." She looked to the door through which the maid had disappeared. "Or else, perhaps, afraid of you, if they are young, pretty things."

"I have never importuned a servant, and do not expect to ever consider it in the future."

"That is good of you."

"Do not attribute more restraint to me than I deserve. I shall never consider it, because I have a wife at my beck and call now. So actually, it is good of *you*."

"Beck and call? I hope you do not plan to bellow through the house for me when you feel randy. Will you send your valet or a footman?"

"More likely I will just walk in the door."

As he had recently done. Unpacking had distracted her from the mood he projected. Interested. Restless and a little dangerous. Ambury, when in pursuit, created a subtle but undeniable disturbance in the air of a space. An exciting one. It assaulted her now, and she stirred in response. Over the last week, her body had shed any inhibitions about meeting desire with desire.

He watched while she set out a few items for her toilet,

on the dressing table. Then she went into the bedchamber. "I think this is the most lovely chamber I have ever used. All the white linens, pale paint, lace trim, and plump pillows make it look like a Boucher painting."

"All that is missing is a beautiful naked woman displaying her pretty bottom on that bed." He lowered himself onto the palest blue chair and reached for her. He turned her around and released the fastenings on her dress. "You will have to paint that in."

"Is that a beck or a call, Ambury?"

"It is a command, Cassandra. Men do not beckon their mistresses."

He was throwing her words from last night back at her. His manner dared her to play the worldly role she had told him he expected.

No, not dared, she decided when she turned around and saw how he waited and watched. Commanded, just as he said. Nor was she certain this would be a game.

She should not like the subtle ways that affected him, but her body did. Lowering her dress titillated her. Ambury's hot, hard gaze caused hundreds of tiny, thrilling shivers when she slid her chemise off her shoulders. Soon she stood in front of him wearing nothing but her hose.

He appeared far too composed to her. Too in command of them both, as he intended. Deciding to even the score a bit, she went to his chair, nestled her knee at his crotch, and angled to kiss him. She did it more aggressively than normal, and she felt the effects in the bulging firmness against which her knee pressed.

She broke the kiss and waited for his mouth to move to her body. Instead, he gave her one small kiss on her cheek. "Get on the bed, Cassandra."

A little disappointed, she walked to the bed. It was a big one that required she climb up. She threw herself down across it. She lay on her stomach and rose on her forearms to watch him.

Ambury stood and undressed. It did not take long. It reminded her of that day on the coast, when he had stripped to bathe in the sea. The drapes in the chamber had not been drawn, so the cool light showed his lean strength just as the brilliant sun had that day. They had seen each other undressed enough, but this was the first time since that day that she had seen him naked in clear light.

He knelt one knee beside her and kissed between her shoulders. Another kiss on her back. One more at the base of her spine. Then she felt him behind her, lifting her hips.

"Kneel."

A profound tremor shook down her center and pooled in her vulva. She knelt, and he arranged her so her bottom rose higher than her back. Her position and vulnerability created a compelling mix of anticipation and fear. Her breasts rasped against the sheets, arousing her all the more.

He touched her, and immediately frantic hunger possessed her mind. It was not a touch designed for pleasure. He did not tease or caress. He stroked deeply, making her ready for him. As soon as she was, he thrust inside her so deeply that her breath caught.

He took her then. Took his pleasure while he held her body for his use. She found hers too, a savagely erotic pleasure stripped of artifice or tenderness. He ravished her, and she reveled in it. She climaxed first, before his final ruthless thrusts brought his own completion. He released her then, and they collapsed on the bed in a tumble of nakedness.

She did not drift in sated bliss afterward. She lay on her side with his strong warmth behind her, starkly awake and alert to the difference in what had just happened.

It had been amazing in its way, but she would not have liked it the first time with him, or every time. She could not ignore that there had been few preliminaries and damned little intimacy. No kissing or caresses. No deliberate arousals of her breasts and body. On occasion, this would be exciting. If it were every night, she did not think she would like the cold indifference it would imply.

She waited for some sign that today did not herald how it would be from now on. Anything at all would do, even a kiss on her shoulder. Surely he did more with his mistresses than ensure they had a climax.

He moved, and she felt the bed respond as he left it. She closed her eyes, and the sounds of dressing came to her. Then his steps crossed the chamber.

She thought he had left and opened her eyes. Instead, she found him standing near her, looking down. He reached over and slid his fingertips down the side of her face in a caress that moved aside some wild strands of her hair. "I will tell them to prepare a bath for you."

Then he was gone.

She sat up in the middle of the damp sheets and erotic smells of the bed. A bath and one caress. It was something, at least.

Yates stopped his horse at the top of a low rise of land. He surveyed the landscape in front of him. It was mostly flat, and the nearby sea had intruded to create an uneven and changeable coast in the distance. Tracks of marsh alternated with farmland that hugged what high ground could be found.

He had to laugh at himself when he saw the unpromising vista. He should have listened to his father and left this alone. No wonder the dispute had never been investigated. If the rest of the property looked like this, he was on a fool's errand. Better if he had stayed at Elmswood with Cassandra.

Since he had ridden this far, he went the rest of the way. A half hour later, he approached a flock of sheep being herded by two dogs and a man. Yates hailed the fellow who gave him a solid inspection before returning the greeting. His garments suggested the man was not a shepherd but a tenant.

He wore a coat that while old still bestowed the appearance of a squire.

Yates swung off his horse and introduced himself. Mr. Harper, who had pointedly taken note of Yates's coats and saddle, brightened when he realized his visitor was a lord.

"Come to see about some defenses here, finally?" he asked. "I don't know what it takes for Parliament and the services to act. I've seen lights on the swamps at night that say someone is up to no good. Some men were here in June seeing what was what, and I told them that. Now with the Irish all but handing their western coast to the enemy—I'm thinking of sending my wife to her family up north, for protection."

Yates gazed to the coast. It was not far from here to Southampton, and he doubted there was any danger. Mr. Harper no doubt felt vulnerable, however. The terrain might not be hospitable to French landings, large or small, but it also meant isolation for the few who lived here.

"I do not speak for the army or navy," Yates said. "But I will report what I see to those responsible."

Mr. Harper decided that was an invitation to show him everything. He pointed to the spots where he claimed to have seen lights, and led to an especially swampy area to point out an abandoned boat. The boat appeared half rotted to Yates, and he guessed it had been there many years already.

He let Harper talk, for the man had much to say. It was not until an hour later, as they walked up to where the dogs kept the sheep waiting, that he broached his real reason for being here.

"Are you a tenant, Mr. Harper? Or is this land yours?"

"I hope if I ever own land it is better than this, sir."

"Who does own it, then?"

"Well now, that is not clear."

"You must pay your rents to someone."

Mr. Harper laughed. "Money leaves my purse, that is sure. Whether and how it lands in another's after that, I do not know."

"Surely it lands in the purse of the person with whom you signed as a tenant."

"One would think so. That is how I expected it. But my family signed with one person, then it was sold to another."

They waded into the flock. The sheep shuffled along like a large, flat, formless animal with many little hooves.

"With whom did you sign?"

"A land agent. My father told me the property was High-burton's when we took it. This was, oh, a good thirty years ago he told me that, and my family has been here twice that long. But at some point another land agent began coming for the rents, back when I was a boy. When I took over, I told him we needed some improvements and to ask Highburton about them. That was when I learned it wasn't his any longer."

Yates judged Mr. Harper to be in his forties. Back when he was a boy was a long time ago. Whatever dispute had entangled this property had done so well in the past.

"What is the name of the land agent who collects now?"

Mr. Harper peered at him skeptically. "You be wanting to talk to him? If you think to buy it, you need to know that it is good for naught but sheep, and barely for that. So there's no point in thinking of more rents."

"No one is looking to raise the rents. I am sure whoever owns this land is grateful for your long tenancy, and any future owner would not want it to end. I am asking for a family member who has expressed interest. I can see it is good for little, but I promised to look into it."

"Well, now, if the rents stay the same, not much difference to me who has an interest. The man I dealt with stopped coming years ago. No one comes now. I send the rents to town now, to the Bank of England."

It sounded as if the property were held in a trust. If so, it might be difficult to learn much more about it.

He thanked Mr. Harper and mounted his horse to ride the rest of the property and see if it had as little to offer as this section did.

* * *

Cassandra rearranged herself on the library's divan and propped her book on her stomach. While she enjoyed Ambury's company, the last two days alone had been very pleasant. These were the first hours she had enjoyed on her own since she went to Mama's house, and she had missed being with her own thoughts and with no obligations for conversation.

Gently crisp air entered the window nearby. It contained just enough of autumn's scents and chill to announce that summer's heat would not return for many months now.

She wondered if Ambury had been glad for an excuse to leave for a few days. He was no more used to the constant company than she was. True, their sojourn here had permitted a variety of sensual explorations, and no man minds that.

In saying he liked having a wife he could treat as a mistress, she had given him permission to do just that, it appeared. The result had been astonishing. A few of his commands had even shocked her, although she never let him know that. There were gestures of affection too. And yet— an essential intimacy had been lost from their first nights together, even if the pleasure more than satisfied on every count.

He did not mind the hours in bed, then. He also appeared to enjoy the dinners to which the county neighbors had invited them, and the long rides to inspect the estate. Still, such frequent companionship was not normal between husband and wife, and she suspected he longed for town and his clubs and more varied activity.

The fair day beckoned, and she set aside the book to go stroll in the garden. Her path took her through the big gallery. It was a tall, wide, and fairly gloomy space. Dark paintings lined its walls, and few of them offered much interest. Many of them could not even be deciphered. She decided that she would ask Emma for instructions on how to clean them.

The light today permitted more to be seen than in her past viewings, and she stopped to admire a landscape that had caught her eye before. Today she noticed it included some tiny figures in the middle ground of the scene. Two of them carried something, perhaps a shrouded body. The lush and extensive landscape overwhelmed whatever burial had been depicted.

Several portraits hung above the landscape, stacked in a vertical row all the way up to the molding. Her gaze followed the line up to the picture of a woman at its top. The woman's eyes arrested her attention, then her mouth and the line of her jaw. The resemblance to Ambury was remarkable. The woman's regalia marked her as a past countess, and from the fashions she wore, perhaps his great-grand—

Her thoughts halted. Her gaze froze on the woman's powdered wig and the earbobs dangling beneath its overwrought curls.

She squinted hard at those jewels. Aging varnish obscured them badly, but—unless her eyes failed her—it appeared that beneath the yellow haze, sapphires hung from settings holding large diamonds.

Piercing disappointment stabbed her heart.

Ambury had indeed been investigating her aunt, but not for some nameless individual. He thought the earrings had been stolen from his own family.

Her mind jolted into a scramble of thoughts regarding what that meant and whether his promise to protect Aunt Sophie had been honest. She cursed herself for carelessness while she strode back and forth beneath the eyes of that ancestor.

I will, however, promise to protect her, no matter what, so long as it does not compromise my honor. A lot of good that would do if he concluded Aunt Sophie was a thief.

She cursed herself again, for not seeing what he was up to and for not understanding how he qualified his promise. She needed to talk to Sophie and be very pointed in demanding the truth, so she would be able to find her own way to offer protection.

While she debated and plotted, a footman entered the gallery. He bore a salver on which a letter rested. She recognized her aunt's hand from five feet away and rushed to take the letter. She told the footman to wait because she intended to jot a quick reply. While he retreated, she opened the seal.

"Danger! Drama! Another Rescue! That is what I write to you about, dear Cassandra," Sophie's letter began. Alarmed, she devoured the rest.

"Your tedious brother came to the house to remove me again. Fortunately, Highburton's footmen refused him entry. Thank goodness you arranged for Angus to replace Sean"— Cassandra had arranged nothing. If one Scot had replaced another, it had been a coincidence. "There is nothing like a Scot built like an oak to send a coward like Gerald running. What a disappointment Gerald is to me!

"He threatened something about the law and a solicitor and a forthcoming summons to Chancery. Angus sent at once for Southwaite. The denouement is I have been moved to Emma's house, but Southwaite cannot ignore a court summons if one arrives, and it is only a matter of time before Gerald discovers I am here. I am sure that I have sanctuary until you return to town, however, and we will decide what to do then.

"You are not to worry, dear. All is well for now."

Not worry? Her brother was acting like a madman. He had to know by now that she had married and was out of his reach. His pursuit of Aunt Sophie should have ended now that it lacked any coercive power.

Instead, he had tried to abduct Sophie again. As punishment for Ambury thwarting him? In retaliation for ruining his plans? Perhaps it had been nothing more than an expression of his pique and anger. Who knew how long he would continue on this path?

All kinds of potential developments raced through her

head. She could return to town next week and find Sophie gone, and Gerald named her guardian.

She dared not risk that.

She strode down the gallery to the waiting footman and sent him for the butler.

London was asleep by the time Yates stopped his horse after a grueling ride with minimal rest. He tied the animal in front of his family home, then let himself in. The servant manning the entry startled out of a dream when he shook the man's shoulder. Embarrassed, the servant jumped to his duties and set about having the horse cared for.

Yates mounted the stairs to his chambers. Inside, he stripped off his coats and shirt and washed with water a servant brought up. Higgins had been left at Elmswood to follow in a carriage, so he did for himself.

Once Yates learned that Cassandra had departed Elmswood Manor in haste, he had himself done the same, even though it was not clear if that were necessary. All Yates learned from the butler was that a letter had come that called her back to town. Her own explanation—a brief note saying the letter had come from her aunt—hardly illuminated matters.

He expected to find the entire household asleep, so it surprised him to see the line of light at the bottom of Cassandra's door when he looked down the narrow passageway. He had assumed he would wait until morning to find out why his bride had bolted without more than a one-sentence explanation. That light raised concerns that banished the irritation he had carried with him all those hours on horseback.

Perhaps her aunt had suffered some accident or illness. Maybe the situation had turned tragic. He did not like to think of Cassandra sitting in her chamber all alone if that were true.

Pressing the door open, he saw her sitting at her writing desk, intent on whatever she scribbled. The light from her lamp gave her profile a golden glow. Her eye appeared very dark, and her lashes very thick, and the tumble of curls falling down her back had already escaped whatever discipline a brush had imposed.

Picking up a small chair by its back frame, he set it down beside the desk so it faced her, then sat. She set her pen in its holder and slid her letter under the blotting paper.

"I did not expect you for several days," she said. "I told the butler to tell you that you should complete what you needed to do in Essex, and that I would manage here on my own."

"He is too discreet, and wise, to ever pass on a message like that. He would worry that I would not take well my wife giving me permission to act this way or that, and he probably feared that I might blame the messenger if I heard it."

Those dense lashes lowered, obscuring whether she hid sparks of humor, regret, or rebellion from his view. "My apologies. I left in such a rush that I did not think of the proper way to do it."

"There was no *proper* way to do it."

Ice entered her tone. "Was there not? Even when an emergency changes one's plans?" She fished through some papers on the corner of the desk, plucked one out, and handed it to him.

He read Sophie's dramatic salutation, then the rest. "It appears that Southwaite had matters well in hand. Your aunt herself writes that you were not to worry."

"She also writes that Gerald threatened to bring the issue to the courts. Southwaite could not disobey any summons to produce her, and had no standing to defend her. It was incumbent on me to find another place for her, quickly, where she would be safe and where Gerald would never think to look."

He tapped the letter against the desk's wood while he decided whether to have the row that was waiting now or later. She stared at him, not cowed in the least.

"Where did you move her?"

"I think it would be better if you did not know."

"You are my wife. I am responsible for your actions. I need to know what you have done, whether you think it a good idea or not."

"You are no more likely to refuse the courts than Southwaite. You might bar the door to Gerald, but you will not disobey a summons."

"And you would?"

"If necessary, yes."

"I cannot permit that."

The look she gave him said what wisdom kept her from speaking aloud. *It does not matter what you will permit.*

"I always knew you were bold enough, Cassandra, and not given to obeying rules that you did not accept. I can't be surprised that you refuse to be an obedient wife, I suppose."

"I am obedient enough, Ambury. Since I married you to protect her, you cannot be surprised that I will disobey you to do so too, however."

The row still waited, like a storm on the horizon. It made the air brittle and their conversation pointed. The gaze she gave him dared him to stir those dark clouds, as if she welcomed a good tempest.

For the first time he wondered if in the name of honor he had condemned himself to life with a stranger. Not because she had so quickly abandoned their honeymoon without a thought for his feelings. Not even because her loyalty to her aunt took precedence over her loyalty to him. And not because she had equated their marriage to the arrangement between mistress and protector, and had tempted him into doing the same.

The real reason he wondered was in the way that she watched him.

She did not trust him.

"Tomorrow I will explain to you what I expect and don't

expect about some of your behavior in the future. For now, let us just go to bed."

She looked at his naked chest and a question entered her eyes.

"I will bid you good night, Cassandra." He stood and walked away. "I have been riding too long to have much heart for giving my wife lessons of any kind tonight."

He strode to his bedchamber. No lamp had been lit there, and he could not be bothered with bringing the one from the dressing room. Without undressing further, he fell onto the bed and was half asleep before his face hit the coverlet.

His hand felt a bulge beneath it. He flexed his fingers and groped. Velvet and lumpy, the bulge gave off various tiny sounds from its contents.

Curious, he got up and carried the discovery into his dressing room. As soon as the lamp there illuminated it, he knew what it was.

He opened the velvet purse's drawstring and poured the contents into his palm. Sapphires and diamonds flashed. A folded paper floated to the floor. He picked it up.

> *I retrieved these from Prebles this afternoon. The thirty days were up. Since our circumstances have changed, I give them to you at no cost. Return them to the family treasury, Ambury. As the future countess, they will eventually be mine again, I expect.*

He set down the jewels and the note that made clear Cassandra now knew why he had been so insistent in wanting to know how they came into her aunt's possession. No wonder she had been so cold tonight, and so wary of him. Of course she did not trust him now, if she ever had.

Chapter 21

Cassandra rose early, putting a merciful end to a very restless night. The reunion with Ambury had played in her head the whole time she stayed in bed, and she hoped that getting dressed would exorcise the uncomfortable memories.

She had never seen him truly angry before, but had guessed he would not be the type of man to bellow and yell. Instead, his mood poured out of him with silent intensity. His face possessed the ability to become quite hard when he did not soften it with smiles and wit. Last night, when he sat down in that chair that he swung beside her writing table, he had appeared carved out of ice.

The depth of his anger made no sense. He knew where she had gone, and why. True, the plan had been to spend two weeks together down at Essex, and become used to each other as a married couple. Theirs had not been some love match, however, and her departure had hardly interrupted a sought-after romantic tryst.

She left the house dressed for the day and strode toward Oxford Street. No matter how much she talked herself through it, his obvious displeasure had left her unsettled and a little sad. Her reaction made even less sense than his behavior. Of the two of them, *she* was the one who had a right to be angry, not him. He had no cause to get all lordly with her about it. He definitely could not claim that she had wounded him.

She paused in her tracks as that word came to her. She had sensed that in him, along with a masculine dismay. She tried discarding the notion as even less logical than all the others. She was incapable of wounding Ambury, of that she was sure. Yet she could not shake the feeling that last night's conversation had revealed a new fissure between them that had not been among the other ones when they said their vows at Kendale's house.

The melancholy swelled inside her again. The sadness included a sense of loss, perhaps for the easy familiarity she and Ambury had shared. She marched on, hoping the dull weight on her spirit would ease as the day wore on.

An hour later, she stepped out of a hackney in front of Fairbourne's auction house. The building appeared cold and still. She trusted Emma had received her letter yesterday and had made the arrangements that she had requested. Upon finding the front door unbolted, she knew it had been done.

Further evidence that all was in order showed on the big gallery wall. A few paintings hung there, including the odd primitive one that had so entranced Emma when it arrived for examination.

Emma came out of the office, looking fresh and lovely in a pale green dress that complemented her golden brown hair. She gave Cassandra a kiss, then stood back and crossed her arms. "What are you up to? Southwaite is not pleased that you spirited your aunt away while he was absent from the house. He instructed me to find out where you took her."

"It would be better if he did not know, which means you should not know either."

"His concern is for her safety. I hope that you know that, Cassandra. He has no desire to see your brother take her away."

"Your husband is a part of the government and sworn to uphold the rule of law. Please do not press me for her whereabouts, Emma. You know I am right to keep it a secret."

"Even from Ambury?"

"Yes." Especially Ambury.

"Will you stand against the whole world, and all alone at that? And now this business with Herr Werner. Am I to know why you had me invite him to see these paintings?"

Herr Werner was the private emissary to Count Alexis von Kardstadt, a member of Bavaria's royal family, who had brought his master's art collection to London last spring. The count's paintings had been the main attraction at the Fairbourne auction where Cassandra also sold her jewels.

Herr Werner knew how Aunt Sophie amassed her jewels, because the count had been one of the lovers who had bestowed some upon her. Cassandra hoped to convince him to explain that to Ambury, to put an end to any suspicion that Sophie had stolen them.

"I assume he is here not only to sell but to buy as well. With the funds from that auction weighting down his purse, I thought your auction house might be a good place for him to lighten his load."

"How good of you to have Fairbourne's best interests at heart. I know there is more to it than that, but I will allow you to keep your own counsel on this matter too, if you insist."

Cassandra took Emma's hands. "Are you hurt that I am not confiding in you? Should I tell you everything and leave you to debate with yourself what you should tell your husband if he demands it of you? I never want to be the reason for you to know his displeasure."

Emma smiled ruefully and squeezed her hands. "It has

become complex, has it not? This friendship we have, now that we are married? I am not hurt, but I do worry about you."

Cassandra began to reassure her, but sounds out on the street distracted them both. The fancy coach that Herr Werner had taken to using in London had stopped outside the building.

H err Werner looked quite different from how he had in the early summer. Some fashionable haircutting gave his blond locks a tousled crop. His garments had lost the military flavor from when he first came. As he approached Emma, he displayed all the deference he had earlier shown her husband, but a twinkle of familiarity entered his eyes, perhaps due to his knowing her when she was merely an auctioneer's daughter.

"Countess." He kissed her hand. "It was kind of you to think of my lord, regarding the rarities your family has discovered. I am eager to see them."

"You will not be disappointed. You remember Lady Cassandra Vernham, now the Viscountess Ambury, I am sure. She has also come to examine the paintings."

"Of course. Lady." He kissed Cassandra's hand in turn. "I am doubly blessed by the invitation now. I am so glad that I was in town. I rarely have been the last few months. The hospitality of so many of your gentlemen has meant that I could tour your fascinating country."

"Let us view the art together, Herr Werner, and chat about your travels as we do," Cassandra said. She accepted his agreement and his arm. She looked over her shoulder at Emma as they strolled toward the wall, and shook her head when Emma took one step to follow.

They stood in front of the little peculiar primitive painting that Emma liked. Herr Werner seemed as befuddled by its value as she was. She repeated what Emma had said about it being very old.

"Have you been shooting in the counties as you toured?" she asked as they moved on.

"How did you guess? The brown of my face, no? Even a good hat does not spare one from hours in the sun. I acquitted myself with the muskets very well, I am relieved to say. As the count's representative, I would not want to appear a clumsy fool."

The count's representative now, no longer the count's servant. Herr Werner had been elevating himself over the months in England, which explained the generous hospitality from those gentlemen.

She bent to examine the Dutch painting that depicted the interior of a house. "The woman in this reminds me of my aunt."

He peered as well. "I trust Lady Sophie is faring well."

"She is as well as when you saw her in March. You were the last person she received, however, and the only one in almost a year. I suppose that makes your friendship exceptional."

"The honor was not mine, but the count's, and the friendship as well."

"He must have been happy to learn you had retrieved the ruby. It was a magnificent piece. I was sorry to lose it." She probably saw a twenty percent decrease from the auction after Sophie made her turn over the ruby and pearl necklace to Herr Werner.

"He was more relieved than happy, I believe. It is an important family piece, with a long history, and it belongs in the family treasury."

"He must have been intoxicated to give it away," she said with a laugh. "I have heard that my aunt had that effect on men. It was good of her to understand that his regrets were not for their passion, but for his intemperate generosity. A different woman might have sent you off empty-handed."

Herr Werner's gaze remained on the Dutch painting.

"The count is very generous, and he had no regrets, that is true. But he is not a fool when it comes to women, and he is never intemperate enough to give away family jewels to a passing lover."

He moved on to the next painting. Cassandra stayed in place, trying to conquer her wrenching disappointment. Herr Werner had just let her know that necklace had not been a lover's gift. The implication was damning to Aunt Sophie. And what about all those other jewels?

She had been blind not to see it, even years ago. Herr Werner was right—counts did not give away the family treasury to lovers and mistresses. They bought new jewels if they wanted to give gifts to those women.

To have family pieces seen bedecking the body of a paramour—she had thought those little notes had been written so Aunt Sophie ensured that never happened. Now it appeared the notes might have only intended to make sure that this peer or that prince did not know who had taken the treasures to begin with.

No. She would *not* think such things of Aunt Sophie. It was unfair and unworthy to do so.

Herr Werner walked back to her. "Perhaps I should have been more discreet. I had assumed you knew, since you gave up the necklace so easily yourself. You must understand—I cannot have anyone saying the count demands the return of gifts he gave freely. It impugns his honor."

"Are you suggesting they were not freely given? I doubt she held a gun to his head before he made a gift of them to her."

"You are distraught now, and angry. I am sorry. Let us say that there was a misunderstanding that resulted in your aunt's acquisition of the jewels. That was the count's way of putting it in the letter he wrote to her, and she accepted his view of it as soon as she read his words."

A misunderstanding? What sort of misunderstanding

could there be? The count was a scoundrel who had regretted his gift after the affair had cooled, that was all. The only other alternative was unthinkable.

A memory came to her anyway. A recent one, of Aunt Sophie all gray and quiet, slipping into Ambury's library while his valet was distracted by someone else.

Then others rushed in, from her tour with Sophie, of being the center of attention at salons, bedazzling nobles the way Sophie used to, while Sophie faded away. Surely her aunt had not been in dressing rooms, poking into jewel boxes. It was wrong even to wonder about such a thing. And yet . . .

Herr Werner offered his arm again. When she blindly took it, he patted her hand. "Let us view the rest of these paintings while you calm yourself, dear lady."

"It was a waste of time, as was the last summons," Kendale said. "Lights on the sea, I was told. If there were any, it was our own naval militia. The sea is thick with them, although it isn't clear what they would do if a French fleet headed their way."

He gave the report while he and Yates stood with Southwaite and watched a young gelding auctioned at Tattersall's. Men of all stripes filled the courtyard, with a thick knot of them near the shed overhang where the auctioneer touted the current offering.

Southwaite had come to sell, and perhaps buy. Yates was here to keep Southwaite company until one of his studs went on the block. He assumed Kendale had joined them so someone would hear him complain.

"They would not know what to do," Southwaite said. "You would, however. That is why it is so wise for you to be the one to answer the summons when it comes."

"Do not insult me with flattery fit for a boy. Any of us would know what to do. I keep going because you are taking advantage of me. Well, next time it will be your ass, not mine."

"It is not as if we are spending our time having fun," Yates said. "Marriage is not all pleasure. You will find out what I mean soon enough."

"Not too soon, after a testimonial like that. Hell, Ambury, you only said the vows a fortnight ago and suddenly you sound like a man married forty years."

"That is because while your ass was in the saddle, mine was on a solicitor's chair most of the day. Since marital duty occupied me, I am not in the mood to feel sympathetic for a man who has no damned obligations in that area." He returned his attention to the men milling around them, keeping his eyes out for one in particular.

"He is in a sour mood, Southwaite, and I do not think sitting in a chair is the reason. Do you know why?"

"I can guess. Have you discovered the whereabouts of Cassandra's aunt, Ambury?"

"I have not even tried yet. I expect to learn all that I require later today."

"Do you now? I expected to learn it all yesterday, and yet here I am, still in the dark."

"Is the aunt lost?" Kendale asked. "If so, you should not be standing around here. Tell me what you know, and I will help you find her."

Yates gave Southwaite a glare for mentioning the topic. "She is not lost as such. I have been assured she is in a very safe place."

"A place known only to one person," Southwaite added. "If *my wife* knew where, I am sure she would have informed me as I commanded. Since she has not . . ."

"Ahhh." Kendale mostly kept amusement off his expression, but his eyes betrayed him. "So this is why marriage is not all fun right now, Ambury. You have had a disagreement with your new bride while I was gone. Surely you are not

too surprised if she is being disobedient, since her spirit is so free of commonplace restraints."

A storm that had been brewing for two days broke in his head. "Be very careful what you say, Kendale. You are treading very close to insulting her, and I will not wait to hear it made explicit before calling you out."

Kendale's vague smile froze. His eyes turned cold. "That would make two men quick to kill for her, which is two too many. Disobedient or not, she has cast her spell. Since you are well entranced, I wish you nothing but happiness with the lovely lady." He turned and walked away.

Yates started after him, to deliver the thrashing he needed to give someone or he would burst. A grip on his arm stopped him.

"You are indeed in a sour mood," Southwaite said. "Do not allow it to turn you into a madman. What are you thinking, speaking of challenges over such a small thing?"

"He insinuated—"

"Nothing untoward. You do not like that she is refusing to tell you what you want to know, but he was correct that you cannot be surprised if she shows the same independence now as she always has."

That Cassandra had not revealed Sophie's whereabouts was the least of it. He resented like hell that she had decided he could not be trusted, and he hated the fact that her discovery about the earrings gave her some cause.

If it began and ended there, time and logic might heal all. He did not think it would, though.

Even as he spent hours today putting in place the promises he had made to her, he had seethed over her manner last night, over her precipitous departure from Elmswood, over the degree to which she intended to remain independent in every possible way. It was if she had examined their alliance, then taken a pen and drawn a box around him, and another around herself, with only one connecting line labeled *pleasure*. He did not like it. She was his wife, damn it.

He shook off Southwaite's hold. "Excuse me. I have been looking for someone, and I am going to the subscription room to see if he is there."

Only Jockey Club members had access to Tattersall's subscription room, and it served as that membership's outpost in London. Yates entered through the courtyard door. The servant standing guard greeted him.

There were no tables nor comfortable chairs. No one played cards here, and no library encouraged intellectual pursuits. A table in the center provided writing implements and paper for recording bets and wagers, but otherwise the paneled walls and high ceiling with its square skylight had spare furnishings. Mostly men came here to gamble, and the odds established in this chamber dictated those all over England for major races.

Yates had won and lost his share of those wagers in the past, but he was not here today to bet again. Instead, he looked over the men chatting and passing the time until the horse they coveted made its way to the courtyard. He spied the man he wanted when a clutch of bodies in one corner shifted, revealing him as the center of its attention.

Yates walked over and joined the fawning group. One by one, they noticed him and slid away, casting wary glances over their shoulders as they left. Soon Yates faced his quarry alone.

"It appears the whole world knows we rarely speak now, and fears this conversation will end badly," Penthurst said.

"Your upcoming trial probably has them expecting the worst. Or hoping for it. Town is dull these days, and could use some good theater," Yates said.

"Did you come over to wish me well in that trial? Or to say that you hope the unthinkable happens and I swing?"

Penthurst would not swing. Dukes never did these days,

least of all for duels. He would say it was a matter of honor, the peers would agree, and it would be over.

"I did not intend to speak of that at all, but something else."

"Of course." His tone implied the refusal to speak of that duel were a failing of character, and predictable.

Yates battled the urge to indeed speak of it, loud and long. He had spent more than six months damning Penthurst in his head for not finding a way out of that challenge, or a means to have it end differently. If he started, he would not stop, today of all days, and the men watching them now would have their drama for certain.

"I wonder if you know if the plans to set up towers on the coast are going forward," he said instead. Penthurst was an intimate friend of Pitt, and while he had refused a ministry himself, he heard almost everything before anyone else seemed to.

"Not towers as such, but the fortifications would serve the same purpose," Penthurst said. "There are some who think it is foolhardy and a waste of money. It has taken on its own life, however, since that business in Ireland."

"Is it known yet where they will build them?"

"That is currently being decided, I believe."

"By whom?"

Penthurst smiled the smile of his that could be confidential if you liked him but damned irritating if you did not. "Does Highburton have some particular location to recommend? If so, you will have to stand in line with all of the other property owners who anticipate leasing at inflated prices to the government and feeding at the trough."

"The money does not interest me. I would like a property on the list for other reasons. It could be removed later. It need never be leased, when all is settled."

Penthurst turned dark, deep-set, thoughtful eyes on him. "You are up to something. Since it is you, I know it is not the first thing that enters my mind, which is fraud. One of your investigations?"

"You could say that."

"On behalf of whom?"

"My father."

Those dark eyes just looked, deeply. "How is he faring?"

"Better. For now."

Penthurst nodded. He walked toward the center of the room, and the table. The sea of bodies parted to make an aisle for him, as if his mere proximity caused men to defer. Or to give him wide berth.

He picked up a pen. "I assume you have the location of this property."

Yates took the pen and jotted down the information. "There is a tenant leasing the most likely location, but he is sure the French come in every night, so he will not object."

Penthurst took the paper and read it. "Now that is peculiar. I can save us both time. I am sure that this property is indeed on the list already. It is not designated as Highburton's, however. It is in trust, as I remember it. The oddity of that is why I noticed it."

"Do you know who pressed to have it included?"

"No. They are not bribing *me*, after all."

"Can you find out?" It killed him to ask. The question stuck in his throat.

Penthurst let the query hang there a good while. He finally shrugged. "Possibly. I will see." He folded the paper. "I have neglected to offer felicitations on your marriage, Ambury. She is a beautiful woman. I always thought the rumors about her were started by less well-endowed ladies who were jealous."

Suddenly they were dangerously close to all that drama again. "If you thought that, why—"

"Why what?"

"Southwaite said Lakewood challenged you because he heard you insult a woman."

"A woman was at the heart of it, that part is true, but he did not challenge me over any insults that I spoke."

Then it was worse than that. The possibilities only made his mood darken. He remembered walking into Mrs. Burton's and seeing Penthurst standing beside Cassandra.

Stop thinking like a madman, or you will end up acting like an ass.

"As a gentleman, I certainly cannot identify her, of course. Not to you. Not to the peers," Penthurst said. "I suppose if it is demanded of me, and my refusal to explain is not accepted, I will swing after all."

"If so, I promise not to dance on your grave."

Penthurst's annoyance flared. "It is understandable that your loyalty was to him and not me. You had been friends for many years. However, he was not entirely the man you think he was, Ambury."

"I am sure the peers will believe that, if you say so. Considering your circumstances, I am the last man you should bother convincing. Now, I must go. I thank you in advance for helping with the property, if you can. In payment, I will give you some advice."

"What is that?"

"Crop your hair. You look antique. What was a sign of independent taste a year ago will appear merely eccentric six months from now."

"I have been thinking I might, although my mistress would pout."

"Then perhaps it is time to make a change there as well."

Chapter 22

After leaving Fairbourne's, Cassandra took a long turn in Hyde Park in order to sort things out. She was sick at heart about how badly her meeting with Herr Werner had gone. Better if she had left the entire matter alone.

He had all but said Aunt Sophie had stolen that necklace from the count. Ambury had always thought she had stolen the earrings from Highburton too, and now the evidence suggested he might have been correct.

Returning the earrings hardly resolved matters. What would Ambury do? Something honorable, which could be very bad for Aunt Sophie. It was possible that she would have been safer at Dr. Wakely's house.

She could take her aunt and run, but to where? She was no longer free and independent. Wherever she went, Ambury would have every right to follow. Nor, she admitted, did she want to run away. She had spoken vows, and honor, her honor, required that she try and keep them.

She began wondering if she could just leave her aunt

where she now resided for a good long while. The snort of a horse near her shoulder startled her out of her thoughts. She turned her head and recognized the animal at once, and his companion pulling the carriage. The coachman reined the horses in.

A footman hopped off the back of the carriage. She did not wait for him, but strode over to the carriage door. The footman hurried to open it and set down the steps, then handed her up.

Ambury sat inside. He moved so she would have the forward-facing seat. She took her time getting settled while she steeled herself for an uncomfortable ride.

"Is there some reason why you did not call for one of the family's carriages today?" he asked.

"Perhaps I thought to take a turn through the neighborhood, then changed my mind and it was easier to hire a hackney."

"I thought maybe you did not want any of the servants to know where you were going."

"That too. Since you found me when you wanted to, it appears I failed. Did you tell them to follow me?"

"I did not have to. Out of concern for your safety, the butler sent two men to keep watch over you. One returned with a report when you came here. Walking out alone is one of the things you should not do any longer, if you have created a habit of it. The town is too dangerous."

She did not like the idea that she would never be able to move without a servant in tow, but of course that was how it would be now. Emma had become accustomed to it already. Someday, however, she and Emma would have to find a way to lose their escorts and have a day to themselves, like they used to.

The park's gates showed through the window, then the houses of Mayfair. "Where are we going?"

"Not far. I have something to show you."

He seemed much like he had last night. Stern and distant. He said nothing else, however. No queries on where Aunt Sophie was. No lectures on the behavior he expected. Not one word or question about the earrings. His silence unsettled her more than a good row would.

They stopped on St. James's Square. She could see Emma's house across the way, through the trees. Ambury stepped out of the carriage, then offered his hand.

She joined him and looked around, perplexed.

"Prebles has had an estate agent looking for houses to let," Ambury said. "This appears to be the best of the lot he proposed. What do you think of it?"

She gazed up at the façade of the house behind the carriage. It was of good size, much like Southwaite's. "It is very nice. I appreciate the location near Emma."

"I thought you would. I signed the lease this morning."

He had the key with him. She stepped through airy chambers with long windows and good proportions. The house was furnished with handsome furniture that would be more than adequate.

They mounted the stairs. "When will we move here?"

"I suppose we can as soon as servants are hired. Those from Highburton's have been cleaning here today, and changing bedding."

The mistress's chambers had been decorated in creams and pale greens, with crisp toile drapes on the bed. They and the rest of the fabrics appeared so clean that she guessed they were the servants' doing.

She especially liked her new dressing room. It was not nearly as expansive as the one she currently used, but the smaller size made it more of a private retreat. It had a cozy window seat from where one could see the back gardens.

She sat down and admired the view. "I think I should like living here very much."

"I am glad." He walked over and looked down at her.

"You are beautiful in the light of this window, Cassandra. I think that I will enjoy seeing you sit here while this is our home."

The flattery surprised her. He sounded sincere, even if he still appeared less than amiable. The way he looked at her made her warm and flustered. For an instant, he did not seem as distant as he had been, even in the carriage. Something of the easy familiarity that they had forged during their first nights passed between them.

They were supposed to be having a row, not a romantic moment.

He reached into his coat and removed something. He took her hand and poured the contents of a velvet sack into her hand. The earrings.

Ah. *Now* they would have the row.

"I found these when I went to bed. And your note. They are the reason for the cold welcome I received last night, I think."

"In part. Your manner inspired a good deal of winter too."

"I had expected to spend a fortnight in private company together with you. I was slow to accept that your aunt would take precedence over all else, even your husband."

There it was. The scold that begged for an argument. Was he wounded that she had not thought of him first? Or was this only about pride and property?

Last night she might have asked, and in doing so shown how foolish his pique was. Her devotion to Sophie should not surprise him. After all, they had married because of it.

Today's events had disheartened her so much that she chose to say nothing at all.

He gestured to her palm. "How did you learn about them?"

"I saw a portrait and the woman was wearing them," she said. "That is how I know they belong to your family. Also how I know that you were investigating my aunt with all those questions about their history. You knew their ultimate provenance better than I did."

"I will not deny it. I should have explained once we married, but the earrings, and that investigation, had faded from my mind for a while."

"Since you have them back now, there is no need to turn your mind to it again."

"It is not that simple."

His tone sounded more soothing than autocratic. She would prefer the latter. He was not going to leave this alone.

"My aunt bought them at a *pawnbroker*."

"My father believes they were stolen before my grandfather died. He thinks the family was betrayed. He does not say whom he suspects, but I think he does suspect someone." He took her hand again, and closed her fingers over the jewels so she grasped them. "He asks about it. It matters to him. If not, I would have never pursued it once I repurchased them at the auction."

She would never win if she had to argue against this duty he felt to his father. "A servant must have taken them and sold them to the pawnbroker."

He looked out the window above her head. She could see he debated something. "Your aunt had a lot of jewels, Cassandra."

"Her lovers—"

"A *great many* jewels."

She could not hold her indignant pose any longer. The day had undermined her confidence in Sophie, and her strength crumbled. Everything had become too muddled. She looked away, defeated and miserable. "I beg you not to tell my brother what you suspect. He would use it most cruelly."

He cupped her chin in his hand and raised her head again.

"I said that I would protect her no matter what, as long as it did not compromise my honor."

Her heart felt like it was breaking. Protecting a thief was probably out of the question then.

"We need to know if any of her jewels were stolen," he said.

"And if they were?"

He sat beside her on the window seat. "Cassandra, if she did this with other jewels, they have to go back to their owners. I cannot have a woman living in my home who I know to be a thief who never even made restitution."

"I do not think that she can live with us now, anyway. Gerald will take her if she does. He will do it to punish me, even though I am now out of reach. It is clear he has not given up."

"I will deal with your brother. He will not dare remove a person from *my* home. Prebles is preparing a petition to Chancery that should resolve the matter for good. Your brother will not succeed in becoming her guardian instead of me, so you are not to worry about that any longer."

She took a deep breath to help her composure, but some tears blurred her sight anyway. Despite his anger from last night, despite her cold welcome, he had spent today arranging to fulfill his promise. "You have done this, even though you know—that is, even though you *suspect*—that she . . ."

"I said I would, didn't I? As for what I *suspect*—I need to find out what we are facing with her. It is time for you to let me talk to her."

"I never kept you from talking to her. She did that all on her own."

"You could have helped. You did not. You delayed and dodged instead. You avoided learning the truth, and I allowed it out of sentiment."

He *had* allowed it. If he thought his family's property had been stolen, he could have found a way to talk to Sophie. He did not have to wait thirty days for Cassandra to pry memories out of her. He could have sworn information to a magistrate, and Sophie would have had to explain herself as best she could.

"That was kind of you," she said. "I had not realized how

you restrained yourself. Was it because you did not want to have to tell your parents that the person who betrayed them was not a servant, but an old friend? Or were you just being considerate of an old woman who is no longer a threat to anyone's jewels?"

He smiled just enough for those lines near his mouth to deepen. "I think I did it to give myself time to pursue you. Also, an excuse to see you."

What a disarming thing to say. Her heart made a little girlish flip.

"So it was all part of your plot to add me to your list of conquests? I am shocked, Ambury. It is perhaps fitting justice that it all worked out so badly."

"I seem to remember you surrendering." He kissed her lips. "So I do not think it ended all that badly, for me, at least."

It touched her deeply that he said that, especially on a day that followed such a bad night. "Not all that badly for me either, if I am honest," she whispered.

He took her face in his hands and kissed her again, long enough for her to stir. Not only her body responded but her raw emotions did too. She felt a lot of care in that hold and kiss.

He watched as he brushed his thumb over her lips. "The house is ours. The bedding is new. I am of a mind to see if it all suits us."

The idea appealed to her for reasons other than pleasure. She needed to hold on to the solace that his touch gave her.

She set the earrings down on the cushion, then accepted his hand and followed him into the bedchamber.

Yates waited while Cassandra's deft fingers released the buttons on his shirt. She stood in front of him, naked, doing for him as he had done for her. Silence surrounded them. Even the sounds of the city did not penetrate this chamber that looked out over the gardens.

No servants. Not another soul on the premises. That

would change very soon, but he liked their isolation and the novelty of this place today.

She looked up at him, her eyes bright with naughty lights, while she unfastened his lower garments. Her touch deliberately worked more than buttons and fabric.

"I expected a terrible argument with you today," she said. "The kind from which couples never recover. I think perhaps you intended one, but chose another path."

He had, and in doing so, had left things unsaid that probably should not have been said anyway. It took more than vows to create trust, let alone loyalty.

She pushed down his garments and took his shaft firmly in her grasp. "I am feeling grateful today, for this house and for that petition, and for your willingness to suspect instead of know. How do mistresses show they are grateful?"

He pulled her into an embrace so he could hold her to his body. Her skin seemed cool, but warmed quickly as flesh met flesh. "A man would have to be an idiot to not be glad his wife tells him to treat her like a mistress. Yet, try as I might, I cannot think of you that way."

"Because I lack experience and skill? You are supposed to rectify that."

A man would have to be a *complete* idiot to do anything other than agree that was the plan, and move on to the next lesson. "Because you are my wife. That makes it different, I have discovered."

"How inconvenient for you."

"Hell, yes. But there it is. Even when the acts are the same, the experience is not."

"By *different*, you mean less scandalous, I suppose, and hence less exciting. More proper, and with lines drawn around what is done. I am flattered, Yates, but it is perhaps too bad for you. I was working up my nerve to be very, very bold in a manner I am told men expect of their mistresses, but I do not want you thinking less of me."

He moved his hands over her, thinking the most ordinary

pleasure would be bold enough for today, or any day, if such lush warmth were his to hold. "Bold in what way?"

She placed a row of kisses to his chest. "I was told once that I have a scandalous mouth. I later learned what was meant by that. It shocked me, but I have perhaps become accustomed to the notion. It is not something that wives do, however."

His arousal doubled in intensity at once. He grasped her bottom and pressed her closer, so his shaft pushed against her stomach. "Actually, I am told that some wives do," he muttered between biting kisses.

"Truly?"

"Mmm."

"Who would have guessed? So you would not mind?"

"No, I don't think so."

"I may do it wrong. I have never . . ." She looked in his eyes and stopped talking. A devilish grin broke. "Oh, you would not mind at all, I think." She looked down. Her fingertips did a little dance up the length of his shaft and tapped the tip. "Let me see if . . ." She bent over and nibbled.

Intense sensations charged through him like lightning. He gritted his teeth so hard that his jaw felt locked.

"It might be easier if I knelt."

"Perhaps." *Yes. Now.*

She lowered herself. Her position made the anticipation unbearable. He saw her elegant back and the round flare of her hips and the erotic rise of her bottom.

The dark cloud of her hair angled toward him. Then velvet heat encased him, and he went blind.

"I think that new pleasure benefits me as much as you," Cassandra muttered between deep gasps. "This is delicious."

He withdrew slowly and thrust deeply again. What she had done did not really require this long, slow joining once he recovered. He could just as easily take her quickly.

He decided it was not in his interests to explain that.

He stopped, her incomparable softness surrounding him up to the hilt. He lowered and angled his head so he could tease her breasts. Her sparkling sigh sang in his ear. She flexed and tightened around him in subtle squeezes. She felt so damned good. He used his tongue to flick at her tight, dark nipples until she whimpered.

She bent her knees and shifted her hips, drawing him in even deeper. She pouted and shifted again.

"You are impatient," he said.

Her lashes rose. "Unlike you, I have not already been in ecstasy this afternoon."

"You know you will be soon. I have never left you discontented." He withdrew and reentered, savoring every instant of the sensation. "It does not always have to be hard and mad, Cassandra. There can be great pleasure in appreciating the nuances."

"Much like forcing oneself to savor a bonbon very slowly?"

"Or keeping good brandy in one's mouth awhile."

"I do not care for brandy, but I do like bonbons."

He felt the tight frustration that had been coiling in her unwind. She kept him deep and close, but no longer from impatience. He moved again, and little signs of delight eddied through her expression.

They did not storm the mountain. They walked up hand in hand, stopping every now and then to admire the view. When the storm finally broke in him, there was no thunder this time. He experienced it as a sudden downpour that drenched his essence with a warm, poignant rain.

Cassandra noticed that the last of twilight was dimming, but she did not move. She remained nestled in Ambury's embrace, afraid she would ruin the mood if she even breathed too deeply.

She did venture a sidelong glance at him. His eyes were closed but he did not sleep. His arms were too alert to her.

Had this pleasure moved him as it had her? She had thought perhaps it had somewhat at least. There were moments when she was sure they had a perfect bond and understanding, and shared the intimacy to the fullest. She wondered now if it were possible for a man to know it quite like a woman, however. She also wondered if he had planned this, for his own purposes. Perhaps he thought to conquer her with tenderness.

That was an ignoble notion, but she could not disregard it. The vows had not bound her enough to make her pliable and obedient, but this sort of chain definitely would. This was why Emma took care to soothe Southwaite's pride and temper, she guessed. Not out of duty or fear or lack of free will, but because she had let him send tethers into her heart that made her want him to be happy.

Ambury rose up on his arm and looked down at her. "You asked me when I proposed if I would accept your having lovers after the heir and a spare. I have decided that I will not."

She rather wished he would not issue decrees like a conqueror so soon. "I trusted that you would be reasonable."

"It is a reasonable answer. You will not take lovers. Ever."

"It is far too soon to decide this. You need to wait until the novelty of marriage has dimmed, and I am more of a nuisance."

"My views on it will not change."

She should explain that he was not being at all reasonable. He appeared uncompromising, however, and at the moment, the idea of another lover did not appeal to her at all. Better to fight battles that counted for something.

They drifted back into the intimate peace they shared. Perhaps if he did not want to share her, he had experienced something similar to what she had tonight. Such as a man could, that was.

"Cassandra, I need you to bring me to your aunt so I can

talk to her. Do you trust me enough to do that?" The question floated to her in the gathering dark. At least he was asking, not commanding.

She had trusted him when he proposed. There was no reason not to now. Except for the earrings. That had not been a small deception, and it touched on everything that mattered to her when it came to trust.

Her mind weighed that heavily. Her heart did not possess the ability to be so ruthless. Trust glowed there, no matter what her thoughts concluded. Acknowledging her heart gave her peace and relief, and brought a smile to her spirit.

"I will take you to her tomorrow afternoon."

Chapter 23

The letter arrived with his breakfast the next morning. It stood out from among the rest of the mail. He recognized the stationery at once, then the seal and the hand. It had been almost a year since he had received a missive from Penthurst.

He broke the seal and unfolded the paper. It bore only one word. Did he imagine that he saw something of his own surprise in the way that name had been penned? Penthurst had to have found the discovery very interesting.

Yates certainly did. Interesting and confounding. Enough that he left the breakfast room, returned to his chambers, and banished Higgins. He took out his violin and trusted that it would not fail him.

The music created its separate world, like it always did. It filled his mind, defining and organizing. He did not think about anything much at all as he played, but lost himself in the purity of sound while the composition worked its magic.

When the piece was over, he set down the instrument.

He still did not have answers, but he at least knew the questions. He merely had to decide if he wanted to ask them. Then he had to decide if he *should* ask them.

He wandered down the little corridor and pushed the door to Cassandra's chambers. The maid in the dressing room shook her head, indicating Cassandra had not risen yet. He went to the bedchamber and stood over the bed. She appeared beautiful lying there. Just looking at her brought calm to the chaos closing in again.

Her lashes rose and she looked up at him. "What is it?"

"Nothing. I thought you were asleep." *I wanted to look at you. I do not know why.*

"I woke up a while ago. I did not move, so I could secretly listen."

It took him a moment to realize she referred to the music. She pointed languidly at her window. "It is open, and yours is too, so the music travels here nicely." She sat up and rubbed her eyes. She looked adorably drowsy and disheveled.

"It is so lovely. Why don't you play for people?"

She did not mean just people. She meant her. He swallowed the inclination to shrug and say he did not know.

"Perhaps because my father did not like it. He enjoys music enough, and admires musicians. He had no moral opposition, nor did he think it below me or inappropriate."

"Then why would he dislike it?"

"He had other plans for my time, especially when I left university. Playing well takes a lot of practice. Hours and hours."

"What did he want you to do instead?"

"Parliament. The Commons, so that I could begin forming the relationships that would give me power when I succeeded him. Inheriting the title only goes so far. I had no interest in that, and resisted, and played—the violin and in other ways." And now when he needed to know what those in power knew, he went to men like Penthurst, who had not followed youthful impulse quite so much.

"I can see how you would not want to play for him, of course. But others—when you played at Emma's grand preview in the spring, everyone was spellbound. Men had tears in their eyes. It is a great gift you have, and that you share when you do perform. They know they have souls when they listen to you play."

She flattered him enormously. She also put a name on the real reason he did not perform. It made him uncomfortable to see people moved like that. It embarrassed him to make grown men weep. He felt inadequate when people said he touched their souls, because his music never did any of that for *him*.

He kissed her for the compliment. "I am going to visit my father. We will go to your aunt in a few hours."

"Do you mind if I listen through the open windows?" she asked. "I do not want to . . . intrude."

"I do not mind." He headed down to his father's apartment, admitting that he found the idea of touching Cassandra's soul appealing.

"How is he today?" Yates asked the valet when he entered the sitting room.

"Tired, sir. But otherwise it is much the same. He is awake now, if you want to see him."

Yates walked to the large chair where his father sat in his robe and cravat. He supposed that the day he came here and found the neck piece gone and the face unshaved, he would know a turn had been taken for the worse.

His father's eyes were closed, and he appeared very calm. Almost beatific in his peace. Perhaps because the valet had opened the window.

"Yates. Good of you to visit."

Yates sat down in the chair all visitors used. He looked at the window again.

"I am wondering if you feel well enough to talk about

the estate. I have some information and also some questions."

"I think sometimes we will never be done with it, but ask what you must."

"I learned more information about those earrings. The ones you kept asking about, that had gone missing after the last inventory. As you know, my wife owned them for a while. She received them from her aunt, Lady Sophie Vernham."

His father reddened with anger. "I am very disappointed in her, to have abused a friendship in that way. Your mother overlooked much with Sophie, and will be distressed to know that her goodness was repaid with common thievery."

"The story about Sophie Vernham's jewels was not that she stole them, of course. She claimed they were gifts from lovers."

"A shrewd ruse on her part, I think now. She does not claim such a thing with those earrings, I am sure."

"No, she says she bought them at a pawnbroker."

His father looked at him, surprised. "Does she? It is possible, I suppose. I would rather not think she took advantage here, and helped herself. The idea of that makes me sad."

Yates leaned forward with his arms on his knees. He caught his father's eye. "Is it possible that she neither stole them nor bought them? Is it possible that Grandfather gave them to her?"

It took his father a few moments to absorb the implication. He struggled to sit upright. The effort and his anger made him red in the face again. "No, it is *not* possible. My father hardly knew her, and he did not have affairs of any kind and did not approve of men who did. If you start one of your tasteless investigations into him, you will come up empty-handed, I assure you. Oh yes, I know about that disgraceful avocation of yours. I forbid you to subject this family to such common meddling and the vicious gossip it engenders."

It was as close to a row as they had come in the last few

months. The earl's indignation looked set to expand even more.

"I expected the answer you gave. However, it was a possibility that I had to inquire about. Remember that you are the one who charged me with finding out how the jewels went missing."

"I told you to find the thief, not have flights of imagination about your grandfather, of all men. With your marriage, you want to think the best of the aunt. I understand that. Let us accept the explanation of the pawnbroker and leave it there." He sighed deeply and seemed to exhale his agitation. He closed his eyes. "Yes, I think that is the kind thing to do all around."

"Do you want to rest? My other questions can wait."

"There is more?"

"Quite a bit more."

Did he imagine that the eyes that peered at him looked more wary than tired? "Best have it out now, then. One never knows about tomorrow, eh?"

"That odd property on the coast—the land with the contestable title—is on the list of locations for the government's new defenses. The rents will be significant."

"The government will never lease land that is not clear. You did not pull strings for this, did you? If so, you wasted your time."

"I did not. Someone else did. Barrowmore."

His father went still. The entire chamber did.

"That is odd," his father said.

"Isn't it? I have to think that Barrowmore thinks to profit somehow. That probably means that his family has the other deed. Don't you agree?"

His father looked out the window for a ten count before nodding.

"It is strange that two pieces of property that left this estate mysteriously ended up in the possession of my wife's family. A logical mind has to assume it was not a coincidence. I am asking you as your son and heir to tell me how it happened, Father."

His father did not return his gaze. Instead, he stared sightlessly with a slack expression.

"I did not know about the jewels," he finally said. "The property, yes. He gave it to her. Your grandfather gave it to Sophie. Tied it up in some trust or other, so she gets the income until I die, then title passes to her and her heirs."

"So there was an affair after all."

"There was not any affair, I tell you."

"It is the only explanation. He may not have admitted it to you, and he may have gone to his grave with his reputation for high morals intact, but gifts of jewels and property to a woman normally mean one thing. Hell, is the Highburton name so sacred that you would let me accuse a woman of being a thief rather than admit your father was fallible?"

"I tell you that I did not know about the jewels. I still do not know if they were a gift too."

Of course they were. His father was being as stubborn on this as he had been during all those old arguments. He refused to accept the obvious because his rigid view of living would necessitate damning his own father.

"Nor, despite your certainty to the contrary, was there an affair between them," his father said again.

Of course there was.

"Ask her, if you think my memory and judgment is ruled by blind sentiment. She will tell you."

He planned to.

He had learned what he needed to know. He stood. His father looked up at him.

"I did not expect you to be so thorough, Yates. I only counted on getting your attention for a while, so you were not ignorant when it all went to you."

"I have enjoyed being thorough, and learning the details about the estate from you."

"You will probably still vote with the damned Whigs when you get the title."

"Quite likely. Do not blame yourself, however. It is a perversion of my character that you did your best to correct."

His father chuckled lowly while he pulled his robe closer.

"The breeze has cooled. I will close the window." Yates went over and shut the casement. "Does my music bother you when you are resting? I realized today that you can probably hear it if this window is open. My chambers are above. I was inconsiderate not to think of that."

"It does not bother me. It is pleasant, and often useful. I never understood all that poetic foolishness about music. I find it is good for clear thinking, myself, not emotional excess. You will think me coldhearted to say so."

Yates turned to look at him. "Not at all. If you ever require clear thinking, let me know, and I will play for you."

His father waved dismissively. "Your mother says you do not like to perform. I'll enjoy what comes through that window there, when it comes."

Yates paused behind the big chair as he walked out. He rested his hand on his father's shoulder. "It is true that I do not like to perform for audiences, but I will gladly play for *you*."

His father reached up, squeezed his hand, then patted it like a father comforting a boy.

"WHat is this place?" Ambury asked. He eyed the blue door, then looked left and right at the mix of common people passing them on the lane. This was not a fashionable neighborhood at all, and Cassandra hoped he would not scold about her coming here in the past.

"It is hard to explain," she said. "It is a home, and also a refuge, and also a place of business. Come and I will show you."

She brought him to the door and sounded the knocker.

Voices from within floated through the open window nearby. Ambury heard them and raised an eyebrow.

"French."

"Yes, mostly."

A thick elderly woman opened the door. Without a word, she turned. Cassandra followed with Ambury at her side. They stepped into the house's dining room, only it was not used for eating.

Rows of tables filled the space. Women sat at them with sheets of paper and saucers filled with colors at hand. Brushes and rags dipped and dapped.

Ambury angled his head to examine one of the papers on the table near them. "They are coloring engravings for the print trade."

Some of the women were young, and others looked quite old, but most were of middle years. Many wore garments that had gone out of fashion in recent years, with fitted bodices and full skirts. A few even sported wigs, although the powder had turned stale and yellow.

"They are émigrés, of course," Cassandra said. "Women of good birth, mostly. They come here and earn a few shillings to keep body and soul together. A few live here, but most do not."

"You put your aunt here? There is not a man to be seen. This is hardly safer than Southwaite's home, or that of my parents."

"My brother would never find this place. If he did, he would never be allowed to enter. These women know how to protect themselves, and each other."

Ambury did not look convinced. He eyed the tables, and the heads bowed over them.

A low chatter filled the space, and occasional laughter. The women seemed to enjoy the work and the chance to gossip and chat.

A door at the far end of the chamber opened, and Marielle Lyon entered, carrying another stack of engravings.

She handed them out to women who had finished their last ones, pausing to bend her delicate face close to inspect some of the work.

Cassandra caught her eye and gestured. Marielle set down her stack and came toward them. She too dressed in the old style, and ink stains marred the torn lace at her elbows. Even so, she possessed an enviable, ethereal elegance.

"That is Marielle Lyon," Cassandra said to Ambury. "She is a friend of Emma's."

"I have heard of her. Is this her home?"

"I do not know if she owns it. She does live here. She certainly is the queen here."

Marielle greeted Cassandra with a kiss, then appraised Ambury while Cassandra introduced them. "You are alone?" she asked. "The other one is not with you?"

"She means Kendale," Cassandra said. "He had taken to following her around town some months ago. She noticed at once. Didn't you, Marielle?"

"I am heartened to hear that my friend had the good sense to admire your beauty, although he should not have followed you like that."

"It was not *l'amour*. He thought I was a spy." The pitches of her accent made the statement charming.

Ambury turned on his own charm. "And are you one?"

"Since you are his friend, I will let you wonder too. It amuses me." She half turned, and stretched out an elegant finger. "You aunt is back there, Cassandra. She is most industrious, and enjoys sitting with Madame Chardin. They gossip about dead friends."

Cassandra spied Aunt Sophie. She wore a white cap that covered her crown, and an apron over her floral-patterned dress. The woman next to her said something, and Sophie threw back her head and laughed.

Ambury joined her as she walked between the tables in that direction.

Aunt Sophie looked up in surprise when they reached

her. She said something to her companion in French, then
smiled. "You are just in time for the most delicious story
about Mademoiselle O'Murphy and that infamous painting
Boucher did of her. Madame says the king insisted that all
his women rouge their bottoms and that explains that rosy
hue in the center of her derriere in the picture. And here I
always assumed it was Boucher's lack of good taste."

"Damnation," Ambury whispered. "We forgot the rouge."

Cassandra stepped on his boot toe, hard. "Aunt Sophie,
we would like to talk to you and explain what is afoot on
your behalf."

"Of course. Marielle will not mind if we seek privacy in
the kitchen, I am sure." She spoke to Madame Chardin, then
stood and led the way out of the chamber. "Such a lovely
child that O'Murphy girl was. Madame Chardin says that
she survived it all, shrewd little Irish minx that she was."

The kitchen afforded some privacy. Cassandra sat with
Sophie at the rustic table. Ambury stood.

Cassandra explained Ambury's petition to Chancery, and
the other efforts on her behalf. "Ambury has let a house,"
Cassandra finished. "As soon as we move there, we will bring
you to live with us. Until then—"

"Until then, it would be better if you came to my family's
home," Ambury said.

Cassandra frowned at him. That was not what she had
planned at all.

"I would prefer to remain here," Sophie said. "I have been
safe, and I am not intruding."

Ambury looked at her very directly. "Would staying there
discomfort you?"

"Not at all. I merely prefer being here."

Silence descended. Sophie and Ambury had eyes only
for each other. Not the friendliest eyes either.

"Aunt Sophie, about the diamond earrings," Cassandra
began, dreading the accusation she was about to imply. "You
said that you bought them at a pawnbroker, but were very

vague. I need you to tell us exactly how you came to possess them."

Sophie opened her mouth to speak, but Ambury interrupted again. "They were a gift, were they not? From a member of my family."

Confused, Cassandra looked from her husband to her aunt and back again.

Aunt Sophie gave Ambury a good examination, taking his measure in all ways. "Yes, now that you remind me, they were a gift."

"They were?" Cassandra blurted. "From whom?"

"It would be a betrayal of trust for me to say."

Ambury did not appear surprised by that answer. Cassandra could barely contain her astonishment.

"It was not the only gift," Ambury said. "I believe there was some property as well."

Sophie hesitated but gave up with a sigh. "There was. Some is in trust, and I receive the income from the rents. Then there is my house—"

"Your house?" Cassandra exclaimed. "You have had that for years. Forever. I thought my father bought that for you."

Sophie reached over and patted her face. "Be calm, dear. Your father gave me money instead. I chose to use it to travel once I had the house and the rents, along with the portion from my mother, to ensure my keep." She turned to Ambury. "So you have discovered that your family was generous to me. You should not bother yourself with such old business. As Cassandra says, it was forever ago."

"I appreciate your tolerating my questions, so there are no ambiguities to the estate. As you say, it was forever ago, and there is no reason to pursue it further."

Cassandra itched to pursue it a lot further. She thought she would burst from the questions galloping through her head.

Ambury finally sat down. He smiled at Aunt Sophie. Suddenly, he oozed charm.

"I have reason to think that Barrowmore will make another try for you. It is wise to accept Highburton's house as sanctuary. I know that my mother will welcome you."

"Do you now? Gerald has become an insolent bother. I should tell his father about him, so he can be put in his place."

Cassandra glanced askance at Ambury. She took her aunt's hand. "Gerald is the earl now, Aunt Sophie. Father cannot help you. Only Ambury can."

Sophie's gaze sharpened on Ambury. "You are not really giving me a choice about where I live now, are you?"

"Not if you want my protection."

Sophie made a little sniff of resentment. "Then I must obey, since I am in need of someone's protection after all these years. I will collect my belongings, such as they are, and trust your word that Elinor will not find me an embarrassment or a burden."

"Do not go and pack quite yet. There is one other thing that we need to talk about before we leave the privacy of this chamber," he said.

"More? What else is there to settle?"

"I need to ask you about your other jewels."

"Who? Why?" Cassandra stammered after Aunt Sophie left to collect her things.

"My grandfather," Ambury said. "And the usual why."

"No." She struggled to keep a giggle from punctuating her astonishment. She did not succeed, and received a very Highburton glance when it emerged. "Forgive me. It is just— refreshing. Don't you think so?" Another giggle bubbled. She almost choked keeping it in. "Do you not find some satisfaction in knowing that you did not fall so far from the tree after all?"

He shrugged. "Some, I suppose."

She pursed her mouth and looked down her nose. "Oh, yes, the Earls of Highburton, bulwarks of moral rectitude and examples for us all." She grinned. "Oh, my, this is rich."

Rather severe blue eyes scolded her.

"Not that I would ever tell anyone," she said. "I can keep family secrets as well as the next person. This one is safe with *me*." She stretched over and kissed him. "Just as I am sure my aunt's revelations about the jewels are safe with *you*, Ambury."

"Are you blackmailing me, Cassandra?"

"Heavens, no."

"Because I will not have it."

"Of course not."

"The two revelations are not equal. And her jewels, the ones she admits to *borrowing*, must go back."

"I agree. Anything borrowed should be returned eventually. I will turn them over to you at once."

They strolled out to the reception hall. French chatter drifted from the dining room. Up above somewhere, Aunt Sophie packed her valise.

"For all my joking, I am a little sad to learn about your grandfather."

"Oddly enough, I am too. It changes my memories of him. Not badly, but it is a change all the same."

Her touch of melancholy had nothing to do with memories. Ambury's grandfather was nothing more than a reputation to her.

Aunt Sophie came down the stairs. A young woman followed, carrying the valise that she handed to Ambury.

Sophie's face showed no expression. Her eyes held that distant, filmy look that worried Cassandra. The talk of forever ago must have sent her thoughts there quite thoroughly while she was upstairs.

Ambury noticed. He offered his arm and spoke gently. "Let us go now, Sophie."

She appeared confused. She looked at him, however, and calmed. "You are sure that Elinor does not mind?"

"I am sure."

Sophie stepped forward. "She has always been the most generous woman I ever had the honor to know."

Chapter 24

His mother did receive Sophie, with open arms. The warm greeting seemed to pull Sophie back from wherever her mind had wandered. The two women banished Ambury and Cassandra and closed the door to the library so they could talk privately. About forever ago, perhaps.

Yates went looking for Cassandra after he consulted with Prebles about the Chancery petition. He found her in her bedchamber, gazing out the window, looking a little lost, much as Sophie had in the carriage. For all her stillness, he sensed turmoil in her.

He embraced her from behind and kissed her shoulder. "What is making you so thoughtful?"

She shrugged. "Many things. Too many revelations, perhaps. I am not happy to learn that my aunt did take some of those jewels, for one thing. I do not think they were all misunderstandings, the way she claimed."

"I think most probably were." It was the sort of lie one says to someone who does not need to know the whole truth.

The type one says to a person one cares about. "You said that learning about my grandfather made you sad too. Why?"

A rueful smile curved her mouth. "I realized that I had started counting on your becoming more like prior High-burtons, in one way. I thought . . ." She turned and kissed him. "It is not important."

He sat in the blue chair and pulled her onto his lap. "You thought what?"

She toyed with his cravat for a few moments. "I thought that with all that righteousness in your blood that I stood a fair chance of eventually not sharing my husband with mistresses."

"But that is not important?"

"It was only a vague supposition regarding your blood. It would certainly be *fair* if you grew more like them that way. You have told me I can never have lovers."

"You think we should be equal in virtue or adultery, in other words. An understandable view, I suppose, but a radical one."

"I expect it is unlikely now that we know your inheritance does not include the inclination to be that virtuous."

He had no idea if it were likely or not. Nor was it clear whether it really mattered to her. He rather hoped it did, he realized. "So all of your heavy thinking was on my inherited inclinations regarding marital virtue?"

"I was trying to sort out many things. For example, as best I understand, my brother has been very cruel for very little gain. My aunt may have had income from a property, but it was not much. Not enough to justify what he tried to do with her."

"He planned there to be more income from that property." He told her about the defense towers and how Gerald had been working to get that land on the list of properties. "If he had control of her, he would control the land and the money it paid. The trustee would not have stood against him, as long as your aunt was being cared for."

"How much more?"

"Hundreds a year, at least."

"He is heartless if he tried to imprison her to control even several hundred. And his behavior to me—so much anger and . . . and hatred . . . yes, hatred—years of it, and for no reason at all other than his own arrogance and pride. There is something very sad about it. Surely a person needs good cause to become so unkind. He was not always like this." She wiped her eyes. "I miss the boy I knew as a child, Ambury. It is as if when I was not looking, my brother disappeared and another person took his place."

He fished out his handkerchief and gave it to her. "When did he change?"

"When he inherited. I did not realize the fullness of it until . . ." She dabbed at her eyes.

"Until when?"

"Do not ask," she said softly.

"Until that business with Lakewood?"

"We are not to speak of it, you said. That was a wise decision, I have come to see."

"Not so wise. You once said no one knows what happened now, except you. I would like to know too."

She shook her head. "You will blame me for tainting his memory, just as you always blamed me for tainting his reputation. I can brave out almost anything, darling, but not your disapproval, I have learned."

He did not believe that she wanted to protect herself from that disapproval. She wanted to protect him from having those memories tainted. It touched him that she would refuse to defend her own behavior in order to preserve those for him.

He embraced her fully, and she laid her head on his shoulder. "I still want to know. Tell me now."

She did not speak for so long that he thought she never would. Then she sniffed again. "As I told you, it was no accident, that day. The boat, our absence alone together, the compromising situation was all planned."

He remembered her claiming that after the party, and his reaction. He swallowed his irritation this time. He had pressed her for all of it and should wait to hear it.

"I saw nothing wrong with that little boat," she said. "In the woods, he seemed incapable of finding our way. I would point out how to go, and he would insist we do otherwise. It was a farce, but at the time, I only congratulated myself for not having accepted the proposal of such a fool. Only when we staggered out of those woods, finally, and my brother and mother and the others on that picnic met us, did I realize the cost of his stupidity."

"I asked to hear this, but I will not have you insult him," he said, fighting the anger her story stoked. He did not know yet if he was furious at her or *for* her, which only made it worse. "He was not a stupid man."

"No, he was not. I was the stupid one, for thinking I could reject his proposal and have it end there."

"He would not do what you are saying, Cassandra. He would not trap a woman so dishonorably. You misunderstood."

She sat up and looked into his eyes. "I misunderstood nothing. That afternoon, he came to me to propose again, to do the right thing. I put him off, but an hour later I went looking for my brother, to tell him that I agreed. They were together in my brother's study, and I heard them laughing about it. Lakewood was regaling my brother with all the missteps. How the hole bored in the wood did not unseal, so he had to use his oars to get water in the boat. How the sun kept coming out and he had to ignore my suggestions we follow it west. It was a great joke to both of them. I decided right then that I would be *damned* before I would be tricked into having a man I did not want."

"Well, you almost managed that, didn't you? Being damned." The words were out before he knew it, spewing from the chaos of reactions he had to this story. *He was not entirely the man you knew him to be,* Penthurst had said. Damn Penthurst and damn Lakewood.

She flushed as if he had slapped her face. "Should I have spared myself by revealing the whole plot? Would the truth of his dishonor have been preferable to vague speculations about it? Or do you think that even knowing what I knew I should have accepted his proposal of obligation? Oh, dear. You do, don't you? You believe that despite it all I should have married him and redeemed him and myself and learned to forget what he was." She pushed away and tried to scramble off his lap. "Well, I didn't, and I am glad even if you are not."

He grabbed her waist before she got away. He held her firmly while she squirmed. "Damnation, of course I am glad you did not marry him. If you had, he would still be alive and you would not have married *me*. It is hellish to think of that, and just as hellish to know I am glad it all happened as it did. How do you think that makes me feel?" He took a deep breath and forced control on himself. "He was my oldest friend, Cassandra."

She stopped fighting him. "I am sorry, Ambury. Sorry that it is hellish for you, and sorry that I told you. I knew it was not wise. You should not have insisted."

"It needed saying. I was tired of having that day forever unexplained." He held her while their emotions calmed. Then he just held her because he wanted to. He tried to picture what she described and fit it on the man he had known. Lakewood's adoring love of Cassandra had been out of character, that was undeniable. And he had a calculating side to him that could be unpleasant.

Even acknowledging those truths created some guilt.

"Why do you think they did it?" he asked a good half hour later.

"It was money for Lakewood. I overheard that too. Talk of the settlement. For my brother—that is what I contemplated when you joined me. A man behaving dishonorably to enrich himself makes some sense. Doing it to marry off a sister seems strange, does it not?"

He set her on her feet and stood. "I will turn my mind to it and see if a less strange answer comes to me. Now we must dress for dinner, so we can welcome your aunt to her stay here."

An hour later, he entered Cassandra's dressing room. The day's drama seemed long ago as soon as he saw how exquisite she appeared in an ivory dinner dress that fell softly over her curves. He offered his arm to escort her down.

"You are your aunt's heir, are you not?" he asked on the stairs. "Perhaps Gerald wanted to control you just as he controlled her. You have noted that he demanded you marry a man of his choosing. Perhaps what he really wanted was to make sure you married a man with whom he had an understanding about that inheritance. He would arrange the marriage, and your husband would share the income."

"I suppose. Only that brings us full circle to my dismay. All of that trouble for a few hundred a year! Gerald needs an avocation even more than I had thought, if it is true."

After dinner, the ladies left Yates to his port. Since his father was too ill to come down to dine, he drank alone and turned over Cassandra's description of that day six years ago.

It changed everything, but damned if he knew how. He did not like to think ill of Lakewood. They had known each other for years. While no one is perfect, and Lakewood had his vices and failings, Cassandra described a level of deception and scheming that most gentlemen would find unacceptable and dishonorable.

It was one thing to compromise a woman and you both married under society's coercion. It was another to trick a woman into appearing compromised so she was required to marry you when she did not want to. The distinction was a fine one, and perhaps, under the circumstances of his own marriage, a self-serving one.

Of course Lakewood could not speak in his own defense now regarding his intentions, and how and whether he had plotted with Barrowmore. A good friend should give him the benefit of the doubt. Much as he wanted to do that, he could not. Cassandra had been telling the truth, he was sure. She would not lie about such a thing.

What a shock it must have been when Cassandra refused his offer to do the right thing. A few hundred a year may have been small recompense to Barrowmore, but Lakewood had inherited an impoverished estate along with his baronage, and a few hundred would have made a big difference.

He was not entirely the man you think he was. Had Penthurst discovered the scheme and threatened to expose Lakewood? It would be humiliating to have the world know the whole story. He could see Lakewood dueling to the death to avoid *that*. It was more in character than issuing a challenge over a woman.

Saddened by the new view of an old friend, he set down his glass and wandered off to find Cassandra. Her spirit would banish his nostalgic melancholy, if anything could.

The drawing room was empty. A footman indicated the ladies had all retired.

On his way to his chambers, he decided to look in on his father. He walked into the dressing room. To his surprise, his mother stood at the bedchamber's door, her profile elegant and regal while she peered through a small opening.

She did not hear him approach, so intent she was on what she saw in the chamber beyond. He stepped behind her and looked over her head.

His father lay on the bed, propped on pillows, his white nightshirt catching the candles' glow. Beside the bed, on a chair pulled close, sat Aunt Sophie.

They were holding hands. And while he and his mother

watched, his father lifted Sophie's hand and kissed it on the palm—the way a lover might.

"Y ou are not to tell him that you know."
       His mother whispered the command as soon as she noticed him. She closed the door to the bedchamber, then beckoned with her hand. She led him across the dressing room to the small sitting room that flanked it.

It took him a few more minutes to rearrange his thoughts. It did not help that his mother did not appear at all surprised by the implications of what they had just seen.

"I had assumed it was Grandfather," he finally said. "Sophie is older than Father by ten years."

"Continue thinking it was your grandfather if it makes it easier, although I cannot imagine why it would matter."

It mattered for a lot of reasons. The immediate ones were because the man in there having a reunion with an old lover had lectured and harped about morality too many times to a son with whom it now appeared he had more in common than he admitted.

But perhaps that was the reason for all those rows to begin with.

"You do not mind?" he asked.

"It was long ago."

"Why do I think you did not mind long ago either?"

She sighed, but it did nothing to alter her straight spine as she perched like a statue on the edge of a bench. "If you must know, I gave my blessing, Yates. I was glad he found someone for a while. It was after you were born, and the physicians had advised against another pregnancy. Well, you know what that means. She was a dear friend back then, and when I saw his interest in her, I . . . let them both know that I did not mind at all."

"Did it last long?"

"Just under a year. Your grandfather was not as understanding when he learned about it. He indeed was a true Highburton, and forced your father to end it."

"And settled property and jewels on her to buy back the family honor. No wonder Father did not want me looking into the land, although I am sure he knew nothing about the jewels."

"He knew about none of it at the time, and only learned about the property when he inherited. He would never have tainted what they shared with such things, like she was a common courtesan. They had true affection for each other. And, I think, true . . . passion. I love him dearly, but . . . I could not deny him knowing *that* kind of love, if he wanted it."

He paced around, fitting this final discovery into all the rest. It closed the door on several questions, and explained why Sophie had not wanted to take residence in this house and had resisted it.

He looked at his mother, who as always appeared every inch a countess, even as she informed him of the love affair that she permitted, and perhaps even encouraged. *You are sure that Elinor does not mind?*

"Father thought those earrings had been stolen. He came to think Sophie was the one who took them. A betrayal of trust, he called it," he said. "His vehemence on the point makes more sense now."

"And you were determined to uncover the truth for him, weren't you? What a nuisance those earrings ended up being. I finally told him the truth a few days ago, so he would not think she had merely used him. I gave them to her, Yates, not your grandfather. They were my . . . parting gift. When it ended, I knew she and I would never be close friends again."

"It was good of you to continue receiving her, and being a friend such as you could be when the stories about her started flying."

"Whatever else is said about me, I hope it is known that I am not a hypocrite."

Not a hypocrite. She might be the only member of the family who could escape that criticism too.

"Did you bring her up here to see him?"

"She hardly found her way here herself." She palmed at her skirt, smoothing the fabric, then folded her hands on her lap. "Neither has much time. Her mind is starting to get lost. Surely Cassandra has noticed. In a few years—who knows? Now, you should go. She will be leaving soon."

He went over and kissed her crown. "It is said that he won the prize of the Season when you accepted his proposal. Even he did not know the half of it."

He left her there, sitting as if stiff corsets still ruled her posture, waiting while her husband reminisced about a great passion with her friend.

She has always been the most generous woman I ever had the honor to know, Sophie had said.

Hell, yes.

Chapter 25

Cassandra swung her leg so she could sit astride Ambury's thighs. He startled awake and looked over his shoulder at her.

"What are you up to?"

"I am just admiring my favorite view of you." She caressed the hard bum that she found so appealing.

"Just never tell me that Lady Lydia also had that view of me. I prefer to think that she shielded her virginal eyes."

"Of course she did. Right away. She saw nothing." She leaned forward and placed a careful kiss at the top of his spine. "You were out of sorts when you came home. Did it not go well today at the trial?"

"It went very well. It is finished. Penthurst is acquitted. The peers accepted his claim that as a gentleman he could not fully explain the reason for the duel without compromising the good names of the innocent. It helped that he had not issued the challenge, I suppose."

"You do not approve of their decision, I take it."

"I am glad it ended as it did. If I was discontented, it is because the truth of it remains a mystery. And because my assumptions may have cost me two friends instead of only one."

"Would Penthurst end the mystery if you asked him?"

"He told me that honor forbids it. Someday, however, perhaps I will see what he will reveal, if he can speak of any of it. In the meantime, I debate telling Kendale and Southwaite what you told me about his plot with your brother to compromise you. Southwaite, at least, will not be surprised, I suspect."

She rested her head against his shoulders. "You want to do that only because of me. For me. It might be better to let them remember him without that story blemishing his honor." She kissed him again, a bit lower. "You do know that it had nothing to do with me, don't you? That is all that matters to me—that you no longer wonder. Penthurst is an acquaintance and nothing more. If I have any feelings for him, it is only gratitude that he treated me with respect and never cut me, when others were less generous."

That created a shifting of the land as Ambury turned on his back. Well awake now, he looked up at her. "Others like me, you mean. In treating you as a woman of the world, I insulted you. I apologize. I have no excuse except desire, which can affect a man's judgment for the worse."

"I can hardly mind that you were bold, and tried to add me to your conquests. Someday I will be the Countess of Highburton as a result."

He pulled her down into an embrace. "I have often wondered what might have been if Lakewood had not laid claim to you so quickly during your first Season."

"Have you started wishing you had courted me back then? That is very sweet."

"I wondered about it long before now. Even before Southwaite's wedding. I always wanted you."

She accepted the deep kiss that accompanied that

declaration. Her arousal flared the way he could so easily make it do. The difference this time, and for the last many times, was the way her chest filled with layers of emotion so poignant that she could easily weep if she were not careful.

She laid her head on his chest and trailed her fingertips over the hard, subtle swells of his muscles. His caresses warmed her back in turn. "I think I prefer that it happened as it did. I was just as silly as most girls, and back then I would have expected more than being wanted in the way you mean."

"And you do not now?"

Her throat burned. She did not expect more, but she ached for it. The pleasure was wonderful, and the intimacy deep, but she wanted to believe that not only her heart experienced this painfully bright joy during their time together.

He rolled, and rose up on his forearms so they faced each other. "There should be no expectation of more, or even great pleasure, in such matches as ours. Duty and loyalty are all one can really expect."

"I know. It is good that you want me in that way, and I you. I am not complaining."

"Nor I. But I wonder if in not expecting more, I accidentally found it."

Her surroundings disappeared, and nothing existed except the two of them and a trembling excitement that frightened her. She felt she balanced on a very thin rope, using only one toe. Merely breathing could send her falling into disappointment. Yet the look in his eyes encouraged her to believe that would not happen if she risked stepping forward.

"My pleasure with you is not only physical," he said. "I know a rare joy with you. It is not only pride that makes me want to hold on to you and keep you for myself." He kissed her sweetly. "You have bedazzled me, and stolen my heart, Cassandra."

She embraced his neck and held him so she could kiss him. "I knew that I loved you, but dared not hope you shared my feelings." She kissed him again and again. They met in sweet passion first, then it turned fierce, as if they tried to consume each other. She felt him enter her, hard and deep, claiming her the way she wanted.

"It is good," he muttered. "Perfect. Love makes it better."

She wrapped her legs around his hips. "Yes. Love makes it wonderful."

Cassandra felt Yates shift on the bed. She opened her eyes to find him looking down at her.

"What is it?"

"Come with me. I need to do something."

They threw on their robes, and he led the way to his dressing room. He lit a lamp.

He pointed to a chair near the wardrobe. "Sit there."

She scrambled onto the chair and pulled her legs and feet up under her. He turned, his hair mussed from their loving, and the raw silk of his robe floating. He fussed with something on a table.

When he turned back to her, he held a violin in one hand and a bow in the other.

"Do not be insulted if I do not appear to notice you while I do this," he said. "I will know that you are there. I am not nearly as lost in it as I may seem."

It flattered her beyond words that he had invited her to listen. She hoped he did not think the gift was required. "I would not want to intrude, darling. Are you sure I will not?"

"That remains to be seen, but I do not think you will. I promise you that I want to do this."

She did not object further. She sat as still as she could and hoped she would not intrude in the least.

There is nothing quite like hearing a violin break the stillness of the night. Its sound filled the small chamber and seemed to emerge from every direction. The notes came cleanly, clearly, purely. The sounds of heaven must be like this.

She watched his strong fingers move over the instrument as if on their own accord, while that bow set the music free. His expression fascinated her. Hard. Thoughtful. His lids remained low over eyes that showed an internal distraction, as if the sounds held a conversation with his mind.

The experience moved her. Exhilarated her. She wished it would not end.

When it did, he lowered the instrument indifferently, as if nothing remarkable had just happened.

"Thank you, Yates. This was the best day of love declarations you could have given me. It was amazing."

He set the violin back in its case, then came and helped her to her feet. With his arm around her, he led her back to the bedchamber. "It was good, wasn't it?"

"Did I manage not to interfere?"

"I was aware of you more than others in the past, but you were not a distraction. Far from it. In fact, it appears that this is something else that love makes better."

Love had made the music better, but not different. Yates acknowledged that the next day as he finished dressing. It had been a joy to have Cassandra there with him. If anyone else had intruded so thoroughly, he would certainly have found it a nuisance. She had fit there, however, as perfectly as she fit against his body when he embraced her. As ideally as she fit in so many ways.

Even so, the music had brought the clarity that he needed. It had organized the thoughts that had kept him awake. While he played, his mind had drifted through the images and impressions of the day, arranging and rearranging them.

People from the past and present had walked through his mind. Slowly, new insights had emerged—that Sophie had mistaken him for his father again today, as she left Marielle Lyon's house, just as she had when he approached her at Dr. Wakely's home. That he would tell Cassandra that he would not take mistresses—he could not foresee ever wanting to, but she had a right to hear a pledge. That the revelations of the day had explained everything, but also had not.

That last thought kept coming back, until a few other memories attached themselves to it. Small ones, mostly. Little oddities that he had barely noted at the time. Then something not at all small became an echo behind the rest— Cassandra's hurt that her brother had treated her and her aunt so cruelly for such little gain.

Perhaps what he really wanted was to make sure you married a man with whom he had an understanding about that inheritance.

It is as if when I was not looking, my brother disappeared and another person took his place

Gerald has become an insolent bother. I should tell his father about him, so he could be put in his place.

"Sir."

He jolted out of his thoughts. Higgins stood there holding his coat. He turned and slid it on.

"I will not be home for dinner, Higgins. Tell the butler."

Before he left the house, he went in search of Aunt Sophie. Hopefully he was wrong, but he did not think that he was.

"Explain again why I am writing this letter," Southwaite said while his pen hovered over the paper. He sat at a writing table in Brooks's.

"Because you are my friend."

"You are not going to do anything stupid with Barrowmore, are you? Fisticuffs or some other bad behavior? Zeus, you do not think to challenge him, I hope."

"Kendale will be with me to pull me away if it looks to be going there."

"Well, *that* is reassuring," Southwaite said dryly. "Tell me what I am to write. I don't like it, but I will do it."

Yates looked over Southwaite's shoulder. "Meet me in St. James's Park this afternoon at four o'clock, regarding a matter of great consequence concerning your family's estate."

Southwaite dipped his pen and wrote. *Please . . . meet . . . me . . . in . . .*

"You added the please."

"I am being polite."

"The man is a scoundrel. I do not choose to be polite."

"My name is signing it, not yours, and I *do* choose to be polite." He scribbled on. "He is not going to like this ruse."

"I do not give a damn, as long as he comes. He will never agree to meet me, that is certain. I realized recently that I have never spent a minute in the man's company without others nearby."

"Does this have to do with your wife?"

"It does."

"Are you going to tell me what it is about?"

"No." Not him. Not anyone, unless there came the day there was no choice.

Southwaite signed with a flourish, then folded and sealed the letter. He handed it to one of the club's servants to post. Then he accompanied Yates to some chairs.

"Have you become accustomed to the married state?" Southwaite asked when they were comfortable.

"I find it suits me far beyond my highest hope."

"The rumor is that it suits your bride as well."

"The ladies have been talking?"

"As is their habit, yes. Emma is delighted that you took the house nearby, so I expect they will be sharing secrets a lot in the months to come. As for your bride, Emma confided at dinner the other day that Cassandra is expressing supreme contentment and thinks you are a wonderful husband."

"How flattering."

"I thought so. My sister then opined that Cassandra had probably been swayed because you are a very hard man, and hard men are preferable. Emma then lectured how a man who is hard is unbearable to live with, lest Lydia had heard differently."

"What did you say?"

"Nothing at all. Do I look like a fool to you? Lydia countered that she had decided she would never marry unless she knew for a fact that the man was suitably hard. At that point, Emma seems to have wondered if they spoke about something other than demeanor. She blushed to her hairline."

"Surely Lydia only repeated some nonsense she had heard, no matter what the double entendre."

"Undoubtedly. I did scowl at my sister, lest she meant hard in a bawdy way and was deliberately speaking recklessly to get my goat."

"She is lucky to have you as a brother, Southwaite. You are very patient."

"I know." He stretched out his legs and crossed his boots. "So how did you manage to start as a man marrying at the point of a sword and end so quickly as a wonderful husband? I had to seduce and woo for months to be wonderful."

"I merely exercised my considerable talents in making women happy."

"She did not stand a chance then, I suppose."

Oh, she had stood a chance. Charm did not get one far with Cassandra Vernham. "The truth is that I am besotted with her, Southwaite. I cannot get enough of her and, thank God, she does not mind. I did the right thing and ended up falling in love with my wife."

Southwaite's teasing smile faded. "I am astonished. Happy for you, but astonished."

"It was hardly expected."

"All the more reason to be happy for you. And I am glad to have a friend who is also enchained. It will make the state more bearable. I have to warn you that not everyone will be congratulatory. There are men who think succumbing is a weakness, and we are to be pitied."

One such man entered the chamber. He saw them and walked over.

"Do not tell him yet," Southwaite said. "Once Kendale hears you are in love, you will never hear the end of it."

Especially if the woman was *that woman.*

"What is happening? Why did you send for me, Ambury?" Kendale asked by way of greeting. "You both look as if I caught you eating the sugar."

Yates kicked out a chair. "Sit and play some cards while we wait, Kendale."

"Wait for what?"

"I have a rendezvous this afternoon. I need you to come with me and make sure I do not kill the man."

Barrowmore wandered through St. James's Park, looking around for Southwaite. Yates had already taken position at a spot where no one could eavesdrop without being obvious, which meant right in the middle of the grass near the canal. Kendale lounged against a tree some distance away, looking like a man without purpose or concern.

Barrowmore saw Yates and halted. His brow knit as he worked out what to do.

"He is not coming," Yates called. "I am here instead."

Barrowmore hesitated, then walked over. "If this is about my aunt, you should know that I have petitioned the High Chancellor to look into the matter and get it settled quickly."

"That is not necessary."

"You intend to relinquish her to me?"

"It is not necessary, because she has already revealed that which you hope to keep a secret by putting her away."

That startled the smug smile off Barrowmore's face. He recovered, but it took a long few moments during which he appeared so frightened that Yates actually felt sorry for him. It must be hell to live every day with that kind of fear.

Barrowmore tried to sound superior, but only managed supercilious. "She is not right in her mind. Whatever nonsense she spoke, her words cannot be taken seriously."

"Her mind is not what it used to be, but most of the time she is as lucid as you are. Nor was her story told while she was not in control of her faculties. Although, your fear was not without cause. She had said things in passing that alluded to this mystery. Enough that I came to wonder enough to ask."

"My aunt has many stories." His jaw kept clenching and his lips thinned. "Endless stories, about princes and dukes and parties and scandals. Half are not true, I am sure, just as this one is not."

"This one was about being with child at the same time as her sister-in-law, and going to the country together for the duration and lying in. A discreet place, because Sophie was not married. I am sure Cassandra's mother recalls all of this story too. Perhaps I should ask her."

"Do not dare go near her."

"Will you put her away as well, if with age she becomes indiscreet? She must be worrying about that now."

Barrowmore's agitation had grown extreme. Yates could not decide if the man was going to swing his fist or crumble into tears.

"You are talking in riddles. I do not have the time for this." He began walking away.

"Only one of them had a child who survived the first day," Yates said loud enough for Barrowmore to hear. "Sophie. The countess took that child as her own."

Barrowmore froze. He looked around desperately, to see if anyone was near enough to have heard. He strode back until he stood less than a foot away. "Repeat that and I will kill you, Ambury."

"I do not think I will repeat it, but I want some answers. My curiosity is my biggest failing. When did you learn the truth that you were Sophie's son, not the countess's? When your father was dying, is my guess. Men like to clear the air at such times." He pictured Barrowmore hearing the death-bed revelation and learning he was not who he had spent his life thinking he was. Shocks like that could turn a man's character, especially if suddenly there was much to lose in addition to one's assumed identity. Barrowmore's behavior had been reprehensible, but at least it made some sense now.

"What he told me was that my sister had too much of her aunt in her and to watch her carefully or she would bring shame on the family. He was right about that, and I am relieved she is your problem now."

Yates saw red on hearing the insult to Cassandra. He maintained his calm with effort. "He also told you that she was not your sister. Not because of any problem with her legitimacy, but with yours. Sophie knows he was aware of what they had done. She knows he intended to tell you."

"I am his son, damn you. His son and heir."

"Under the law, yes. He did not repudiate you. The title was yours. The entailed lands too. Any inheritance that designated a direct blood descendant of his, instead of the usual line of inheritance, however—it was contestable by Cassandra. It still is."

"Are you threatening me, Ambury? So that is what this is about. You married a slut that you tumbled, and now you want a settlement after all."

He almost reached for Gerald to throttle him. Out of the corner of his eye, he saw Kendale go rigidly alert, then take one step. He gestured behind his back for Kendale to stay away, and found some sense within the fury that urged him to thrash Barrowmore soundly.

"I should demand the biggest settlement England has seen after the way you treated her, you scoundrel. That was your fear—that she would marry a man who would learn the truth and go after whatever he could in her name. Better she be married to some fellow you had in your pocket."

"If you try for anything, I will fight you every step. I will have it tied up in Chancery for decades. She will not see a penny."

"Probably not, but she will see you humiliated, and known as a bastard before the whole world. That may be worth more than money to her."

Enraged, almost bursting from it, Barrowmore strode away again, then turned and strode back. His fists were clenched this time. "What the hell do you want? How much?"

"No money. You need only withdraw your petitions regarding your mother and speak nothing but praise of Cassandra in the future."

"Praise?"

"Glowing praise. What a delight she is. How much you love her. How you regret the breach of the last years. You should write her a letter to this effect, to start. Be sure to grovel and beg her forgiveness in it."

"Are you mad? I am not writing or saying anything of the kind."

"Then I will expose the truth of your birth, and you will challenge me, and I will end up killing you. That alternative is not without appeal, but for my wife's sake and that of the others involved, I will forgo the pleasure."

Gerald still looked like a man who wanted to hit something. Over beneath the tree, Kendale maintained an alert pose.

"Damnation, if all you want is a letter full of lies and taking on the trouble of a dotty old woman, you can have it, Ambury. But I swear if you ever tell anyone any of this, if I ever hear it so much as whispered, I will see you dead."

"I have no interest in telling anyone. Not even my wife."

Gerald stared at him. Yates gazed right back, looking for—he did not know what.

Gerald turned to leave.

"Do you know who he is?" Yates asked. He had to know.

"Who? Oh, you mean the blackguard she raised her skirts for. No, thank God." A scowl formed, then darkened with suspicion. "Hell, do *you*?"

Yates looked at the brother fate had given him. He branded his memory with the way the Highburton arrogance and righteousness could get twisted, so he would never forget its dangers.

"Sophie did not say and I did not ask. I have no idea who he was. None at all."

Chapter 26

Cassandra snuggled under Yates's embracing arm and fitted her head against his shoulder. She laid her palm on his naked chest. She could feel his heart beat if she paid close attention. It thrummed like a vague physical echo sounding through his body.

Autumn's crisp air chilled the chamber, but they were cozy under down. The toile drapery around their bed held out the worst of night's cold. She never closed the drapes all the way, however. Her new home still fascinated her. She liked being able to see the silver light break through the night at dawn from where she slept.

"Will you go to Fairbourne's early, to help Emma?" Yates asked. He often remained in her bed until morning like this. He seemed to enjoy the peaceful hour after waking when they held each other and listened to the household start the day.

"I will arrive an hour before the auction. She does not really require my help, except to keep her from worrying.

It will kill her to be unable to do anything useful. Her brother plays his role today, and the world must assume she is no more than a patron like I am."

"Will your aunt join you?"

The question referred to one of the more interesting developments since they had moved into the house on St. James's Square. Aunt Sophie had come out of her retirement. Most notably, she had taken to visiting Yates's parents. Yesterday she had agreed to receive Southwaite's Aunt Hortense.

"I think an auction would tire her. Nor do I know that she even enjoys them. She never spoke of acquiring jewels that way." The way she had acquired them was being rectified. Discreet letters from Mr. Prebles were on their way to various locations on the Continent. Sophie had cooperated with the plan of restitution, to the extent she could. She really did not remember where some of the jewels had come from.

He pressed a kiss to her crown. "She appears contented here, with Merriweather as her companion. Her insistence that Senora Paolini be retained as one of the cooks is not the disaster I expected, although I find the woman's food a little odd. Not bad, mind you."

She decided not to mention that Aunt Sophie's interference might account for any oddities.

A discreet cough interrupted their lazy bliss. A delicate knock sounded. Yates sat up and looked toward the dressing room. "What is it, Higgins?"

"A letter, sir. Special delivery for madam. Should it wait until breakfast?"

Yates threw aside the covers and walked to the dressing room. He returned with the letter. "It is from Anseln Abbey." He handed it over and climbed back into bed.

She sat up and pulled a cocoon of warm bedclothes around her. "I hope Mama is not ill." She opened it to find a lengthy missive from her brother.

It proved to be the last kind of letter she ever expected

to get from Gerald. Full of apologies, he begged her forgiveness for his past behavior and promised to reform. He went on and on about how mistaken he had been, and expressed his hope that she would find more time for Mama. He offered to arrange his own absence from any family property if she required it in order to visit. He even admitted that she had many fine qualities, and included a little list of them.

He thanked her for taking care of their dear Aunt Sophie.

She let the letter fall onto the bedclothes and stared at her brother's scrawl. Her initial astonishment gave way to a deeper emotion. She almost wept. It was as if her brother had returned from wherever he had disappeared. Excitement built, and she pictured seeing Gerald and talking and laughing like other women did with their brothers. She imagined family gatherings to which she brought her children, and a closeness that filled the vacant spots the last years had left within their family.

She became almost giddy with happiness.

Then a very different reaction took over.

She picked up the letter. She looked at it closely. Not one correction could be found. It was as if Gerald had made multiple drafts and kept copying the final one until it was perfect, much like they did for their governess when young.

The more she reread the letter, the odder she found it. She could not believe Gerald had written this. All this effusive praise would not be like him on his kindest day. Gerald would never admit he had made all these mistakes, unless someone stood next to him and held a pistol to his temple.

She turned her head. Yates gazed up at the toile canopy. It looked like he counted the figures depicted on it. He displayed no interest in this special-delivery letter. None at all. He had not even asked if in fact Mama was ill.

She folded the letter and set it on a table near the bed. She turned and snuggled back down and looked at her husband.

"It was from Gerald. An attempt at rapprochement. He is very apologetic."

"That is good, isn't it?"

"Very good, although I do not think he really wants much to do with me. I am glad, because I do not want much to do with him. Too much has happened between us to ever have it right again. Seeing Mama more often, and more easily, is welcomed, however."

"After all the hurt, his attempt at an apology should make you happy, I would think."

"It makes me very happy. Did you not see how over-whelmed I was? I nearly wept." She looked in his eyes. "It was unexpected, but a wonderful surprise on this glorious day."

"It probably means that he will not create trouble for your aunt too. That is good news. Prebles said Gerald has removed his petition to Chancery. This must explain why."

"It is a great relief that he has seen the light." Other good things would come from this, even if she and Gerald would never be friends. She could visit the home of her youth without enduring scorn. She could reclaim memories lost, of her youth and of her family before Papa died.

She stretched and kissed Yates, and felt profound relief and gratitude for all of those things. She did not know how he had accomplished this. Whether he had bribed or threatened or talked reason, he had convinced Gerald to write that letter, however. She just knew it.

"Are you hungry for breakfast?" she asked. "I am thinking I could lie abed for quite a while still." She kissed his chest once, twice, three times, tasting his skin. His hand went to her head, holding her there with her lips sealed to his warmth.

"I am hungry, but not for breakfast. For you. As I always am. For your beauty and your passion and your humor, but mostly for your love."

"My love is always here for you, Yates. We will feast on love together."

"An unending feast." He rolled and rose above her, then dipped to kiss her deeply.

She savored that kiss, and all that came after. She relinquished herself to his heart and his body. She enjoyed the pleasure immeasurably, and with each touch acknowledged the truth they knew and shared—that love made it different, and better.

Keep reading for a special look
at the first novel in Madeline Hunter's
latest Regency quartet

The Surrender
of Miss Fairbourne

Now available from Jove Books

MAY 1798

The final sale at Fairbourne's auction house proved to be a sad affair, and not only because the proprietor had recently fallen to his death while strolling along a cliff walk in Kent. It was also, from the viewpoint of collectors, comprised of very minor works, and hardly worthy of the reputation for selectivity that Maurice Fairbourne had built for his establishment.

Society came anyway, some of them out of sympathy and respect, some to distract themselves from the relentless worry about the expected French invasion for which the whole country had braced. A few flew in like crows, attracted to the carcass of what had once been a great business, hoping to peck a few morsels from the body now that Maurice did not stand guard.

The latter could be seen peering very closely at the paintings and prints, looking for the gem that had escaped the less experienced eyes of the staff. A bargain could be had if a work of art were incorrectly described to the seller's detriment. The victory would be all the more sweet because such oversights normally went the other way, with amazing consistency.

Darius Alfreton, Earl of Southwaite, peered closely too. Although a collector, he was not hoping to steal a Caravaggio that had been incorrectly called a Honthorst in the catalogue. Rather, he examined the art and the descriptions to see just how badly Fairbourne's reputation might be compromised by the staff's ineptitude.

He scanned the crowd that had gathered too, and watched the rostrum being prepared. A small raised platform holding a tall, narrow podium, it always reminded Darius of a preacher's pulpit. Auction houses like Fairbourne's often held a preview night to lure the bidders with a grand party, then conducted the actual sale a day or so later. The staff of Fairbourne's had decided to do it all at once today, and soon the auctioneer would take his place on the rostrum to call the auction of each lot, and literally knock down his hammer when the bidding stopped.

Considering the paltry offerings, and the cost of a grand preview, Darius concluded that it had been wise to skip the party. Less explicable had been the staff's failure to tell him of their plans. He learned about this auction only through the announcement in the newspapers.

The hub of the crowd was not near the paintings hung one above another on the high, gray walls. The bodies shifted and the true center of their attention became visible. Miss Emma Fairbourne, Maurice's daughter, stood near the left wall, greeting the patrons and accepting their condolences.

The black of her garments contrasted starkly with her very fair skin, and a black, simple hat sat cockily on her brown hair. Her most notable feature, blue eyes that could gaze with disconcerting directness, focused on each visitor so completely that one would think no other patron stood nearby.

"A bit odd that she is here," Yates Elliston, Viscount

Ambury, said. He stood at Darius's side, impatient with the time they were spending here. They were both dressed for riding and were supposed to be on their way to the coast.

"She is the only Fairbourne left," Darius said. "She probably hopes to reassure the patrons with her presence. No one will be fooled, however. The size and quality of this auction is symbolic of what happens when the eyes and personality that define such an establishment are lost."

"You have met her, I expect, since you knew her father well. Not much of a future waiting for her, is there? She looks to be in her middle twenties already. Marriage is not likely to happen now if it didn't happen when her father lived and this business flourished."

"Yes, I have met her." The first time had been about a year ago. Odd that he had known Maurice Fairbourne for years, and in all that time he had never been introduced to the daughter. Maurice's son, Robert, might join them in their conversations, but never Robert's sister.

He and Emma Fairbourne had not spoken again since that introduction, until very recently. His memory of her had been of an ordinary-looking woman, a bit timid and retiring, a small shadow within the broad illumination cast by her expansive, flamboyant father.

"Then again . . ." Ambury gazed in Miss Fairbourne's direction with lowered eyelids. "Not a great beauty, but there is something about her . . . Hard to say what it is . . ."

Yes, there was something about her. Darius was impressed that Ambury had spotted it so quickly. But then, Ambury had a special sympathy with women, while Darius mostly found them necessary and often pleasurable, but ultimately bewildering.

"I recognize her," Ambury said while he turned to look at a landscape hanging above their heads on the wall. "I have seen her about town, in the company of Barrowmore's sister, Lady Cassandra. Perhaps Miss Fairbourne is unmarried because she prefers independence, like her friend."

With Lady Cassandra? How interesting. Darius considered that there might be much more to Emma Fairbourne than he had assumed.

He did not miss how she now managed to avoid having that penetrating gaze of hers connect with his. Unless he greeted her directly, she would pretend he was not here. She surely would not acknowledge that he had as much interest in the results of this auction as she did.

Ambury perused the sheets of the sale catalogue that he had obtained from the exhibition hall manager. "I do not claim to know about art the way that you do, Southwaite, but there is a lot of 'school of' and 'studio of' among these paintings. It reminds me of the art offered by those picture sellers in Italy during my grand tour."

"The staff does not have Maurice's expertise, and to their credit have been conservative in their attributions when the provenance that documents the history of ownership and supports the authenticity is not clean." Darius pointed to the landscape above Ambury's head. "If he were still alive, that might have been sold as van Ruisdael, not as follower of van Ruisdael, and the world would have accepted his judgment. Penthurst was examining it most closely a while ago, and will possibly bid high in the hopes the ambiguity goes in van Ruisdael's favor."

"If it was Penthurst, I hope it was daubed by a forger a fortnight ago and he wastes a bundle." Ambury returned his attention to Miss Fairbourne. "Not a bad memorial service, if you think about it. There are society luminaries here who probably did not attend the funeral."

Darius *had* attended the funeral held a month ago. He had been the only peer there, despite Maurice Fairbourne's role as advisor to many of them on their collections. Society did not attend the funeral of a tradesman, least of all at the start of the Season, so Ambury was correct. For the patrons of Fairbourne's, this would serve as the memorial service, such as it was.

"I assume everyone will bid high," Ambury said. Both his tone and small smile reflected his amiable manner, one that sometimes got him into trouble. "To help her out now that she is alone in the world."

"Sympathy will play its role in encouraging high bids, but the real reason is standing next to the rostrum right now."

"You mean that small white-haired fellow? He hardly looks to be the type to get me so excited I'd bid fifty when I had planned to pay twenty-five."

"He is astoundingly unimpressive, isn't he? Also unassuming, mild-mannered, and unfailingly polite," Darius said. "Unaccountably it all works to his advantage. Once Maurice Fairbourne realized what he had in that little man, he never called an auction in this house again, but left it to Obediah Riggles."

"And here I thought that fellow over there was the auctioneer. The one who gave me this paper listing the things for sale."

Ambury referred to the young, handsome man now easing the guests toward the chairs.

"That is Mr. Nightingale. He manages the exhibition hall here. He greets visitors, seats them, ensures they are comfortable, and answers questions regarding the lots. You will see him stand near each work as it is auctioned as well, like a human signpost."

Dark, tall, and exceedingly meticulous in his elegant dress, Mr. Nightingale slithered more than walked as he moved around the chamber, ushering and encouraging, charming and flirting. All the while he filled the chairs and ensured the women had broad fans with which to signal a bid.

"He seems to do whatever he does quite well," Ambury observed.

"Yes."

"The ladies appear to like him. I expect a bit of flattery goes far in helping the bids flow."

"I expect so."

Ambury watched Nightingale for a minute longer. "Some gentlemen seem to favor him too."

"You *would* mention that."

Ambury laughed. "I expect it causes some awkwardness for him. He is supposed to keep them coming back, isn't he? How does one both encourage and discourage at the same time?"

Darius could not swear that the exhibition manager did discourage. Nightingale was nothing if not ambitious. "I will leave it to you to employ your renowned powers of observation and let me know how he manages it. It will give you something to do, and perhaps you will stop complaining that I dragged you here today."

"It was not the where of it, but the how. You deceived me. When you said an auction, I just assumed it was a horse auction, and you knew I would. It is more fun to watch you spend a small fortune on a stallion than on a painting."

Slowly the crowd found seats and the sounds dimmed. Riggles stepped up on a stool so he showed tall behind the rostrum's podium. Mr. Nightingale moved to where the first lot hung on the wall. His perfect features probably garnered more attention from some of the patrons than the obscure oil painting that he pointed to.

Emma Fairbourne remained discreetly away from the action but very visible to everyone. *Bid high and bid often,* her mere presence seemed to plead. *For his memory and my future, make it a better total than it has any right to be.*

Emma kept her gaze on Obediah, but she felt people looking at her. In particular she felt one person looking at her.

Southwaite was here. It had been too much to hope that he might be out of town. She had prayed for it, however. He went down to his property in Kent often, her friend Cassandra had reported. It would have been ideal had he done so this week.

He stood behind all the chairs, dressed for riding, as if he had been heading down to the country after all, but had seen the newspaper and diverted his path here. He towered back there and could not be missed. Out of the corner of her eye she saw him watching her. His harshly handsome face held a vague scowl at the doings here. His companion appeared much more friendly, with remarkable blue eyes that held a light of merriment in contrast with the earl's dark intensity.

He thought he should have been told, she guessed. He thought it was his business to know what Fairbourne's was doing. He was going to want to become a nuisance, it appeared. Well, she would be damned before she allowed that.

Obediah began the sale of the first lot. The bidding was not enthusiastic, but that did not worry her. Auctions always opened slowly, and she had given considerable thought to which consignment should be sacrificed like this, to give the patrons time to settle in and warm up.

Obediah called the bids in his smooth, quiet fashion. He smiled kindly at the older women who raised their fans, and added a "Quite good, sir" when a young lord pushed the bid up two increments. The impression was that of a tasteful conversation, not a raucous competition.

There were no histrionics at Fairbourne's auctions. No cajoling for more bids, and no sly implications of hidden values. Obediah was the least dramatic auctioneer in England, but the lots went for more than they should when he brought down his hammer. Bidders trusted him and forgot their natural caution. Emma's father had once remarked that Obediah reminded men of their first valet, and women of their dear uncle Bertie.

She did not leave her spot near the wall, not even when Mr. Nightingale directed the crowd's attention to the paintings and objets d'art near her. Some of the people in the room would remember that her father stood here during the sales. Right in this spot where she now was.

As the final lots approached, Mr. Nightingale retreated from his position to stand beside her. She thought that odd, but he had been most solicitous today in every way. One might think his own father had taken that fatal fall, from the way he accepted the condolences of the patrons during the preview, almost losing his composure several times.

As soon as the hammer came down on the last lot, Emma exhaled a sigh of relief. It had gone much better than she had dared hope. She had succeeded in buying some time.

Noise filled the high-ceilinged chamber as conversation broke out and chairs scraped the wooden floor. From his place beside her, Mr. Nightingale spoke farewells to the society matrons who favored him with flirtatious smiles and to a few gentlemen who condescended to show him familiarity.

"Miss Fairbourne," he said while he bestowed his charming smile on the people passing by. "If the day has not tired you too much, I would like a few words with you in private after they have all gone."

Her heart sank. He was going to leave his situation. Mr. Nightingale was an ambitious young man and he would see no future here now. He no doubt assumed they would just close the doors after today. Even if they did not, he would not want to remain at the auction house without the connections her father had provided him.

Her gaze shifted to the rostrum, where Obediah was stepping down. It would be a blow to lose Mr. Nightingale. If Obediah Riggles left, however, Fairbourne's would definitely cease to exist.

"Of course, Mr. Nightingale. Why don't we go to the storage now, if that will suffice."

She walked in that direction with Mr. Nightingale beside

her. She paused to praise Obediah, who blushed in his self-effacing way.

"Perhaps you will be good enough to meet me here tomorrow, Obediah? I would like your advice on some matters of great importance," she added.

Obediah's face fell. He assumed she wanted advice on how to close Fairbourne's, she guessed. "Of course, Miss Fairbourne. Would eleven o'clock be a good time?"

"A perfect time. I will see you then." As she spoke she noticed that two men had not yet left the exhibition hall. Southwaite and his companion still stood back there, watching the staff remove the paintings from the walls in order to deliver them to the winning bidders.

Southwaite caught her eye. His expression commanded her to remain where she was. He began walking toward her. She pretended she had not noticed. She urged Mr. Nightingale forward, so she could escape to the storage chamber.

He wouldn't settle for less than
her unconditional surrender.

From *New York Times* bestselling author
MADELINE HUNTER

The Surrender of Miss Fairbourne

As reluctant business partners, Emma Fairbourne's defiance and Darius Stainthorpe's demands make it difficult to manage one of London's most eminent auction houses. But their passionate personalities ignite an affair that leaves them both senseless—until the devastating truth behind their partnership comes to light, threatening the love they have just begun to share . . .

"Hunter's books are so addictive."
—*Publishers Weekly*

madelinehunter.com
facebook.com/MadelineHunter
facebook.com/LoveAlwaysBooks
penguin.com

M1193T1012

Penguin Group (USA) Online

What will you be reading tomorrow?

Patricia Cornwell, Nora Roberts, Catherine Coulter,
Ken Follett, John Sandford, Clive Cussler,
Tom Clancy, Laurell K. Hamilton, Charlaine Harris,
J. R. Ward, W.E.B. Griffin, William Gibson,
Robin Cook, Brian Jacques, Stephen King,
Dean Koontz, Eric Jerome Dickey, Terry McMillan,
Sue Monk Kidd, Amy Tan, Jayne Ann Krentz,
Daniel Silva, Kate Jacobs...

You'll find them all at
penguin.com

Read excerpts and newsletters,
find tour schedules and reading group guides,
and enter contests.

Subscribe to Penguin Group (USA) newsletters
and get an exclusive inside look
at exciting new titles and the authors you love
long before everyone else does.

PENGUIN GROUP (USA)
penguin.com

M224G0909